THE SUMMER WITCH

Also by Louise Cooper from Headline Feature

The King's Demon
Sacrament of Night
Our Lady of the Snow

THE
SUMMER
WITCH

Louise Cooper

HEADLINE
FEATURE

First published in 1999
by HEADLINE BOOK PUBLISHING

A HEADLINE FEATURE hardback

10 9 8 7 6 5 4 3 2 1

British Library Cataloguing in Publication Data

Cooper, Louise, 1952-
Summer Witch
1. Suspense fiction
I. Title
823.9'14 [F]

ISBN 0-7472-2145-6

Typeset by
CBS, Martlesham Heath, Ipswich, Suffolk

Printed and bound in Great Britain by
Mackays of Chatham PLC, Chatham, Kent

HEADLINE BOOK PUBLISHING
A division of the Hodder Headline Group
338 Euston Road
London NW1 3BH

www.headline.co.uk
www.hodderheadline.com

THE SUMMER WITCH

Chapter I

From her early childhood, everyone in the district had known that Powl Miller's youngest daughter, Carys, was going to be a beauty. She had that rare, fine skin that the sun turned honey-hued rather than florid, hazel-brown hair with eyes to match, and a figure that promised to be trim and not run to too much muscle. A lovely girl, they said, and a good girl, bright and diligent and obedient to her father as any daughter should be. A few more summers and the lads from a good many miles around would be following her. Powl would have more choices for a son-in-law than a sow had piglets, and unless Carys did Something Foolish he'd make a good match for her, just you wait and see.

Powl Miller was well aware of his daughter's virtues; not least the potential effect that her future marriage could have on his own purse. With only three girls of his own union, and the eldest two unremarkable however generously you tried to look at it, Carys was, to Powl's way of thinking, the insurance for his old age. The mill made a modicum of profit, but a good bride-price for Carys would make the difference between a passable retirement and a comfortable one.

So by the time Carys was sixteen, Powl had begun to keep a weather eye open for suitable candidates. By the time she was eighteen, he had dismissed many of the village lads out of hand, on the grounds of lack of money, lack of standing or, in one case, plain imbecility; one or two others were, regrettably, too far above his family in status for any hopes to be entertained. But Powl watched and speculated, and (as he told his wife, Tibba, one evening when he had enjoyed a couple of sociable hours at the local inn, and was thus more forthcoming and benevolent towards her than usual) he was satisfied that, with a little time and patience, the right match would be found.

One prospect that Powl Miller had never thought to consider, however, was Jone Farmer.

Jone's holding lay on the southern slopes of Crede Hill, the great rise of mixed wood and pasture that dominated the surrounding landscape for miles. It was a favoured and fertile location, and the farm had been in Jone's family for generations, making him about as native to the district as it was possible to be. Jone was a quiet man, a few years older than Powl; self-contained but not unfriendly, and as honest as Midsummer Day was long. Carys had been thirteen when Jone's wife of twenty-something years was carried in sad procession to the village graveyard and laid in her final bed. Jone had accepted the cut of fate as he accepted everything: uncomplainingly and with quiet resignation. Sympathy had been widespread, but when it was expressed he had only lifted his high shoulders and, looking into the middle distance with his soft, brown eyes, said in his thoughtful way that that which was ordained must come to pass, and life would continue whether or no.

So for five years now the people of the district had grown accustomed to seeing Jone alone, walking his lands, driving his cattle to the monthly market, riding in his cart with Faithful, the shaggy-fetlocked bay gelding, clopping sedately in the shafts. A pity Jone had had no children, they said. Doubtless he had a good few years left in him yet, but when his time did come, as it eventually and inevitably must, it was a shame that there would be no son – or even daughter, though that would naturally have been less satisfactory – to carry on the farm of his ancestors. Not for one moment did anyone ever imagine Jone remarrying; he simply wasn't the kind.

So when, one market day in late winter, Jone Farmer made a point of seeking out Powl Miller's company, nobody was more surprised than Powl himself to hear what he had to say. The proposition was simple, and made with the same open, modest candour with which Jone conducted all his business. He had a mind to take a new wife. And he would be pleased if Powl would consider the bride-price he was prepared to offer for Carys.

Powl spent upwards of four hours in the market tavern that night, and by the time he left, half the district knew every detail of the contract that he and Jone Farmer had entered into. His friends packed him into his cart and slapped his horse's rump – the animal could have found its way blindfolded, so there was no cause for concern – and Powl went home in a daze of happy inebriation.

Tibba could make no sense of his drunken excitement at first. Only in the morning, when the worst effects had worn off with nothing much worse than an aching head to show for it, did she finally hear the tale in some semblance of order, and realise what her husband had done.

'Well, now!' Her small, sloe-black eyes glinted eagerly. 'Well, now! Just think of it, Powl! Our Carys and Jone Farmer – whoever would have thought?'

Powl beamed expansively. 'A comfortable widower, with one of the best parcels of land for many a mile around,' he said. 'And no children to complicate the picture by making claims on his estate. I can think of nothing better, Wife. Nothing at all.'

'There is the matter of children, of course.' Tibba's face fell a little. 'We've the mill to think of, as well as Jone's farm, and grandsons—'

'Will come in time,' Powl interrupted. 'Jone's vigorous enough; there's nothing amiss with him that a fecund wife won't put to rights. And he's got a good few years in him yet, if I'm any judge. Time enough for a whole brood of grandchildren.'

'All the same, I see no cause to delay the wedding,' said Tibba.

'Jone has no wish to delay. Sooner the better, he said, sooner the better.'

'Then we must tell Carys.' Tibba clasped her hands together and looked at them contentedly, already making embryonic plans for the invitations, the feast, what she herself would wear. 'She'll be that pleased, Powl. Pleased and grateful.' She smiled trustfully up at him. 'Pleased and grateful.'

Carys, though, was far from pleased. Later, Tibba could only give thanks for the fact that the mill was isolated enough for no neighbours to have been able to witness the scene that took place that evening. There were tears, there were tantrums; and when the screaming and shouting failed to move Powl, Carys had pleaded with him on her knees not to make this bargain. Tibba, shocked and sorrowful, had told her that she was an ingrate to break any mother's heart, and at that Carys had turned on her – on *her* – and shrieked that if that was so, then let them turn her out of the house in the clothes she stood up in, for she would rather tramp the roads than be forced into marriage with a withered old man.

For a few dreadful moments Tibba had feared that Powl would rise to that challenge and turn Carys out. But Powl had more sense than that, and with relief she saw him, instead, unbuckle his belt and draw it ominously through his hands. That was the tacit signal for her to leave, and she busied herself in the kitchen, humming a little tune she had heard the musicians play in chapel a few days ago, until Powl emerged from the parlour, the belt back in its loops and a sour but satisfied expression on his face.

'She'll do as she's told,' was all he said. And Tibba, knowing it to be true, set her pot of potatoes on the trivet to finish and go floury, and went upstairs to fetch out the family bridal dress, which she and her mother and grandmother had all worn in their time, and which would very soon be used again.

The wedding of Jone and Carys took place on a dank and dreary winter afternoon. A biting east wind blew fitfully, and the weather had been sulky for so long that they had been hard pressed to find enough flowers to decorate the bride, let alone the cart in which she was carried to her nuptials, so it was a subdued and shivering procession that turned out of the mill yard, crossed the stone bridge and set off along the rutted road towards the village and the chapel.

Carys sat stiff and pallid on the seat beside Powl, draped in the green sateen of the family dress, which fitted her in all the wrong places, and with a chaplet of damp primroses crowning her veil. In the back of the cart rode Tibba and her elder daughters, both plain and unmarried, seething at their sister's luck and jealously longing to change places with her. But Jone Farmer had not offered for them. Their only consolation – as their mother had pointed out with little subtlety – was that, if all else failed, Carys's bride-price was at least enough to buy them husbands before they were doomed entirely to lifelong spinsterhood.

The road wound on, with the bare fields of small farms stretching away beyond the hedges to either side. Carys wondered if it would rain. That would seem fitting, matching her mood and adding its own tacit comment to her feelings about this day. Able for once to see over the hedge-tops (she was more used to walking to the village than to riding), she stared without interest at the fields. In the middle of one, a scarecrow hung from a pole. It looked stark and lonely on the slope of straight brown furrows; its shoulders were hunched, its arms outstretched in a parody of menace, and the pole had tilted to a tipsy angle so that the figure leaned towards the road. Momentarily it seemed to Carys that the scarecrow possessed its own, alien sentience, that it was watching her as she passed by, mocking her plight. A shiver that was not entirely due to the weather went through her, and she looked quickly away. But as the cart rolled steadily on, leaving the still shape behind, she couldn't shake off the feeling that invisible eyes in the head of rotting straw gazed after her, and a gust of unheard laughter was snatched away on the wind.

A mile further on, they reached the outskirts of the village. The cart now attracted a straggling tail of children who ran or toddled in its wake; the younger ones shrieked excitedly, while the older ones chanted rude rhymes until a granfer with a blackthorn stick chased them off. Neighbours and villagers were already gathered in the little graveyard – Powl smiled his satisfaction at the size of the turnout – and by the chapel door, a little apart from the rest, the groom and his party were waiting.

Carys had thought she could not feel more miserable, but something inside her shrivelled utterly and finally as she saw Jone Farmer's tall, spare and slightly round-shouldered figure. How many times had she ever spoken to him? Five? Six? She didn't *know* him. And for all his kindly reputation, he was older than her father. Yet in the next few minutes she must stand beside him and pledge herself to him, and somehow, *somehow*, she must force herself not to scream aloud when he placed the brass ring on her finger and the cheerful little preacher pronounced them man and wife.

She could, of course, have refused to take Jone in wedlock. But even during her one small rebellion when Powl announced the marriage contract, that option had never truly existed in her mind. It wasn't that she had been cowed by the strapping her father gave her; that had happened before, on various occasions and for various reasons, and she was accustomed to it. It was simply that, ultimately, one did not disobey one's parents. If they said a thing should be so, then it was so, and there could be no argument. In the bedroom she shared – *had* shared – with her sisters, she had sobbed long and bitterly into her pillow, but she had accepted because any other course was unthinkable.

The cart jolted to a halt. Powl alighted first and, for the only time in his life, reached to help his daughter down. For today, and only for today, Carys was someone special, to be treated with at least the pretence of respect and deference. Carys didn't look at anyone as she awkwardly accepted Powl's hand. A fold of the dress caught in the cart wheel and her chaplet and veil slipped sideways as she struggled to disentangle it, and by the time that business was over with she was feeling distinctly sick. And now it *was* raining, a dull drizzle with a threat of sleet in it.

The groom's party had gone into the chapel ahead of them. Carys stood passively while her mother fussed and tweaked her draperies back into place, then, with the sickness like a lead weight inside her, she walked on Powl's arm under the low arch of door, to the sealing of her fate.

It all went off very properly and unremarkably. The words were said, the promises and pledges made. The preacher then handed Powl a small rope of plaited straw, and Powl symbolically struck Carys on both shoulders before passing it solemnly to Jone Farmer for him to do the same. Jone's touch, Carys noticed, was lighter than her father's; whereas Powl's token scourging carried a tacit warning, Jone's was simply to satisfy the old custom and meant nothing more ominous. She glanced sidelong at him, a little surprised; seeing the glance Jone smiled faintly then turned his attention to the preacher once more. The brass ring had been carefully made to fit Carys's finger without pinching. With dull bemusement she watched it slide on, then the preacher pronounced the indissoluble bond, and from the choir the sound of viol, pipe and shawm struck up a hymn, more or less in tune. To the accompaniment of enthusiastically scraping instruments and lustily singing voices, Carys Jonewife wrote her name in the marriage book beside that of her new husband, and with the congregation falling in row by row behind them, they walked together out into the dank day.

The wedding breakfast was held at the meeting hall near the chapel. Apart from the chapel itself, it was the only building large enough for everyone in the village to squeeze into; and, invited or not, everyone did. Powl, increasingly flushed with drink and triumph, played the host with a jovial bonhomie that seemed to swell in inverse proportions to Carys's unhappy discomfort, and the company ate and drank themselves nearly to bursting point. Finally, the last speeches were made and the last toasts proposed, and the tables were cleared for dancing, to shake the food down and make room for more.

Carys had always enjoyed dancing, but her husband, it seemed, did not share her liking, for as the musicians clambered to their places and argued over the first tune, he leaned slightly towards her, smiled, and said in an undertone, 'I think, Wife, that this should be our cue to leave.'

Carys felt something akin to panic take hold of her. She wanted

7

to protest that she would like to stay a little longer. She wanted to coax him, cajole him, persuade him to take the floor; anything to put off the moment when she must be alone with him. Instead, she heard herself say meekly, 'Yes, Jone,' and allowed him to take her limp fingers as he rose from the bridal bench.

The movement was seen immediately, of course, and the departure of the newly married pair was a protracted affair of congratulations, back-slapping, ribald jokes and all the other necessary paraphernalia. They were escorted out into the chilly night (it had, at least, stopped raining) and all but bodily lifted into Jone's market wagon, which was decorated with evergreens, good-luck charms and a few less savory items provided by the village wags when no one else was looking. Faithful, Jone's elderly bay farm horse, turned his head and watched the antics bemusedly; then Carys's bride-trunk (which didn't contain very much at all) was heaved into the cart well behind the seat, and to a last volley of shouts and whistles, Jone Farmer and his new wife left for home.

The cheerful noise and lights of the meeting hall fell away into the dark behind them, until the only sound was the steady clop of Faithful's hooves on the rough road. Jone had lit a lantern, and its small pool of brightness bobbed and swayed, reflecting from the cart's big wheels. Carys found the reflection hypnotic, and stared fixedly at it as Faithful plodded along. She could think of nothing to say to Jone. There was nothing *to* say.

Jone, too, was apparently no great conversationalist, and seemed content to travel in silence. They passed the field where the scarecrow stood; it was too dark, now, to see any sign of the angular shape on its leaning pole, but in her jangled imagination Carys believed she could feel its presence, and its gaze, on the other side of the hedge.

She had seen Jone's farm – her new home – before, but only from a distance as she passed its boundaries on her way to or from somewhere else. The house, as far as she could recall, was a substantial one, with a proper yard, upper rooms in the eaves, and barn and byres built to last. She did not know the acreage, but it was good land, as her parents had repeatedly told her. As Carys Jonewife she would live more comfortably than she had ever done before. Other women would envy her.

She would eagerly have changed places with any one of them.

The cart turned on to the track that led to Jone's holding, and a few minutes later they were home. As Jone handed her down, Carys stared at the stone façade of the house, but she took little in; all she truly saw were the three lit windows on the ground floor, and the single candle burning in a room upstairs. She stood back, hesitant, as Jone went to open the front door, then he paused and she realised that he was waiting for her to go in first. Drawing a deep breath, she made herself walk forward and step over the threshold.

She entered a large, L-shaped room, furnished with good pieces of heavy oak: a long table, four chairs, a settle near the inglenook. A fire burned sluggishly in the hearth, and the embers glinted their reflection in copper pots and pewter plates on and around the mantel. In one corner a long-case clock, taller than Carys, ticked with stately complacence. There were thick curtains, two rugs, and on one wall an embroidered picture of a red cow with a text beneath that said something about 'the Milk of Humanity'. Below that, on a smaller table, lay a single book with no visible title on its dark cover.

'Does it please you, Carys?' Jone asked quietly.

She jumped a little at the sound of his voice, and glanced nervously up at him. 'Yes,' she said. 'It's . . . very fine.'

He looked pleased. 'Izzy has left a cold pie for us, but I've eaten my fill and more. So unless you are still hungry . . .?'

'No.' Carys had barely touched a scrap at the wedding feast and wanted nothing now. 'Thank you,' she added faintly.

'Good. Then we shall sit by the fire for a while and enjoy our solitude.'

She nodded, and lowered herself on to the settle as he raked up the embers and put two more logs on to burn. Who was Izzy? Jone's servant? Did she live in or out? What was she like – and what would she think of the household's new mistress?

With a faint grunt and a creaking of knees that made Carys recoil inwardly, Jone straightened and took a chair on the other side of the ingle. Picking up the book that Carys had noticed earlier, he weighed it in his hands for a few moments before saying, 'Your father tells me you can read and write.'

'Ye-es,' Carys admitted hesitantly, 'but I'm not learned. Not like a teacher or scribe or—'

'No matter. You know your letters.' Jone smiled at her again. 'Read aloud to me. It will please me.'

She was astonished. Jone, she knew, was perfectly able to read and write on his own account, yet here he was asking – telling – her to please him with her own poor abilities. She didn't want to do it but felt too intimidated to refuse, so reluctantly she took the book from him and opened it at the page he had marked with his thumb. It was, she saw, a volume of parables and moral tales, and very dull; but as she haltingly began, Jone closed his eyes and leaned back with a look of contentment on his face. He didn't interrupt once as Carys floundered her way to the end of the passage, and when she finished he uttered a small, satisfied sigh.

'You read well, Carys, I enjoy hearing your voice. I think I would like you to read to me often. It will make these dark winter evenings pass very pleasantly.'

Surprised and, she had to admit, a little encouraged, Carys ventured, 'Shall I read more now?'

'No, I think not. It's late, and we should be abed.' He stood up stiffly. 'I'll carry your box to our bedroom, and then I expect you'd like a few private minutes, hmm?'

This was the moment Carys had dreaded most of all, and she only hoped that her feelings didn't show too clearly in her face as she nodded mutely. She watched Jone disappear with her trunk up the shallow, twisting staircase, then listened to the sound of footfalls overhead and the thump of the trunk being set down. A few private minutes. During that time she must take off her bridal dress (which was to be returned to her mother in the morning), put on the white dimity nightgown (a wedding present from her family, and thus hers to keep) and prepare herself for the duty that she could not shirk. Carys knew what men did to get women with child. In a rural community it was impossible not to know; if children didn't see for themselves how it was with the cows and pigs and horses, they were enlightened soon enough by older or more observant friends. Of the girls in the village who had experimented, some said it was the greatest fun to be had while others claimed it was a dull disappointment; but they had all tested the water with young men of their own age. To Carys's knowledge, none had given herself to a man ten years older than her own father, and the prospect of what she must face filled Carys with dread.

Jone came down again to find her standing before the fire, trying to warm hands that were suddenly ice-cold. Helplessly Carys tried and failed to smile at him, then, feeling that her legs were made of putty, she gave in to the inevitable.

Up the stairs and into the bedroom. She knew which room it was, for Jone had thoughtfully left the door open. There were more curtains, another rug; a dark wood dressing-table with a stool set before it; another sampler on the wall: she didn't look at this one. And the bed. The bedstead was of painted iron and the mattress looked very large. When she sat on it, she found it soft and thick; in fact its thickness made the bed so high that her feet barely touched the floor. There were linen sheets, two pillows, and a patchwork counterpane, beautifully stitched and very old, doubtless a family heirloom. Carys thought of Jone's first wife, whose name she couldn't remember. She had lain with him, in this bed and under this counterpane, but he had never sired a child on her. Carys wished that he had. She wished the first wife had had ten children, and not died, so that Jone would have had no reason to look at her.

But the wife *had* died, and Jone *had* looked, and there was nothing in the world that Carys could do about it. She started to unfasten the buttons of her dress, and once the process had begun she rushed at it, terrified that Jone would come up earlier than expected and see her naked. The trunk was flung open and the nightgown scrabbled over her head in frantic haste. Tugging it down over her ankles, she scrambled under the bedclothes and huddled

11

there, pulling the counterpane to her chin. She wanted to pray, but didn't know what she could possibly pray for.

Then came the sound of footsteps on the stairs.

Jone did not speak when he came in. Carys shut her eyes as he removed his own clothes and put on a nightshirt and cap, and when he climbed into bed beside her she held her breath for fear that she would scream.

Jone blew out the candle. He shifted his weight, ponderously, a little awkwardly. Their bodies had not yet made contact.

Then he said peaceably, 'Good night to you, Wife', turned his back to her, and fell sound asleep.

Chapter II

Within two months of her marriage, Carys realised that she was the envy not only of her sisters, but of half the women in the district. She saw it in the eyes of unwed girls when she rode with her husband to market, sitting high beside him on the driving seat of his wagon with old Faithful plodding sturdily before them. She saw it in the eyes of older women, those of an age with Jone, who had never worn a man's brass ring upon their finger. She even saw it in the slantwise looks and wistful smiles of Olma Carnwidow, thirty-five and handsome and with a prosperous holding of her own since Carn had taken shelter under a tree during a storm and been killed by lightning.

Olma had called on Carys several times now; on the first occasion in the company of Gyll, wife of Merion Blacksmith, and her good friend Juda. Carys was unlikely ever to forget that visit. The three women had arrived unannounced and in fine style, driving up to the house in Olma's gig, and Carys, seeing them from the window, had been struck near dumb with terrified awe. But where she feared disapproval and patronage, she found instead only friendship and kindness. Her new neighbours were curious, of course; they quizzed Carys about herself, her skills and her opinions, but they seemed to like what they saw. It didn't matter that in her flustered state she let a batch of cakes overcook and didn't leave the tea to brew for long enough; every young wife made mistakes to begin with, and the women welcomed her into their circle.

Gyll in particular had become a friend, which pleased Jone, as he and Merion Blacksmith had been comfortable companions for a long time. Sometimes Merion and Gyll would visit the farm of an evening, and while Jone and Merion played dominoes by the fire, Gyll would take Carys into a corner and recount all the latest gossip, which always seemed to reach the smithy before it spread anywhere else. Under Gyll's tactful guidance, Carys's cooking improved out of recognition. And she was learning other skills: she sometimes milked the cows now, almost always fed the pigs, and was in sole charge of tending the chickens and ducks. Jone joked to Merion that she must have second sight, for she always knew where to find eggs that the hens had laid in out-of-the-way spots under the hedgerows.

Jone made no effort to hide the fact that he was extremely proud of his new, pretty wife. And Carys, in turn, had discovered much that was unexpected in her new husband. Jone was a good and gentle man, slow to anger, and generous in his dealings with the world. His five fields were well tended and well nourished, and yielded plentiful harvests; his cows were sleek and contented and gave milk in abundance. There were chickens for eggs and for festive meat, two fat pigs to be raised each year, and barley for the brewing of beer. Jone stinted Carys nothing; she had good clothes in plenty, a blue dress for special occasions, and new and well-made boots that were more comfortable than any she'd ever worn before. The farmhouse was warm and well appointed, Carys had plentiful fuel for her fires, and as Jone employed a man and a woman from the village to help in byre and house respectively, she even had a little free time to call her own.

But what she did not have from Jone Farmer was the one thing she had dreaded, and now, lacking it, was perversely beginning to crave.

Lying awake on her wedding night, with Jone snoring gently and contentedly beside her, Carys's initial relief at his lack of sexual interest had turned first to puzzlement and then to faint indignation. *Why* wasn't he interested in her? Did he find her uncomely? Repulsive, even? Had she done or said something that displeased him? Or was there something wrong with *him*, some failing that no one knew about? It could explain the lack of children from his first marriage. Had she tied herself, she wondered, to an impotent man?

The thoughts had turned and turned in her mind, until finally, tiring of them, she had mentally shrugged her shoulders and decided that time would tell. The most likely explanation was that Jone was simply tired after a long and eventful day. She should be grateful rather than offended. She didn't desire him, far from it, so it was better to give thanks that he had made no demands on her. Tomorrow might see a change, and if it did she would face it as she must, but until then she had nothing to complain of.

The next night had not brought a change, nor the next, nor any of the nights that followed. Jone's routine was unswerving: when bedtime came he would rise from his chair and say: 'It's growing late, Wife, and tomorrow we must work.' Always the same words; Carys could have recited them along with him. She would then go up to the bedroom before him, and he gave her enough time to change into her nightgown before a tread of feet on the stairs announced that he was coming to join her. He would climb into bed at her side, say, 'Good night to you, Wife,' and blow out the candle.

And that was that.

It didn't take long for Carys to realise that it would take far more than mere patience to alter the pattern that Jone had established. With a youthful mixture of curiosity, challenge and contrariness, she began inwardly to rail against the situation in which she found herself. As time went by it mattered less and less to her that Jone was old and she would never have chosen him of her own free will. He was her husband, and husbands had duties just as wives did; duties which Jone was singularly failing to fulfil. Relief was turning to resentment, thankfulness to pique. She felt rejected, neglected, deprived of the one thing that would have finally confirmed her new status as a married woman. Though Carys herself would not have been able to name the instincts within her, she was suffering all the frustration of a young woman ripe for awakening but denied the chance of that fulfilment.

15

She couldn't speak of it to anyone, of course. To raise the subject directly with Jone was unthinkable, and she didn't know Gyll or Olma well enough to confide in them, even if she could have forced herself to say the necessary words. If a remedy was to be had at all, Carys decided, it lay in her own hands. She must try to *make* Jone love her as a husband should.

So she tried. She had no experience, but she had all the instincts of her eager youth, and night after night she tried to find some way of kindling a spark in him. But her efforts were a complete failure. Night after night Jone Farmer slept the sleep of a contented man, and rose with the dawn to begin another day's steady and diligent work. He was still kind to Carys. Oh, he was *kind*. He never beat her as her father had done. He talked to her almost as though she were his equal, and he asked her for her opinion about this and that. Once, he even kissed her brow, on Plough Night when their neighbours and her parents and sisters had come to make merry and mark the beginning of the new year's sowing. Carys hoped then, briefly, that there might be more, but when the guests were gone and the single candle in the bedroom had been blown out, he only said, as always: 'Good night to you, Wife,' before turning away.

As the third month of their marriage began, Carys stopped trying. All her wiles had achieved nothing, and there was simply no point in persevering. If Jone noticed any difference in her behaviour, he showed no sign of it, and Carys began to consider other possibilities.

At first she wondered if she could look for salvation in the world around her. But who had she to choose from? The man Jone employed to tend his cattle was forty, with a wife and nine children to keep him busy, and not fool enough – even had she been willing – to give more than a good day to the mistress of the farm. Old Izzy, who helped Carys in the house and never looked askance, had a young and strapping son, but that son was also a gangling half-wit who drooled on good days and gibbered on bad. And among the neighbours, traders, barterers and tinkers who came day by day to her neat front door, Carys saw no one who might provide her with a means of deliverance from the warm, protected, virginal and utterly frustrating prison of her existence.

Finally she concluded that any experiment along these lines was doomed to failure. Besides, it was too great a risk. She might cuckold Jone under his own nose once or twice, but – even if there had been any possible candidates in view – a long-term illicit liaison was sure to be found out eventually. It must be Jone or no one. And as Jone remained unwilling or unable, no one was the only option.

As if to reflect her mood, spring was reluctant to arrive that year. Winter clung on with a cold, wet, dogged persistence that felt as if it would never end, and though the early crops were sown and the new lambs born as usual, the advancing season was held back in a mire of relentless grey dreariness. One such morning found Carys trudging across the fields, heading for the lambing pens on the west side of Crede Hill, where Jone and Garler Shepherd were busy with the latest crop of new arrivals. She carried a basket on her back, packed with enough bread, cheese and ham to relieve two tired and hungry men. Izzy had been scandalised at the idea of Missus taking it in person, but Carys turned a deaf ear to her arguments. For days she had seen nothing but the interior of the house or cow-byre, and with Jone away all the daylight hours, there had been only Izzy's voice to listen to, grumble, grumble, grumble, like a rickety cart wheel, wherever she went. Rain or no rain, she needed a change. So in stout boots, and with one of Jone's working coats over her dress, she toiled along the path. The clay clung stickily to her feet, making every step an effort. Though the seeds had been in nearly a month now, the fields were still stubbornly and blankly brown, and as she looked sidelong through the drizzle at the bare furrows, Carys gloomily imagined the land becoming more and more waterlogged until one day it and everyone on it floated away into oblivion, like the unrepentant transgressors of chapel sermons.

Trudging on, she almost began to enjoy this self-indulgently miserable mood, relishing it as a hypochondriac might relish pain. For some reason she had suffered a bad, restless night, and the little sleep she had managed had been filled with vague, disturbing dreams of need and frustration. In the small hours she had heard, in the distance, a vixen screaming to the moon (which, but for the clouds, would have shown full last night). Screaming for a mate. It was that time of year, and in the wake of her dreams Carys had shut her eyes against the tears that welled in them, bunched her fists under the goose-feather pillow, and curled tighter beneath her blankets as an answering thrill coursed through her own body and mind. Jone, of course, had slept on undisturbed. If a knife had been to hand in those minutes while the vixen cried, Carys would have been sorely tempted to use it, though whether on him or on herself was a question to which she had no answer. But there was no knife, the vixen had eventually fallen silent, and in the hour before dawn Carys had slipped back to sleep and her aching dreams, until she woke to the slow creep of dawn over the eastern hill and the sharp chill of another late winter morning. And the big, calm, placid voice of her husband saying, as he always did, 'The sun will be rising soon, Wife, and we must be rising too. I shall rake up the fire for our breakfast, my dear, then you may cook it while I get about the milking.'

Always, *always*, that same little speech. Carys wanted to shout, to scream, to rake her nails down the lines of his quiet and pleasant face; anything to make it different. Instead, she had turned her bitter face from him and said mildly, as *she* always did, 'Yes, Jone.' And so another new day had begun. As it always would.

She grew tired of looking for green shoots that weren't there, and focused her gaze instead on the ground before her. Lost between brooding on her lot and taking care of the ruts, she didn't notice the scarecrow until she was almost level with it. Then, without any obvious cause, something made her raise her head and look.

She had forgotten about it. Forgotten the mocking, satirical dumdolly that had watched her over the hedge on the day she rode to her wedding and silently laughed at her. She hadn't known, then, that the field it guarded was one of Jone's own; now, though, she stopped and stared at the scarecrow with narrowed eyes. In the

18

waterlogged earth it had sagged further on its pole, so that now its face pointed towards the mud. One push, Carys thought, and it would slump tipsily forward to squelch ignominiously into the sludge. She smiled. A small revenge, petty perhaps, but it would be something.

She picked her way across the furrows, not caring that she might be trampling the first struggles of new seedlings, until she stood squarely before the figure. The scarecrow's hat was beginning to rot away, and birds had pecked at its straw-and-sacking head so that unlikely tufts sprouted from its nose and cheeks. Carys smiled again. Then she laughed, surprising herself with the sound.

'You!' she said contemptuously. 'You're no more use than *he* is! What are you – Jone Farmer's son, is that it? The only son he's capable of getting?'

She kicked out at the wooden pole. It rocked, but didn't fall. Instead, it lurched and swung and rolled on its axis, so that the figure spun round in a jerking dance and fetched up with what passed for its face looking at the sky.

An anger that she couldn't explain and couldn't control welled up in Carys. 'There's nothing for you up there!' she shouted viciously. 'Nothing, do you hear me? You can't fly away any more than I can! You're here, and you'll *stay* here, and you'll *rot* here, just like me!'

A distant rook cawed a sardonic comment and her gaze snapped round, fixing on the grey-brown wall of the wood beyond the path and the narrow strip of uncultivated ground. There they were, among the bare branches: flapping black carrion, useless things, squawking and nesting and mating and preparing for the arrival of their young . . . she hated them.

'*You!*' Swinging back, she attacked the scarecrow again with renewed energy, grabbing at its tattered coat, shaking it with hands that were suddenly hot. 'Come on, then, come on! I'll put you with them, because you're as useless as they are! Come and scare the rooks, come and *do* something!'

One final, violent jerk and the ragged doll came free from the pole. It flopped in a contorted heap at Carys's feet, and for a few moments she stared at it, torn between pleasure and dismay at her own small act of vandalism. She almost expected the scarecrow to open wide, human eyes and look reproachfully at her as it lay there in the mud. It didn't, of course it didn't. But as the tide of her fury ebbed, she felt suddenly sad and sorry.

Setting down her basket, she tried to pick the scarecrow up. It was too heavy for her; straw and hemp and wool soaked by months of rain would have been a challenge to a fit man twice her size. But after a few minutes' wrangling and heaving, she managed to get it into a position whereby she could drag it along behind her, like Faithful pulling the market cart, and resolutely set off with it towards the wood. Across the path, through a gap in the hedge (not easy, but she persevered), then into the borderlands of the trees, where at last she let it drop and stood grunting and gasping as she surveyed her handiwork.

She didn't know why she had done it, but the doing had made her feel better. The scarecrow lay supine in the wet mass of last autumn's rotting leaves, deaf, dumb and blind, leaking straw, the remains of its hat tip-tilted like a sot's salute.

'Go on, then.' But there was less venomous energy in Carys's voice now. 'Do what you were made to do. Scare them. Scare them far away so they never come back. Make spring come. Make things grow.' Silence then for a few moments, as she stared down. 'But you can't, can you? You're not a man. You're just a *thing*.'

Carefully, deliberately, she scooped up a handful of the leaf mould, with a clod of earth for good measure, and threw it at the scarecrow's face. She wanted it to respond in some way, to cry out, protest, ask her forgiveness. That would have helped. But of course, it didn't; it *was* just a thing.

She left it lying there and went to retrieve her basket and continue on her way. The field looked different, somehow, without its half-comic, half-threatening presence, and as she walked on Carys tossed her head like a coquette disdaining a suitor. Good riddance. Let it lie. Let it moulder. It would not mock her again.

She composed herself as she approached the lambing pens where Jone and Garler Shepherd were working. If his wife's cheeks were a little flushed and her speech a little breathless, Jone was too preoccupied to notice. The wet was taking an oppressive toil on the lambs this year, and he and Garler faced a long, hard toil if they were to save the majority. He would not be home to his bed tonight, Jone told Carys, but would stay here with Garler to do what must be done. Deenor Garlerwife would see for their night's victuals as Carys had seen for daytime food, and she was to go home directly and instruct Lob, Izzy's son, to bring Faithful and the smaller hay cart – too wet for the larger, it would bog down – to fetch the most vulnerable little ones and their dams back to the farm.

Carys took all this in on an instinctive level that barely touched her conscious mind, and said 'Yes, Jone,' and 'No, Jone,' and repeated her instructions clearly when he asked her to. The lambs were crying like lost souls and the ewes milled anxiously. With a last uneasy, pitying look at them and the men on whom they depended, she set off back towards the farmhouse at a faster pace than she had come.

Back on the rutted track beside the fields, back along the perimeter of the wood . . . and her steps slowed, without her intending it. Where was the scarecrow lying? That sapling oak with the oddly contorted branch, that was surely the marker, and from there it was just by the hedge, a few steps into the wood to find the place . . .

She went through the gap in the hedge and found the scarecrow where she had left it. A robin, surprised by her sudden appearance, flitted up from the sacking face and flipped away into the denser branches. Carys gazed down, again, at the still and silent mannikin.

Suddenly, she felt sorry for it. Not sorry as she had done for the lambs, for the scarecrow had none of their bewildered innocence; in fact, if she had had the learning to understand it, she would have recognised the underlying, seductive nature of the pity it aroused

21

in her. All she did feel was that she had wronged it, used it as a whipping-boy for a confused tangle of unfathomable feelings which had no possible connection with its own puppet existence.

'There, now.' Heedless of what the wet might do to her skirts and stockings (Izzy would lament, but she had no thought of Izzy, either), Carys dropped to her knees beside the fallen thing. 'This is no proper place to lie, is it? Even for you.' She lifted back the brim of the mouldering hat, half expecting to see a face staring back at her. There was no face, of course. Just the sacking. Carys smiled a small smile, then picked two scraps of bark from among the litter on the ground and pressed them into the misshapen head. There; it had eyes now. Maybe later she would find something for a mouth.

She began to stroke the scarecrow with an odd, jerky movement, speaking half to it and half to herself. 'You could be strong, couldn't you? Oh, yes, I think you could be strong. Stronger than *he* is. Was he your master? Well, there's no more of that. He's not your master now, is he? I've found you another place. A new place. So you're mine now, aren't you?' Leaning close, she pressed her mouth to where the scarecrow's ear would have been, had it possessed one. 'You're *mine*. And I can do whatever I please with you.'

The ragged thing, the dumdolly, gave her no answer. But to Carys' fevered senses it seemed that there was a response of another kind. A stirring, a flickering, something old and primitive and deeper than she could begin to understand. It had no voice; it could not and would not communicate in any way known to her. But she *felt* it. And a sensation she had never experienced before filled her like a flood.

She stared for perhaps a minute more at the sodden creature of straw and sacking and worn-out, unwanted clothes. Then, quickly, like a child surprised at some forbidden activity, she scrambled to her feet and brushed at the dirt that clung to her legs and skirt. She didn't speak again; instead, she pressed three fingers to her mouth, like a silent compact, a conspiracy of secrecy between herself and the scarecrow. The gesture might also have been taken for a blown kiss.

Then she turned about and was gone, back to the farm and her work and the urgent business of Jone's message.

And that was how the make-believe began.

Chapter III

She didn't mean to go back to the place in the wood. By the time she reached the farmhouse she had already dismissed the whole episode as a silly game, a momentary, childish diversion that had no significance worth thinking about. Ignoring Izzy's henhouse flutterings at the state of her clothes, she delivered her message to Lob and helped him to harness Faithful to the cart before retreating indoors to set about preparing her own evening meal.

Jone and Garler Shepherd saved all but six of the newborn lambs, an achievement, as Jone wearily said later, that in this weather owed more to Providence than to human effort. Barring two brief visits to change his soaked clothes, he was away from the farm for a total of three days and four nights, which for Carys was a new and intriguing experience. With Jone absent, she was the undisputed chatelaine of both house and farm. It meant more work as a consequence, but Carys had never been work-shy, and found herself actually enjoying her new, if temporary, responsibility. Throughout the day she was brisk and busy, a bubbling well of enthusiastic energy that would have astonished her mother had she been there to witness it. And at night she slept the deep, sound sleep of one exhausted by honest labour, alone in Jone's bed and free to move and writhe and indulge her most secret dreams.

For two nights and the day between, she did not venture away from the closed world of the farmyard. Lob carried food to Jone and Garler at midday, while Deenor Garlerwife took care of their evening victuals. But on the second day of Jone's absence, word came via one of Garler's sons that his mother had a touch of the

ague, and begging pardon but could Missus Jone be so kind as to
see for the men's needs tonight, there being no daughters in Garler's
household to know what had to be done. Carys smiled and
consented, and felt a disturbing stir in her loins as she watched the
tall, well-built youth depart. She kept watching until he was out of
sight. Then she turned from the door and went in search of Izzy.

She didn't send Lob that evening, but delivered the basket of food
herself, timing the walk so that she could be home again before
dusk turned to darkness. There was a hint, today, of a gentling in
the weather; intervals between bouts of rain had become longer,
and though there was no trace of the sun yet, the biting, dismal
chill was at last beginning to relent. As she passed the wood on her
outward journey, Carys thought of the distorted oak sapling, but
she did not look.

When she returned, however, her steps slowed, almost (or so
she convinced herself) without any conscious intention. She
stopped, lingered, gazing at the cryptic tangle of the wood. Then
she glanced right and left. No one in view. The only eyes to see her
were those of a hare loping slowly across the next field, and the
hare wasn't interested.

Abruptly she turned from the path, went through the gap in the
hedge and entered the wood.

It took her a few minutes to find the scarecrow. At first she
thought that someone must have moved it – or, more fancifully,
that it had moved by itself. But it was simply that she'd mistaken
the spot. One tree looked much like another, and at last she saw the
angular figure sprawling in the leaf mould where she had left it,
looking for all the world like a sleeping drunkard.

She didn't touch it immediately, but stood a few paces back,
looking, and mulling over the strange thoughts that were forming
in her mind. For all her derisive thoughts of the other day, this did
not feel like a foolish game. Or, if it was, why should she not have
a game of her own? A secret of her own? It harmed no one, so no
one need ever know. And in an obscure way it would please her to

26

see this doll, this thing, come to a proper semblance of life.

She looked around, wondering if she might find an early flower or two among the debris of the woodland floor. There was nothing – the weather had seen to that – so instead she looked down at herself. She was wearing a scarf, tucked in to the collar of her coat to keep out the damp. It was an old one, worthless, but brightly coloured, and she took it off and wound it around the scarecrow's neck, carefully arranging the two ends on his straw-stuffed chest. With the hat adjusted to a different angle it gave him a jaunty air that made her smile.

'You look ridiculous,' she told him. Never mind. That could be put right, in time. It was, at least, a beginning.

A small, cold wind stirred the bare branches and rustled the leaves at her feet, and she realised that the daylight was failing. The last half-mile home would be arduous in the dark; best that she should go quickly.

But she would come back. Soon.

Jone made no direct reference to Carys's efforts about the farm in his absence, but when they returned home from the next market day, he gruffly – and surprisingly – presented her with a new hat. It was quite the fashionable thing: straw, with a small brim, a dark blue band to match her blue dress, and a sprig of blue linen daisies pinned to the bow. Gyll Merionwife had one much like it, and Carys guessed that Jone had copied the idea from her. She was delighted, and in a rush of appreciation flung her arms around his neck and kissed his chin, which was already shadowed with the day's beard growth. Jone seemed pleased, smiling and blinking rapidly before asking what time his dinner would be ready, and with a renewed stirring of her dissatisfied longings Carys wondered if tonight, at last, something might occur. But when they went to bed, Jone only said his usual 'Good night to you, Wife,' turned his back to her, and fell asleep.

Carys lay awake in the dark for a long time. She was learning to stifle the worst of her disappointment, but she could not crush it altogether. She doubted if she would ever be able to do that. Carefully, tentatively, she touched herself, first her breasts through the folds of her nightgown and then lower, towards the forbidden, unfulfilled place. She didn't have the courage to explore too far; modesty, and her mother's dire warnings of what befell girls who committed such wickedness, were thoroughly ingrained. But she felt the stirrings again, and with them the now familiar reactions: frustration, curiosity, and a deep, abiding resentment of Jone for his neglect.

The vixen wasn't screaming tonight. Doubtless she had found what she wanted, and Carys resented her, too, for her better fortune. She turned over in the bed, trying not to notice Jone's heavy, regular breathing that would soon become snores. Eyes wide open but with no light to see anything, she made a decision. A plan. It wasn't a dramatic plan, and in the greater term would make not a jot of difference. But it would help, a little, and so would be better than nothing at all.

Carys closed her eyes at last, and, eventually, slept.

In the morning she was awake an hour before her usual time. It was still pitch dark, but as she dressed (quietly, not wanting to disturb Jone) and tiptoed downstairs with a candle to light her way, she could feel a change in the atmosphere. It was warmer, and the house was no longer besieged by the sound of rain swilling in the gutters. Peering through the kitchen window she saw stars in the western sky, and when she squeaked the window open the air had a new and different smell to it; the smell of change, and of spring.

To Carys, it was an omen, and as soon as she had riddled up the range and put on the barley-meal for breakfast, she lit a lantern and ran out to the cow-byre. The cows turned their heads to stare at her, pausing in their slow, meditative chewing and obviously wondering at this early visitation. One of the younger heifers uttered a long *mer-er-er*, like a question. Ignoring them, Carys hurried through the byre to the store-barn beyond. Here were kept the hay and corn, cattle-cake and salt licks, and on the far side, looming dimly beyond the lamplight, the great stack of straw bales for the animals' bedding. Setting the lantern well clear, Carys took a hemp sack and went to the bales, disturbing four of the six cats that lived in the barn and made short work of the rats and mice. Two of them, Tabby and Little Black, came treading across the straw to greet her, purring and with their tails raised in the hope of milk.

'It isn't time for milking yet.' Abstractedly Carys scratched Tabby behind the ears and gently wound Little Black's tail around to tickle his own nose. 'Later, now. I'm busy.'

The cats watched with puzzled interest as she started to pull pieces of straw from the bales, examining each one before rejecting it or pushing it into the sack. When she judged that she had enough, she picked up her lantern again and was gone in moments, hastening back to the house. In the doorway she paused, listening, but there were no sounds of stirring overhead. Still safe, then. Now . . . where had she put that old jacket that Jone had said could go to the chapel poor-box . . . ? She found it in the cupboard under the stairs. It had been a good jacket in its time, kept for feast days and other celebrations. Jone must have had it for twenty years or more, and if you ignored the threadbare patches there was still a fair amount of wear left in it. But it was a younger man's garment; Jone said that for him to wear it now was like putting gosling's feathers on an old gander, and it was time for it to go to some more needy soul who either wouldn't look a fool in it or wouldn't mind if he did. Carys, though, had another use for the jacket, and it disappeared into the sack along with the straw.

Next came some scraps of patching leather, a needle and thread from her work-box, and the kitchen scissors. Jone might notice the scissors' absence, but they would be back in their place before he could ask any questions, so no real risk there. Now, what else . . . Standing hands on hips in the middle of the kitchen floor, Carys gazed around for inspiration, and was still looking when a floorboard creaked in the bedroom directly above her. Jone was awake. Carys muttered a word that she shouldn't even have known, snatched up the half-full sack and whisked out into the yard again. She hid her spoils in the barn, burying them out of sight between two bales to the cats' renewed interest, then – to make the thing look right – unhooked her milking apron from its nail in the byre and tied it round her waist.

Jone was coming down the stairs as she arrived back in the kitchen. He looked at the apron in surprise, then smiled his slow smile.

'You're abroad early, my dear.'

Carys smiled brilliantly back at him. 'I woke early, Jone, and there didn't seem any point in wasting time lying abed when I knew I'd not go back to sleep.' She went into the scullery and returned with clean udder-cloths and a bucket. 'I'll make the cows ready, shall I, and then you can milk while I fetch our breakfast?'

She knew he was nonplussed by this sudden rush of industry, but hoped he'd put it down to the habit she had acquired while he had been away at the lambing. Turning so that he wouldn't see her face (she had an unpleasant feeling that she was flushing noticeably) she continued, 'It's going to be a much better day. Clear, even. We've all waited long enough for that, haven't we? So I thought . . .' Nibbling her lip she glanced at him over her shoulder. He wasn't watching her as she had feared; instead he had gone to the weather-glass on the wall and was tapping it, squinting a little to see the pointer with his increasingly long-sighted eyes. But he was listening, for when she stopped he said, 'Mmm? What did you think?'

'I thought . . . that perhaps I might walk down to the mill and see Mother. If the day *is* clear. It's a while since I've visited, what with the weather and us being so busy.' She paused. 'We could take tea, and I could wear my new hat. I needn't be gone long.'

Jone said, 'Mmm' again, which didn't signify anything one way or the other. Carys waited. She knew by now that he always took his time in considering even the most trivial matters. Then at last he smiled again.

'I think that would be very well. Go this morning.' He smiled again. 'And yes; wear your new hat, and have it admired.'

He thought, Carys surmised as she left the house later, that the hat was her main, if not only, motive for this sudden impulse to call on Tibba. The few social meetings they had had with her family since the wedding had been ordeals of stilted small-talk punctuated by long, uncomfortable silences when no one could think of anything else to say, and so far she had shown no anxiety to repeat the exercise more often than was necessary. Well, if the hat gave her an excuse, that was all to the good. She would have to call at the mill, of course, or complications might arise later, but she needn't stay long. And before she went, she could complete her other task with no one any the wiser.

By a happy coincidence, the field track to the mill road was the same one that led past the oak wood, so Carys needed no subterfuge as she set off in bright sunshine and a brisk wind, with a basket on her arm. The basket contained two bottles of Jone's cider brew for Powl – and, underneath and squashed as small as Carys could make it, the hemp sack and its contents. Carys's pace increased as she left the farmhouse further and further behind, and as her steps quickened it seemed that her heartbeat was quickening with them, beating in rhythm like a marching drum. Her gaze was fixed on the grey-brown curve of the wood coming closer with every moment, and by the time she reached the gap in the hedge where the contorted sapling grew, she was stumbling and almost running over the rutted ground.

The scarecrow was there, wetter and more bedraggled than ever, but with the bright scarf still in place and the hat still rakishly tilted.

'Well, then,' Carys said to it, standing arms akimbo and smiling slightly as she gazed down. 'You're a sight to behold, aren't you? Not fit for any company. But perhaps we can make a change.'

One of the two scraps of bark that were the scarecrow's makeshift eyes had vanished, dislodged, probably, by a bird or mouse that mistook it for something worth eating. So it looked at though the unfinished thing was winking at her. Carys tried to wink back, but couldn't; she had never mastered the trick of shutting one eye without the other closing, too. Her smile became almost a grin. Then she set down her basket, lifted aside the covering cloth and the bottles of cider, and set about her work.

Tibba was surprised to see her youngest daughter. She was also pleased. Carys's new hat wasn't even noticed, let alone mentioned, for Tibba had momentous news of her own.

'Hus-BAND!' she shrilled into the dusty, sun-and-shadow depths of the mill, ignoring Carys's protests that there was really no cause to disturb her father from his work.

'What's to do, woman?' Powl's burly figure appeared on the upper platform, where he was filling the great hopper with a new consignment of winter oats.

'Carys is here to see us!' Tibba called. 'Come down, come down!'

Carys expected Powl to bawl back that he was busy and what did he want with women's chatter, but instead, to her astonishment, his face broke into a broad smile. He came creaking down the ladder and strode into the kitchen, filmed with dust as he was and – even more astonishingly – drawing no protest from Tibba.

'Well, daughter!' He looked Carys up and down, nodding with satisfaction, though not, she suspected, at what he saw. 'You've heard the good news, then?'

Carys echoed, 'Good news?' and Tibba flapped her hands agitatedly. 'Powl, I haven't had the chance—'

Powl had lifted a corner of the cloth that covered the basket, and interrupted her as he saw the cider.

'What's this?' he demanded, almost jovially. 'For the celebration?'

'Jone sent it, Father,' Carys said, more mystified than ever. 'The brew's just matured, and he asks that you sample it and give your opinion.'

'That I will – and with reason now, eh, Wife?' He jabbed Tibba playfully, and painfully, in the ribs. 'Go on then woman, as you're plainly on the point of bursting at the seams. Tell her.'

'It's your sister, Carys,' Tibba said, as soon as she could get her breath back. 'Nellen.' She beamed. 'She's to be wed.'

'Oh!' Carys blinked, then hastily made herself smile. 'That's – that's brave news, Mother. I'm greatly happy for her.' In truth, she was largely indifferent to anything connected with her eldest sister, for they'd never got on. But her parents were too enthusiastic to notice any lack on her part.

'We thought it would take her longer to be offered for,' Powl was continuing, 'and I can't say that the match is as good as I might have hoped. Nellen hasn't got much in looks or temper and there's no point pretending she has. Takes after your mother's side of the family, more's the pity. But Jemp Holder's a steady sort, and an only son; when his father dies he'll have all of their holding, so she'll be well set up.'

Carys tried to put a face to the name of Jemp Holder, but couldn't. She did recall, though, that he was very far from handsome, which went some way towards explaining his choice of a bride. That, and the portion – or bribe – that Powl would doubtless have dangled as bait. Part of the settlement that Jone had made upon her . . .

'We'll have tea,' said Tibba suddenly. 'I'll put it on to brew. Sit down, Carys, there at the table. And you too, Powl, I'm sure you can leave your work for a few minutes.' She glanced at Carys over her shoulder, her look meaningful and with a faintly coquettish hint. 'After all, who knows but that Carys hasn't got news of her own?'

Powl had opened his mouth to say that he had no time for such flummery, but closed it again as he realised what his wife was hinting at. It had, after all, been four months now since Carys and Jone were wed; high time for the anticipated announcement to be made. So he sat down and gave his daughter a quizzing scowl.

'Well, then, girl. What *is* your news, since last we saw you?'

Carys knew precisely what they were hoping, and indeed expecting, to hear. She looked down at the table.

'That's a fine new hat, Carys,' Tibba commented, making a point of noticing it at last and putting entirely the wrong interpretation on it. There was a pause. Carys still didn't speak, and at length Tibba prompted, 'Did Jone give it to you?'

'Yes,' said Carys tersely.

'That's kind of him! And was there a . . . reason?'

Something darkly furious rose in Carys's heart and mind. She looked her mother directly in the face and repeated, much more clearly, 'Yes. There was.'

The abiding silence was like waiting for the first explosion of thunder on a sultry summer day. Carys was wrestling inwardly, desperately, to keep her self-control and not scream in their faces that she had nothing, nothing, *nothing* to tell them, and most certainly not the news that they were so agog for, and tell them *why*, and tell them *everything*. Rationality won. She blinked and smiled, a fixed, artificial smile.

'Jone and Garler Shepherd had trouble with the lambs in the foul weather. Jone was away from home over four nights, and I ran the farm on my own. He was grateful to me. So he bought me a gift.'

Tibba's face fell like melting treacle. 'Oh,' she said. 'Yes. I see. Well, that *was* kind of him, wasn't it?'

'Yes,' said Carys.

Silence again. The kettle started to hiss and sputter, and Tibba made tea. Powl was studying the cider bottles, as if they held the answer to some unasked and baffling question, and at last Carys couldn't stand the suspense any longer.

'When's Nellen's wedding to be?' she asked, trying her best to sound cheerful, normal. 'Is it decided yet?'

'We thought' – Tibba sniffed, and rubbed a finger quickly under her nose – 'We thought Hawthorn-month. At the beginning. That will give her the best of the summer to settle to her new life, won't it, Powl?'

Powl grunted assent. 'No point in delaying. Nellen's not getting any younger.'

The barb went home and Carys's cheeks flamed. When the tea was set in front of her she started to gulp it down immediately, wanting only to get through this miserable encounter and leave.

'Nellen will be sorry to have missed you,' Tibba told her, watching with mute and misplaced sympathy as Carys grimaced over scalded tongue and mouth. 'She's over to the holding this morning, to see everything and . . . well . . .'

'Yes,' said Carys. 'Of course. Tell her I'm glad for her. And I'll see her at the wedding.'

'Yes, yes. You'll be one of the bride-maids, I'm sure Nellen will want that.' A forced smile. 'Bride-matron. That's the thing. Bride-matron.'

Carys drained her cup and rose to her feet. 'I can't,' she said in answer to Tibba's hesitant invitation to stay longer. 'There's work to do. I mustn't neglect . . .'

Tibba saw her to the door. Under the porch, she reached out and touched Carys's arm.

'Daughter . . .' Her expression was earnest, and a little pinched; quickly she looked back to make sure that Powl wasn't in earshot. 'These things, they . . . sometimes take a while. Don't lose heart, Carys. You're young. There's plenty of time. Plenty.'

Carys wanted to rake her fingernails down Tibba's cheeks, like a raging cat. Instead, she delivered a formal, dutiful and cold kiss to her mother's cheek, mumbled her goodbyes, and left. She could feel Tibba watching her until she had turned the curve in the road and was out of sight, then she stopped in the middle of the track as a flush of furious heat sang through her body, reddening her cheeks and bringing sweat prickling to her forehead and hands. She felt humiliated, mortified. As if she were a fair-day exhibit, some freakish thing to be carried around in a cage for pointing and gawping and prodding at . . . The shame and anger of it brought tears to her eyes; she clenched her teeth against them, forcing them away, and stared around at the road and the hedges.

A primrose, just one, was flowering at the roadside. Carys felt a violent urge to tear it from the earth and crush and rip it to shreds, taking out her venom on something that couldn't strike back. She had already taken three steps towards it, hand outstretched, when reason won over blind fury, and instead she slowed and her movements became more gentle and considered. She picked the flower, very carefully, and for a few moments stood holding it up to her face, studying its delicacy and beauty. The very first flower of spring. It would be an ill thing to spoil it for the sake of spite. She could find a far, far better use for it than that.

Clutching the flower in one hand and cupping it with the other to protect its fragile stem, she set off again along the road. When she reached the gate into Jone Farmer's fields she was walking at a rapid near-jog, and by the time she came to the gap in the hedge, and the twisted oak sapling, she was all but running.

As she approached the scarecrow on his seat of dead leaves, she saw him with fresh eyes. He looked very different. The jacket had confined and moulded his bulky straw body into something slimmer and much more human and the effect pleased her, as did the new straw hair that she had painstakingly shaped to frame his face, smoothing it and gathering it into a single plait down his back. The leather patches that she had cut and sewn to his face to make eyes and mouth were not so successful; stitching into sacking and wet straw had not been an easy task, and one eye was lower than the other, while the mouth was too big and grinned crudely, like the mouth of a turnip lantern on Hollow Night. He had no real expression, which was a disappointment, but, in time, improvements could and would be made. Already – and if Carys had asked herself, she could not have said why – he was something more than a dumdolly. And he was *hers.*

She placed the primrose in the top buttonhole of his jacket, and wrapped the stem in a piece of damp moss so that it should be preserved for as long as possible. Her head was close to the scarecrow's head, and as she arranged the flower petals she thought for one fleeting moment that his face, blurred on the periphery of her vision, changed. It gave her a startling jolt, and she jumped quickly back, staring at him like a rabbit surprised and mesmerised by a hunting fox. Then light and shadow danced again on the sacking features and she realised that it was only the effect of the sun, making shifting patterns through the branches above her.

Experimentally, Carys blinked, but the scarecrow did not blink back, and the leather eyes remained as blank as ever. She laughed at herself, and quickly smothered the sound, though there was no one in the vicinity to hear it. Then, feeling bold and ridiculous, mocking and playful all at once, she kissed the scarecrow on his witlessly smiling mouth. He tasted of tanning-oil and hemp and mildew, a combination that made her grimace with revulsion. But she made her lips linger for a second or two before she broke the contact. Then she straightened up, wiping her mouth and then rubbing at it to get rid of the last residue. She giggled as she wondered what Jone would think if he were to kiss her and find that taint on her lips, then reminded herself that Jone did not make a habit of kissing her. She remembered Nellen's forthcoming marriage, and the giggle faded and darkened into a frown.

Turning, she snatched up her basket. The scarecrow, mute and motionless, watched her as she tramped away through the forest debris, where one or two green shoots were now beginning to appear. As Carys's steps faded, a robin came down and alighted on one of the scarecrow's limp hands, pecking busily until it had extracted a generous beakful of straw. Then it flipped away with its quick, bouncing flight. A few minutes later, the full-throated music of its song flowed from a distant branch.

But there was no one to hear it.

Chapter IV

'Father and Mother are greatly pleased for Nellen, of course,' Carys said. Cautiously she raised her gaze from her plate to Jone's face. 'They hope for grandchildren before long.'

Jone's peaceable expression didn't waver. He only nodded and said, 'That will be pleasing. I trust the union will be blessed.'

They were at their evening meal. Izzy had gone home an hour ago, towing Lob – who had been having one of his less rational days – with her like a dog on a lead, and the farmhouse was a quiet, comfortable haven with nothing to disturb its tranquillity. Jone enjoyed this private ending to each day; as he often said to Carys, it was a time of pleasant companionship and peaceful ease before the next day's work must begin. Tonight, though, Carys felt neither pleasant nor peaceful. She kept up the pretence, as to do otherwise would be impossible, but inwardly, silently, she was howling.

Jone's knife clicked on the plate as he cut his meat. A roasted fowl. Jone had suggested it when Carys told him her family's news, as a token of celebration for Nellen's good fortune. He had killed the bird, and Carys had plucked and cooked it, snapping at Izzy when she tried to help. Jone had also opened another of his cider bottles, which now stood on the table between them. Only a small part of its contents had gone; Jone's large mug was still half full, and though Carys had drained her own smaller mug and would dearly have liked much, much more, she could not ask, but must wait for it to be offered.

They continued to eat. Neither spoke again for a while, and the ticking of the clock began to grate on Carys's nerves. Slow, ponderous, inexorable, marking the seconds of her life away one by one; she wanted to jump up from the table and wrench its hands from its face, bending and twisting them, then pull out the pendulum and throw it through the window, and—

'We must put our minds to the thought of a suitable gift,' said Jone meditatively.

Carys forgot the clock and scowled, replying before she could stop herself, 'Haven't they already had enough from you?'

He looked at her in surprise. 'What do you mean, my dear? I don't understand.'

She shrugged resentfully. 'Well . . . Father hasn't much money. I don't doubt that part of my bride-price has gone to buy a husband for Nellen.'

She regretted saying it the moment it was out, but there was no undoing it. Jone looked at her with a blend of astonishment and sorrow, and said, with something approaching severity, 'Wife, that is not a kind remark. Especially about your own sister.' He paused, frowning. 'It isn't like you to be uncharitable.'

No, Carys thought, it isn't. Meek, obedient, docile, yes, but not *uncharitable*. How little he knew . . .

But she could not argue with him. For all his even-tempered kindness she dared not, for he was her husband and she his chattel.

'I'm sorry, Jone,' she said indistinctly, clasping her hands under the table and digging her fingernails painfully into the flesh. 'I didn't intend . . . that is I meant only . . .' Then the attempt at a false explanation failed and she hung her head. 'Forgive me.'

'Of course, child,' said Jone. She hated it when he called her that. He smiled. 'Perhaps it's only natural that you should feel some small rivalry. It's in the character of women, and in a small way there's no harm in it. But be assured, by giving a gift to your sister I am not slighting or belittling *you*.' He raised his mug, as though to toast her. 'I would never, ever do that.'

Carys was defeated. She finished her food in silence, was grateful for a second mug of cider (though to her disappointment it wasn't enough to make her feel drunk) and, when Jone too had had his fill, cleared the dishes, washed them, and put the rest of the fowl away in the larder.

By the time these tasks were done, Jone had moved to the ingle and was sitting in his favourite chair. He had the book, his one book, open on his lap and was thumbing through it. This was a familiar signal for a now familiar routine. Carys was to read to him, and then he would say, inevitably and invariably, 'It's growing late, Wife, and tomorrow we must work,' and they would go to bed, and he would sleep, and she . . .

Carys suppressed a sigh and asked, 'What passage would you like tonight, Husband?'

She read to him in her halting, stumbling way, while Jone sat gazing idly at the fire, listening to the words and enjoying the sound of her voice. Carys's mind, though, was even less focused on tonight's tract than was usual, and abruptly the pressure of her thoughts grew too great to be borne any longer.

She paused in mid-sentence and looked up.

'Husband . . .'

Jone raised his eyes from their sleepy contemplation of the fire's flickering. 'What is it, my dear?'

A snake moved down Carys's spine, and she tried to ignore the feeling. 'Why . . . did you choose me?'

The question surprised him, she could see that from the slight but distinct change in his expression. Then, as usual, he smiled.

'What manner of idle question is that, Carys?' He nodded towards the book in her hands. 'Read on. I like to hear you.'

Carys wasn't daunted. She drew a deep breath and said: 'Jone, do you love me?'

He blinked at her, slowly, thoughtfully. 'Why yes, I believe I love you dearly. Do I not provide for you, and are we not the best of companions?' Then he leaned forward and patted her hand where it clenched and trembled on the arm of her chair. 'If I've let you go wanting, then tell me how and I shall make amends.'

He was thinking of their earlier conversation, but this had nothing

to do with Nellen. 'No,' Carys said. 'No, it isn't . . .' Her lips were
dry. She licked them quickly, but the fire's heat seemed to scald
them again. He wasn't angry, wasn't about to upbraid her for
impertinence. She could say it. She *must* say it.

'Jone – why did you not choose someone else?'

There was a pause. Then, to Carys's surprise, Jone laughed.

'Carys, my dear.' His voice was warm, amused, complacent.
'You don't think I have regrets? Is that what you're fearing? No,
no, not at all! You please me greatly, my dear; you have a pretty
face to grace my table, and a pretty voice to read to me when our
day's work is over. You feed me well, and you are diligent and
good and obedient. I am *proud* of my new wife, and I wouldn't
trade her for another.' He smiled again, at the fire this time, and
sighed the sigh of a contented soul. 'What more could a wise man
want?'

Carys didn't speak. She longed to leap at him, to claw his face
with her hands, to tear at him, rail at him, scream at him: *what of
me? I am young, I am yearning, I am ALIVE! Touch me, you fool,
you old man, you worthless, useless, withered thing, or if you won't
touch me, then let me go to another who will!* But the words were
no more than a surging, rolling agony inside her and she couldn't
give them form. Rebellion – *open* rebellion – was beyond her. She
could do nothing and say nothing, and so she fell silent.

Jone Farmer, her husband who was no husband at all, stretched
his arms and yawned. 'Enough now, wife. It's growing late, and
tomorrow we must work,' he said, not noticing how Carys silently,
savagely mouthed the litany along with him. 'Go up to bed, now.
I'll see to the fire and take a last look at the animals. Good night to
you, my dear.'

Carys said, very quietly, 'Good night, Jone.'

Within a few days, the longed-for spring had well and truly arrived.
And as if to make up for the time it had taken in coming, it was the
warmest and kindliest spring the district had seen in years. Crops,
trees, hedgerows and wild flowers burgeoned under lengthening

days of sunlight, and the winds blew lightly from the south or west, with no sign of the vicious and unpredictable easterlies that so often disrupted the season and spoiled its promise.

It was a busy time for Jone and Carys and their neighbours. The lambs were growing quickly, and other new arrivals weren't far behind them. Four calves were born within a month, three of which – to Jone's delight – were heifers. The hens were laying, and several had gone broody over clutches of eggs, which soon hatched out into energetic balls of yellow fluff that had to be protected from the attentions of the farmyard cats as well as from wilder predators. At market one day, on the spur of the moment, Jone bought a small flock of piebald ducks to populate the pond in the hollow by the largest barn, and it was Carys's task to accustom them to their new home and cure their determined instinct to return to their old one. Then there were the rapidly sprouting crops to be weeded, the last of the winter's roots to be lifted and stored, all in addition to the regular work of the house. Carys had barely a waking moment to rest, and each night she slept the sleep of healthy exhaustion, with hardly a fleeting thought for her personal predicament.

But still, now and then, she stole a little time to return to the oak wood and the scarecrow.

She went there on the eve of her sister's wedding, which, as Tibba wanted, had been set for the first day of Hawthorn-month. Carys had seen little of her family since the announcement of the betrothal; she had – thankfully – been too busy. But she and Jone had driven once to the mill, riding in the gig and taking Jone's choice of a wedding gift: two good yew-wood chairs, with curved arms and wheel-shaped backs, which Jone had commissioned from Bartel Carpenter in the village. Carys suspected that they had cost a pretty penny, but Jone could afford to be generous, and as she would not have to go without as a result, she had no cause to carp. All the same, a niggling worm of self-pity was awake inside her as she made her way down the field track to the wood. On that one visit to the mill she had met Jemp Holder, Nellen's husband-to-be. He certainly wasn't much to look at: his hair was sparse and receding

– and red into the bargain – and he had a large and unsightly birthmark on one side of his face. He would also, she guessed, become very overweight before many more years had passed. But for all his defects, he was young. No more than thirty, which put him much of an age with Nellen. And the look Carys had seen in his eyes stated quite clearly that he had no intention of neglecting a husband's natural duties. Even while thanking Jone effusively for the gift, he had been glancing sidelong at Nellen with a thinly-veiled and hungry anticipation. Twice, Carys had caught him looking at her in that way, too, and she had turned hot under the scrutiny. She was not attracted to Jemp, nor ever could be. But simply to be looked at in that way, by any man, was enough to set the old stirrings alight again – and light, too, the spark of her envy. She didn't believe for one moment that either Jemp or Nellen was marrying for love. But there was no doubt in her mind that they would have compensations in plenty.

So, then, her discontented mood that evening, and the reason why she had to go to the wood. For as the spring advanced, on the few visits she had managed, Carys had elaborated on the game she had begun to play on that first wet and dreary day when she had vented her frustration on the scarecrow and dragged him from his rickety pole in the field. In her imagination he had become, first, her friend and confidant, to whom she bitterly whispered her secrets safe in the knowledge that he could never repeat them to any living soul. Then, after a while, the 'friend' had begun to turn into something more. He looked very different now, for she had carefully worked on his improvement, concentrating most of her attention not on his clothing but on the body beneath. She had reshaped his face, giving it proper contours, and replaced the primitive eyes and mouth with a contrivance of sewing and patching that resulted in a tolerably good imitation of real features. He even had a nose now, new sacking for skin, and his hands were no longer mere tufts of straw bound with twine; she had found a pair of old leather gloves, and these, stuffed with soft hay, were vastly better. He looked almost . . . *human.*

And, incited by that resemblance, Carys's fancies had begun to grow.

She didn't – not truly – *do* anything. At least, nothing that was shocking or shameful or, to use her mother's favourite execration, *wicked*. She only sat astride his outstretched legs, there among the drying leaf mould, gazed into his face, smiled at him, and pretended, just a little, that he was not a lifeless doll but a handsome, living, young man. To help the pretence along she sometimes manoeuvred his arms so that the glove-and-hay hands touched her, coming to rest on her waist or shoulders, or once, more boldly, on her breasts. That experiment had brought her out in a sweat of shame and excitement, and afterwards she hadn't dared return to the wood for days. But the rest was harmless. Even the kisses she planted artlessly on his mouth or cheeks were innocent enough, though recently they had started to become longer and more intense, leaving her breathless and pink-cheeked and feeling just a little like a coquette.

She hadn't given him a name. She would have liked to, but she could not think of one that was right. Besides, a name was personal and would have made him more real, and she was still afraid to let this fantasy go too far. So nameless he remained. But in her dreams, both waking and sleeping, he was beginning to fulfil the role of the lover she yearned to know.

On the wedding eve, she didn't kiss or caress him, but only sat in the undergrowth by his side and talked to him, trying to express her confusion and envy and increasingly complex longings. He was a passive, mute companion, but at this moment that was what Carys wanted, and it didn't matter that he made no reply, or that when she held his hand and squeezed it there was no answering response. Tomorrow, she told him, she would dance at Nellen's wedding, and must smile at her and wish her well, and try not to think of what she and Jemp Holder would do when the festivities were over and they were alone with the whole night ahead of them.

'I wish you could be there,' she said, turning her head to regard the scarecrow with eyes that were suddenly very dark and intense. 'You would come in at the door, and I would be among the guests, and when you saw me you would have eyes for no one else. You would ask me to dance, and I would say yes, and then we would take to the floor, and afterwards we . . . we . . .'

The daydream collapsed into a strangled scream of rage and frustration, and Carys jumped to her feet, almost kicking the scarecrow aside, and paced up and down the clearing. She knew few swear words, but she wanted to say them all, shout them, run down to the village, knock on every door and *shriek* them brazenly at everyone who answered! The impulse passed, dying down to a simmer, and instead she gave a sigh of exasperation as common sense took control once more.

'Nellen Jempwife,' she said aloud, and smiled a small, contemptuous smile. Nellen Jempwife. Hardly a name to flaunt. It sounded clumsy. Carys Jonewife had a much better ring to it. Or Carys . . . She looked at the scarecrow again. Carys *What*wife? *Who*wife?

'Carys Scarecrow-wife,' she announced pompously, and giggled. If she could keep refilling her cup without Jone noticing, she would get drunk tomorrow. Why not? A toast to the newly wed couple. A toast for the spring, for a good harvest. And a toast, or two, or three, for her friend. Her scarecrow. Her secret. Why not?

Feeling unsteady on her feet, as if something within her was already anticipating the plan, she weaved to the edge of the clearing, adjusted her skirt, hat and shawl, so that they did not look so dishevelled, and gave the scarecrow a last, appraising stare.

'Wait for me,' she said softly. 'I'll come back soon.' She would, for she had no other choice, not now. These interludes were more than a relief to her, they were a *need*. Without them, she did not think she could keep up the pretence of contentment for much longer.

The scarecrow returned her stare blankly. Carys smiled, then turned to face home and work and the steady familiarity of real life.

When it came to it, she didn't have the courage to get drunk at

Nellen's wedding. Her father did, though, to the embarrassment of Tibba and the huge amusement of almost everyone else. Powl made a lengthy speech, climbing on a table for emphasis and rambling happily on until one of the trestle legs suddenly gave way and pitched him into the laps of Merion Blacksmith, Elios Carter and Elios's wife, Juda. Jone smiled at the antics, but Carys, who had stayed dutifully at his side rather than dancing as she wanted to, saw that his eyes reflected discomfort rather than mirth.

After Powl's performance, the wedding feast grew steadily more riotous. Ribald jokes abounded, crude songs were sung, even the preacher was persuaded to get up and perform a ditty that had nothing to do with chapel principles. The normally dour Nellen was laughing uproariously, while Jemp, increasingly impatient, fumbled at her under cover of the table. Only Thomsine, Carys's middle sister and one of the bride-maids (Carys had managed to avoid that ordeal), was sulkily ignoring the fun. Thomsine was jealous of both Carys and Nellen, and today her jealousy was fuelled by disappointment that Garler Shepherd's third son had steadfastly ignored her efforts to catch his eye. As the boy was very handsome, and five years younger than Thomsine, Carys was hardly surprised, and Thomsine's discomfort gave her a small, shameful feeling of pleasure.

Jone chose to leave not long afterwards. Courteously but firmly pleading tiredness, he made his farewells and, with Carys obediently at his heels, headed for the door. They drove home under a rising, gold-tinged moon, with the scent of thorn blossom on the air. Every now and then Jone made some pleasant observation on the success of the occasion, the obvious happiness of the bride and groom, the quality of the food and music. Carys said yes or no as was appropriate, and watched the moon as it climbed higher above the distant dark outline of the woods. They would not pass her secret place; the field track wasn't suitable for the lightweight gig, and Spry, the young driving-pony whom they had used tonight instead of Faithful, was better suited to the level road.

They did, however, pass the gate to the field track, and as they drew level with it the sound of someone whistling floated on the breeze from far off. It was a cheerful tune, and as she heard it and realised the direction it was coming from, Carys felt her skin prickle. Who would be abroad, and whistling, at this hour? Reason told her that it could be any number of men: a travelling tinker making camp for the night, a shepherd making a late round of his flock, a rabbit-catcher satisfied with his night's work and wending his way home. But still her skin prickled.

She wasn't aware that she had turned her head to look back, straining to catch every nuance of the sound, until Jone on the seat beside her said equably, 'Is something amiss, Wife?'

Carys hastily jerked round to face forward once more. 'No,' she said. 'No, Jone. I just wondered who might be whistling that tune . . .'

Jone chuckled. 'A contented man, by the sound of it. And on such a pleasant night, who can fault him?'

The breeze capriciously changed then, and the whistling faded away, leaving only the clip of Spry's hooves and the comfortable whirr of the gig wheels. A contented man, Carys thought. Doubtless Jone was right. Only just for one moment, she had nearly allowed herself to believe that it might not be a man at all. Not a *man*, but . . .

She sighed, causing Jone to glance at her again.

'Tired, my dear? Take heart, we're nearly home. And then you can sleep undisturbed until morning.'

A small cloud covered the moon then, darkening the way, and Carys was glad that, at that moment, Jone could not see her face.

Chapter V

To the chagrin of the pessimistic weather prophets – of whom there were a good many in the district – the fine spring became an equally fine summer. Crops and livestock flourished, there were no epidemics, and with abundant grass and just the right degree of rainfall, haymaking began nearly half a month early.

For all that it meant hard work, when the weather was good everyone enjoyed haymaking. Like the later corn- and then apple-harvests, it was a time not only for neighbours but for the whole district to join and work and socialise together. Teams of willing hands moved from one farm or holding to the next as the fields ripened, and soon the stooked sheaves stood like hundreds of miniature thatched cottages among new stubble, and the stack-bases were going up in farmyards, and the great wagons were being oiled and prepared ready for the carrying. Tradition held that the stooked hay should stand in the fields for three chapel-days before it was taken home, but even with this wait, by Midsummer-feast all was done.

There was to be a midsummer celebration in the village, with food and musicians and a great, beribboned pole for dancing. All the young people would be there and not a few of the older ones. Carys, though, would not be going. Instead, she and Jone were to entertain a small party of their nearest neighbours: Merion Blacksmith and Gyll, Garler Shepherd and Deenor (their sons would be at the village festivity), Elios Carter and Juda, Gyll's – and now Carys's – good friend. This private celebration was a habit Jone had had for many years and he would not break it now. Carys was disappointed, but tried to make the best of it. She liked Gyll, Deenor and Juda, and at least Jone had not invited her parents.

Three days before the feast, however, Jone came in from the cow-byre with a troubled look on his face.

'It's Placid,' he said in response to Carys's concerned inquiry.

'Is something amiss?' Placid was the best milker of all Jone's cows, and a particular favourite of Carys's, for her temperament matched her name.

Jone nodded. 'It's some kind of malaise, that's certain, but I've not seen anything like it before. She's staggering in the byre, twisting and twining her legs about as though they've hardly the strength to support her. Then every so often she'll stop still and shiver, as if she had an ague.'

Carys frowned. 'Should we ask Merion to look at her?'

Merion was farrier as well as blacksmith, and knew more about animal ailments than anyone else for miles around.

'I've no wish to trouble him unless there's need,' Jone said dubiously. 'He's a busy man. But if she's no better by morning, then yes, I think we must.'

Placid was indeed no better by morning. In fact she was worse – hardly able to stand, and the shivering was almost continuous. She would not touch food, and, strangest of all, there seemed to be a kink in her tail, about half-way down its length.

Jone set Lob to fetch Merion, who came and subjected the cow to a long, careful examination, while Jone and Carys watched anxiously over the partition of her stall. Eventually Merion straightened up, dug the knuckles of one hand into the small of his back to ease an ache, and said, 'I'm sorry, Jone. I've seen many different sicknesses in cattle in my time, but this one defeats me! I've no idea what it is.'

Jone sighed. 'Then I'm at a loss, Merion. If you don't know, there's not another man I can name who will.'

'I'm sorry, my friend. I only wish I could help you – and Placid.'

Carys spoke up. 'Maybe it's not so serious as it looks, Jone. Maybe she'll get better by herself . . .'

Jone nodded sombrely. 'Well, that's something we can only hope for, Wife. Hope, and pray.' He paused, looking at Placid with sorrowful eyes. 'She's a fine animal. It would grieve me to lose her.'

By the evening of Midsummer-feast Placid had not died, nor really deteriorated any further. But she was clearly very sick, and Jone held out little hope of a recovery. When their guests arrived, Merion took another look at the animal but declared himself as baffled as ever, and neither Garler nor Elios had anything of help to add. So it was a more subdued party than it might have been. Thanks to Carys's and Izzy's efforts, the meal was splendid, and though he drank little cider or beer himself, Jone never stinted his guests. When the food was gone, the women helped Carys to clear the table while the men settled themselves around the fire, refilled their mugs, lit their pipes and began to talk.

By the time the clearing was done, they had moved on from discussing Placid in particular and were on the subject of animal ailments in general. Merion Blacksmith recounted the tale of a smallholder who had come to him some months ago for help for a sick pig. Recognising the sickness, Merion had prescribed a dose of medicine that was to be mixed with apple-brandy; he had provided the brandy as well as the dose, and two days later had heard that the pig was still ailing, while the smallholder was at home nursing a sore head. The burst of laughter at this brought Gyll Merionwife to the fire saying that they must share the joke, so the tale was told a second time.

The clearing completed, Carys, Gyll, Juda and Deenor joined their menfolk at the hearth, and under their influence the talk became more general. Juda said that the preacher, who was unmarried, had been seen several times talking to Tally Rigswidow at her cottage door, and as he was personable and Tally lonely, she predicted an announcement before too long. Speaking of the preacher, said Gyll with a smile, had any of them seen his new pony? It looked handsome enough, but – as Merion could vouch – it was flighty and ill-trained, and only last quarter-moon it had apparently reared in the shafts, upset its gig and sent the preacher and two passengers cat-in-the-pan over the side. Merion grunted, suppressing a grin, and commented that if he was the preacher, he'd have the beast made into dog's-meat and buy the little bay filly that Padlow Holder over to the north side of Crede had for sale.

Then Deenor Garlerwife said: 'This talk of horses reminds me – I'd quite forgotten to tell you.' She leaned forward, lowering her voice as though she half expected some other, unseen presence to be listening. 'The Wayfarers are back.'

There was a moment's silence before Gyll, too, leaned forward in her chair. 'So early? Are you sure, Deenor?'

Deenor nodded. 'I've seen them for myself. They're on that piece of common land beyond the village; you know, the place where they made camp last year. Nine wagons, a string of horses and a herd of goats. I was visiting Olma Carnwidow, and she'd heard the rumour, so we drove out to see.'

Garler looked uneasily at his wife. 'You didn't talk to them? Didn't go too close?'

'No, Husband, I didn't,' Deenor assured him. 'Though they're harmless enough. Kindly, even. And we've had cause to be grateful to them before now. That time when those stray dogs had scattered the flocks and we were in dire need of help finding them again.'

'I know that, I know,' said Garler. 'But all the same, it doesn't do to get too friendly, like.'

Jone took his pipe out of his mouth, studied it, and frowned. 'I can't say that I approve of the Wayfarers,' he said. 'In my opinion, they bring nothing but trouble to any parish where they set their camps. Begging food and water with never a groat paid in return, taking up good common land to graze their skinny animals . . . and their children swarming anywhere and everywhere, and likely as not leading the children of decent folk into wild and savage ways.'

Merion rubbed his own chin thoughtfully. 'Well, Jone, I take your point, but I'm not sure that I can agree with you. I'll not deny a lot of what you've said, and you and Garler are right to counsel caution. But then again, I've had dealings of my own with the Wayfarers, and I've never found them anything but fair. Whenever they return to the district they come to me to shoe their nags, and they always pay on the nail.'

'Not with money,' Elios Carter pointed out. 'They don't hold with money, and they sneer behind their backs at those who have it.'

'True. But they pay in equal kind – more than equal, sometimes. Truly, I've no complaint to lay at their door.'

'And of course it doesn't do to overlook the *other* things,' Gyll put in quietly.

The women exchanged meaningful looks at that statement, for they all knew what Gyll meant. Each and every body present knew someone, or someone who knew someone, who had had occasion to be grateful to the Wayfarers' *other* abilities before now.

'Remember Shal Nainwife?' said Deenor. 'Years back, when her father's potboy had – well, you know what he'd done, and there she was in dire trouble, and not even old enough to be legally and properly wed. The Wayfarers gave her a spell, and the thing she didn't want was got rid of.'

'Or just five years ago,' Juda added. 'Our own youngest was taken with the quartan fever, and the apothecary despaired of him. We were desperate, and Elios went to the Wayfarers for help. They cured him, and asked nothing in return.'

Elios looked sideways at Jone, embarrassed. 'Like Juda says, we were desperate,' he repeated, as though trying to justify himself.

Juda nodded. 'So, begging your pardon under your own roof, Jone, we can't deny that for all their strange doings, the Wayfarers aren't bad folk.'

'They've got skills and powers beyond the wit of our kind,' Gyll added.

'And they're honest enough to sell them at a fair price,' said Merion.

Jone hesitated, then laughed, a little self-consciously. 'Yes, well . . . it seems I'm outnumbered by all my good friends!' He leaned down to light a spill from the fire. 'I suppose I must admit that there's good among the dross. Besides, it's not for us to judge our fellow men, as the preacher says. They have their ways, we have ours. They're different ways, that's all.'

Carys, who had taken no part in the conversation so far but had been listening intently, suddenly spoke up. 'Husband . . . what of Placid? Might the Wayfarers not be able to help her?'

She glanced uneasily at Merion as she said it, wondering if he would think the remark a slur on his abilities. But far from being offended, Merion raised his eyebrows with quick interest.

'It's a thought, Jone. I've done all I can and failed. So why not try the Wayfarers? It's either them or leave the animal to Providence, and I'd say that Providence is the lesser hope.'

Jone frowned. 'It goes against the grain . . .'

'Maybe. But to see Placid suffering goes against the grain too, doesn't it?'

'Yes . . . yes, that's true, I'll allow it.'

For reasons which she couldn't yet interpret, Carys's heart had started to beat like Merion Blacksmith's hammer on the anvil. She reached out and laid a hand tentatively on Jone's arm. 'Even though you've little liking for the Wayfarers, Husband, it's like Merion says: we've nothing to lose by going to them.' She paused, just long enough to let that thought sink into his mind. Then, 'If you don't want to ask them yourself, Jone, send me. I'm not afraid. They'll know me for your wife. They'll respect me if I speak to them with your words.'

Jone considered her suggestion. It was true that the Wayfarers *did* respect the women of the parishes, more, from what he'd heard, than they respected the men. Certainly there would be no danger in sending Carys to them unescorted; better, in many ways, than going himself, for they would be sure to sense his innate hostility and would react accordingly.

He said dubiously, 'Well . . .'

'I'd let her go, Jone,' Merion urged. 'For Placid's sake.'

That was the weak link in Jone's argument against the venture, and he knew it. He turned to face Carys. 'Very well then, Wife. We shall ask the Wayfarers – and you shall carry the message.' He looked back at the fire. 'Something must be done for poor Placid, no matter what.'

Carys's racing heart gave an extra, exultant thump, (Why she didn't know . . .). 'I could go tomorrow, Jone,' she said. 'First thing.'

Jone nodded. 'Yes,' he said. 'First thing.'

The next morning, Carys was awake even before the midsummer dawn had started to break. She didn't rise immediately, but instead lay still and quiet, aware of but not listening to the sound of Jone's breathing beside her, and thinking.

She knew, now, the cause of the lurching excitement she had felt last night, when she had diffidently suggested enlisting the Wayfarers' help for Placid. It was as if a hidden instinct had guided her – that or the Providence that, as Merion had said, was Placid's only other hope. Providence, too, that the Wayfarers should have come to the district earlier than usual this year. Their normal custom was to arrive at harvest time, when there was always casual work in plenty to be had. The fact that they had broken with custom now seemed, to Carys, deeply significant. She believed she was being guided, shown, that the Wayfarers held not only the answer to Placid's plight, but also the solution to her own.

Carefully, so as not to wake him, she turned her head and looked at Jone. Old though he might be, he wasn't an ill-favoured man. She did not find him repulsive. And he *was* her husband . . . Her games and fantasies in the wood were all very well, but they were not a cure for what ailed her, nor ever could be.

So, if she could muster the courage, why not ask the Wayfarers for a spell, to make her husband *be* a husband to her at long last?

If she could muster the courage. That was the stumbling-block, the thing that might balk her at the last and bring her scheme to nothing. To confess the truth to a stranger, and to ask for what she wanted, would be far from easy. But then, as one of the tracts in

Jone's book pointed out, the faint of heart never won the day. Carys *wanted* to win the day. Surely, surely she could overcome her abashment and humiliation for the sake of future gain?

Her fearful self argued then that there was another potential problem: the fact that the Wayfarers would surely ask for payment in some form for the services they rendered. Carys had a little money, but the travelling people scorned that. What else, then? Some goods or clothing? She could offer her new hat, but they were unlikely to want it, and anyway, Jone would notice. A coat or warm shawl? That was a possibility. Or perhaps some preserves from her larder. Izzy might wonder, but she wouldn't dare ask.

And Carys would have what she yearned for . . .

Jone stirred then, grunting as he began to wake. Quickly Carys slipped out of bed, wrapped her robe around herself and glided out of the room before he should open his eyes and see her. Downstairs, in the lamplit kitchen where dawn's first glimmer was starting to lighten the window, she riddled up the range and put on the big kettle. The excitement was back, making her feel queasy and restless and eager all at once. She must be calm, appear normal. If Jone thought she was nervous, he would change his mind and forbid her to go, or insist on coming with her. That must not, *not* happen. But the excitement would still be there, bubbling like a cauldron beneath the surface of her mind.

For today, her life was going to be changed, irrevocably and for ever.

Carys set out as the sun showed its face over the eastern shoulder of Crede Hill. Shadows of the hedges and trees formed long, gaunt fingers between shafts of dusty gold, and the day was already warm. Carys's own shadow skimmed along with her, flickering occasionally with the skip of elation in her step.

She took the field paths to skirt the village, which cut out a good deal of distance, and approached the common land from the south side instead of the west where the road ran. The Wayfarers' camp was clearly visible: nine wagons as Deenor had said, all painted in a motley of vivid colours, and behind them the tethered horses and goats, heads down and grazing. It seemed that the entire camp was already up and about. Three cooking-fires burned, looking pallid and silvery in the sunlight, and human figures in bright-coloured clothes moved hither and thither. A woman was hanging out washing on a line stretched between two caravans, two men were crouched over a wagon wheel making some repair or adjustment, and children ran and played among the clutter, their shrill voices carrying clearly.

The dogs saw Carys first, and they came running and barking. Carys wasn't afraid of dogs, and anyway their tails were wagging; this was just a show of bravado with no threat in it. All the same she stood still and let them come up to her. They sniffed her clothes, her feet, her hands when she outstretched them, then as she walked on they trotted beside her like a small escort.

The children's reaction was very different. They stopped their games and fell silent, staring at the approaching stranger. Then the bolder ones came gathering round, still silent, their eyes wide with interest and a wary curiosity. Carys almost faltered then, but when the children suddenly began to talk, at her and about her, in their strange, half-recognisable tongue, her courage came back at the sound of human voices, and she went on.

As she reached the first of the vans, she became aware that the adult Wayfarers were looking at her, too. Probably they had watched her from the moment she set foot on the common, though unlike the dogs and the children they had the skill not to let her know it. A young, brash-looking woman who had been tending one of the fires rose to her feet and ventured a reserved smile. Carys smiled back nervously and nodded a greeting, and the woman sauntered towards her.

'Good day to you, Mistress. And a fine one it is.'

'Yes . . .' said Carys.

The woman waited and, when nothing more was forthcoming, prompted, 'You have business with us?'

Carys swallowed. 'Yes, I . . . was sent. My husband . . . we've a trouble, and he hopes that, by your kindness, we might . . .'

She was stumbling and stuttering over the words Jone had told her to say, and her confusion was made worse by the look of tolerant but mocking amusement growing in the woman's eyes. Carys paused for breath and was about to try to continue when the sound of a latch clicking halted her.

She looked up. The door of the nearest caravan had opened, and on the threshold another woman, much older, stood looking down at her. The scrutiny was a long one and it fixed Carys to the spot. She couldn't move, couldn't speak. Suddenly she felt no bigger than a blade of grass.

Then the gaze broke and the old woman glanced at the other by the fire. Her head jerked a little and her eyes slid briefly, expressively, sidelong. It was a signal, a command, and it was instantly obeyed. The younger woman made what looked suspiciously like a curtsey, and without another word or look in Carys's direction, hurried away.

Carys stayed motionless. Then the caravan creaked, and the old woman came stiffly down the steps to meet her. In her day the matriarch had obviously been handsome, and there was still some echo of those long-lost looks about her. Her hair was longer than Carys's own, grey now though lovely once, and she wore it in five braids. Her eyes were grey, piercing, and she wore grey, too, a stark and startling contrast to the bright clothes of the rest of her clan. She stooped, but Carys couldn't dispel the feeling that the stoop was something she affected with a purpose; something to reassure the Rooteds – which was what the Wayfarers called folk not of their kind – that she could do them no harm. Carys knew better. She knew that, if she chose, the old woman *could* harm her, for everything about her spoke of knowledge and abilities far beyond her comprehension. This matriarch had power, and Carys, her heart quailing inside her, wanted to turn tail and run like a frightened rabbit, away from the camp and the common and her own fear.

But then the old woman smiled at her, and the smile changed

everything. The fear slid away, and in its place came a surge of longing that caught in Carys's lungs and throat and made her feel as if she would choke. The matriarch folded her long-fingered hands together. And the first words she spoke, in a soft voice that made Carys think of cobwebs, were uttered with the calmness of arcane and unshakeable certainty.

'Good morning to you, Carys Jonewife. Which will you ask of me first – the cure for that sick cow of yourn, or the cure for your own longing heart?'

Chapter VI

Carys stood very still, staring as blankly as a half-witted calf as a terror of realisation crashed into her mind. All the way here she had rehearsed and rehearsed what she would say, how she would edge slowly and carefully around to the thing that she wanted to broach, how she would explain. But without a single one of those words being spoken, her secret and her desire were known. *How?* she thought frantically. *How?*

The wide mouth in the hazel-brown face smiled again, though this time with more than a hint of sardonicism.

'You needn't fear that it'll reach the ear of your husband, Carys Jonewife. That isn't our way. Do fair by us, and we'll do fair by you. Yes?'

'Yes . . .' Carys whispered.

The woman nodded briskly, confirming that part of the bargain. 'So, then. As this is such a private thing, you'd best come in, and we'll see what's to be done for you.'

She led the way up the steep steps of her wagon, and Carys, following, shivered as she saw the strange, tiny figures painted on the panels, and the carved wooden charms and fetishes hung over the low door. Inside were cushions and the smell of herbs, and pools of sunlight full of sluggish dust motes. The old woman sat down in a chair by the pot-bellied stove and gestured for Carys to take a stool on the other side.

'Well, Carys Jonewife.' In the gloom her face looked strangely young, and not quite human. 'The sick cow it shall be first, yes? What payment does your goodman offer for a cure?'

61

Carys's heart was pounding under her ribs and when she tried to stammer Jone Farmer's message what came out instead was: 'How do you know . . .?'

'About the cow?' A soft chuckle impinged as the woman turned aside the real meaning of Carys's question. 'A word here and a word there, that's how. And a nod from Merion Blacksmith's woman, and a little of something else that's beyond your understanding. Now. There's a cure for your Placid, sure and simple. I've seen the malaise before, and I know what must be done. Give me a pair of new boots, or put the word and the price to Corl Shoemaker in the village, I don't mind which, and you can put the cow right by tomorrow morning.'

Carys knew the price of new boots, and the fee was well within the limits Jone Farmer had set. She nodded. 'Yes. Yes, that's well.'

The matriarch reached for a leather satchel and delved within its depths. 'Five grains of this, then, in the water that Placid takes to drink, and you must boil an onion in salt water and be sure that the beast eats it, willing or no. Give it to her in the hour between sunset and moonrise, and when the moon comes up tell your man to turn about three times and say a luck-prayer. He won't like it and he'll call it a fool's play, but it must be done if the cure's to work.' She measured the dose into a twist of paper, which she pressed into Carys's unresisting hand. There was a long pause. The paper was a nothing, an emptiness in Carys's palm. She waited, and at last the matriarch spoke again.

'Will you tell me of it, then? Or will your secret wither you before your time and make an old maid of you for all your life?'

Carys's face flamed scarlet and she turned her head sharply away. 'I don't want that!'

'No, you don't, and that's only natural. Spring and winter don't lie easy together and never have.' From a shelf beside her she took a long-stemmed clay pipe and stuffed it with a hank of tobacco from a pottery jar. Carys had never seen a woman smoke before, and she watched, mesmerised and at the same time grateful for the brief diversion. Pungent, slate-blue smoke began to curl up from the pipe's bowl; the matriarch closed her eyes, puffing appreciatively, then took the pipe out of her mouth and said, 'Well then, lass. You'd best try to explain to me what it is you *do* want.'

Slowly, haltingly, Carys began to tell her story. It came hard at first; she faltered and stammered and blushed, hoping against hope that the matriarch would take pity and say the words for her. She had proved that she knew the nature of Carys's misery, so she must surely know the rest. But the old woman only listened in silence. Then, as the pipe smoke began to spread like a canopy over the ceiling of the caravan, the words Carys had floundered over suddenly came. Words she hadn't dreamed were in her: the whole tale of her forced marriage to Jone Farmer, her early dread of lying with a man more than three times her age, then of her change of heart and the hope that was born with it, and lastly of her misery when Jone Farmer proved no true husband. She began to cry then, hot, helpless tears of confusion and frustration and a desire that was only half formed but nonetheless agonisingly powerful.

She did not, could not, speak of the scarecrow. To reveal the depths to which her desperation had brought her would have been the ultimate humiliation, and for all her gentle and calm manner she could not believe that the old woman would not have mocked. So that part of it remained hidden and buried, and at last the flow of words and tears tailed off and Carys fell silent.

The silence lasted for some time. A little to her surprise, Carys felt better. Simply to speak, to *tell* someone of her misery, had brought her a sense of release, like cool water soothing fevered skin. She sat mute, passive, waiting.

Then, from the shadows of the old woman's chair, a strong, brown hand reached out, and Carys felt her wrist taken and held. 'So,' the matriarch said, very softly, 'what would you have me do for you?'

Carys bit her lip hard enough to draw a bead of blood. 'I want Jone to be a husband to me,' she whispered. 'For him to change, to – to *desire* me, as a man should desire a woman. I want that.'

Silence again. The old woman's pipe had gone out but she did not relight it. She was looking at the stove but her eyes weren't focused on it; they gazed somewhere else, somewhere invisible and unreachable to Carys.

Then she said, 'It can't be done. Or if it can, I'll take no part in the doing of it.'

Carys's swelling hopes crashed like shattering glass around her. 'But—' she began desperately.

'Hold.' The matriarch raised a commanding hand, silencing her. 'And listen. What you ask for is wrong. To use magic to force a man – or woman – to act against their nature is a shameful and wicked thing, and dangerous into the bargain. No one has the right, Carys Jonewife, not me, not you, not any living soul, no matter how good their intentions or how just their cause.' Her shrewd grey eyes took on a flinty quality, with a tinge of wry humour. 'Rouse your man with your own womanly wiles, or not at all.'

Carys looked away again. 'I've tried,' she said, with a catch in her voice. 'Oh, I've tried.'

'Then it seems he's past his ordained time for such pleasures. Spring and winter, like I said; it comes to all of us eventually.'

It seemed to Carys that the old woman was trying to give her comfort, but comfort of such a harsh and cryptic kind was of no use to her. She started to get to her feet, nearly knocking the stool over as distress made her clumsy, and her voice quivered. 'I'll not trouble you any further. Thank you for the cure for Placid. The new boots will—'

The matriarch said: 'Wait.'

Carys stopped. The old woman was watching her.

'You didn't pay full heed to my words, girl. I said, *what you ask* is wrong. But that doesn't mean there isn't another way for you. One question only you'll have to answer to yourself, and that is: have you the will for it?'

Carys stared at her, too afraid to acknowledge the hope that was beginning to resurrect itself out of ruin. 'The will . . .?' Her face crumpled and grew ugly with renewed tears. This time she suppressed them. 'Of course I have the will! I have the will for nothing else!'

The matriarch was unmoved by her vehemence. 'You must be sure,' she said. 'Once done, it can't be changed, and the responsibility will be all your own. Think hard on that, Carys Jonewife, before you take it on.'

Carys stood very still. 'Take . . . *what* on?'

'The thing you desire. The thing you crave.' The woman smiled a strange, unfathomable smile. 'The lover that your heart and your loins ache for.'

Carys's eyes opened saucer-wide. '*Lover . . .?*'

'You're fond of echoing my words, aren't you? Yes, that's what I said.'

'But there isn't anyone!' Carys protested. 'No man in all the district! Do you think I haven't – that is—' The words cut off as she realised abruptly that she had been about to give away another shameful secret, and her cheeks turned scarlet again.

'Looked?' the matriarch supplied for her. 'Of course you've looked. Wouldn't be natural if you hadn't. And what did you find?'

Carys turned her head away. 'Nothing.'

Though Carys didn't see it, the matriarch's smile became a shade grim. 'Think again,' she said. 'And I ask you again: what did you find? In your husband's field, that wet day in the worst of the lambing?'

From hectic red the colour of Carys's face drained to a pallor. 'How do you know about that?'

The old woman shrugged. 'Maybe I know a little and I guess a little, and the rest is easy from there. Or maybe there's more to it than either of us knows. So, then. You've invented a dream for yourself. Do you want the dream to become real?'

'Yes . . .' Carys whispered.

'*Think*, girl. And remember what I said. You must have the will, for once it's done, it can't be changed.' Again she reached out and gripped Carys's wrist. 'Are there any doubts in your heart?'

Carys felt as if the real world, the mundane world, was spinning away from her into an impossible fantasy. Yet the old Wayfarer woman said it was *not* impossible . . . It was the answer to her prayers, to her longing . . .

'No,' she said, with a new and almost harsh note in her voice. 'There are no doubts.'

The woman made a sound like a sigh. 'Very well, then. I must accept your word. Now—'

'Wait.' Even in the first giddy rush of eagerness, one thing anchored Carys to earth, and perhaps it could not be resolved. 'Your price. You haven't said your price. I may not be able to pay it.'

A pause. 'There'll be no price.'

'No price?'

'Mistress Echo again. No. Not for this. It's a wish, see, and wishes are best given freely to those who ask for them. I'll take the new boots for curing your cow, but for what you want I'll have nothing in return.' The old, shrewd eyes regarded Carys steadily for a few moments. 'Well? Is it to be a bargain between us?'

'Yes,' Carys said. 'Oh, *yes*.'

'It's done, then. Now,' she released Carys's wrist, 'were you schooled? Can you make your letters?'

The question took Carys by surprise; she hadn't expected such a change of subject, and for a moment she was nonplussed. Gathering her wits, she nodded cautiously. Her writing was a poor thing at best, far worse than her reading, but she feared to say so, in case admission of her failing should snatch this chance away.

The matriarch nodded too. 'Good, that makes matters simpler.' She looked directly into Carys's eyes. 'You must write it down, see. Write down the thing you want. I'll give you a piece of parchment, and you must carry it with you, day and night, from new moon to full. That gives it power, gives it time to grow. Then when full moon comes, write your wish on it. I'll tell you the words, and they must be *exactly* the same; any mistake and nothing will happen. Then when you've written it, you must put the parchment in your hearth fire and say the wish aloud – again, mind they're the same words, don't get it wrong – as it burns.'

Carys waited but the old woman said no more. At last, in a bewildered voice, Carys asked, 'That's all?'

The matriarch chuckled sourly. 'What more do you want? A spell that calls you to dance and sing naked in your own farmyard so that half the world learns your secret?' Chastened, Carys blushed and the old woman delved again in her satchel.

'Here it is.' She produced a scrap of yellowed parchment, folded twice, the edges rough and frayed. 'When the time comes, you must write on it: "Please to waken the power of the woods, and release me from my pain". Say it, now. Say it aloud, until you're sure of remembering.'

As though in a trance, Carys recited the words. She repeated them six times before the matriarch was satisfied that they were secure in her mind and wouldn't be dislodged, then, with no ceremony, the scrap of parchment was handed to her.

'Here's your wish, Carys Jonewife,' the matriarch said. 'And be sure you make good use of it, for you won't get another from me.'

Carys stared at the parchment, unable to believe that such an ordinary thing could have the power to grant so much. Suddenly she wondered if the old woman was deceiving her, having fun at her expense, and she looked up with new suspicion in her eyes.

'He'll come? My lover . . . he'll come to me?'

'Oh, yes, he'll come to you. And that'll be your responsibility, like I said. Don't ever forget that.'

Carys didn't understand, but she wasn't given the chance to ask the matriarch's meaning, even if she could have formed the right question. The old woman rose stiffly to her feet and gestured at the door.

'Go, now. Go and cure your husband's cow, and think hard on your wish.'

Carys moved towards the door. Then, on the top step, she stopped and looked back with an abrupt surge of fear.

'What if he—' she swallowed. Dear life, she hadn't thought of this until now, but suddenly it was there in her mind, a spectre, an ogre, a terrible peril. 'What if he should – get me with child?'

The matriarch laughed softly, a laugh that was neither humorous nor unkind but simply, strangely, resigned. 'Don't be a fool, girl,' she said. 'Only a *mortal* lover could do that.'

And the door of the van closed in Carys's face.

Carys made a wide detour on her way home to avoid going near the place in the woods where her scarecrow lay. With the Wayfarer matriarch's words still whispering through the vaults of her mind, she was afraid to face the stiff, silent figure, afraid of what she might see or not see, afraid of losing her nerve. Instead she fixed her gaze on the smooth green slopes of the pastures where the grazing sheep looked like white boats on a rolling sea, then later on the fields of corn and barley, and lastly on the distant, comfortable bulk of the farmhouse and barns. She tried to blank her mind and think of nothing, but that proved impossible, and when she reached the house she was almost glad to find Izzy in one of her martyred moods, waiting for her with a long list of grumbles and complaints, which mostly seemed to concern her son's latest idiocy, or her suffering feet. Carys listened more sympathetically than usual until Izzy had talked herself out, then the two of them went about preparing the evening meal in a relatively satisfied silence.

Jone, as the Wayfarer had predicted, was not pleased when he learned what he must do to cure Placid. He called it foolery and superstitious nonsense, and muttered darkly about what the preacher would think to see him demeaning himself with such antics. But for all his objections, Placid was still suffering, and with great reluctance Jone steeled himself to do what was required.

Carys boiled the onion in salt water, her eyes stinging from the smell of it, and at the appointed time, between sunset and moonrise, she carried it to the byre. Making Placid eat it was not easy, and eventually Jone was obliged to tether and hobble the cow, and forcibly hold her mouth open while Carys dropped the onion, piece by piece, down her throat. Then five grains of the old woman's powder were put into her bucket of water, and as she nosed fitfully at it Jone and Carys stepped outside.

In the yard Jone paused, frowning. Guessing his thoughts, Carys ventured diffidently, 'The luck-prayer, Husband . . . She said it must be done.'

Jone grunted. 'I suspect it means nothing. The woman's mocking us, that's all.'

'Maybe,' said Carys, 'but should we take the chance?' She glanced eastwards. Beyond the brow of the fields, a faint silvery-grey glow was visible, and she added uneasily, 'The moon will be rising soon . . .'

Jone sighed irritably. 'Oh, very well! If it pleases you, let it be done and over with!' His expression mellowed and he smiled at her a little sheepishly. 'You're a kindlier and more trusting soul than I am, Wife. You put me to shame.'

Carys turned her head away as her conscience gave a twinge. Fortunately for her, Jone misinterpreted the movement, as he often misinterpreted the things she did. 'Yes, yes, I'd prefer it if you don't watch me making a fool of myself.' He paused. 'And not a word of this to anyone, mind. If Merion Blacksmith asks what we were told to do, tell him only about the onion and the powder, nothing more!'

Carys said meekly: 'Yes, Jone.'

She heard his boots scrape on the yard cobbles as he turned around, and heard him mutter the luck-prayer, though his voice was too low and indistinct for her to catch the words. Then he said, more loudly and with evident relief, 'There. It's done. And Providence alone knows what will come of it!'

Carys's heart was palpitating like a trotting horse as they walked back to the house. She was desperate to find out what Providence knew, for Placid's cure – or otherwise – would surely be a measure of the success she could anticipate. If the cow did not recover, then hope was gone.

But if she did . . .

'What's amiss, Wife?' Jone asked. 'You're sweating.' He looked alarmed. 'Have you taken a fever? Did you catch some sickness at that camp?'

'No, Jone,' Carys said hastily. 'No, no. I'm well as ever, truly.

It's just the air – it's close tonight.'

He relaxed. 'That's true enough. We shall sleep with the window open.' He smiled at her again. 'Jem Apothecary says that open windows bring the wet-lung disease, but apothecaries don't know everything, do they, hmm? Fresh air does no harm.'

'Yes, Jone,' said Carys, as the sweat continued to trickle down her spine.

Chapter VII

Within two days, Placid was entirely herself again.

'It's little short of a miracle!' Merion Blacksmith declared when he came to see the animal for himself. 'To look at her now you'd think there was never a thing amiss with her.' He scratched the back of his head wonderingly. 'And you say it was just powder and a boiled onion, Jone? No mummery or fal-lal at all?'

'None at all.' Jone stared inscrutably at the byre wall while Placid chewed her cud.

'Well, now. I'm impressed, and I don't mind confessing it!' Merion chuckled. 'You should have asked the Wayfarers for another wish or two while you were about it, Carys – no rain for harvest, heifer calves for every farmer's cow, or some such!'

Carys forced a smile, quailing inwardly at the thought of how close he had unwittingly come to the truth. As she struggled to find an innocuous reply, Jone said, 'Doesn't do to be greedy, Merion. This is enough, and I'm satisfied.'

Carys was satisfied, too – and terrified. Placid's recovery was proof that her own wish would not fail, and the parchment – which, as instructed, she was carrying with her day and night, concealed in her small-clothes – seemed to burn against her skin as she listened to her husband's words. She had sixteen days to wait until the moon was full, and she truly didn't know whether, when the time came, she would have the courage to carry out the instructions the matriarch had given her. What she wanted, what she *needed*, was to be able to take the plunge now, while her nerve still held, rather than risk a failure that would condemn her to a lifetime's bitter regret.

But wait she must, there was no other option. So as the days passed she went about in a daze of fear, sickness and excitement all combined. Sleep was hard to come by; ever aware of the parchment, her mind boiled day and night with the thoughts of what she had been told to write upon it, the words marching through her head in relentless repetition until she half believed the litany would drive her mad. There was certainly no chance that she would forget the instructions she had been given: several times she almost caught herself repeating them aloud in Izzy's or – worse – Jone's hearing. Luckily that calamity was avoided, and Jone appeared to notice nothing untoward in his wife's behaviour. He was, anyway, out of the house through all the daylight hours, which at this time of year also meant most of his waking hours. But Izzy was another matter. For all her grumbling self-preoccupations, she had sharp eyes and an inquiring mind, and as she shuffled about her duties, her continuing complaints about her feet and her son gave way to unspoken but acute curiosity at Carys's increasing distraction. However, she couldn't quite summon the boldness to ask a direct question, and so nothing was said, and to outward appearances life on the farm continued as sedately as ever.

The fine summer weather also continued, and each night was brighter than the last as the moon began to wax. With each rising Carys watched for its changing face, experiencing a strange, sick inner tumult as she mentally recorded its slow, steady growth. Then, at last, the white circle in the sky was all but complete. Tomorrow, it would reach its culmination.

And then the thing, the terrible thing, must be done, or forgotten for all time.

In a few brief interludes when she could be sure of being alone, Carys had been fetching the stub of pencil that Jone kept in his box of accounts, and a page from the monthly broadsheet taken by those in the parish who could read, and practising her neglected letters. The results of her efforts were consigned to the kitchen range lest Jone should see them and wonder at her sudden taste for scholarship, and Carys could only hope that what she had achieved would be enough.

To her surprise, she slept soundly that night, though her sleep was fringed with elusive, unnerving dreams that, unusually, she clearly recalled on waking. Dawn heralded another perfect day. Jone said, unchangingly, 'The sun will be rising soon, my dear, and we must be rising too,' and smiled his invariable smile at her as he rose ponderously from the bed and began to dress.

Feeding the pigs, letting the chickens out of their arks, fetching the cows for milking; all these tasks Carys performed while the breakfast oatmeal simmered and the kettle brewed on its trivet. She had no real conscious awareness of what she was doing, it was merely an automatic routine that skimmed past her dazed mind while her hands and feet worked unprompted. She fetched a new loaf from the larder, cut several slices from the bacon on its slate in the cold-room, and was laying out plates and knives when the clank of the milk-buckets outside announced Jone's return from the byre.

He talked to her through the open door of the scullery as he strained the milk into the waiting churn. Carys hadn't the least idea of what he said, but her occasional responses seemed to content him, and they sat down to their usual uneventful breakfast. She forced herself to eat, though her stomach did not want it, and watched the patterns made by the strengthening sunlight on the scrubbed table top as she waited for Jone to finish. At last he did, stood up with his customary sigh of satisfaction, and said, 'When Lob comes, send him to the east pasture. I want to trim the feet of some of the sheep, and I'll need a second man for the doing of it.'

Fortunately Carys heard this, and promised to send Lob the moment he arrived. She watched her husband trudge away across the yard and through the gate, and even when he was out of sight she still stood at the door, staring into the quiet, warm morning as though she were hypnotised. One of the barn cats, trotting on some mysterious business of its own, saw her and paused, staring, but she did not give her customary chirrup to it, and after a few moments it continued on its way. Only when the yard gate clanked again did

73

Carys start and blink, shaking her head as the real world came suddenly back into focus. Izzy's waddling shape was bustling towards her, with Lob shambling a pace behind. Izzy called out a brisk, 'Good morning,' and Lob grinned his vacuous grin. On some reflex level Carys noticed that Lob was only drooling a little, meaning that this was one of his better days, and by association she remembered Jone's instruction. She smiled at Izzy, smiled at Lob, and with a great effort forced her mind to shake itself out of its paralysis and concentrate on the routine of another day.

The routine was upset early that afternoon by the arrival of uninvited and unannounced visitors.

Carys was in the dairy, skimming cream from the previous evening's milk to make butter, when Izzy's head appeared around the door.

'There's callers,' Izzy said.

'Oh?' Carys looked up. 'Who?'

'Your sisters.' Izzy radiated disapproval with every syllable. 'Wed to Jemp Holder, that elder one is now, en? You'd think a Holder's wife had more to do than go gadding about the country paying calls!'

Nellen had obviously already said something to cause Izzy offence, and Carys was tempted to agree. Of all the people she could have wished not to see today, Nellen and Thomsine would have been almost the highest on the list. Neither of them had troubled to come near her since Nellen's wedding; she couldn't imagine what had prompted them to do so now, and she would very much have liked to tell them to go away.

But common decorum, as well as the lingering imposition of being the youngest in her family, squashed the temptation, and with a sigh she put the skimmer down, wiped her hands and composed her face into what passed for a welcoming smile as she went to greet them.

Nellen and Thomsine had arrived in Nellen's – or rather, Jemp Holder's – gig. They were both dressed as if for a fair or market

74

day, and Nellen sported a new hat suspiciously like the one Jone had bought for Carys during the lambing season. She looked smug. The three of them exchanged insincere kisses while Izzy, still disapproving, made a great and pointed to-do about filling the kettle and banging it on to the trivet. Not wanting any trouble, Carys dispatched her to finish skimming the cream, and the sisters were left alone.

'Well, Carys.' Nellen looked around the kitchen, which she had hardly ever seen before, her eyes missing nothing. 'And how is Jone's farm? Prospering?'

'Indeed.' Carys was having difficulty maintaining her smile. 'And Jemp's holding?'

'Oh, we are doing very well. Very well indeed.' Nellen and Thomsine exchanged a conspiratorial look, then Thomsine giggled and Nellen slapped her arm. 'Hush!' she added. 'Or she'll guess.'

'Guess what?' Carys asked. Then she did guess; knew it, in fact, beyond any shadow of doubt. It was the only thing that could have brought Nellen to her door today, and Thomsine would have been unable to resist the chance to witness Carys's reaction and chagrin. Nellen had succeeded where Carys had failed, and after barely two months of marriage she was to provide Powl and Tibba with their first grandchild.

'The birth will be in Ash-month, Jem Apothecary says,' Nellen told her proudly. 'And he's *sure* it will be a boy. He held a pendulum over me, you know, and he can tell by the way it swings. A boy, for certain.'

'Father and Mother are overjoyed,' Thomsine chimed in, looking for discomfiture in Carys's face. 'It's what they wanted above all else. Oh, and Mother sends you her love,' she added as an afterthought.

Carys did not want love, or any other kind of message, from Tibba, for she could well imagine the spirit in which it had been sent. Manufacturing another smile, and praying that her cheeks weren't flaming with humiliation, she said, 'I'm that pleased for you, Nellen.'

Nellen beamed graciously. 'I knew you would be.' She laughed. 'Isn't it strange how life turns out? You were wed before me, but now it seems I'm to be ahead of you after all.' A pause. 'That is, if you don't have news of your own . . .?'

'No,' said Carys stiffly. 'Not yet.' *And you may tell Mother so, and I wish you all joy of it!*

'Ah, well. Providence can't be hurried, eh?' Nellen glanced towards the trivet, where the kettle was now hissing and spitting like an angry cat. 'Is there tea . . .?'

There was tea, and the ordeal of it lasted a full hour, until Nellen had had her fill of triumph and said that they had taken up enough of Carys's time and must go. More hollow kisses, and Carys saw the gig through the yard gate before turning back into the house and slamming the door with a ferocity that nearly shook it from its hinges.

She wanted to cry, but tears weren't in her. Only an anger, so deep and so painful that it all but took her breath away. She could hear Izzy in the dairy, chanting some tuneless doggerel to the slap-slap of the cream as she worked the butter-churn, and she was sorely tempted to rush in there and overturn Izzy, churn and all, just to vent her bitter fury on something that could not retaliate.

She had clenched her fists without realising it, as if preparing for the first savage strike, when a new noise from outside snatched her attention. Rapid footsteps, a hurrying figure moving across the square of the window, then the door juddered open again and Jone stood on the threshold.

'Husband!' Colour swelled and fled again in Carys's cheeks, and she groped for something mundane to cover it. 'Did you see the gig? My sisters—'

Jone wasn't interested in Carys's sisters. Sweeping her words aside, he said, 'Wife, fetch the slingshot and my heaviest blackthorn stick.'

He strode into the parlour and began to unleash his hunting knife from where it hung over the ingle. Carys ran automatically to do

76

his bidding, then with the stick and slingshot in her hands she too went to the parlour. 'Jone, what's amiss?'

'It's those dogs again,' Jone told her curtly. 'There were two lambs and a ewe dead in the field this morning, with their throats torn out. And not half an hour ago, Garler Shepherd saw the brutes on the north pastures.'

'No!' There had been trouble with the dogs before: a pack of strays, half wild and roaming. During the winter they had made several attacks on sheep, but for the past few months nothing had been heard or seen of them, and everyone had thought them gone from the district. Clearly, they were wrong.

'Garler's gone to muster his sons and any other men he can find,' Jone continued. 'We'll get up a hunt, and we won't rest until those dogs are dead at our feet!' He thrust the knife into his belt, then turned to look at Carys. 'See to the farm, Wife, the way you did at lambing. And don't wait up for me; I doubt I'll be home before the small hours.'

'I'll fetch you food,' she said quickly. 'You'll need sustaining—' She flew back to the kitchen and put half a loaf and a hunk of cheese into a cloth which she tied into a bundle. Jone nodded his thanks, said, 'If any neighbours call, tell their menfolk to join us if they can,' and was gone again before she could reply.

As he hastened away, Izzy emerged from the dairy. 'What's to do, Missus?' She peered after Jone's rapidly retreating back.

Carys told her, and she clucked like an agitated hen. 'Them curs! If you ask me, it's the Wayfarers to blame, coming here with their wild ways and mangy beasts. No better than savages, any one of them!'

Carys knew that the Wayfarers kept their dogs under strict control, and besides, they had not been in the district when the attacks began. But there was no point in saying so to Izzy, so she left the older woman to mumble and mutter her outrage, and escaped to the barn. There, among the rich scents and dusty sunlight and with three somnolent cats for company, she felt a sense of calm steal over her, like a quiet sunset after a summer storm. Mere minutes ago, when her sisters departed, she had been on the verge of volcanic rage. Then Jone had come, and Nellen's news had been swept aside by the matter of the dogs. Now, with her part in the emergency over and the goad of her sisters' presence gone, she had time for rational consideration – and with it, a new realisation.

For Nellen, today's visit had been a victory over the sister who, as she viewed it, had outdone her in the race for marriage and now was being paid back. It was petty, and typical. But Nellen had unwittingly achieved something else, that neither she nor Carys could have anticipated. Carys's mind was clearing – and as it cleared, so the uncertainties and fears that had plagued her since her fateful visit to the Wayfarers' camp finally and irrevocably vanished. She *would* have what she wanted. She would not quail, she would not balk, she would not take the coward's way. Jone would not come home until the small hours, or possibly not even until morning. The house would be her sole domain, and time her own, to do with what she pleased. No need for subterfuge, for sneaking and creeping about in constant terror of discovery. She would be alone.

So tonight she would take the piece of parchment and she would write her wish, and she would send the wish curling up in the smoke from the fire. No doubts now. None. Tonight, the thing *would* be done, and the longing, the craving, the time of hopeless frustration, would finally come to an end.

Lob came back in the early evening, bringing word from Jone – so far as anyone could make sense of what Lob said – that a large group of men were engaged on the hunt for the killer dogs, and did not expect to see their beds tonight. Carys had the impression that Lob had proved more of a hindrance than a help, so she told Izzy that, if the indoor and outdoor tasks were completed quickly, they could both go home at an earlier hour than usual. Izzy was surprised, but she wasn't about to spurn such an opportunity, so she chivvied and scolded Lob out to the yard and set about her own work like a whirlwind. Well before sunset all was completed, and Izzy made her farewells and went, with Lob trailing behind her like a puppy on an invisible leash.

Carys was alone. She stood for a long time in the parlour, staring at the ingle where no fire burned and letting the atmosphere calm and settle around her. All that must be done was done, in the house and farm alike. The butter was made, the floors were swept, and enough water had been carried in to see through to tomorrow. Carys and Izzy had baked enough bread for four days, and made pound cake and pasties, and a stew simmered on the range ready for Jone's eventual return. The cows were in, milked, fed and watered, the pigs had clean straw, the chickens were shut up safe, with a lantern by their arks to keep the foxes away. Nothing stood between her and her desire. Nothing but her own resolve.

She went to the kitchen, cut a piece of bread and made herself eat it; she had had little else all day and an empty stomach would not stand her in good stead. Then she washed her plate, wiped the crumbs from the table and carried the basket of logs that Lob had brought in earlier to the parlour hearth. Izzy had raised her eyebrows at the idea of a fire in this weather, but Carys had said sharply that a man could get cold on the hills on even the warmest of nights, and a good wife should always consider her husband's needs above all else. Jone's needs, though, had no part in it as she knelt down, set logs and kindling in the grate and carefully began to coax the fire to life. The clock ticked, like the tread of slow, heavy boots, and it seemed to have been ticking for half a lifetime before at last the flames caught and she felt safe to leave the fire to its own devices.

Now, the parchment. Pushing a hand down the bodice of her dress, Carys pulled it from its hiding place. It was crumpled now as well as folded, and she laid it on the floor and smoothed it out as best she could. The fire burned up suddenly, brightening the ingle, and she realised how sharp was the contrast between its light and the gathering shadows in the room. The sun was near setting. Before long, the full moon would rise . . .

Then, far away in one of the coppices on Crede Hill, a vixen screamed.

Carys jolted, and her heartbeat quickened to a rapid, painful throb. She had not heard that sound since winter, and then only in the deep of night. It was a sign – she knew it, it *must* be. Some power, beyond her ken, was telling her that this was right. And the sensual hunger of the vixen awoke a surging response in her own body. Heat coursed through her; ice consumed her. She wanted to run and jump and roll and dance and scream, wild as any wild animal.

But she did none of these things. Instead, she rose and went to Jone's accounts box and took out the stub of pencil, then returned to the ingle and sat quietly down on the flagstones. A part of her felt like a thief and a betrayer, but another part, far stronger, was pulsing with excitement that grew and grew in a dark, steady tide. How long to wait? Over her shoulder, she could see the sky turning crimson. Minutes more and the sun would sink behind Crede Hill. Then the fiery display would fade through gold and green to the indigo of late evening. And, at last, the moon would appear.

She jumped up again, too restless to sit and wait as she had first resolved. The parlour's shadows were turning from dove grey to charcoal, their outlines wavering in the unsteady firelight. Carys paced the room, looking at the clock but not seeing what it told her. She touched the polished horse brasses, one by one, as if they were talismans that would bring her good luck. She picked up Jone's pipe-whistle, which she had never heard him play, and turned it over and over in her hands, but did not have the courage to try to conjure a reedy note from it. Then, lastly, she took up the book from which she so often read to her husband, and opened it at random. A title confronted her: 'The Love between Youth and Beauty', and she shut the book with a snap as a fresh hot-cold wave chased over her skin. Jone had never asked her to read *that* text aloud, and, like the vixen's cry, it seemed to her to be another omen.

The sun was truly out of sight now, and the glory of the sky was starting to drain away as twilight crept from the east. Carys returned to the ingle and crouched down on the edge of the firelight's reach. She smoothed the parchment one last time, took up the pencil, licked it. Then slowly, laboriously, and filled with an awful thrill of defiant anticipation, she wrote the words that the Wayfarer matriarch had taught her.

'Pleas to wayken the powre of the Wodes, and rellayse mee from my Payn.'

She looked again and again at what she had written, trying to ignore the spring of terror that bubbled inside her. She *would* do it. She *had* done it. And no one else in the world, save for an old woman whose people would soon be making ready to move on to other roads, could ever know her secret.

Carys crushed the parchment in her hands. She drew a deep breath and cast it on to the fire, and as the flames caught hold of it she whispered, with all the inner power she could muster, the same words that her shaking hand had written.

The parchment burned first yellow, then scarlet, then purple, then blue. Within seconds it was gone. A few last charred fragments spiralled up the chimney, then the fire continued to hiss contentedly as though nothing untoward had happened. Carys was disappointed. She had expected more than this; she had expected some sign that her wish had been heard. White fire, or the cry of heavenly voices—

Then, in the distance, faint but clear from the darkening outside world, she heard someone whistling.

Shock stabbed at Carys's vitals and spread outwards until her entire body tingled. *That sound* – she had heard it before, on the night of Nellen's wedding as she and Jone drove homeward. Was it the same tune? She couldn't remember, for she couldn't bring the other tune, the first one, back to mind. But the intuition she had felt then was suddenly and sharply reawakened.

She scrambled to her feet and ran to the window. Moonlight flooded the yard (how had so much time passed? It had seemed like only minutes!) and at the far end, by the gate, she thought she could make out an indistinct figure. Her heart lurched and thundered. There *was* someone there – he was opening the gate, he was coming through, he—

The wild surmise froze as a second and then a third figure joined the first, and the quiet was broken by the unmistakable tramp of boots. Men's voices rose on the still air. And Carys's rioting imagination collapsed as she recognised the tall, stooping shape of Jone Farmer.

He came into the kitchen with Merion Blacksmith and Elios Carter behind him. Carys was there to meet them, standing in the parlour doorway, striving frantically to appear normal as bitter disappointment curdled inside her.

'Wife.' Jone looked tired and a little grim, but there was a satisfied light in his eyes.

Carys's mouth trembled and she had difficulty making her tongue obey her. 'Have you – did you—' she managed.

'Six of them.' Jone nodded over his shoulder to the open door. 'The carcasses are in the yard. We'll bury them in the morning, and trust that will be an end to it.'

'Two more ewes they killed before we got to them, though,' Elios added. 'And one – you know, Jone, that brindle-grey brute, the ringleader – attacked Garler's own dog. Terrible fight, terrible, and Garler's animal coming out of it torn and bleeding and hardly able to walk.'

'He'll mend soon enough,' said Merion. 'None of the wounds are serious, and I'll fetch Garler some ointment to stop them going bad.' He smiled a hard smile. 'The brindle's dead meat now, and that's what counts.'

Jone looked at the stewpot bubbling on the range. 'There's a good smell in here, Wife,' he said to Carys. 'Enough, do you think, for three hungry men instead of just one?'

Carys snapped out of the trancelike state in which she had received the news, and nodded hurriedly. 'Yes, Husband, yes, of course. Sit you all down, now – there's a fire in the parlour, I thought it would be a comfort – and I'll prepare the table and fetch the new butter and some beer . . .'

She fled to the dairy, leaving the men to make their way to the parlour. As they trooped through, Jone's voice carried back to her.

'A good wife, my Carys, a good wife. She always thinks of my comfort before all else. No man could ask for better.'

Guilt hit Carys like a blast from the north wind, and she shut her eyes and pressed a clenched fist to her mouth, biting the knuckles hard. The feeling passed, though it took some moments. Then she opened her eyes again, drew a deep breath in which she tasted bile, and continued soberly with her task.

Chapter VIII

The terror caught up with Carys in the middle of that night.

Against her expectations, she had slept like the dead at first, as if sleep was a necessary rescue. But in the darkest hour, she woke again and realised fully, for the first time, what she had done.

She stared into the bedroom's moon-silvered gloom, feeling as though all the breath in her body had been sucked chokingly away. At her side Jone lay as peaceful as always, and for a moment Carys had a powerful impulse to reach out to him, wake him, confess her secret and beg his forgiveness and his help. She did not. Instead, she slid from under the blankets and groped her way to the window, where she hacked back the curtain and pressed her forehead against the glass, trying to settle her pounding pulse.

It was far, far too late for regret. Even the Wayfarers hadn't the power to turn back time, and nothing could be changed. She recalled the matriarch's words: *the responsibility will be all your own*, and understood, belatedly, that it had been a warning. Well, she had not listened to the warning. She had cast the spell, set the wheels in motion, and must accept the consequences, whatever they proved to be.

But that was the thing that frightened her above all else. What *would* the consequences prove to be? The spell she had performed had been unspectacular, and in its aftermath, thus far, nothing out of the ordinary had happened. The stew had been eaten, Merion and Elios had left, she and Jone had retired to bed. All was as usual. She felt no different and sensed nothing different in the air. There had been no further omens; even the whistling had a mundane explanation, for it had been Merion, who had been feeling cheerful about their success with the wild dogs.

Carys frowned down at the moonlit, empty yard. Though she wasn't consciously aware of it, her thoughts were beginning to turn around, shifting from terror and regret towards disappointment and, almost, a sense of pique that the Wayfarer woman's promise had not immediately come true. She wondered if she had been duped, taken for a fool and sent on her way like a troublesome child pacified with some worthless trinket. If her spell had awoken 'the power of the woods', as the matriarch said, she could see no sign of it.

But the matriarch had promised, and part of the Wayfarers' reputation was that their word was their bond. So what would happen? And *when*?

'When . . .?' Without knowing it she whispered the question against the window pane. An opaque circle appeared on the glass as her breath warmed it, obscuring her view of the yard, and suddenly she was afraid again; afraid to look lest she *should* see something – or someone – out there under the moon, where there should only be stillness.

She scuttled back to the bed like a hunted animal, and huddled under the covers with her eyes tightly shut and the eiderdown pulled up over her ears. Not to see, not to hear, not to know. *'Let me sleep!'* she prayed silently. *'Please, please, let me sleep now. Oh, dear life . . . what have I done . . .?'*

Days passed, and still nothing happened. With the haymaking finished there was a brief lull in the busyness of work before the corn harvest began, and Jone, as always, used the respite to take stock of the farm and see to the less urgent tasks for which there had been no time through the early summer. The market cart and the big hay wagon were checked carefully and small repairs made here and there, some broken tiles on the barn roof were replaced, the pond where the cattle and horses drank was dredged out and the muddy edges made good. Carys fed the pigs and chickens and brought the cows in twice a day and worked in the house and saw her neighbours and went to market and to chapel; all the routine and uneventful things to which she had become accustomed.

But in her heart, the pressure of apprehension was growing like ivy beginning to strangle a tree.

She hadn't dared go back to her secret place in the wood. Why she was suddenly afraid to return was a question that, if asked, she would have been unable to answer, but she went out of her way to avoid the place, telling herself that the scarecrow was of no significance to her. By now some vagrant, passing through, had probably found the stupid dumdolly, taken the jacket and the scarf and the hat and been grateful for them, and the woodland birds and animals had pecked or nibbled away the rest. It didn't matter. Carys didn't care. And when another part of her tried to claim that she *did* care, she quelled it by arguing that there was no reason, none at all, for her to go to the wood just to satisfy idle curiosity.

Then the Wayfarers packed up their camp and left the district. Carys was bringing the cows in for milking early one morning when she saw a procession of wagons in the distance, making their slow, dignified way along the road from the village. Their vehicles' bright colours made them instantly recognisable, and Carys stopped and stared after them, oblivious of the cows who had started to meander and graze when they should have been moving on towards the yard. From here she could make out little detail and certainly no individual figures, but there could be no doubt that the entire group was on the move. They had helped with the haymaking and been paid in kind; they had dispensed wisdom or nostrums to those who asked and been paid in kind; and they might or might not be back later in the year when work was plentiful again. Still watching them, Carys was torn between regret and relief. The leading wagon passed out of sight behind an interspersing belt of trees, and one by one the rest followed until they were all gone. A flutter of panic went through her, then faded and died, leaving an odd, dull ache in its wake. She didn't move for another two minutes, though there was nothing to look at now. Then one of the cows ambled across her field of view, and reality came back with a small, sharp shock. Picking up her stick, which had slipped unnoticed out of her grasp, she called harshly to the cows, and began to round them up and herd them on towards the yard.

Twice on the way she looked back. She didn't see the Wayfarers' convoy . . . but her gaze lingered for a little longer than it should have done on a particular part of the woodland, all too familiar to her. She told herself again that she must not go back.

And she knew inwardly, without the smallest doubt, that she would.

That day was the hottest the summer had yet seen. By noon the light was like brass, so bright that it hurt the eyes, and the landscape faded to a mirage-like golden pallor, its contours dithering from horizon to horizon in the heat. With hardly a breath of breeze, let alone wind, it seemed that there was not enough air to fill the lungs. Even when Carys flung open every door and window, the farmhouse was stifling and the kitchen almost unbearable, and she tried to find work for herself in the barn, where little sunlight came in and the lofty, raftered shadows gave at least an illusion of relief.

Even Jone was affected by the weather, and broke completely with custom by coming home for his midday meal.

'Any man who tries to work outside in this is a fool to himself,' he said to Carys as she cut him a piece of cold bacon pie, with leaves from the garden, newly picked but already limp from the withering heat. 'There's nothing to be done but wait until the day cools.' He sighed with frustration at the thought of time wasted.

'It'll do you no harm to rest for an hour or two, Jone,' Carys told him. 'You work hard enough. Too hard, I sometimes think.' She glanced covertly at him, wondering how he would react to the remark, but he was frowning at the window and did not seem to have heard. She was disappointed. The weather had had an effect on her, too, though not in a way that Jone or anyone else could have guessed. She felt languid, but not torpid; the heat and the light, the barn shadows and the slickness of sweat on her skin had conspired to kindle – or rather, rekindle – the hankerings of desire in her, formless but rife with imagination. The sensation of wanting, of craving, was awake in her, and for a moment, lacking any other outlet, she had focused them on Jone, wondering if perhaps, were he to think a little less of work and a little more of leisure, matters might possibly take a turn, and he might . . .

But Jone was still looking out of the window, and had not heard her. Even if he had, what difference could it have made? He would not change, and there was no point in pretending that he would.

Carys cast her eyes down, fixing her gaze firmly, miserably, on the table. She heard Jone stand up, then he said, 'There'll be tasks enough to attend to in the barns or byre. I'll work there through the worst of the afternoon, then I'll go out on the pastures when the sun westers.' He paused, looking down at her. 'You, too, should find cooler work than in the kitchen, my dear. You're flushed with the heat, and it won't do to make yourself unwell.'

Carys's high colour had little to do with the heat and she wanted to tell him so, but instead she only nodded agreement. She didn't look up as he left the house, and when he had gone she shut her eyes and her tongue clamped down on her lower lip, biting until the pain drove other thoughts out of her mind. Then she stood up and began slowly, methodically, to clear the table.

For three more hours the tension in Carys built and built, until she was like a wire tautened almost to breaking point. She tried to work, but it was a sham of apparent industry that actually achieved very little. Thankfully, Izzy was not at the farm. Yesterday she had taken a fall on the rutted path to her home and was laid up with a twisted ankle. Lob was around, but this was one of his vaguer days and Carys had no need to concern herself with what he might see or think. She could concentrate on nothing, because she was waiting. Waiting for Jone to decide that the day was cool enough to make outdoor work possible again, and to bid her farewell and walk through the yard gate and away to the pastures. She willed him to go, she *ached* for him to go. For only when he was gone would she dare to give in to the impulse that was goading her and, this time, could not be ignored.

At long last Jone emerged from the barn and stood in the yard, looking up at the sky and testing the humours of the air. The heat was still fierce, but as though in answer to Carys's unspoken prayers, a tiny breeze had sprung up, just enough to ruffle a few stray strands of his hair. She waited, trying to control her impatience, and after what seemed like an endless thoughtful pause he said, 'I'll be off to the sheep then, Wife. I doubt that I'll be back until dusk.'

He smiled his customary smile at her and she replied with her customary, 'Yes, Jone,' and gave fervent, silent thanks as she watched him go. As soon as he was out of sight she ran back into the house, flung off her apron and went to fetch her new hat and her walking shoes.

The sunlight and heat seemed to touch Carys like a lover's provocative caress as she made her way down the sloping track. The corn in the field alongside her was green-gold now, and dazzlingly bright; it rustled and whispered as she passed, and the sound of it seemed to heighten the inner fever that drove her on.

The gap in the hedge was almost invisible, tangled with the summer's green growth, but the sapling oak showed the place and Carys pushed her way through. The green wall of branches and lush undergrowth was darker than it had been, showing that the season was advancing, and there were fewer flowers now, though the ropes of wild honeysuckle and old-man's-beard were in full bloom. The honeysuckle's scent was rich and cloying, mingling with the earthier smells of the wood; parting a curtain of hanging strands that stroked her face and shoulders, Carys looked into the dimness ahead, searching for the place where the scarecrow lay.

He was not where she had left him. She recognised the patch by the paler colour of the grass, starved of light by the scarecrow's bulk. But he was not there. Carys stared around, remembering her scornful thoughts about vagabonds and regretting them, as though the mere notions had somehow made this happen.

Then, deeper in to the wood, she saw a glimmer of unnaturally bright colour near the base of one of the oldest oaks. Frowning, she started to pick her way through the vegetation towards it, then stopped again, peering harder. It was her scarf, the one she had tied around the scarecrow's neck. And there, below it and half obscured by shadow, was something the colour of Jone's old jacket . . .

She stood beside the scarecrow and looked down at it for a very long time. Questions came, stirring a peculiar, queasy excitement. Who had moved it? When? Why? It had been placed in a different posture, too; sitting rather than lying, propped against the tree's bole with its legs drawn up and its straw body slumped forward over them, so that the disreputable hat obscured its face. In this pose it could almost have been human, a living man who had sat down by the tree to rest and had fallen asleep. Only the stiffly artificial angles of its legs, and the fact that one of its gloves had split and was leaking straw, gave away the truth.

At last Carys moved nearer, until her feet touched the scarecrow's feet. She pushed experimentally, quite hard, with her toe. The scarecrow's leg wobbled passively, and one shoulder slipped a little way down the tree trunk. Carys was reassured, for she had almost believed the illusion, and she dropped to a crouch beside the mannikin, meaning to straighten the hat and the jacket and set everything to rights.

A robin began to sing, shrill but melodious, as she reached out to take hold of the scarecrow. Though this was not the time of year when robins were in full song, Carys was preoccupied and hardly noticed the sound. Her fingers touched the figure's arm.

And the scarecrow raised its head, turned, and looked her full in the face.

Shock and terror slammed like an explosion into Carys's mind. She recoiled with a violence that sent her sprawling into the undergrowth; in a wild, animal reflex her feet and hands scrabbled for purchase, propelling her to get up, *up*, it didn't matter how, or if she twisted every sinew in the doing of it; her only need was to flee. On hands and knees now, gasping, moaning as if in hideous pain – *but it wasn't pain, it was fear; panic of an order she had never known in her life* – then her feet pushed her upright and she plunged blindly at the trees in the direction that instinct told her was homeward. Trailing tendrils of honeysuckle reached for her, but she ripped at them and flung them aside and careered on, colliding with tree trunks, rebounding, tripping over her skirt, reeling like a drunkard. Light flared ahead and she burst out into the open. There was the hedge: through it, *through* it, forcing and pushing and neither knowing nor caring that the gap was five paces to her right. Amid a litter of broken twigs she fell out on to the track on the other side, grazed hands and knees in her desperate, uncoordinated struggle to get upright again, and ran. Sobbing in terror, breath raw in her throat, Carys raced in the sweltering heat under the sun's calm, impersonal glare, pelting for home and for sanctuary. She didn't look back, dared not. If she had, she would have seen only the empty path and the rustling cornfield and the somnolent stillness of the wood. Nothing else. Nothing at all.

The farmhouse came into sight, shimmering in the afternoon haze. The yard was deserted and silent; only the cat called Little Black, in a cool cranny behind a water-butt, saw Carys's chaotic arrival and her headlong flight towards the house door. The door slammed behind her with a crash that echoed across the yard, then all was peaceful again.

And inside the house, Carys had collapsed into Jone's chair in the ingle, and there she stayed, rocking involuntarily back and forth, with her hands covering her face and her sobs blending with the steady, soothing ticking of the clock.

Carys lay motionless in bed, listening to the night. The breeze of this afternoon had dropped away again and a deep hush had settled on the world. Far away she could hear a lamb bleating, the sound high-pitched and answered occasionally by the deeper note of an adult ewe. The farmhouse roof creaked a little as it breathed out the day's store of heat, and somewhere there was a faint scratching that might or might not be a mouse in the wainscoting. But nothing else. Nothing to set her fear leaping again.

When dusk fell, Jone had returned home to find all, apparently, as normal. Carys had greeted him with a pleasant smile, a late supper ready on the range, and they had eaten it and she had read to him – just a few minutes – and they had made their way to bed. He knew nothing of the terrified turmoil that had raged in his wife for more than an hour before she finally managed to calm herself, and nothing of the thoughts and images that still roiled and tumbled in her head, making sleep an impossibility.

She did not know what she had seen. Whether it had truly happened, or whether it had been a moment's mad delusion brought on by the heat and her own inner fever, was a question Carys was hopelessly ill-equipped to answer. All she did know was that the face that had turned to her and looked at her had not been the sacking-and-stitching face of a doll, but unequivocally and irrefutably real. Though she had confronted it for only one brief moment, it was imprinted on her mind like a picture etched in acid. A sharp, narrow face, too narrow to be truly handsome, but with a dangerous charm to it. Smooth skin, young skin, tanned brown and with an underlying glow of health. A wide mouth, smiling as though at a secret shared. And the *eyes* – blue as the summer sky, and filled with a sly, sardonic mischief that was utterly unhuman.

A shudder racked Carys as the image swam into mental focus yet again. It *couldn't* have been real. Yet the shock of it had been enough to make her bolt like a rabbit with ten foxes snapping at its heels. And even though nothing had followed her, the memory of that face kept coming back to haunt her, and each time it did, the icy sweat broke out again and she could feel the fear, the dread, the . . .

excitement . . .?

. . . rising again and clutching at her vitals.

She must never go back there. Never, ever, not even to destroy the scarecrow, which seemed to her the safest, wisest thing to do. Let it decay and become one with the woodland debris; it would take time, but it would happen eventually. Mould and detritus couldn't harm her. Mould and detritus couldn't turn its head and look at her and smile that terrible, alluring smile—

The chain of her determined thoughts snapped then, as from a distance and direction that was impossible to determine came the sound of someone whistling. It was only a fragment of a tune that drifted on the air and then vanished, but it paralysed Carys. Eyes wide as a staring corpse, she lay rigid, listening, until her lungs felt as if they would burst with the air pent-up in them. As her breath finally came out in a stabbing rush, she heard the whistling again. Just two notes this time, but repeated over and again. The first note was long, the second shorter and pitched lower, and an awful realisation crept on her that they sounded like the pattern of her name. *CAR-ys. CAR-ys.*

She couldn't seem to stop herself shaking, and now something else was taking hold of her: a terrible need to see what was out there, what was calling. Her legs moved of their own volition, then her whole trembling body, and she stood up and lurched across the room to the window. Jone had left it open but she had closed it later without his knowing, needing the safety of a physical barrier between herself and the night. It had not worked; she was not safe. She had to look.

Hands and face pressed against the glass, Carys stared towards the yard. Tonight the darkness was strong, because this was the night of the new moon, and only the stars gave a thin scattering of illumination. That, though, was enough, because as she gazed down she saw immediately that there was someone standing by the yard gate.

And she knew without any room for doubt who – what – he was. For on his head was a battered, familiar hat. And, muted in the starlight but still recognisable, gleamed the colour of Jone's old coat.

Very slowly, one unsteady step at a time, Carys backed away from the window. By a twist of chance the curtain did not fall again but snagged on the rough wall and stayed, exposing the window and making her feel horribly vulnerable. The terror was back, but this time there was nowhere to run. There was only one possible way to sanctuary, and in her panic Carys grasped at it.

'Jone!' She reached towards his slumbering shape, clasping his shoulder, shaking it. 'Jone, oh Jone, wake up!'

But Jone did not stir. He slept on, unmoving, and after a few moments Carys realised the truth. Some power beyond her knowledge was on her husband, holding his mind and body in sleep and putting him beyond her reach. He would not wake until the power chose to release him. And it would not choose, until she had answered its call.

In trepidation, Carys forced herself to look towards the window again. The angle was wrong and she could see only the stars . . . but as her head turned, the two clear whistling notes came again to break the silence.

CAR-ys. CAR-ys.

She couldn't resist its influence. The pull was too strong, and she found herself moving to the bedroom door, lifting the latch, easing it open. The door creaked but still Jone did not stir. Barefoot in her nightgown, Carys moved like a silent wraith to the stairs, down through the parlour, into the kitchen. The flagstones struck chill into her soles, but she did not notice. She reached the back door, lifted the latch. No creaking this time, only a waft of night air scented with the smells of animals and hay and something else, undefinable.

He was no longer by the gate. Now he stood in the middle of the yard, slight and angular and out of place in the homely setting. For there was nothing homely about him. Under the hat brim, a glimmer of light showed, an inner light, from his eyes, and she thought, though the darkness made it hard to be sure, that she saw him smile.

Then he raised one hand – a real hand, a human hand – and held it out towards her.

'Come, then, love.' His voice was warm and gentle, and it set invisible knives of longing twisting in Carys's heart. 'You have called, and you have waited. Now you need wait no longer.'

Chapter IX

The sky to the east was showing the first signs of lightening when Carys returned to the farm.

She approached the gate slowly, laid her hand on it as though to open it, then paused, gazing with a strange, clouded gaze at the comfortable solidity of the house. It did not look real to her, but seemed to have sideslipped into another world that no longer had any meaning. A dream, a limbo, from which she had awoken. *It* had not changed, but *she* had. Nothing would ever be the same again.

In the slowly growing greyness she turned and looked back along the path that meandered away across the fields, but he was not there. He had gone back to the wood and the land and the inscrutable enchantment that had conjured him. But he would return. That, he had promised. And Carys knew his word could not be doubted.

One hand moved, tracing a slow pattern over her own body: breasts, stomach, hips, and finally *that* place, which even now she hardly dared acknowledge. The ache of him, the glory of it, still burned like a small, hot fire, and she welcomed and savoured it, knowing that it would not last but wanting to hold on to the awareness for as long as she could. Jone would not know; he would not see or sense. That was another promise, and it made her secret safe.

In the first moment when she had faced him in the yard, her nerve had almost broken and she had wanted to turn and run back to the house's protecting walls, to lock every door and window and hide herself away until he was gone. But then he had held out his

97

arms, and at the sound of his voice, his words, *Come, then, love*, the fear had evaporated and she had gone to him, and when she looked into his eyes, on a level with her own, the die had been finally and irrevocably cast. He had said nothing more then, but had taken her hand, and together they walked from the farm out into the night. Not to the woods below the fields, her secret place, as Carys had expected; instead, he had turned aside from the track and led her on to the sloping shoulder of Crede Hill. They climbed upwards, over the springy, nibbled turf where sheep raised wary heads and watched them pass, and came at last to a gentle ridge of stonier ground. Four mature oak trees marked the start of the ridge, and in the starlight it was just possible to see the stones' paleness curving upwards to a stand of ancient hawthorns that hunched black and ragged against the sky.

They stopped, as if by some unspoken agreement, under the first of the oak trees. Carys leaned against its bole, feeling the rough bark pressing against her back. He drew close to her, and in the star-shadows cast by the leaves her eyes searched his face wonderingly, uncertainly.

'Are you . . .' Her voice caught and cracked and she struggled to bring it back under control. 'Are you . . . real?'

He smiled, and for a disconcerting moment she seemed to see the doll-face of the scarecrow that she herself had stitched, underlying his human features. Then the illusion vanished and he replied, 'As real as you can imagine, Carys.'

'But not . . .' She swallowed. 'Not *human* . . .'

A brown hand, the fingers warm and firm, touched her cheek and stroked it. 'I am whatever you want me to be. You called me, love. I'm yours. Only ask, and I shall serve you as your heart wishes.'

Carys, standing at the farmyard gate, recalled the sheer, shuddering power of the sensation that had gone through her as he spoke those words. Knowing her heart's wish, he had kissed her then. It was a true kiss, her very first, and when finally it ended and they drew apart, her mind was tumbling in helpless ecstasy. As he kissed her again she lost all hold on reality, and gave her entire self up to the moment and to him.

They had stayed then, unmoving, for what might have been a minute or an hour. The leaves above them rustled and whispered like voices, urging, cajoling, until at last he had stepped back and taken both her hands in his. Carys understood, and instead of the fear she had expected, she felt only the aching pull of joyous anticipation. She went with him, on up the ridge to the stand of hawthorns which formed a half-circle like enclosing arms around a hollow where the grass grew more luxuriantly. There, with the ground for a soft mattress and the silent sky for a canopy, she had offered herself like a gift upon an altar, and the man, the scarecrow, the strange and magical lover of her dreams, had fulfilled the pledge of the Wayfarer woman's spell. There had been fear at first, and then pain, but both were short-lived, and what took their place was the fulfilment for which she had prayed and yearned and hungered. He was gentle, he was skilful; every touch and every moment was an enchantment that set Carys's soul soaring. And when it was complete, he gazed with his strange, sky-blue eyes into her face, smiled his secret smile, and in the voice that she already worshipped said to her: 'My Carys. My love.'

She had cried for a long time afterwards, huddled in his arms while he rocked her tenderly and understood without the need for words. Eventually he kissed her yet again and dried her tears with the cuff of the old jacket (which now, for Carys, had no link with Jone but only with him), and then they sat for a while, looking up through the hawthorns' crowding branches to where the stars glimmered and flickered. Carys's heart was so full that she thought it must burst; she wanted to ask him and tell him a hundred, a thousand things, but none would come to her in any form that she could make sense of, so she stayed silent, feeling the warmth of his body against hers and the zephyr of his breath on her cheek, trying to commit this perfection to a safe and precious part of her memory, from which it could never be lost.

She wanted the night to be never-ending. But even the Wayfarers' magic could not grant that wish, and the time came when he rose from the grass and lifted her to her feet, and they began to walk slowly, hand in hand, down the hill's smooth slope. The thought of returning to the farm and the routine of ordinary life weighed leadenly in Carys, and as they passed the last of the oak trees she could bear it no longer. She stopped, turned to him and began desperately, 'When—?'

'Will you see me again?' He finished the question for her, his fingers tightening around hers. 'When you will, love. At any hour between sunset and sunrise, only call to me in your mind, and I'll know, and I'll come to you.'

'Sunset and . . . and sunrise?' Her eager expression clouded a little. 'Not in the daytime?'

He shook his head. 'That isn't possible.'

'Why?'

'Because . . . things are the way they are. Be content, my Carys. Isn't that enough?'

She hung her head, looking at the ground but not seeing it. 'The summer nights are so *short*.'

'True. But the winter nights are long. All things change, and what is lost now can be gained in another season.' Leaning forward slightly, he kissed the crown of her head. Even through her thick hair she felt the touch, and it comforted her. Things *would* change. They might have little time together now, but autumn would come, then winter. For the first time in her life she longed for winter.

They walked on. Soon the farmhouse was in sight; she thought he might leave her then, but he continued on with her until they reached the place where the narrow hill path met the field track. There he stopped, and, wanting to delay the unwanted but inevitable moment of farewell, Carys said, 'Your name – I don't know your name!'

He shrugged, an odd, stiff little gesture that for the first time tonight made her think of the scarecrow. 'I have no name, or many names, or any name. It doesn't matter.'

She didn't understand. 'But what can I call you?'

'Anything you choose. Whatever it is, I'll be content with it.' Humour glinted suddenly in his eyes. 'What shall I be?'

But Carys could not answer. No name came instantly to her mind, and no amount of effort could force one. Dismayed, she tried to persuade him to make the choice for her, but he only shook his head and repeated, 'None or many or any,' and would say no more.

So they had parted at last. He had kissed her once again, then told her to turn away and cover her eyes and count to thirteen before she might look back along the track and wave him farewell. She obeyed, though there seemed no reason for the game, putting her palms to her face and slowly reciting the numbers aloud. When she was done, and looked, there was no trace of a moving figure on the track. She had waved anyway, in case it was simply the grey darkness that made him invisible, but she felt instinctively that he was no longer there.

And now, coming out of her reverie she found herself leaning against the gate, head on her folded arms, staring at the yard, but, until this moment, unaware of it or of anything else. The eastern sky was perceptibly lighter, and faint shadows were beginning to form. Then, from somewhere beyond the barn, a sweet trill of birdsong broke the quiet. A robin . . . He sang again, an ebullient little melody, and from a greater distance a blackbird answered. The dawn chorus was beginning. But the robin had been the first. Robin, Carys thought. *He* was like a robin: slight and lively and vivacious, with his heart-warming smile and his mischievous eyes. Robin. It would suit him well.

She smiled, pleased that the answer she wanted had come to her, and was still savouring it when a cockerel crowed from the arks in the nearest field. This was the unequivocal herald of dawn – and the customary signal for Jone to wake. Alarm clutched her, and Carys pushed the gate open and hurried across the yard to the house. In at the door, through the warm, drowsy kitchen, up the stairs, quickly, *quietly*, to the bedroom. Easing the door back, she peered in and saw Jone's dim shape still sleeping peacefully in the bed. Emboldened, she crept to look at him more closely as the cockerel crowed again. He didn't wake then, nor did he stir while she pulled off her dust-and grass-stained nightgown, hid it under the bed and put on a clean one. Even when she slid into bed beside him, he only sighed a little and did not move.

Carys lay still, her back to him, gazing at the window, thinking. Minutes passed, perhaps five, perhaps ten. Then there was a shifting behind her, a grunt, and Jone opened his eyes.

She turned to look at him, feigning sleepiness. He smiled.

'My dear,' he said by way of greeting. 'The sun is rising, I think, and we should be rising too.' He paused. 'Have you rested comfortably enough despite the heat? Is all well with you this morning?'

'Oh yes, Jone,' said Carys. 'All is *very* well with me.'

Oak-month ended, Holly-month passed, and by the time Apple-month began the corn stood high and had ripened to a rich, deep gold. The farmers walked their crops, looked with quiet satisfaction at the rustling acres spreading away under the sun and agreed among themselves that in three more days, if Providence remained bountiful, the harvest would begin.

The bounty of Providence so far showed no signs of changing. The shimmering weather had continued almost unbroken, save for a few fierce but short-lived thunderstorms that rolled in from the west, drenched the district in brief, spectacular cloudbursts, and moved on, leaving the parched land refreshed and ready to greet the sun again. On one smallholding a pig had been killed by lightning, but it was the storms' only casualty. So, trusting to the sky's optimism and backing the trust with some private prayers, preparations began. The Wayfarers were gone, but there was no shortage of labour to be had; men who could spare the time helped as a matter of course, and though the old men, women and children couldn't work with the same speed or efficiency, they still made up useful numbers for the tying, carrying and stooking.

On the appointed day, as the sun started to climb above Crede Hill, the small army of toilers spread themselves among the farms and steadings, and the work began. Three great wagons were mustered in Jone's yard, with Faithful and two loaned horses harnessed in their shafts, and Carys stood at the kitchen door to wave the procession off, the carts creaking and swaying in the vanguard like great, dignified ships.

She was not to be among the harvesters. Her duty was here, at the farm, baking and preparing the small mountain of food needed to sustain the hungry workers. It would be hard work, but Carys welcomed it, for she was in dire need of distraction. Last night she had wanted to meet Robin, but circumstances had conspired against her. In the early evening Merion had come to the farmhouse to sharpen Jone's scythes, then Gyll had arrived, and Garler and Deenor; the six of them had shared a late supper, and by the time their neighbours left Carys was too tired to do anything but fall into bed. This morning she felt pent-up, and as edgy as a fox. Little wonder: three nights had passed since she had last seen her lover, and she missed him, *wanted* him. But the farm had to come first. She must give Jone no cause for suspicion.

The fact that Jone continued to suspect nothing was, Carys felt certain, another marvel of the Wayfarers' magic. Each time she sent her silent call to Robin, Jone slept like the dead and did not stir throughout her absence, or when she crept back in the small hours to slip into bed beside him as though nothing had happened. At first she had been terrified that, one morning, she would return to find him waiting for her with a face like doom. But that had never happened, and now she knew that it never would. She was free of dread, free of doubt, free of constraint. And for the first time in her life, she was truly happy.

In the past month or so she had met her lover twelve times. Each occasion had been a new and thrilling experience for her, and each had been different from any other . . . except in one regard, for always, *always* before the end of the night there had been the passion, the cleaving and the coming together, and a surge of release from the ache of frustration that had blazed in Carys for so long. She did not know whether Robin was a skilful lover, versed in all the arts and tricks of pleasure; all she did know, and cared about, was that he gave her everything that her imagination could desire. 'You make me complete,' she had said to him one night, as they lay together in an old, old place in the woods that he had shown her, where moonlight filtered through gnarled, ancient branches to cast fantastical patterns in the grass, and the silence was so intense that she believed she could have reached out and held it and kept it like a memento. And he had smiled his wide, gentle smile, and laughed a little at her, ruffled her hair, and replied: 'And what would I be without you?' A question to which she could find no answer.

Oh, she had learned about love from Robin. But she was learning other things, too, and in those he was no less a teacher. For it seemed to Carys that Robin knew everything there was to know about the world around them, its ways and its lore and its mysteries. Before Passion was aroused, or after it was spent, they walked together, roaming the hills and the pastures and the woods, and as they walked he showed her small and fascinating things which she had never thought to notice before. A lowly flower, growing almost invisibly in a hedge-bottom, which, he said, had the power to heal moon-madness if used in the proper way and at the proper time. A forgotten and all but completely overgrown track, leading to an equally forgotten cleft in the hills where the purest spring in five parishes bubbled from the earth. When a white owl glided past them on silent wings, he told her that owls knew the future, and their calling in the coppices at night sometimes foretold a death. Carys had laughed nervously at this, saying that she had been brought up not to believe such superstitions. Robin had only smiled, then raised a finger, signalling to her to listen. Distantly, she heard the call of a screech-owl: two quick, eager *kee-wicks*, ringing out from somewhere to the south. 'There!' Robin had said, 'but that's not an ill omen. The owls say many different things, if you learn to listen to their voices.'

What *was* he? At first, Carys had asked and asked the question of him, but always he answered with banter or diversion. At last she had given up, and tried to find the explanation in her own mind.

But that, too, proved fruitless. She did not know, and could not know. And as time passed and she came to love him more, she no longer cared. He was Robin, and he was *hers*. What else mattered?

And this morning she wanted him so much that it hurt, physically, like an ache inside her bones. As the carts diminished she withdrew into the kitchen, picked up the broom and, closing her eyes, stepped out a slow, small dance of her own devising. *He* danced with her sometimes, on the hill under the stars, and when he did, she heard the lilt of music in her head and it seemed so real. But here in the kitchen she couldn't conjure the illusion back to mind. The floor was stone, the room was hot, and she held not Robin's hands but only a stick of wood; and Izzy would soon be here and there was work to be done . . .

As if on cue, she heard the sound of the yard gate, then the unmistakable tramp of Izzy's footsteps. Carys sighed, opened her eyes, and when Izzy came in she was sweeping the floor with a good deal more industrious energy than necessary. Pausing in the doorway to take off her hat, Izzy said, 'No point to that, Missus, if you ask me. Floor'll be sloven again soon enough, and we got more to do than four hands can rightly be asked without making more.'

Carys glowered sidelong at her. 'Where's Lob?' she demanded.

'I sent him over to the fields. That's supposing he can find the way without getting hisself lost.' Izzy took her apron from its hook and wrapped it around her ample middle. 'Tisn't one of his good days, so I reckon he'll be more use there than lummocking around under our feet. Now, then—' She paused, looking at Carys keenly. 'You all right, Missus? You're sweating something terrible.'

'Don't be stupid,' Carys said sharply. 'Of course I'm all right. I'm just hot.'

Izzy grunted agreement, and started on a long tale about how her leg had been playing up as well as her feet, and if anyone should think to ask her, which they wouldn't, she could tell them that more ailments were due to the weather than to any of Jem Apothecary's fancy notions, which he only put about to dupe fools into parting with money better spent on other things . . . Carys let the monologue fade into the background as she went to fetch flour, salt, lard and the water pitcher. Work. She must concentrate on it and forget everything else. Until the harvest was in, the farm must come first and there could be no more meetings with Robin. A few days, no more. She could bear it. She would have to.

Izzy's droning voice paused suddenly, and belatedly Carys realised that she had moved on from the subject of her health and asked a question.

'What?' she said.

'The King, I said.' Izzy sounded affronted. 'You haven't forgotten? It's to be made here this year, and we're to have the charge of it.'

Carys stared at her. She *had* forgotten, and Izzy's reminder took her completely by surprise. The Harvest King was a tradition set in time; from her earliest childhood Carys could remember the thrill of excitement she had felt each year as she watched the bizarre figure coming down into the village. The making was women's work – no male hand must ever touch the King until he was complete – and every female involved in the harvest had a part to play, however small. Using the sheaves that the farmers provided – the best of the crop – they would weave and plait and mould the shape, slowly and carefully creating the life-sized mannikin with his crown of wild flowers and his flail of corn-ears. They would secure him to a litter made from newly cut hazel branches, make a canopy of leaves behind and above him, and surround his feet with loaves of fresh bread. When the last of the harvest had been brought in, the King would be carried in procession round the fields, then down to the village and the chapel, where the preacher would bless him before he was set in his place of honour at the communal feast.

And this year, the making was to take place under her own roof.

As a miller's daughter rather than a farmer's child, Carys had never played a part in the making before. Three months ago, she had been looking forward to it. Now, though . . . she couldn't explain the discomfiting, almost frightened *frisson* that went through her.

There was no rationality to it – the making was an occasion for fun, and all her good women friends would be here to help her: Gyll and Juda, Deenor and Olma, and others from the outlying steadings. But Carys felt only a sense of dread. Something was wrong, and though she couldn't place a finger on it, neither could she push it away.

Izzy was warming to her new topic. 'It's twelve years or more since the making was done here,' she informed Carys. 'I don't reckon they've had one as good, not since. Last year – you recall last year? No better than a pig's breakfast, that was, and when it come time for preacher to bless it, he could hardly tell which end was which!'

'It was a poor harvest last year,' said Carys uneasily.

'So maybe it was, but all the same I reckon we'll have something to show 'em, eh?' Izzy rolled her sleeves back. 'Something to make up for that old misbegot!' She plunged both hands into the crock and scooped a small mountain of flour on to the scrubbed table. As she started to make a well in it she added, 'It was a shame on the parish, and we'll all be glad to see it go to the burning. Good riddance, that's what I say!'

Carys's disquiet slipped into focus with a mind-shaking jolt. *The burning*. That was the other part of the ritual, the final act to celebrate harvest's end. The new King was carried to the village, blessed, set in his place of honour. Then the feast: music and dancing and drinking, continuing until the first signs of dawn came. Then, at the moment when the sun rose, the old Harvest King, carefully preserved since the previous year, was set up in the rough square outside the chapel meeting hall, and burned to ashes. The old King is dead, the new King reigns. Part of the tradition, immovable and unchanging.

Carys had witnessed the burning every year throughout her life. But this year she did not, did *not*, want to be a part of it.

She didn't understand. *Why* should she fear the old ritual now, as she had never done before? It made no sense, and she wanted to push Izzy aside and run from the house, out to the woods, and call with all the strength she possessed for Robin to come to her and explain. Only the fact that it was day, and she would not find him, held her still. But she wanted to *know*, and he was the only one who could tell her.

She felt sweat break out anew, all over her body, and quickly she turned to the water pitcher, plunging her hands in past the wrists in an effort to cool herself before Izzy noticed her state. Seeing what she was doing, but thankfully not the reason for it, Izzy said, 'You'll want some hot; can't make bread rise with cold. Shall I put on the kettle?'

'Yes,' said Carys tersely.

There was a sound of horses' hooves outside then, and Izzy craned through the window. 'Well, now, here's Missus Merion Blacksmith, and Missus Elios Carter with her by the looks of it. Come to help with the baking, have they? That's neighbourly!'

The hooves stopped, there was a jingle of harness and Carys heard Gyll's cheerful voice calling her name. Gyll and Juda. They would help her. They would distract her. She had never been more glad of their arrival.

She withdrew her hands from the pitcher, wiped them on her apron, and went to greet her good friends.

Chapter X

The making of the Harvest King took five days, and by the time it was done Carys didn't know whether exhaustion or strain had the greater grip on her.

With so much else to do, the women had worked on the figure only after sunset, and into the small hours the great barn – which for the time being was forbidden to the men – rang with the sounds of chatter and laughter and singing. Up to twenty at a time were present; they came and went as time and tiredness allowed, but Carys, in the responsible position of hostess, was obliged always to be there. She alone had seen the figure at every stage, from the first rough shaping when Jone and two more men left the sheaves at the barn door, to the making of the final details of form and feature. And the dread that had lodged in her at Izzy's first careless remark still remained, like a fever for which there was no cure.

Twice, when all but one or two sleepy diehards had admitted defeat and gone home, she had hoped that the chance might come to escape, if only for an hour, and go to Robin. But Fate had worked against her; the diehards had worked on and she had no choice but to do likewise. And when finally they did leave, she was too weary for anything but sleep.

On the fifth night, dawn was close to breaking when the last piece of straw was tucked into place and the King was complete. Ten women had stayed on to the end: the skilled ones, the experienced ones. Gyll, Deenor and Izzy were among their number, and they and Carys sat together on a hay-bale, flexing their aching fingers and gazing silently at their handiwork. They had set the

King on more bales, stacked three high, and in the light of lanterns the strange, silent figure towered over them like something from a disturbing dream. Izzy's prediction that, 'We'll have something to show 'em' had come emphatically true. Though no one could have said why if asked, there was a ferocious energy, a *life*, to the King of this blazing year. Proud, regal, as if he was already liege of his lowly creators, he embodied the spirit of the harvest in a way that none of them could remember ever having seen before.

And he embodied something else. For his shape, his face, his whole aura, reminded Carys disquietingly of Robin.

She sat staring at the King, not speaking, feeling distinctly unreal. Her eyes prickled with weariness and kept trying to close of their own accord; every few seconds she had to shake her head to pull herself back from the borders of sleep and a half-formed dream in which Robin and the King became confusingly and impossibly entangled one with the other. The dread had sunk to a dull, shapeless sensation somewhere below the level of clear consciousness, but she felt miserable, uncomfortable, and a little afraid.

'. . . her doing, if you ask me.' A voice impinged on her muddled thoughts, and a friendly elbow nudged her in the ribs. 'What do you say, Carys?'

Carys turned her head dully to find Gyll looking at her, smiling, waiting for an answer. 'I'm sorry . . .' she said indistinctly. 'I didn't . . .'

'The poor child's near exhaustion, Gyll,' Deenor Garlerwife put in. She stretched her arms and rubbed at the biceps. 'We all are, I reckon, and we'll be glad to see our beds.'

'I'm sorry,' Carys said again to Gyll, rousing herself with some effort. 'What did you say?'

Gyll nodded at the straw figure. 'Just that he's a King to be proud of. I think it must be your influence, him being your very first.'

'Oh.' A cold river moved in the pit of Carys's stomach. 'I . . . don't know.' Then, belatedly, remembering good manners, 'But thank you, Gyll. Yes, thank you.'

110

'Well, I don't know about anyone else, but I'm for home,' Olma Carnwidow declared, standing up and brushing the clinging straw-dust from her skirt. 'The men say the harvest should be home in two more days. So we meet again the morning after, yes? For the crowning?'

There were murmurs of agreement, punctuated with yawns. Gyll rose and started to extinguish the lanterns. Their glow faded and the colder, pearlier light of pre-dawn took its place. The King seemed to become yet more real, and Carys avoided looking at him as the whole group moved out into the yard, closing and fastening the barn door behind them.

The air was cool and refreshing, reviving her a little as she made her farewells, thanked all her companions and tried her best to join in with the last-minute chat and pleasantries. She thought that Gyll looked curiously at her once or twice, as if suspecting something untoward, but no questions were asked and at last the company were all gone and she was alone.

She didn't go into the house, but instead stood gazing at it for a minute or two. Jone would be awake soon, but not quite yet. She had a little time. And suddenly she no longer felt like sleeping.

She turned, left the yard and started along the field track. There wasn't time enough to go all the way to the woods, or to any of their other special meeting places, so after fifty paces or so she turned off the path and hurried to the edge of the sheep pasture, where a blackthorn hedge grew tall and impenetrable. Birds were stirring and twittering in the hedge. Carys stopped by the pasture gate and strained her eyes to peer into the grey world beyond.

'Robin!' Her voice drifted softly into the field. 'Robin, I need you! Come to me, my love – come to me!'

She could see the sheep, like ghosts on the pasture slope, but nothing else moved, and nothing answered her. Carys called again, urgently, reinforcing the words with a surge of her will to draw him to her. But she knew as surely as she knew her own name that he was not there. She was too late; the sun was close to rising, and he would not – or could not – come.

At last she accepted defeat, turned from the gate and walked slowly back to the farm. The light was strengthening rapidly, and the curtains at the bedroom window had been opened, indicating that Jone was up and about. Another day, another round. It no longer mattered to Carys that she had had no sleep; all her desire for rest had gone.

She moved past the barn, trying not to think of the Harvest King alone and waiting in the shadows of the interior, and turned her heavy steps towards the kitchen and breakfast.

The feast to celebrate the completion of harvest took place three days later, and still Carys had not seen Robin.

She had had only one opportunity to look for him, on the eve of the feast day, when the hectic pace of work finally slowed as the end came in sight. With the weather still perfect, the last loads would be brought home in the morning, the farmers could relax, and, as Carys had hoped, Jone wanted nothing more than to eat a good meal and seek his bed early for the first time since the reaping began.

As her husband snored gently under the patchwork counterpane, she stood at the open window and sent out a silent summons to her lover. *The wood*, her mind said. *The clearing, by the great oak.* Tonight, there would be no need for haste. And she wanted and needed him so much.

She was there waiting as the moon, which had just begun to wane, cleared the shoulder of Crede Hill and turned the wood to a magical, grey and silver kaleidoscope. But Robin did not appear. Hunched down on an oak root that protruded like a grandfather's knee, Carys counted the minutes, her unease growing until it was a hard, tight ball lodged above her heart. Again and again she called to him, sometimes in her mind, sometimes aloud, but her only answers were the chirp of a sleepy bird disturbed by her voice, and a furtive rustle in the undergrowth as some small nocturnal animal scurried by on its foraging. Robin did not come to her.

Eventually, she had no choice but to go home. She lingered on the way, stopping every few moments to look around her, hoping against reason that he would step suddenly out of the shadow of a bush, or form from a patch of the night gloom and smile and laugh and take her hand. He did not. *Why?* Carys asked herself. Where was he? Had he chosen not to answer her, or was something keeping him away? She didn't know, couldn't understand, and anger and fear warred for the upper hand.

In the farmhouse, she climbed the stairs listlessly and got into bed. She did not expect to sleep, but after perhaps half an hour of restless worry, tiredness took over and she was aware of nothing more until dawn came and with it Jone's familiar greeting and the start of another day.

From the beginning there was an undercurrent of excitement in the atmosphere around the farm and fields, as everyone waited for the word that the final load was ready to be carried home. The word was eventually brought by Garler's eldest son, who came running down the hill, waving his hat like a signal flag. Izzy saw him first and shrilled the news to Carys; soon afterwards the first of the women arrived and they all hastened to the barn to prepare the Harvest King for his triumphal procession.

Under the shimmering noonday sun, the litter with its precious burden was carried out into the yard. Here the men waited to take over, and with Jone at their head they carried the King through the gate and away up the track towards the fields. The procession grew and grew; first a trickle, then a spate, as young and old, the workers and the gleaners, people from every part of the parish, joined in the jubilant march.

Carys walked behind the litter, with all the women who had taken part in the making. Ahead of her the King swayed with slow dignity on his throne, his head half hidden under a great crown of flowers and leaves. The scents of the flowers and the hedges and the cut stubble combined into a sweet, heavy perfume that made her dizzy and a little disorientated, so that the broad vista of the fields seemed to swell and fade by turns, one moment closing in, the next impossibly distant. She felt as if she had lost control of her body and moved like a puppet on invisible strings, and when they reached the crown of Crede Hill and the litter-bearers began to sing the age-old Summer Song of celebration and thanksgiving, it sounded to her like something from a feverish dream.

Across the great expanse of the hill, field to field and farm to farm, the procession wound on its long and cheerful journey, until, three hours and no one knew how many miles from their starting place, the vanguard turned at last down the stony lane that led to the village. The sky was hazing over to the south-west, giving the afternoon a brassy tinge, and the small breeze of earlier had vanished, leaving the air breathless and utterly still. The singing died away to solemn silence, punctuated only by the occasional whining of a fractious child, and Carys tried to clear her head, rally her energy and not allow herself to think of Robin.

The preacher was waiting outside the chapel, and with him was another crowd of people; all those who had been unable to follow the procession but would not dream of missing this great occasion. Carys caught sight of her parents, with Thomsine as sullen as ever beside them. Nellen was there too, and she waved to Carys, who did not wave back. The chapel porch was decorated with sheaves and straw plaits, and on the grass were heaped the villagers' harvest gifts: trugs of fruit, baskets of loaves, sides of bacon, cheeses, preserves, fresh vegetables, beer, cider, all piled together to honour the King.

The chapel could not possibly have accommodated such a throng, so the ceremony of blessing was conducted outside. Carys listened dully to the familiar words, while her eyes scanned the crowd around her, looking for something without knowing what it was she wanted to find. Now and then she frowned at a flicker of bright colour among the press of people, but by the time the last hymn was sung and the ceremony drew to a close, she was no nearer to satisfying her restlessness.

The preacher pronounced his last benediction, and the formalities were done. The King on his litter was lifted once more, and the mass exodus began towards the adjacent meeting hall.

Tables laden with food and drink had been set up both inside and out, and the harvest gifts were carried from the chapel to augment them.

Carys would have preferred to stay out of doors, but Jone took her arm and led her into the hall, where the older and staider villagers were gathering. The King was there, in the place of honour prepared for him. Through the smoke already hazing from several granfers' pipes he looked more lifelike than ever, and Carys turned her head away from his blank, blind stare. As Jone fell into conversation with two of the village elders, she surreptitiously poured herself a mug of cider from one of the pitchers on the nearest table, drank half of it in one draught, then quickly topped up the mug before anyone noticed. Milk yields and market prices . . . she *wanted* to drink. She wanted to get drunk, and dance all night. She wanted to dance with Robin, but Robin wasn't here, and wouldn't come, and he hadn't answered her call last night, and she didn't know why, and—

The chain of her thoughts was snapped by a sudden wail nearby as Ina Bartelwife's little boy, a toddler, missed his unsteady footing and sprawled face-first on the hard floor. Ina, who was barely older than Carys and known as a scatterbrain, tried to pick the child up, but he immediately started to yell in earnest, and Carys saw that he had grazed both knees and the palms of his hands.

'There, then! There, then!' Ina flapped her own hands ineffectually. 'Oh, stop crying, do!'

A few of the older women were watching with pitying cynicism; one said: 'Leave him be, Ina. A few knocks won't harm the lad; teach him to be more careful.'

The little boy howled anew, and something – she didn't know what; couldn't name it – awoke in Carys's head.

She touched Ina's arm. 'He's grazed himself. Knees and hands – see?'

'Oh, yes!' Ina's eyes widened, then her mouth started to quiver. 'Oh, my lamb, he's hurt, then! What shall I do?'

Before she knew it, Carys said, 'Flowers of morning-gold. Crush

115

them in your hand and rub them on the grazes. They'll soothe the pain.'

Ina stared blankly at her. 'Flowers of . . .?'

'Morning-gold. You know, like daisies, only bigger and yellow-orange.' Abruptly and unexpectedly brisk, Carys added, 'They grow everywhere; they're even outside in the verge – wait here and I'll fetch you some.'

She shouldered her way through the increasing press of people, found the plants where she expected to find them, and returned with a handful of flowers. With Ina worrying and dithering at her shoulder she crushed the petals and rubbed them firmly on the child's wounds, gentling him with a smile and a clucking of her tongue when he started to protest. Within less than a minute his howls subsided to hiccupping sobs, then after a final sniffle he fell silent, staring at her in awed wonder.

Ina was staring too, with a blend of admiration and confusion. 'Th-thank you, Carys,' she got out at last. 'That was . . .' But she didn't quite know what she was trying to say, so the sentence hung unfinished.

Carys blinked and came back to earth. She felt startled. It was as if, for a few minutes, another personality altogether had stepped into her mind and taken the place of her familiar self. Without any conscious effort she had known exactly what to do for the little boy, and the remedy had worked. That wasn't like her. She knew nothing about herbs and simples and cures; they were the province of Jem Apothecary, or Merion Blacksmith in the case of animals. She had never been wise in that way.

But then it occurred to her that she was no longer quite the person she used to be. She had changed. Robin had changed her. In his company she was learning about life in a way that she had never dreamed before. And now, it seemed that the lessons he taught her were taking root . . .

Ina was still trying falteringly to express her gratitude, while the watching women had taken keen notice and looked suitably impressed. Suddenly Carys experienced a secret, delighted flush of pleasure and pride. Smiling at Ina, and looking a good deal more modest than she felt, she said, 'There's nothing to it, Ina, and no need to thank me. Just remember the morning-gold flowers, eh?'

'Yes, Carys.' Ina nodded emphatically. 'Yes, I will.'

She was still staring as Carys returned dutifully to Jone's side.

She did not get drunk. It wasn't that the opportunity eluded her; Jone became so engrossed in his talking that she could have swallowed down a whole pitcher and more without his noticing it. But after the first two mugs she lost the taste for cider or anything else. What she had had lay sour and heavy on her stomach, and neither did she want anything to eat. Even the sight of the laden tables was off-putting.

She did dance a little. She joined Olma Carnwidow and her twelve-year-old twin nephews for one of the squares, helped make up the numbers in a step-dance, and was invited by Merion Blacksmith to partner him for the fourth set of jigs. The invitation, she suspected, was Gyll's doing; Jone did not dance, and Gyll felt sorry for Carys and was trying to do her a good turn. It was a kind gesture, but it made Carys feel depressed. She did not want to be here: she wanted to be out in the fields, in the woods, on the hill, with Robin.

But last night Robin had not answered her call . . .

The night and celebration went on, and to Carys it seemed endless. She harboured hopes that Jone might fall asleep, but perversely he seemed to have found a reserve of strength to keep him going, probably, she thought, because he would have considered it a poor show of manners to do otherwise. The midnight chimes of the chapel clock were greeted with a wave of cheering (much of it highly inebriated by this time) and calls for the four musicians, who were taking a well-earned rest, to strike up again for more dancing. This they gallantly did, and Garler Shepherd shyly asked Carys if she would consent to partner him. Garler was no dancer; he was ponderously slow, and tended to forget the steps and tread on everyone's feet, but Carys thanked him prettily, looked to Jone for permission and tried to join in the fun.

The hall doors stood open, and from outside came occasional bursts of noise; shouting and laughter and, once, a huge mass roar of approval. Carys knew what it meant, and the thought of what was being prepared made her shiver inwardly. This year she did not want to see it. She wanted to look away, hide her head and cover her ears, until it was all over. This year, she was frightened.

However, there was nowhere to hide and no excuse that she could have made. This was the last rite, the final seal set on the harvest's success, and for anybody not to witness it was unthinkable. So when the stars began to fade and the first signs of light appeared in the east, another great shout from the revellers outside summoned everyone from the hall.

The bonfire was ready. A royal funeral pyre, logs and faggots and brushwood piled like a truncated pyramid and standing a head higher than the tallest man in the crowd. The old Harvest King was already in place on the top of it. He had been ill-made at the start and the year had taken its toll, so by now he was a sorry sight: lumpen and misshapen and sagging to one side, the straw shrivelled and the weaving coming undone. He looked tired of life, as if his departure was overdue. Carys could not bear to face him, but kept as far back among the crowd as she could, sheltering behind the bulk of two burly men who had linked arms to hold each other upright and were swinging their empty mugs in erratic rhythm.

The buzz of noise subsided to something near silence as the moment approached and the pent-up excitement grew. Then somewhere beyond the chapel an owl hooted, and was answered by another in the direction of Crede Hill. Carys's head came up sharply, and she listened. She had the uneasy feeling that the two birds were speaking to each other across the distance, and she remembered what Robin had told her: that owls knew the future and their calling sometimes heralded a death. Was this such a portent? A cold current was set flowing in her veins, and her mouth moved in a silent but fervent plea: *No harm can come to Robin . . . it can't, it can't . . . Oh, please, don't let this dread get the better of me!*

She listened again, but the owls no longer spoke and the only sounds were the restless, eager shuffling of feet. A minute passed, two. The eastern horizon was paling by the moment.

Then the sun began to rise.

The first glimpse was the signal for the greatest yell of all. The torch-bearers' brands flared into life with a *whoof* and a glare of yellow light, and the throng pressed forward as the brands were thrust into the heart of the woodpile. The kindling caught instantly; for a few moments small tongues of flame crackled and danced, then with a roar echoed by almost every human throat in the crowd, the pyre went up. Carys covered her face with both hands, trying not to hear the noise of the flames as they surged skywards, but she felt the fire's heat, and her eyelids seared with the red glow filtering through her fingers. Voices rose suddenly in the Farewell Song, the King's last eulogy, and her breath caught chokingly in her throat, making her gasp with a pain that wasn't physical but still felt horribly real.

Suddenly, as though something had torn down the mental fortress she had tried to build around herself, she knew that she *had* to look. Beyond conscious control, her eyes snapped open and she stared straight at the blazing pyre.

The old King was in his final death throes. To the jubilant strains of the Farewell Song, he burned like a shooting star. A great corona of sparks streamed upwards from the straw figure, which was twisting and writhing as though in a macabre dance. Scraps of flaming straw whirled above the heads of the singing throng, then the King's arms disintegrated, and the entire figure began to collapse in on itself.

And, superimposed over the charring travesty of a human face, Carys saw the face of Robin.

An awful, mewing sound broke from her throat. The scene swelled in on her, receded, swelled again – then she uttered an agonised cry and her unconscious body dropped like a sack to the dusty ground.

Chapter XI

'These summer fevers are always at their worst around harvest time.' Jem Apothecary packed his nostrums, together with the silver spoon and listening tube, into his satchel, then smiled reassuringly at Jone. 'But in your wife's case, there's no cause for alarm. Indeed, Providence has been kind to us this year. Mercifully few have been stricken, and those that have, have made a rapid recovery. A day or two of rest and she'll be herself again.'

Jone nodded dubiously. 'Mercifully few, you say . . . why Carys, though? She's young and fit. I thought it was usually the weakly ones that took these ailments.'

'We-ell . . . doubtless she's been working long hours, what with the season and the King-making?' Jone nodded again. 'There, then, all that with the excitement of the harvest-feast on top, and even the strongest can succumb. Don't worry, Jone. Rest and my elixirs will soon set her to rights.' He looked up, as if he could see through the ceiling to the bedroom above where Carys lay. 'She's sleeping now. Instruct Izzy to let her be until she wakes naturally, then she should have a bowl of the broth I've prescribed, and another this evening. Send word if you need me, of course, but I'm confident that all will be well. Good day to you, now, Jone.'

Carys was not sleeping. Lying flat in the bed, she listened to Jem's departing footsteps, then to Jone's heavier tread as he returned to the parlour and stood there in silence for a few moments. She could picture him, thoughtful and puzzled and a little worried, beset by a man's uncertain helplessness in the face of illness.

Not that she was ill. For all Jem's pronouncements and

nostrums, she knew that there was nothing wrong with her. It had been a fainting fit, that was all. But if Jem told Jone otherwise, and Jone believed him, that was all to the good, for it had saved her from what might otherwise have been some very awkward questions.

She turned her head and looked at the empty mug in which the apothecary had mixed her sleeping draught. It hadn't worked, and she had not expected it to. Redspear and star-flower she would have chosen, with perhaps a leaf of tissel from the hedgerow to make her sweat away the fever more quickly; *if* she had a fever, which she did not. Jem had not remarked on the lack of sweating, so perhaps, when a little time had passed, she should find some tissel and chew it to keep up appearances, so that everyone would be satisfied.

She rolled over so that she was facing the window, and thought about the events of a few hours ago. She remembered little of what had happened in the minutes before she fainted. Her one clear recollection was of opening her eyes, looking up at the blazing King on his pyre and seeing Robin's features in the disintegrating face of straw. Now, at a few hours' distance, the intensity of her reaction seemed nonsensical. Two mugs of cider and no food, the overheated hall and the airless night, all combined with bone-weariness in the wake of the harvest – it was enough to unhinge anyone and give them delusions.

As for the rest of it . . . Carys had come to in the meeting hall, whither she had been carried and laid down on a bench. Opening her eyes, she had been confronted with a blur of concerned or curious faces staring down at her. For one instant she had thought that Robin's face was among them, but of course it was a delusion, and she had shut her eyes again, willing them all to go away. They did, or almost all, drawing back as Jone and Gyll and Merion helped her to her feet and led her outside. Jone fetched Spry with the gig, they lifted her into it, and with Gyll still at her side to keep her from falling, she had been driven home, Merion following in his own market cart. Gyll put her to bed, and for a long time Carys had lain listening to the low murmur of voices in the room below. At last she had fallen asleep, and dreamed of owls, and when she woke again it was mid-morning and Jem Apothecary had arrived to make his diagnosis.

Abruptly, as the thought of the owl dreams skimmed across her mind, she remembered the calls she had heard last night, and the fear they had engendered in her. The owls' portents, Robin's face in the fire . . . and the mystery of why he had not come to her when she summoned him. A sick sensation cramped her stomach as she realised the possible link, and this time rational arguments about cider and tiredness couldn't banish it. Her hands clenched, gripping the hem of the counterpane, and a sweat that would have vindicated Jem Apothecary's diagnosis started to break out on her face. If something had happened to Robin – but surely it wasn't *possible?* Robin was not . . . she struggled to find a word and managed an approximation. He was not *ordinary*, not *mortal;* at least not in the way that she was. What could harm him? What could wish to? It made no sense.

She had to find Robin, or, if she could not, then she had to search for any clue, however small, to his disappearance. The clearing in the wood was the obvious place to begin, so as soon as she could be sure that no one would know—

A footfall sounded on the stairs. Carys froze momentarily, her thoughts collapsing, and as the steps came closer she shut her eyes and tried to make her breathing slow and shallow, feigning sleep. She heard the door open. Then came a long silence in which she felt Jone's presence on the threshold, gazing at her. Time passed, until at last he sighed, the doorlatch tapped gently back into place and the footfalls went slowly away, along the landing towards the other bedroom that was used only for storing lumber. *Good . . . good . . .* There was an old couch in that room; Jone must mean to rest for a while, so he would not come back in here to disturb her. Count the minutes, Carys thought, give him time to fall into a sound sleep. An hour or two she would need, no more.

Her ears were sharp, and it was not long before they picked up the faint sound of snoring from the far end of the passage. With a small smile she slipped out of bed, dressed herself and pushed one of the feather pillows down into the bed's depths, pulling up the counterpane so that, if Izzy should look in, it would seem that she was still there and asleep. Avoiding Izzy would be the hardest part, but Fate was on her side, for when she peered out of the window she saw the older woman crossing the yard, carrying a bucket of vegetable peelings and heading for the chicken arks. Grasping her chance, Carys flitted down the stairs and was out of the front door in less than a minute. Round the house to the far side, and by the time Izzy came stumping back she was out of sight, running down the field track towards the wood.

The air was closer and heavier even than yesterday, and the haze thicker, obscuring the sun. There was something threatening about the quality of the light, as if an immense thunderstorm was building up. If that was so, Carys wished it would break and have done. She was a little afraid of thunder and very nervous of lightning, but this ominous stillness was preying on her, oppressing her mind and body. A storm would at least clear the air, in every sense.

She looked south-westwards, half expecting to see a great anvil-head of cloud forming in the sky, but there was only the same flat, brazen cast from horizon to horizon. The green shades of the wood ahead of her were losing their brightness and becoming dull and dusty; before long, she thought, their colours would begin to change in earnest, the reds and golds creeping in as summer gave way to autumn. Then the fruit and potato harvests would begin, followed by leaf-fall, and before anyone knew it, it would be winter once again. Carys's heart fluttered under her ribs at the thought that the nights would then be at their longest; time for her to be with Robin, to love him, to learn from him, to indulge in all the delights that he could show her.

If she found him . . .

She frowned, trying to quell a renewed surge of fear by pretending it was anger. Robin had no *right* to hide from her. Hadn't he said himself that he was hers? Hadn't he said: *Only ask, and I shall serve you as your heart wishes?* That was a promise, and he had no right to break it.

Her lower lip started to quiver and she bit it hard, feeling momentarily as foolish as Ina Bartelwife and resenting it. Clues. She would go to the place where the scarecrow had lain, and where she had not ventured since the night Robin first came to her. If clues there were, that was surely where she would find them.

She pushed through the gap in the hedge, harder now to penetrate, and with scratched hands and several small tears in her skirt hastened to the trees. Then, between the first of the oaks, she stopped as she asked herself just what she would find here. The connection – or possible connection – between Robin and the scarecrow was something that she had thrust away from her consciousness these last few months, but now it rose afresh in her mind. That very first night . . . he had been wearing Jone's jacket and the battered hat; she had seen and recognised them in the moonlight before she took in any other detail. And on other nights, too . . . didn't he always wear them?

Suddenly, as if certainty had been snuffed out like a candle, she couldn't remember. She could picture *him*: his sharp, almost foxy face, his vivacious eyes, his hair, his *body* – but all recollection of his trappings was gone. Because the trappings didn't matter and she cared nothing for them? Perhaps that was it. Perhaps it was.

But what would she find when she reached the scarecrow's resting place?

Carys had a simple choice. She could go on as she had planned, find the scarecrow, see what was there and if it told her anything; or she could turn tail and scurry back to the farm with her quest unresolved. There was no third option, and no one to help her make up her mind. For perhaps a minute or two she wavered, torn between courage and cowardice. Then, looking down, she saw something at her feet among the undergrowth. A small plant called the Pathfinder, rare in these parts, with a single bloom growing on it. Robin had told her about the Pathfinder, and about the significance of its name . . .

125

She bent down, picked the blossom and laid it on her palm. The petals were white tinged with pink; carefully, one by one, she pulled them from the flower head, cast the head away, then raised her hand as though offering the petals to the sky.

Show me, she said in her mind, as Robin had taught her.

The smallest breath of breeze stirred in the wood. Leaves rustled above Carys's head, and she felt a tickling touch on her palm, as though a feather had been brushed lightly across it. The petals quivered, fluttered – and the breeze lifted them, blowing them from her hand and away to scatter to the ground, deeper in among the trees.

Their message was clear. She should go on.

She looked, first, for the scarecrow's original resting place, though intuition told her that the figure would not be there. How he had moved, or been moved, was still a conundrum, but she ignored that. As expected, there was nothing at the spot, so she worked her way deeper into the wood, seeking the ancient oak. Her nerve nearly failed her a second time when the great bole came into sight, and she halted, narrowing her eyes and scanning the area around it as though suspecting signs of a trap or ambush. There were no such signs, of course, nor, as far as she could tell, any trace of the scarecrow. At last Carys gathered her courage and walked up to the tree. As always, there was a good deal of detritus scattered around its foot, even some immature acorns which had fallen before their proper time. (Jone should be told of that, said a detached, practical part of her mind; soon they would fall in earnest, and then it would be time to drive the pigs to the wood to forage . . .)

Then, among the detritus, she saw wisps of straw. And something else – an old glove, half buried, two of the fingers either worn or chewed away.

Carys crouched down and touched the glove. She recognised it at once as one of the pair with which she had fashioned new hands for the scarecrow. There was even some hay left inside, though it was green with mildew now, and two earwigs and a spider scuttled out of it when she picked it up.

She let the glove drop back into the litter, and straightened up. Nothing else of the scarecrow was left here; the glove and the straw were the only signs that it had ever existed. Again she gazed all around – and stopped as her eyes focused on a shape she had not noticed before.

Something was protruding from the far side of the oak tree's massive trunk. At first glance it looked like a thin branch or twig, but it was too even, too straight. It wasn't a natural growth; it had been deliberately cut.

Avoiding a low-growing bramble that tried to snare her ankle, Carys walked round to the far side of the tree and saw what had been propped there.

It was – or had been – a pole, with a second, shorter bar lashed crosswise to it. The pole had been snapped in half, and the lower half, which was sharpened like a stake, lay at the foot of the tree. Both sides of the bar were snapped too, so that their outer ends hung down like broken arms. And from those broken ends some scraps of frayed twine dangled.

It was a scarecrow's pole, there could be no mistaking it. The sharpened end was dark where it had been driven into the ground, and traces of clay soil still clung, while the twine showed where the manikin's arms had been tied to the crosspieces. Carys picked up the sharpened end of the pole and turned it over in her hands. Whether this was the same pole on which her scarecrow had hung, and which she had left lying in the field when she dragged the figure away, she did not know, but there seemed to her to be an awful significance in its presence here. She turned her head, first to the right, then to the left, taking in the tangled patterns of the wood, looking for, but failing to find, something that might tell her what was afoot. She had the distinct sensation that the wood, or rather some force that embodied the wood, was watching her, and laughing silently at her bewilderment.

Then from somewhere nearby came a quick trill of birdsong.

Carys looked up into the crowding leaves, but all she saw of the robin was a brief and tiny blur of red as it flipped from its perch on

127

a branch and flew away deeper into the trees.

'Robin!' she called out, not to the bird but to *her* Robin, a sharp, fearful cry that was half demand and half desperate entreaty. 'Robin, where *are* you? Why didn't you come to me when I called?'

The wood had no answer for her. Dropping the pole, hands clenching until her knuckles strained, she cried, 'Just tell me that you're all right! Tell me that nothing has happened to you! Oh, Robin, come *back!*'

Silence and stillness. The wood breathed, but nothing more.

Slowly, her steps dejected and her face bleak, Carys left the enigmatic, useless traces she had found, and went home.

'Truly, Jone. You're kind to think of me, but truly, I'm well enough!' Carys looked across the table and conjured a convincing smile.

Jone tapped his fork on the side of his plate. 'Nonetheless, we must remember what Jem Apothecary said, Wife. You're not to overexert yourself, and I still believe you would be better for being in bed.'

She shook her head. 'I don't believe I could sleep. It's so hot and airless, and worse upstairs under the rafters. I'd much better prefer to stay here.'

'Well, it's as you wish. But if you feel tired or sickly, you're to tell me at once. Air or no air, you must have your rest.'

Carys said, 'Yes, Jone,' and returned to her meal.

He took another mouthful, chewed, swallowed. 'It was wrong of you to dismiss Izzy for the night. She could have stayed and been a help to you.'

Carys drank some water. 'Izzy *fusses* so. And she never stops talking; she's more tiring than doing the work myself.'

Jone started to smile with amusement, then quelled it. They continued to eat in silence. Jone's eyes were heavy; he had woken soon after Carys's stealthy return to the house and had worked through the long afternoon, only stopping when it was near on sunset and Carys sent Izzy to call him in. Even before his plate was empty he began to nod, and when Carys rose to clear the dishes and asked him if he would take some fruit pie, he roused himself only with an effort and said, 'Thank you, Wife, but no. I think I shall sleep now, and be refreshed for the morning.'

'Very well.' Carys tried not to look pleased. She let a moment pass, to make the thing seem casual, then added, 'I'll stay up a little while. Just to wash the dishes and tidy the kitchen.'

He frowned. 'If you're tired—'

'No, Jone, really I'm not. I slept more than half the day, remember. You go on. I shan't be very long.'

She thought he might argue, or even order her to bed, but he only smiled a weary smile at her before kissing her brow and making his way upstairs. Carys saw to her kitchen tasks, then when all was done returned to the parlour. No sound from overhead; Jone was probably already asleep, and she went to the front door and opened it wide to the night. The air that wafted in was no cooler or fresher than that of the house, and when she tried to fill her lungs with it, it was as if it had no substance.

Carys gazed out into the hot darkness. The anticipated storm had still not come, and there were none of the tell-tale signs – menacing little breaths of wind, far-off grumblings – to suggest that it was on its way. For all the oppressiveness, she was relieved. If the weather held just for tonight, then tomorrow it could rain blood and fire for all she cared.

She cocked a careful ear to the upper floor again, then, still hearing nothing, slipped outside and walked until she was well clear of the house. Then she closed her eyes and sent out a message: *Come to me. My Robin, come to me. I call you. Answer, Robin. Answer!*

A surge of tiredness washed over her as she completed the summoning, but she pushed it away. Waiting was the hardest part, especially now, when she did not know what would happen. Moving back to the front door, Carys stood on the threshold, leaning against the doorframe and watching, though without stars or moon she could see little. She could hear the clock ticking in the parlour, and she tried not to count the time passing, but it was impossible to ignore. Five minutes. Ten. She couldn't stop yawning. Fifteen.

And as the clock ticked gravely on towards the sixteenth minute, she saw a silhouette in the gloom ahead of her.

She ran to him and flung herself into his arms, almost sobbing, incoherent with relief. Robin held her tightly for a few moments, then disentangled her clinging arms and took hold of her hands instead.

'Come,' he said quietly, urgently. 'Away from the house.'

They skirted the building, and Robin would have headed towards the path that led on to Crede Hill, but Carys tugged at his fingers, halting him. They were behind the barn, concealed by its bulk from the house or yard, and she turned him to face her, looking intensely into his eyes.

'What happened?' she asked him. 'I called you, but you didn't come!'

'I couldn't, love.' Though his features were vague in the darkness, she thought that he looked very serious.

'Why not?' she demanded. 'You said—'

'I know, Carys, I know. And I would have kept that promise if I could. But . . . I couldn't come to you, and I don't think you'd understand if I told you why. Not yet, at least.'

'I thought – I feared—'

'Yes. I know that, too. I'm sorry. Forgive me.' His arms went round her and he drew her against him once more. Carys pressed her face against his shoulder, smelling the familiar scents of him, the scents of the wood and the land and something else that was sharp and sweet and especially his own. Forgiveness was not relevant, he was back now, he was here and safe. She was no longer afraid.

She asked no more questions, but let him lead her away to Crede Hill. They went again to the ridge with its crown of hawthorn trees, and their lovemaking seemed to Carys to have a new dimension, some extra beauty and exquisiteness that struck to the core of her soul. She had not cried at his passion since their first night together, but now she did, and the release of it was a balm. Afterwards they lay together, staring up at the sky, until Carys turned to him and said, 'Robin, are you tired?'

'No, love,' he said. But he *looked* tired, Carys thought. There was a shadow in his eyes, and his face showed lines that she had not seen before. She traced one of them with a forefinger, lightly, gently, pushing up the skin at the side of his mouth to make him smile.

'I'm exhausting you,' she told him, trying to be a coquette.

He turned his head to look at her. 'No,' he said again. 'You couldn't exhaust me, Carys. It isn't possible.'

She laughed, thinking he was teasing. 'Don't you ever sleep?'

'Oh . . . sometimes. But never for long.' Abruptly, startling her, he sat up. 'Tell me about the harvest feast. Was the King blessed, and were your friends and neighbours pleased with him?'

She was a little nonplussed by the unexpected change of subject, but rallied. 'Yes and yes. They say he's the best King we've had for years.'

'And the old one – he went to the burning, as always?'

'Of course. But Robin, something h—'

She had been about to say, *'Something happened',* and go on to tell him of her frightening experience and ask for his help in explaining it. But before the words could come out, Robin sprang to his feet. His face turned to the sky again and for a second or two he was motionless, as though listening to something that he alone could hear. Carys had an extraordinary, disconcerting feeling that time had stopped – then, just as suddenly, the illusion fled and Robin swung round to face her again. The strained look and the shadows were gone, and his face wore its familiar smile, broad and lively as ever.

'Past midnight,' he said. 'The world has turned over in its sleep.'

Carys remembered her grandmother, dead now, using that expression. 'How do you know?' she asked. But he didn't answer. Instead he snatched hold of her hand and pulled her upright.

'Run with me, Carys! On the ridge, along the path – race me and see who's faster!'

Her fingers slipped through his, losing their hold, and Robin was away, darting up the slope of the hollow and in among the hawthorns. She shouted, *'Wait!'* but he took no notice. For a few moments he vanished altogether, then the trees shook and he reappeared on the crest of the ridge, beckoning to her.

'Come, Carys! Run!'

Afraid of losing sight of him completely and being left alone out here in the night, Carys scrambled up the slope. She was panting by the time she reached the top, and Robin, outdistancing her, was a dancing silhouette on the skyline. 'Come on!' he called. 'Come on!' Carys went after him. She was no runner, though, and soon her calves were aching fiercely and her breath had deserted her. Before long she had to stop, bending forward, hands on thighs, gasping.

'Was I too fast for you?'

Robin spoke so close by her that she started.

'Where did you come from?' Only moments ago he had been far ahead – how could he *possibly* have returned to her in so short a time?

He laughed, mischief glinting in his eyes. 'Here, there and everywhere. I'm sorry, love – I'm elated, excited. I didn't mean to leave you behind.'

He put an arm round her shoulders, helping her to straighten up, and she asked, 'What are you excited about, Robin? A little while ago you were so serious, and now you're – you're like a boy, a child. What's *happening?*'

'Ohh . . .' He shrugged. 'The summer. The season. The night. The weather.'

'The *weather?*' Carys echoed.

'Yes. Don't you like it?'

She shook her head. 'It's too hot. I can't breathe, even now. I wish a storm would come and clear the air.'

'Do you?' Robin gestured to the sky. 'Then call one.'

Carys laughed. The laughter was intended to be scornful, but it didn't quite come out in that way. 'You're teasing me.'

'Oh, no. No, no.'

'You are! I can't make the weather do whatever I want it to.'

'Not quite that, perhaps. But you can help it along, if you know how.' He caught hold of one of her hands, tugging. 'Come with me, and I'll teach you. Come on!'

She went with him as he turned off the ridge and down the slope of the hill, back towards the lower-lying pastures. Where a hedge divided two fields he stopped and began to forage in the hedge-bottom.

'There!' He picked up something small and showed it to her. 'This is what you need.'

'This was a piece of flint, one face sheared away to show the smooth, shiny core. 'We must find four of these,' Robin told her, 'all of the same size, or as near as possible. Help me to search.'

Intrigued, Carys began to rummage beneath the hedge. They found what they wanted within a few minutes, and, holding the stones in a clenched fist, Robin led her back a short way up the hill.

'We must be in the open, or the spell has no chance to work.' He looked up, drew a deep breath, and his tongue appeared, flicking like a snake's. 'Taste the air, Carys. There's a storm in the sky somewhere, waiting to break, just waiting to be called.'

Dubiously Carys put out her own tongue and immediately understood what he meant: the air had a flavour, hot and slightly metallic, like licking a copper spoon. Excitement squirmed somewhere deep down in her vitals. She recalled what she had done for Ina Bartelwife's little boy; this, though, was something very different. Something *powerful*.

'Show me,' she said softly. 'Teach me, Robin. Will you?'

He smiled, an odd, private, and almost, if she had noticed and interpreted it in that way, sad smile.

'I'll give you anything you ask for, if I can,' he said. 'You know that, love.'

They sat down together on the short, sheep-grazed turf, and Carys took the stones from him, and he told her what she must do. Words

133

and gestures, the stones in a pattern, but above all how to catch hold of the feeling; the atmosphere and aura of the night and its potential. When it was done, Carys's head swam with tiredness and the night seemed unreal. She didn't argue when Robin raised her to her feet and, with a supportive arm about her, guided her down the hill and through the fields and finally to the yard gate of her own home.

He said: 'Goodnight, dear love. Dream sweetly.'

Carys went into the house, closing the door softly, not looking back. She climbed the stairs and entered the bedroom. Jone was sleeping peacefully, as she had known he would be, and she undressed as quietly as a moth in the darkness before sliding under the coverlet beside him.

The storm broke an hour later.

Chapter XII

The storm lasted well into the morning, drenching the land with a downpour the like of which had not been experienced for months. The parched ground gratefully soaked up the rain, dry streams and ditches ran again and the air came back to life with an invigorating freshness that seemed to liven the entire countryside. Everyone praised the largesse of Providence for timing the respite to perfection, and the praises grew louder when the sun appeared again in the wake of the rain. Only Carys knew that Providence had had nothing to do with it, but that was a precious secret to be kept and nursed and mulled over only in her most private moments.

She was deeply impressed by what she had done. At first she was also a little frightened, but the fear soon wore off, giving way to a glow of pride. Summoning storms was something that even the Wayfarers could not do, as far as she knew, yet she had succeeded at her first attempt. Robin had guided her, of course, and had been at her side while the magic was performed. But the will, the power, had been her own.

For some days she was in such a state of excitement that no one who came to the farm could fail to notice the change in her. Gyll Merionwife suspected and hoped (as she confided to Juda and Deenor) that the announcement of an addition to Jone Farmer's family was about to be made. Izzy thought it was a result of the fever, and no good would come of it; Jem Apothecary basked in the satisfaction of an expeditious response to his remedies; and Jone simply accepted the fact of his wife's new exuberance, indulged it in his quiet way and allowed Carys to enjoy it as she chose.

For half a month in the wake of the storm, Carys spent as much time as she could with Robin. Inspired by her success, she was hungry to learn anything and everything she could from him, and night after night she plied him with questions, cajoling him to tell, explain, demonstrate, teach. She proved an apt and quick pupil as she mastered the lore of wild plants, where and how and when to gather them, and how they could be used. She learned how the sound of the wind or the flight of birds or the calling of the sheep could allow her to see, just a little way, into the future. And she learned of the real power of the moon, under whose light so much of the old magic was best done.

She never tired of learning; indeed, it was close to becoming an obsession with her. The sensual pleasures that she had so enjoyed with Robin, and which at first had been her sole focus, were not entirely forgotten, but they meant far less to her now. And if, sometimes, Robin seemed saddened or troubled by the change, he said nothing and she did not think to consider it.

Carys's new-found knowledge was also starting to have wider repercussions. First it was Deenor, who had a troublesome whitlow on her finger and asked if Carys might know a cure. Carys did, and the whitlow healed within a few days. Then Faithful developed a troublesome dust-cough; before Jone could consult Merion about it, Carys dosed the horse with a decoction of her own making, and the cough ceased. Then Izzy started to complain that the butter turned faster and more thoroughly when Carys made it than when she did. Carys smiled, and said nothing about the small spell Robin had taught her, and which never failed to work. One day, she even turned her attention to Lob. Lob was having one of his bad intervals, twitching and yammering and almost impossible to communicate with in any way. Carys waited until no one else was about to see, and put a calming enchantment on him, backing it up with a very special drink. By evening, the fits were gone and Lob was as near normal as he could be. Izzy thanked Providence and swore to attend chapel more regularly, while Providence in the form of Carys only smiled and kept her own counsel.

Small kindnesses, the gratitude (even if sometimes unwitting) of her neighbours; it all helped to make the wheels of life turn more smoothly. But one thing was too close to home for Carys to foresee, let alone prevent. And when it happened, it was like lightning from a clear blue sky.

The lull after harvest came to an end when the first apples ripened, and within a matter of days the farms were buzzing with activity again. Jone and Garler Shepherd shared a large orchard between the boundaries of their lands, and each morning Jone left the house at an early hour to begin work with Garler and an assembly of pickers. On this particular morning – which promised, again, to be hot – Carys was upstairs, reluctantly attending to the dull but unavoidable task of cleaning rooms and changing the bed linen. Izzy, alone in the kitchen, was humming in her usual tuneless way as she mixed dough for a batch of bread, when a distant flicker of movement through the wide-open window caught her attention. Looking out, she saw what appeared to be a small procession winding across the fields towards the yard gate. A strange, sure instinct set the hairs at the back of her neck rising and prickling, and she edged to the door, on to the threshold, shielding her eyes against the brightness . . .

'*Missus!*' Izzy's shriek rang shockingly to the rafters. '*Missus, come quick! Fate preserve us all, oh, come quick!*'

Carys had never heard such a cry, and she almost fell down the stairs in her haste to reach the ground floor. Izzy was in the doorway, her face white and her eyes filled with horror. She seemed to have some thought of blocking Carys's way, and even her view, but the impulse collapsed and she stepped aside as Carys hurried past her and out to the yard.

The little procession had just reached the farm gate, and Carys froze as her gaze took in the sombre figures of Garler Shepherd and his eldest son, who carried a wattle hurdle like a litter between them. Something was lying on the litter, and following in its wake came Deenor and three sombre-faced women pickers.

Deenor saw Carys and Izzy. She stopped, and for a moment

stood motionless. Then with a cry of grief she rushed forward and embraced Carys, unable to speak coherently. Over her shoulder Carys saw the men setting the hurdle gently down. Detaching herself from Deenor's arms, she took a step, a second, a third, towards it, until she had a clear view of the supine figure lying there. Not that there had been any doubt in her mind; the conclusion was all too obvious.

'Oh, my dear . . .' Deenor tried to touch her again, but Carys moved out of reach and Deenor's hand fell back. 'I'm so *sorry*.' She swallowed. 'We found him at the foot of one of the apple trees. There was a ladder there, and a basket beside him, and . . . and he was simply . . . *lying* there, with his back against the tree trunk. He looked so peaceful, at first we thought he – he had simply fallen asleep. But when we touched him . . .' She turned away, biting her lower lip hard.

'He knew no pain and no suffering, Missus Jone, I'm sure of it.' The eldest son twisted his hands awkwardly together. 'It was a kindly going, and I reckon no man could ask for more than that.'

Garler nodded agreement. 'Peaceful,' he said in his slow, thoughtful way. 'Peaceful. Like he'd fallen to sleep. Just like he'd fallen to sleep.'

Izzy was crying in noisy, gulping sobs that tore at the air and set Carys's teeth on edge. She wanted to cry, too – or felt at least that she should – but there was no trace of tears in her. She only continued to stare down at her husband as the words that Garler and Deenor and their son had spoken sank into her mind and eddied there, trying but failing to form a coherent whole. He *did* look peaceful. There was even, or so she thought, a slight smile on his face that softened the lines and creases and stripped years from him. He looked so well. Yet he was dead. Jone Farmer, her husband. Dead. Gone. For ever.

'We've sent for Merion Blacksmith,' Garler's son told her, almost apologetically. 'Father says he'll know what to do for the best, this being such a shock and all . . .'

Carys found her voice at last. 'Yes,' she said thinly. 'Thank you.'

Should they send for Jem Apothecary, too? No, no point. Jem could do nothing. The preacher, perhaps? She wasn't sure what the proper thing was. But Merion was coming; Merion would know. She hoped he would bring Gyll.

Suddenly she didn't want to look at Jone any more, and she didn't want to be out here in the yard, in the sunlight, surrounded by all these kindly people. Without a word she turned and walked back into the house, leaving them staring after her in sympathy or embarrassment or confusion according to their natures. Into the parlour, where she stopped in front of the grandfather clock and took careful note of the time, though without knowing why that should matter in the least. The clock's ticking only served to emphasise the quietness; that, and the sound of a fly buzzing as it tried to find its way out of the window.

What to do now? In the peculiar, practical way that the human mind sometimes buffers itself against shock, Carys thought of the people in the yard, and of Merion and (possibly) Gyll who would soon be arriving. She would offer them tea, that was the proper thing. And the baking should be done, so that there would be bread. Had she finished her work in the bedroom? She couldn't quite remember, though of course all must be neat and clean for when the men carried Jone upstairs. They would do that, wouldn't they? Not that he would know about the fresh linen . . . Or would he lie here, in the parlour? When should she send for Bartel Carpenter, to measure and to make the . . . the . . . But her mind balked at the word *coffin* and she pushed the thought away. Tea, yes. Fill the kettle and put it on the range. That much, at least, she could do.

She looked down at herself. Her apron had dust-streaks on it, and a stain where she had splashed herself while washing the breakfast dishes. Breakfast seemed such a long time ago . . . she must change. Just her apron, or all of her clothes? She had nothing suitable for a new widow, so perhaps it was best just to attend to the apron.

A harsh, hiccupping sound spoiled the quiet then. It took Carys a few moments to recognise that it had come from her own mouth, and seconds more to realise that tears were streaming down her cheeks and falling to the floor at her feet. When she did realise, all she felt was relief that she was displaying the expected grief, even if there was no real emotion inside her. But maybe that would come, in time. For all the failings of her marriage, Jone had been a good man.

A footstep sounded, and a shape blocked the sunlight from the door. Carys turned to see Deenor on the threshold of the room. Deenor said nothing, but her compassionate look spoke volumes. Carys sniffed, then summoned up a wavering smile.

'Deenor . . . I must change my apron. Would you – would you be so kind as to put the kettle on? I think we should all have tea. Isn't that the right thing to do . . .?'

Merion arrived within half an hour. Gyll was with him, and she and Deenor sat with Carys in the kitchen while the men saw to the sad necessities. Jone's body was carried upstairs and laid respectfully on the bed behind closed curtains, then the men joined the women at the table, nodding sober thanks as Gyll set tea before them. For a little while there was a strained silence. Then Merion looked at Carys and said: 'He had a good life, and a good wife to care for him. We'll all mourn him, my dear, but he is gone now to his right reward.'

Carys returned his look for a moment or two before casting her eyes down. She did not speak.

Merion sighed. 'It's hard for you at this moment, Carys, I know, but there are certain things that must be done. The preacher . . . arrangements for the funeral. And – forgive me – but someone should speak with Bartel Carpenter . . .'

'Husband,' Gyll said gently, 'wouldn't it be the neighbourly thing for us to take care of all that?' She glanced at the silent girl. 'Would you prefer it, Carys?'

'Yes,' whispered Carys. 'If it's not . . . not a trouble . . .'

'Of course it's not. And if there's anything else we can do, you only need say.' She paused. 'Would you like me to stay with you tonight? Juda will come too, I'm sure, if we ask her.'

Carys shook her head. 'No thank you, Gyll. I'll be well enough.'

'Or you could stay with us – that would be best of all, perhaps. We could—'

'No,' Carys said again, firmly. 'It's kind of you, but . . . I'd rather stay here.'

Gyll opened her mouth to try again, meaning to say more about the perils of loneliness at a time like this, but a shake of the head from Merion stayed her tongue. Merion's look clearly said, *Leave her be,* and reluctantly Gyll subsided.

'Well, if you change your mind, send word straight away,' she finished.

'To any of us,' Deenor added.

Garler cleared his throat. 'And don't worry for the apples,' he said diffidently. 'It will all be done whatever, the way Jone would have wanted.'

The apples could rot on the trees for all Carys cared, but she had the self-control not to say so. She wished they would leave her in peace, do what had to be done and then go away to their own homes to grieve in their own ways. Their sympathy and kind words were all intended for her good, but she did not want them. She only wanted this day to end and darkness to fall.

She tried, however, to rally herself enough to play her part in dealing with the things that could not be postponed. Garler's son was dispatched to the village, and shortly after noon Bartel Carpenter drove up to the house with his neat black pony, his slate and measuring stick, and a suitably woeful expression. Carys managed to accept his flowery condolences with a measure of dignity, and he went upstairs with Merion to view his new customer and discuss patterns and woods and brass bindings. Shortly afterwards the preacher arrived, hot and flustered and brimming with abject apologies for his tardiness; he had been visiting in the parish and had not received the message until his return, and he was sorry, so very sorry to hear the news, and if there was anything at all that Carys should wish for, or if he could offer spiritual comfort

. . . Gyll tactfully managed to cut short his speech, and said they had thought perhaps the funeral might be held in three days' time, would that be convenient?

So the plans took shape: the coffin was ordered, the funeral arranged complete with flowers and village choir and the bell to be tolled, until at long last Carys's wish was granted and she was left alone. Izzy was long gone; her weeping and wailing had been driving Carys to distraction, and Lob, knowing something was wrong but unable to properly comprehend it, had kept intoning 'Poor Missus, poor Missus!' and trying to stroke Carys's hair. Garler had eventually driven them both home in his market cart, and then returned for Deenor. Merion and Gyll were the last to depart. When their gig was out of sight, Carys walked out into the yard and gazed around. All was clean and in good order, thanks to her neighbours. The cows were milked, the pigs were fed, the chickens were shut in their arks. In the house there was new bread and hot barley broth, though Carys wanted nothing to eat. The kitchen was swept, the parlour tidied.

And Jone lay still and cold upstairs in the bed that they had shared since their wedding a mere few months ago.

She did not want to go up and look at him. The sheet would have been pulled over his face, so there was nothing to look at anyway, unless she should lift it back. She shivered a little at that thought. Bartel Carpenter would be back in the morning. And Merion had offered to take over the running of the farm until Carys had recovered from her shock, for which she was grateful. No doubt Gyll would come too, and probably Juda. And of course her parents would soon get to hear of it. She should have sent them word; her father would be angry and her mother upset that they had not been told immediately. Well, well. Let them come, and let them scold her. She would cope with that when it happened, not before.

There was nothing to be done out here, nothing to take her attention, so she turned her steps back towards the house. Half-way there she paused and looked westward. The sun was lowering, giving a melancholy cast to the daylight, and something in Carys echoed the mood of it, so that she almost began to cry. Almost, but not quite. Another two hours and darkness would fall. Then, only then, could she seek the ease she needed.

She walked on. By the barn, a small shape detached itself from the lengthening shadows and glided towards her. Little Black was the most demonstrative of the farm cats, and as Carys reached the door he intercepted her and rubbed against her ankles. Carys bent to stroke him – something she did not often do – and, emboldened, he followed her into the kitchen and thence to the parlour. When she sat down, he waited for a minute or so, then, finding his presence tolerated, jumped on to her lap. Carys smiled, detachedly but with a trace of warmth. Her fingers started to move gently, rhythmically, over the cat's sleek fur, and Little Black purred. It was a kindlier sound than the ticking of the clock, and it soothed Carys as, quietly, patiently, trying not to think too deeply about anything in the world, she waited for the time to pass until the sun set and she could at last share her trouble and her sorrow and her confusion with Robin.

He was waiting for her by the yard gate, in the exact place where she had set eyes on him for the very first time. Carys did not run to him but walked, quite slowly, head down, hardly daring to raise her gaze to his.

With the gate between them she stopped and said quietly: 'Jone. He . . .'

'I know.' Robin reached across the gate's top bar and touched her cheek, tracing the line that her tears had taken hours ago. 'I grieve for him.'

'For him?' Despite herself, Carys felt a twist of something like jealousy. 'What of me?'

'For you, too, yes. But you still live.' His other hand moved, indicating the quiet night world around them. 'You haven't left all this behind.'

'He had a good life. Merion Blacksmith said that and it's true.'

143

Carys took refuge in a kind of defence, and on its heels came a challenge that made her stare Robin directly, hard, in the face. 'You know what had happened before I told you. How?'

Robin's shoulders drooped a little. 'The owls told me last night.'

'I didn't hear them.' A hint of resentment.

'Perhaps you didn't listen. Or perhaps they thought to spare you.'

She laughed, harshly. '*Spare* me? From what? If—' Then abruptly her anger collapsed and she hung her head. 'I'm sorry. Forgive me . . . this is none of your fault, and I shouldn't speak so to you.'

'You may speak to me however you wish,' he said gently. 'You know that.'

'All the same, I . . .' Oh, what did it matter? Robin understood, and he was kind. That, perhaps, was what her conscience found hard to bear.

'I didn't *expect* this,' she went on, floundering to find words that might go some small way towards explaining the inexplicable. 'He was strong, fit – not a day's sickness, nothing. And now—'

'You cared for him, didn't you?'

Carys nodded miserably. 'I think I did. I think I – I *came* to care for him. He was always good to me. Now he's gone, and it feels . . . strange.'

The gate was still between them; neither had moved to open it and bridge the gap. Robin said: 'Come to the hill with me.'

Carys glanced back at the house and felt her conscience stir again.

'Just to walk, that's all,' Robin coaxed. 'To walk, and to think of Jone and wish his soul good speed.'

She wanted to be with him, needed him, and her conscience quieted. 'Yes,' she said. 'Please.'

The gate creaked mournfully as she drew it back. She closed it carefully behind her, and felt Robin's fingers entwine with hers. Her throat constricted suddenly, she caught her breath, and then she was leaning against him, crying quietly.

'Come,' he said. 'The hurt and the confusion will heal, I promise.

I'll teach you, love. I'll help you.'

He led her away under the stars, away from the silent, empty, unlit house.

Chapter XIII

Jone Farmer went to his last rest at noon on a bright day that reflected the coming change of season. A fitful wind was blowing, with a chill to it that had not been present for months, and in the hedgerows past which the funeral procession wound its way to the chapel, the first signs of autumn colour were showing.

Nearly the whole parish turned out for the solemn occasion, all in their best clothes and forming a quiet procession through the village. Six girls dressed all in white and wearing flower chaplets on their heads attended the coffin carriage, which was draped with willow and ivy, and behind the carriage came a market-chaise bearing the young widow. Carys wore brown, as was proper, and flanking her were Gyll and Deenor, doing neighbourly duty as Widow's Comforters. Merion drove the chaise, and throughout the journey Carys looked neither to left nor right but stared unswervingly at his broad, taut back.

In the chapel she sat quietly with her attendants, listening – or appearing to – as the preacher spoke of Jone's kindness and piety, and the choir sang psalms. Now and then her gaze strayed to the nearest window, through which the sun shone fitfully as clouds chased each other across its face, but her composure did not falter. She even joined in the final psalm, though her voice trembled a little and she seemed unsure of the words. When the time came for the burial itself, Gyll and Deenor held her hand tightly until the thing was done, then thanked the preacher on her behalf and led her to the chaise.

A convoy of vehicles and people on foot returned to the farm, where women friends had joined together to prepare a fine funeral tea. The parlour was almost too small to accommodate the entire company, but somehow everyone squeezed in. Among the guests were Carys's parents and sisters, with Nellen's husband, Jemp, accompanying them. Powl and Tibba had not been asked to play any part in today's arrangements, and were privately glad of it. They had visited Carys on the day after Jone's death and the customary sorrows had been expressed and accepted, but Carys had not asked them for help, and Powl had pragmatically decided to leave well alone. Carys's immediate neighbours had rallied round to give her all the assistance she could possibly need; extra hands were superfluous, and Powl's role in this (he considered) lay in quite a different direction. But there would be time enough for that. So when they arrived he patted Carys's shoulder in gruff consolation, while Tibba dabbed her eyes, then they drank tea and ate cake and made polite small-talk with the rest.

It all passed off very well. When the first flush of conversation faded a little, Merion and Garler each made a little speech about Jone and their sorrow, and then Juda, who had a fine contralto voice, stood up and sang an old ballad that had been one of Jone's favourites. It wasn't only Tibba who had to dry her eyes when the song was finished, and Carys, seated in the best chair by the ingle, kissed Juda's cheek, held her hands tightly and thanked her.

As evening approached, Merion had a quiet word with Garler and Elios Carter. The everyday running of the farm couldn't be neglected; there were cows to be milked and a range of animals whose food and comfort must be seen to, and Merion suggested that they should attend to the work without needing to trouble Carys. Carys saw them leave the room, guessed what they were about and wished that she could have gone with them, to escape from the well-meaning but stifling company in the parlour. That was not possible, but the three men's departure acted as a tacit signal, and at last the guests began to take their leave. Powl and Tibba were among the first to go. Nellen seemed inclined to linger, until a warning shake of the head from Powl made her change her mind.

148

Carys noticed that and wondered at it, but when Nellen came to make her farewells she said nothing, only kissed Carys's cheek and gave her an artificial little smile before following her husband outside.

Powl said goodbye to Carys, then cleared his throat. 'If you should need anything, Daughter . . .' He let the sentence hang unfinished.

'Thank you, Father,' said Carys. 'I'll be well enough.' Unable to resist, she added, 'I have all my good friends to help me.'

'That's fine and good for everyday matters,' said Powl, 'but there are some things that are better kept within your own family.' He paused as if waiting for Carys to respond, and when she did not he grunted, 'Well, there's time enough . . . Your mother and I will call on you again in a few days. That's for the best.'

Carys didn't meet his eyes. 'Yes, Father, as you wish. Good night.'

More goodbyes followed then, and more, until finally only Gyll, Deenor and Juda were left with Carys in the parlour. Their husbands were still busy in the yard and cow-byre, and Gyll turned to Carys with a smile.

'They'll be a while yet. Sit down again, Carys, we'll clear up and put the kitchen to rights.'

'Let me—' Carys began, but Gyll shook her head.

'No, no, you deserve a little time to yourself. Leave all to us.'

She didn't argue. In truth, she wanted nothing more than to forget everything and everyone around her, if only for a few minutes. So many faces, so many words, so much to try to absorb and cope with; it had been a greater ordeal than she had expected, and she was thankful that it was almost over.

She rested her head against the back of her chair as the other women went out, and, closing her eyes, thought back over the past few days. Much of it had passed like a vague dream. Even the funeral seemed unreal now. The only thought, the only memory, that stood out clearly in her mind was that of her last encounter with Robin.

She had walked with him on the hill that night following Jone's death, taking the high path to the ridge and following its crest for several miles. Carys had wanted to talk, but when it came to it had found something blocking the words she might have said. Then, somewhere near midnight, her conscience had besieged her again, and with it came a wave of sadness so strong that it had stopped her in her tracks.

'I have to go back!' She could hear her own voice now, shocked and unsteady yet utterly resolved, and she recalled the feelings that had beset her. Jone, lying alone in the farmhouse, with no light and no hearth fire and no one to keep vigil with him. The thought was unbearable, and without waiting for Robin to respond, Carys had turned in distress towards the homeward track. She ran all the way, and he ran with her. He had not tried to dissuade her from her decision, but as she ran through the gate and away from him across the yard, he had called out to her: 'Carys!' It had sounded like the distant cry of a bird. 'Don't forget me . . .'

She had looked back to where he stood, a lonely figure in the moonlight. 'Of course I won't forget you!' she had cried back to him. 'But I must go. Tonight, I must!'

He had raised his hand in a farewell salute, blown her a kiss, and she knew that he understood. Since then she had not seen him. But he would understand that, too. She knew he would. She prayed he would.

A footstep in the kitchen doorway alerted her then, and she opened her eyes in time to see Gyll coming in.

'All's done in the kitchen, and the men have finished the farm work,' Gyll said. She glanced at the window. 'Just in time, too, it's growing dark.'

'Is it?' Carys sat up. How long had she rested here? It had seemed only a few moments . . . perhaps she had fallen asleep?

Gyll went to light one of the lamps, and with an effort Carys said, 'You'll stay for a while longer, Gyll? You and the others?'

'Well . . . if we're not imposing on you . . .'

Carys shook her head. 'I'd be glad of the company.' The crowd was gone and that was a relief, but these close friends were another matter. Though she didn't know why, there was a small dread in Carys's heart at the prospect of being left quite alone. And as for Robin . . . she wasn't ready to face him again. Not yet, not quite.

Gyll smiled. 'Then I'll put the kettle on, shall I?'

'Yes,' said Carys. 'Thank you, Gyll. Thank you.'

Seven was a comfortable number for the size of the parlour, and for an hour or so they sat around the inglenook (where Merion had lit a fire, just for the friendliness of it), drinking yet more tea and talking of this and that; small, unimportant things to ease them after the strains of the day. Carys did not say a great deal. Whenever she was moved to speak she instinctively looked towards the empty chair where Jone used to sit, forgetting momentarily that he was no longer there to influence her. The surprise each time was small but sharp, so after a while she avoided talking and simply listened to the others as they discussed this person's deeds and that person's good or bad luck, the apple harvest, weather predictions for the winter and other trivial matters.

Then, unwittingly, Juda threw a stone into the pool of her quietness and set it rippling. Turning, she asked, 'And what of you now, Carys, with a farm to call your own? What shall you do – stay or sell?'

Carys stared at Juda in shock, then the implications of what she had said slowly began to dawn. Since Jone's death she had not given a thought to her long-term future, but now, for the first time, she faced the fact that she was in a very unusual situation. If Jone had been to her what other husbands were to their wives, then by now she would doubtless have been with child, and, son or daughter, that child would have been the rightful heir to all its father's property. But it had not happened, and neither did Jone have any children from his first marriage. So the house and the farm belonged to Carys. Not to her father, for on the day of her wedding he had lost all claim to her, but to Carys, and Carys alone.

She swallowed, feeling as if her last sip of tea was clogging her throat. 'I – I hadn't thought . . .' she said, sounding as stunned as she felt. 'Not at all . . .' She looked to Merion, confused and needing confirmation. 'Is it true, that I – that the farm—'

'Is yours? Oh, yes,' said Merion. 'That's the law.' He smiled kindly. 'Juda is being a little hasty; no one expects you to make your choice so soon. But whatever you do choose, you're well set now.'

Carys bit her lip and stared into the fire. She felt quite giddy with the enormity of this new concept and what it could mean. A woman of property in her own right, with the freedom to make her own decisions . . . It was an extraordinary thing, and as yet she could barely take it in, let alone make sense of it.

Merion spoke again. 'If you decide to sell the farm, there'll be no shortage of willing buyers. It's good land and it's been well tended. The house and buildings are sound, the livestock healthy – you'll have enough money from it to live comfortably for the rest of your life, if you use it wisely.'

'And of course you might marry again,' Gyll added, and shrugged apologetically. 'Maybe I shouldn't say such a thing, but . . . well, life goes on, doesn't it? The time of mourning will end, and you're still very young.'

Carys looked at them both. 'Do you think I *should* sell?'

Merion and Gyll exchanged a glance. Gyll said, a little hesitantly, 'I'm being selfish, I know, but . . . There's a lovely cottage close to the smithy that's lain empty for a year now. It would suit you well, and we would be close neighbours. I would like that very much indeed.'

Merion nodded agreement. 'A little repair is all it needs, and that can soon be seen to. I, too, would be glad to have you as a neighbour.' He paused. 'And there's a more practical consideration. I dislike to say it, but it's best faced. A young woman living alone and unprotected on a farm – it isn't wise, Carys. You'd be undefended, too far from the nearest help.'

'There's Izzy and Lob,' Carys said.

'Izzy and Lob couldn't safeguard you against vagabonds or

thieves. I've heard stories – no, I'll say no more of those, for I don't want to alarm you. But think on it. In the village, you could turn to us in a time of trouble. Here, you'd have no one. It isn't right.'

Garler cleared his throat in the diffident way he had. 'I agree with our good friend Merion,' he said. 'In fact, I'd be ready, myself, to make you an offer for the farm and land. A good offer of course, very fair, that's only proper . . .'

'Our eldest son's family is growing, you see,' Deenor added, 'and it's likely the other two will wed before too long. They'll inherit our farm in the fullness of time, just as they should, but between three of them . . .'

'Two farms would suit us all very well.' Garler nodded slowly. 'Very well. If you should be willing.'

So, Carys thought, they had already discussed this among themselves, and in their own minds they had decided what she ought to do. Perhaps she should not be surprised . . . and certainly not resentful, for they were her friends and they had her best interests at heart. Merion was right; there were potential dangers in continuing to live here without a man or even a proper household to protect her. And Garler would certainly pay her a fair price – more than fair, she suspected – and the farm would continue to be run as Jone would have wanted. It was the obvious solution, and meant for her benefit.

But she was not yet ready to make a decision. As Merion himself had said, it could not be expected of her yet; it was too soon. She needed time.

And she wanted advice from a very different source.

They were all waiting for her to respond, and when the silence began to grow just a little tense, she spoke at last.

'You're all so kind to take trouble for me,' she said. 'And I'll think hard on what you've said. In a few days, maybe, I'll be ready to decide.'

Gyll leaned forward and patted her knee. 'Take as much time as you need, my dear,' she said. 'There's no need for haste.'

'In the meantime, though, the farm can't be neglected,' Merion pointed out. 'The animals, the apple harvest—'

'I'll see for that,' said Garler placidly. 'It's near on done anyway, and I can manage Jone's pickers along with my own. The sheep, too, no need to worry about them.'

'I can do enough about the farm,' Carys added. 'Feeding, milking, the byre—'

Merion shook his head. 'It's too much for a woman, with the house to keep as well. No, you'll have help, Carys. I'll do what I can. Elios too; I believe I can speak for him?'

'Certainly, my friend,' Elios said firmly. 'Certainly.'

The women joined in, Gyll and Juda pledging help in the house, Deenor promising to bring loaves from her baking each day. There would be others, too, Gyll added; Carys must never forget that she was among friends.

Carys was touched by their generosity, especially as she felt that she had done little to earn it. She was, effectively, a newcomer among them, a child who had been slotted suddenly into their adult world without their having any say in the matter, and to be accepted so warmly and unequivocally was a thing of wonder to her. With a catch in her voice she thanked them all. She would repay them, she thought. In one way or another, she would repay their goodness.

They left at last, under a high, pale moon flecked with scudding clouds. Garler had offered one of his dogs as a companion and protector; he would bring the animal over in the morning. Gyll and Juda and Deenor all kissed her, and Carys waved them off from the doorway with a fullness in her heart.

When they were gone, she went back inside, and as she closed the door she realised how desperately tired she was. She wanted sleep, craved it as a starving man craved food. Not upstairs, though; she had not yet had time to make the smaller bedroom ready, and she would never lie again in the bed she had shared with Jone. These past few nights she had fared well enough on the settle, with blankets for warmth and pillows for comfort. That would do again.

She wound up the weights of the grandfather clock – that was

154

one task which must never be neglected – then fetched her bedding and extinguished the lamps. The fire's embers glowed, and its warmth radiated gently over her as she curled up on the settle. She could hear the wind outside. Its voice was not quite a whistle and not quite a moan; strangely, she found it soothing. *So* tired . . . she could do no more tonight.

Carys sighed, closing her eyes. 'Forgive me, Robin,' she whispered, half to herself. 'Tomorrow, I'll see you again. I promise. Good night, my love. Good night.'

Fleet was a handsome, lop-eared black-and-white dog, one of Garler's best, and he took to Carys from the start. Garler advised her not to allow him into the house but to keep him chained in the yard; Carys nodded, said she would take his advice and thanked him earnestly, all the time aware of Fleet's intense gaze on her face. Garler departed, and when Carys turned to go back into the house, she found Fleet like a shadow at her heels.

She stopped on the threshold and gave him a stern look. 'Now, Fleet! You heard what Master said.'

Fleet barked, once, and waved his plumed tail hopefully. Then he pressed himself against her leg and whined. Carys was undone. The dog's message of affection was so clear, and what Garler did not know surely could not hurt him . . . Smiling, but saying no more, she went indoors, and with another triumphant wag of his tail, Fleet followed.

It took Fleet only half the morning to ingratiate himself thoroughly with his new mistress. In truth Carys was glad of his company; wherever she went around the farm, he was there too, but his was a silent, undemanding presence that did not intrude on her in any way. The fact that Izzy disliked dogs and thus went out of her way to avoid him was an added bonus, and by the time the morning work of the farm was completed Carys felt better than she had done for some time.

At noon she sent Izzy to the fields with provisions for the apple-pickers, and savoured the chance to set out her own meal and sit

155

quietly in the kitchen for a while with no one to disturb her. Fleet lay at her feet, and she fed him pieces of bread and cold bacon from her plate; then, as she idly stroked his long ears, a thought came to her. The dog was just another example of her neighbours' kindness; kindness which she had resolved to repay but without any concrete idea of how she might do so. Now, a notion was beginning to form in her mind, and the more she considered it the more sense it seemed to make. The things that her friends did for her were the things they were best at, the things they *knew*. Money was not involved; if she tried to thank them with coin they would be offended. So what skills did she, Carys, possess that would be of use to her good friends?

The answer was perfectly clear, and Carys smiled to herself. Take Gyll, for example. Gyll had fine, thick, black hair, but it was starting to grey prematurely, and Gyll had once privately confided that she disliked the change, for it made her look older than her years. From Robin, Carys had learned of a particular plant whose leaves, carefully prepared, would return Gyll's hair to its splendid blackness.

Then there was Garler's troublesome cough, which according to Deenor came on him every autumn and which Jem Apothecary's nostrums had so far failed to cure. Carys knew a surer cure than anything Jem could prescribe, for Robin had told her of it.

And then there was the potato harvest. People hereabouts were concerned that the summer's drought might mean a poor yield this year. They needed rain now; not so much as to make the land sodden and rot the tubers in the soil, but enough to help them swell and be plentiful. With Robin's guidance Carys had influenced the weather once. Could she do it again . . .?

Fleet whined suddenly and put a paw up to dab at her knee. Carys looked down at him, and saw – or imagined – something conspiratorial in his expression. It was as if he had understood her thoughts and was encouraging her. Well, hadn't Robin told her many a time to watch and listen to the creatures of the land, and take heed of what she observed? A fool she'd be if she failed to take that advice when it was staring her in the face . . .

Her pulse had quickened into an excited and slightly erratic rhythm. Standing up, she gave Fleet the last piece of bacon from her plate as a reward, then started to clear the table. She had no desire to sit quietly now. She wanted to finish what must be done here, then go out to the fields and search for the ingredients she needed. Gyll's potion first; she could mix it tonight and find an opportunity to give it to Gyll tomorrow, out of Merion's sight. It did not do, as Juda had once slyly said, to let men be privy to *all* a woman's secrets.

Carys smiled to herself as she washed her dishes and put them in the wooden rack. Gyll would be very surprised to receive her gift, and more surprised still if it worked. Just a small repayment. And possibly it would be the first of many.

Time would tell.

Chapter XIV

Gyll came to help in the house the following morning, and was indeed surprised – and delighted – when Carys presented her with a stoppered glass bottle and whispered its purpose in her ear.

'Carys!' She gazed at the bottle, wide-eyed. 'Will it really work?'

'I don't know,' Carys confessed. 'I've never tried to mix it before, so I can't promise. But it should.'

Gyll put a hand up to touch her hair. 'I can't think what Merion will say . . .'

Carys smiled conspiratorially. 'Then don't tell him. The change will be slow, see, so he probably won't notice. And even if he does, why shouldn't he be pleased?'

'Yes . . . yes, why shouldn't he?' Gyll giggled, then her expression sobered. 'Where did you learn to do this? Was it something your mother taught you?'

'No. Oh, no.'

'How do you know about it, then?'

'Ohh . . . I can't really remember,' Carys lied. 'It's just a small thing. I saw it once in a book, maybe.'

'Of course, you learned your letters, didn't you? Since I married and memorised all the words in my scrip of recipes, I've all but forgotten reading. Not that I was ever good at it anyway . . .' Gyll's hand clenched round the bottle. 'I'll try it this very afternoon, Carys.' She grinned. 'Merion has a whole team of carriage horses coming for shoes, so there's no danger of him returning to the house and catching me! Now, tell me again, what must I do . . .?'

Carys glowed with the satisfaction that Gyll's pleasure gave her.

159

She said nothing of the fact that she had been up half the night making her concoction and waiting for it to simmer to readiness. What mattered – all that mattered – was that she had made a contribution, albeit small, to the debt she felt she owed.

The afternoon found her out among the hedgerows once again, searching for the ingredients for Garler's cough medicine. These proved a good deal harder to find, and it was some hours before she returned to the farm, tired, dishevelled and scratched, with all that she wanted. Izzy was avidly curious to know what Carys had been doing, but Carys ignored her broad hints, put her treasures in a high cupboard which Izzy could not reach, and returned calmly to her work.

When evening came and she was left alone at last, Carys ate a hasty meal (which she shared with the ever-attendant Fleet) and cleared the table ready for her new experiment. Some of the house tasks had been neglected, but they could wait until tomorrow. This, if not more important, was certainly far more interesting. She was setting out her bowl, pestle and mortar and sharpest knife when Fleet got up, ran through to the parlour and started to bark. Between barks Carys heard the sound of hooves and wheels outside, and she frowned. She was not expecting visitors; company was the last thing she wanted tonight, and with a frown she followed the dog into the parlour and went towards the front door.

'Quiet, Fleet!' Hand on the latch, she spoke sharply, then pulled the door open. A market chaise with three people in it was pulling up outside, and Carys's heart sank as she recognised her father and mother, accompanied by Nellen.

'Daughter.' Powl climbed down from the chaise. 'I decided it was time we paid a call on you.'

Carys forced back the surge of resentment she felt. Of all the times to choose . . . But she couldn't argue. Powl was already handing her mother and sister down, and her mother was carrying a large and generously full basket; it was neither polite nor practical to turn them away.

She stood back to allow them all in. Tibba kissed her, handing over the basket and saying, 'It's nothing special, child: salt pork and a cake, and two jars of my own preserves just made two days ago.' Powl and Nellen did not kiss her. Powl looked her up and down and grunted, while Nellen smiled insincerely and turned her attention to a covert scrutiny of the parlour.

'You'll all take tea?' Carys hoped they would say no, but they did not, so she retreated to the kitchen, Fleet at her heels, to put the kettle on and cut some pieces of her mother's cake. Tibba followed her, looking around much as Nellen was doing in the other room. The state of the kitchen obviously did not match up to her own exacting standards, but she didn't comment directly, saying only, 'You must be finding it hard, Carys. The house to see for, and all the work of the farm as well. I fear it might prove too much for you.'

'I have neighbours to help me, Mother,' Carys replied a little frostily. 'Between us, we manage very well.'

Tibba's mouth curled slightly and she changed tack, nodding towards Fleet. 'You have a dog, I see.'

'Garler Shepherd gave him to me, for company and as a guard.'

'That's prudent. You can't be too careful, especially in an outlying place like this. Where do you keep your cups?'

Carys pointed. 'There.'

'Ah.' Tibba fetched four down, examining each one to ensure that they had been properly washed. She set them in a neat line on the table. 'Not that *I* would let it in the house. Dogs aren't clean animals, they don't belong in houses.'

Carys didn't answer that, but her grip on the cake knife tightened.

Tibba went to the window (Izzy had washed the glass this morning, which gave Carys sour satisfaction now) and looked out at the yard. 'Who helps you with the farm work?' she asked.

'Merion Blacksmith, Garler Shepherd, and Garler's son.' Carys's voice was becoming a little terse.

'That's neighbourly of them.' A pause. 'I hear that Garler is interested in buying the farm.'

So word had got about. Carys wasn't surprised; once any rumour reached the village it invariably spread like a summer weed. 'He's spoken of it,' she said. '*If* I choose to sell. I haven't decided yet.'

The kettle began to sing. Tibba took it from the range before Carys could, and poured water into the big pewter teapot. 'As to that . . .' she said, 'you mustn't let yourself be pressed, Carys. Remember, the choice is yours.'

Carys stopped cutting and looked at her in surprise. Tibba was the last person from whom she would have thought to hear such advice; she had expected her mother to hold firm views and to try to impose them. This was something quite new.

She smiled, hesitantly but more warmly than before. 'I feel the same, Mother, and I'm gratified that you agree with me. Thank you.'

Tibba made a self-effacing gesture. 'We're family, when all's said and done. If families don't keep together and help each other, who will? Now, where's the honey for the tea? You know your father likes it sweet . . .'

They carried in the brew and the cake. Powl was sitting in Jone's old chair (Carys flinched a little at this, but reminded herself that he couldn't have known), while Nellen occupied the best part of the settle. The coming child was showing quite noticeably now, and Nellen's face had become distinctly fudgy. Carys noticed the pitying glance her sister gave to her own waistline, but ignored it.

'Well, then,' she said as she and Tibba sat down. 'And how is Thomsine? Could she not come with you?'

Nellen raised her eyebrows, and Tibba said, 'Thomsine is taking supper at Tally Rigswidow's this evening. The preacher has been invited, too. And, of course, Tally's son.'

'Oh,' said Carys, beginning to see the lie of the land.

'Yes.' Tibba's look became complacent. 'A personable young man. We think there will be an arrangement before long. And what with the preacher being so gallant to Tally, it will all make for a very respectable connection.'

'That's happy news for Thomsine,' said Carys. So, all three daughters off her parents' hands at last, and the prospect of more grandchildren. No wonder her father looked so pleased.

'It is,' Powl agreed. He made himself more comfortable in the chair. 'However, respectability and money don't always go hand in hand. Tally Rigswidow only has the one son, but the inheritance her husband left is small. I've been considering that, and I've come to a decision.'

Later, Carys realised that she should have seen the light at that moment. She didn't. Lulled by what Tibba had said in the kitchen, she only looked politely interested and said, 'Have you, Father?'

'Yes.' Powl gave her what passed, with him, for an affectionate smile. 'The solution's obvious. There can be no question of you continuing to live here, without a husband to govern you and take care of this farm. So you shall return to us, your family.'

'You'll be our own dear child again,' Tibba added.

'Of course you will. Just as you used to be before you were wed.'

Carys expression had begun to change markedly. 'And the farm . . .?' she asked.

Powl did not recognise the dangerous note in her voice. 'Naturally, you will yield it to me. A girl of your age can't be wise enough to make her own way in the world, and besides, I'm your father and I brought you up to know your proper duty. I shall take charge of your husband's property—'

'Poor, dear Jone,' Tibba interjected with a sniff.

'—and use it for the good of us all.'

There was a pause. Then: 'The good of us all,' Carys repeated slowly, thoughtfully. 'Including Thomsine and her potential husband.'

'Of course.' Powl nodded complacently. 'As I said, Tally Rigswidow has little to leave to her son. And we'll not forget Nellen and Jemp, either. With their first child coming soon, it would suit them well to have the extra asset of their share.'

'Especially as my child is a boy,' Nellen added. 'You remember, Carys, I told you, Jem Apothecary held his pendulum—'

Carys's head turned quickly and she said with venom, 'Your child is a girl.'

She didn't know how she was so certain; it had simply come to her mind unbidden, a flick of intuition so sure that she would never dream to doubt it. Nellen stared at her in surprise and annoyance, and Tibba said, 'Now come, Carys, if Jem says—'

'Jem is wrong. It's a girl.'

There was an uncomfortable silence that lasted for several seconds before Powl cleared his throat.

'Now, then, enough of this. Boy or girl, it makes no difference to the situation. Jone's farm will fetch a good price in its entirety. On the other hand, it might be better to keep some of the fields, and—'

'Father,' Carys said sharply. 'You forget something.'

Her voice was shaking; *she* was shaking, inwardly, violently, with a fury so enormous that she felt she could barely contain it. Powl looked annoyed. 'What, Daughter? And I don't care for being interrupted.'

Carys's ribcage heaved with the effort of controlling herself, and her breath became ragged in her throat. 'No,' she said, 'you don't care for it. But *I* don't care for being told what I shall do with *my* farm.'

Tibba exclaimed, 'Carys!' and Powl's face flushed with anger. But the tide of Carys's rage had reached its height, and before her father could utter another word the floodgates opened. She didn't know where she found the words she said to him then; it was as if some deep, untrapped force came surging to the surface to give her strength and a ferocious eloquence which she had never before possessed. Fuelled by the memories of how he had dominated and used her, his harshness in forcing her to marry, for his advantage, an old man whom she barely knew, she flung the full sting of her resentment and contempt in his face. Neither his outrage nor her mother's hysteria moved her, and when he tried to resort to his old custom of physical threats, he was confronted by Fleet barking and snarling between him and his errant daughter.

Powl, Tibba and Nellen finally left the house, all three of them white-lipped. In an atmosphere of deadly silence Carys held the

164

door open for them, and when her mother seemed about to speak she received such a look that she instantly and prudently changed her mind. Carys watched them into the chaise, not from courtesy but because she wanted to be sure of their going, and as Powl wrenched the pony's head round and drove away in a scatter of stones, she felt a diabolical urge to send a silent curse in their wake, to follow them home and bring them bad luck. She fought it down, knowing it was wrong. Then, as the chaise disappeared she slammed the door violently and strode back to the parlour. Her father had sat there, taking Jone's chair without so much as a by-your-leave . . . Carys snatched the cushion from the chair and flung it on the fire, thrusting at it with the poker as it blazed and not caring about the stink of burning feathers. *Damn* him. Damn and rot and three times curse him! Who did he think he was, to invade *her* house, and *her* life, and try to tell her what she should do?

She drew a huge, gasping breath, and the rush of air into her lungs sobered and calmed her a little. Fleet came crawling and fawning at her feet, aware of her state and unsure of the right thing to do. Carys looked down at him. 'Good boy,' she said, and the ghost of a smile caught at her mouth. A pity that Fleet hadn't bitten her father. But he had played his part, and a real attack would have made complications.

'They're gone now,' she told the dog. 'All's well. They won't come back.' No, they would not, not ever again. She would see to it that they didn't. But this visit – which might, she acknowledged unconcernedly, have been the last contact she would ever have with her family – had achieved one good thing among all the bad. It had focused her mind on her dilemma, and suddenly she was resolved.

Jone's farm was not for sale, and neither was Carys Jonewidow. This was her future, and she was free to do with it as she pleased. Let her friends worry, let her enemies sneer, let anyone who cared to say what they would. She was going to stay.

The ingredients for Garler's potion were still waiting where she had left them. Carys smiled. She carried the aftermath of the calamitous tea out to the kitchen, dumped the pots unwashed in the sink and put on her apron. Pestle and mortar, bowl, knife. Good. Time to do something worthwhile.

'Lie down,' she ordered Fleet, who had followed her. He whined happily and flopped in his favourite spot in front of the range, his brown eyes watching her contentedly as, singing to herself with a lightness she had not felt for many a day, Carys began her work.

With dawn less than two hours away, Carys was finally forced to admit defeat. No matter what she did or how hard she concentrated, the brew simply would not come right. She couldn't understand; the procedure was perfectly straightforward and she was certain she had memorised it correctly. But the results of her labours, instead of simmering into a smooth, clear potion the consistency of set honey, remained stubbornly liquid and opaque. Something was wrong, but Carys could not for the life of her guess what it might be.

Only one person could help her, and so she sent out her psychic summons and waited impatiently for Robin to appear at the yard gate. When he did, and she went to greet him, his face looked sad and a little lost.

He said, 'My love . . . I've missed you.'

Carys was faintly surprised to realise that the last time she had called him to her had been on the night of Jone's death. But how could she have done otherwise? There had been so much to think of, so many people around her; she had barely had a moment to call her own. Besides, in the wake of what had happened it would surely have been . . . *improper* was the word that came to mind. Improper to tryst with her lover while her husband (even if Jone had never been a true husband) waited to go to his grave. Now that the funeral was over, of course, matters were different; it was simply that she had had no time . . .

'I'm so sorry, my dearest.' She stroked his cheek, an affectionate gesture she had learned from him early on. 'I've been so busy . . . the funeral, and the farm work, and all my neighbours . . .'

'Yes,' Robin said. A pause. 'I saw Jone Farmer's spirit depart. He is at rest.'

A *frisson* went through Carys. 'You . . . saw? Were you there?'

'In a sense. You could not see me and I could not reach out to you. But I was aware of your sadness, and I hope it's a comfort to you to know that there's no need for grief now.'

It was not a comfort to Carys, though she could not have said why. She looked away from him, feeling a sudden and strong desire to change the subject, and said, 'I need your help.'

'Yes?' His voice became more animated. 'Anything I can do for you, I will.'

She nodded, knowing that, and told him of her plan to repay her kind friends, and of the potion that refused to behave as it should.

'You can show me where I've gone wrong,' she said eagerly. 'Come to the house and see.'

His expression changed. 'I can't, Carys.'

She stared at him. 'What do you mean?'

'I mean, I cannot enter your house. If I could, I'd do so, and gladly. But it isn't possible for me.' He drew breath with a sharp, hissing sound. 'A house is a human place, far more than any other, and I . . . I am not human. If I tried to step over your threshold, I . . .' He shrugged. 'I couldn't.'

Carys was dismayed. Though she had not yet permitted herself to acknowledge it consciously, she had already begun to anticipate a new place for Robin in her future life. She had imagined him coming to her door when the sun set; they would sit together in the parlour, lie together in her bed, *be* together all through the night until he took his leave of her at dawn. Just like true lovers. Just like husband and wife. Now, in the space of a moment, her budding plans had been thwarted, her hopes crushed, and suddenly she felt let down and almost angry.

'I don't understand!' she protested. '*Why* would it be as you say? What is it about you that makes it so? Are you incomplete, is that it? Are you flawed, an unfinished thing?' And before she could stop it, a spiteful impulse made her add, 'Like the scarecrow?'

167

She saw the pain in Robin's eyes and instantly regretted those last words. Putting a clenched fist to her mouth, she said indistinctly, 'I'm sorry . . . oh, Robin . . . forgive me, please!'

Robin had turned his head away, but now he looked at her again. 'Of course,' he replied, his voice quiet. 'Besides, what is there to forgive? You have the right to speak as you feel.'

'But it isn't what I feel! I was wrong, I didn't mean it, it was just a moment's anger, the disappointment . . .'

'Yes,' he said. 'I know. And I share that disappointment.'

Carys hung her head. 'I don't want to be cruel to you, Robin. Never, ever, in all the world.'

He smiled, but the smile held a bleak note. 'And I am here only to serve you.' His fingers closed over her hand, which still hovered near her mouth. 'Tell me about your potion. Explain what you did, and we'll try to mend it together.'

Carys grasped thankfully at the chance he offered her. The tale came out haphazardly, but Robin understood and, when she was done, said, 'Bring me the brew. And a long spoon, and your salt jar.'

She ran to do as he bade her. When she returned, he had ventured into the yard – just a little way, not far from the gate – and a small fire was burning at his feet, though where he had found the wood and how he had made it blaze up so quickly was a mystery. Carys did not ask; she only crouched beside him and set down the things she had brought.

'Look up,' he said. 'Tell me where the moon is now.'

She turned her face to scan the sky. There was a rack of cloud, but the moon's glow was a smudge in the darkness away beyond the house.

'Westward,' she told him. 'It's near setting.'

'And that's what you've done wrong. Don't you remember, when I taught you? This medicine must be prepared in the last hour before the moon sets. Try it now. Set your pot on the fire, yes, that's the way. Stir it slowly, with the track of the moon and sun, you must never stir against, never widdershins, that's the way of evil.'

168

Carys took the spoon and began to stir as he instructed. The brew came gradually to the boil, and as it started to seethe Robin touched her arm and said, 'Now, cast in some salt, just a little, to ask for the moon's strength. Good. Stir now. Yes, that's the way. Stir, and let your will focus on what you wish to achieve.'

'When I was making it before, in the kitchen, I sang,' she said. Robin shook his head. 'Don't sing now. Only concentrate.'

The liquid in the pot was changing, altering its consistency and becoming thicker, like clear honey. Carys watched it with a growing sense of elation, then abruptly Robin touched her wrist and said, 'Enough. It's done.'

She drew the pot from the fire, set it aside and sat back on her heels with a sigh. 'Thank you,' she said, and gave Robin a smile so sweet that he was visibly affected.

'My love . . .' he began.

'Ohh . . . you are *wonderful*!' Carys reached to him and flung her arms around his neck. 'My saviour and my hero! What should I do without you?'

'You'll never be without me, Carys,' Robin told her solemnly. 'For as long as you wish it.'

'And I always shall wish it, you know I shall!' She kissed both his cheeks, soundly, warmly, then for the third kiss found his lips. That lasted a long time, and when finally they drew apart, she said, 'I won't leave this farm. Tonight, I made my decision.'

'When your family came?' Robin asked.

She narrowed her eyes at him. 'How do you know that they came?'

'I was watching. From a distance.'

First at Jone's funeral, now during her parents' visit . . . How often, she wondered, was Robin there, invisible but aware of her, what she did, whom she saw? The speculation produced an ambiguous sense of discomfort, and to allay it Carys looked out towards Crede Hill and said fiercely, 'I don't care what anyone else says or what anyone else wants. *I* mean to stay. For *always*.'

'You're free to choose, love.'

'Yes. Yes, I am, aren't I?' She turned to him again, appealingly this time. 'Do you think I'm right, Robin? In my place, would you do the same?'

'I never could be in your place. But for you . . . yes, I think it's right and good.' He ventured another smile. 'And *I* am glad of it.'

'You'll help me, won't you?' she asked him. 'Oh, I know I have neighbours and friends, but I need more than that. I need *you*; to teach me, to talk to me, to be with me.'

'I'll do all that, and more.'

He meant it, she knew, and she didn't doubt the promise.

Though if only he could have stepped over her threshold . . .

Carys pushed that thought away, not wanting to resurrect the disappointment again. 'It's nearly dawn,' she said, not consciously aware of the small, tight knot of resentment that was lurking deep inside her. 'I suppose you must go.'

He nodded. 'I must go. But tomorrow . . .'

'Yes. Oh, yes.'

'Call to me.'

'I will.'

She did not watch him leave; she never did. She only stared at the remains of the fire he had made, which now was only embers and soon would be nothing but ash. Then she picked up the pot, the spoon and the salt, and walked slowly back to her house.

Chapter XV

The news that Carys Jonewidow intended to stay on at the farm was the talk of the parish. The first reaction was astonishment and, in some quarters, disbelief; then when it became clear that the rumour was not false, discussion began in earnest.

The arguments ran fierce and deep. Most said that Carys was a fool both to herself and to the district; some went so far as to speculate that the shock of her husband's death had addled her brain and turned her as mad as Lob. But a few, even though they found her reasoning impossible to understand, pointed out that if nothing else she had courage, and that was surely to be respected.

Carys heard most of the talk at second hand from Izzy. She showed no outward interest (though she was well aware of the inquisitive looks and whispers that followed her every time she ventured into the village), but with those closest to her – Merion and Gyll, Garler and Deenor and Olma and Juda – she was more open, confiding many of her thoughts and her hopes. Yes, she would stay on at Jone's farm, which now would be known to all as Carys's farm, and with the help of Providence and her good friends she would continue to run it as Jone had done. That, she told them all with a pensive little smile, was what Jone himself would have wished. And Carys knew, and the parish knew, that whatever men might think and women might whisper in the privacy of their own homes, no one could contradict her.

Though her friends resolved to support her in any way that they could, they were still disappointed. Gyll had fervently hoped that Carys would come to live in the cottage near the smithy, while

171

Merion felt a fatherly concern for her safety in what was, by comparison with village life, an isolated place. Garler and Deenor regretted that they would not now have the chance to buy the farm for their expanding family. They all pointed out, though gently, that the course Carys had chosen would be far from easy. But they *were* her good neighbours, and when they finally accepted that nothing they could say would sway her, they stopped trying to persuade her to their way of thinking and offered their open-handed help.

Of them all, Gyll and Olma Carnwidow were the only two in whom Carys might have been tempted to confide the entire truth; Gyll because she was Carys's best friend, and Olma because she also knew the sweet freedom of childless and prosperous widowhood. But Olma longed only to trade her freedom for a new husband, and even Gyll, kind, loyal Gyll, believed that no woman could be happy without a man to order her days and be her constant guide and mentor. They would not have understood why Carys rejoiced in her own liberty. They would not have understood about Robin. So Carys covered her hair with a widow's white cap, took possession of her inheritance, and held her precious secret close to her heart as she opened the door upon a new life.

She soon discovered that she had a great deal to learn. She could feed pigs and tend chickens and milk cows and sweep the yard, and had been doing so since her marriage. But these relatively simple skills did not qualify her to be sole mistress of a busy and well-ordered farm. The local gossips smiled behind their hands and said that the gilt would soon wear off the gingerbread. One lonely winter, they predicted, and Carys Jonewidow would marry again or sell, and with the farm surely gone to rack and ruin by then she would be lucky to receive half its present worth. But for every soul who prophesied doom there was another who rallied to Carys's cause. Izzy stayed and became chatelaine of the house, and if the dusting of the parlour was sometimes neglected as a result, no one minded. Lob, too, proved more useful than anyone had imagined he could be. Carys discovered that the more repetitive his task, the better was his ability and memory, so she patiently schooled him to drive the herd back and forth between pasture and byre each day, and before long he could be relied on more often than not to achieve it. Then she took on a village girl, a child of twelve from a poor family, to feed the chickens, collect the eggs and help with the milking. The girl was grateful to be paid in kind, so that saved money. And Carys herself began to glean the harvest of knowledge and experience that, when it was all gathered in, would make her a farmer and not merely a farmer's wife. Merion Blacksmith taught her first how to groom the horses and harness Faithful to the plough or wagon for workdays and Spry to the light trap for chapel or visiting; then how to look for the signs that would tell her if either horse was unwell or in need of new shoes. Garler Shepherd, rallying from his disappointment, schooled her in the lore of sowing and gathering, and told her which wild plants would choke her crops and which should be left to make the hay sweet and the butter yellow. Garler had also taken charge of Carys's sheep and merged the flock with his own. This arrangement meant less profit for Carys's farm, but with so much else to concern her Carys saw the wisdom of handing over the responsibility, and the bulk of the dividend, to someone more expert than she could ever be. Besides, it was a small way of recompensing Garler, and thus helped to oil the wheels of friendship and cooperation. She was content enough.

Vine-month passed into Ivy-month; the apple picking was over but for a few varieties that hung late on the tree, and the root-crop harvest got under way in earnest. Local interest in Carys's doings had died down as newer subjects worthy of gossip came along, but with winter now only a caprice of weather away, it began to revive. People recalled their own predictions that winter would burst the bubble of Carys's plans, and the signs were that the coming season was going to be a harsh one. Granted, they said, the young widow had done well enough so far, but what when the freezing winds came, and the ice and the snow and the long hours of darkness? There'd be a change to Carys Jonewidow's tune then, they said. Marry or sell. That's what she would surely do. Marry or sell.

As before, Carys was aware of what was being said about her, and as before she paid no heed to it. For one thing, she was far too busy to concern herself with the village's petty preoccupations, and for another, she knew very well that – except, perhaps, in the vicinity of Powl's mill – there was no actual malice behind the talk. Certainly not now. For other, kinder tales were beginning to circulate about Carys Jonewidow, as a growing number of people had occasion to be grateful to her.

The potion to bring the colour back to Gyll's hair had worked very well indeed. Gyll was overjoyed – it had made her feel young again, she said, and she bashfully confided to Carys that Merion was taking quite a renewed interest in her these days. Garler, too, had benefited from his medicine. He was set in his ways and had been reluctant to try it at first, but Deenor had persuaded him, and so far his cough showed no sign of returning.

Carys's next customer was Olma Carnwidow, who had heard from Juda, who had had it from Gyll's own lips, that Carys might help her where Jem Apothecary had failed. Olma suffered from headaches that, when they struck, laid her low for a day or more. Jem had bled her four times – a very distressing experience – and prescribed poultices and bandages tied tightly around her skull, all to no avail. Could Carys help? *Would* she . . . ? Olma would pay, and gladly, for anything that might bring her relief.

Carys made a show of reluctance, but Olma pressed her and at length she gave way. The remedy was a simple decoction, but Carys stressed that it must always be taken during the hours of daylight, preferably when the sun was shining.

'The hours of daylight?' Olma repeated, and laughed nervously. 'You make it sound like witchcraft, Carys.'

'Oh, no, indeed it's nothing of the kind!' Carys protested. 'It's the nature of the plant, see. The pollen is used, and pollen's strongest in sunlight, so the same rule should be followed for the medicine.'

Olma nodded, fascinated and impressed by Carys's knowledge.

Carys flatly refused any idea of payment, and the older woman went away with her preparation.

The headaches had not troubled her since.

After Olma came others: friends who had heard about Carys's remedies and wondered if she might have something for their own afflictions. They were only small troubles, like headaches or whitlows or cuts that were slow to heal, and no one actually asked Carys directly for help, but dropped hints and hoped they would be taken. They were taken; a potion here or a salve there changed hands, and in almost all cases relief from the trouble followed.

Like Olma, her other friends wanted to pay her, but Carys would have none of it.

'Oh, fudge!' she said, her cheeks flushing, when Juda, whose eldest daughter had just been through a difficult birth and had been eased by one of Carys's nostrums, tried gratefully to press money on her. 'Truly, Juda, I won't hear of such a thing! After all your kindnesses to me, it's the very least I can do. Sit down and take tea, and let's talk of something else.'

They drank tea, but Juda did not want to change the subject.

'You've been hiding your true light from us, Carys,' she said as she sipped. 'These healing skills, and you never told anyone. How did you learn them?'

That was always the most difficult question to answer, and Carys had devised a means of putting people off the scent. Books were her excuse, and she had made up a tale about Jone having a modest collection of volumes, from which she had taken instruction. She embroidered the story by pretending that Jone had encouraged her, but declared that what she knew was very little and should never be taken as a true talent.

She repeated the practised story to Juda, finishing with a shrug and a self-effacing smile. 'So you see, it's as simple as that. No craft or skill, nothing special at all.'

Juda wouldn't accept that. 'Olma says the cure you gave to her worked like magic,' she persisted.

'Oh, nonsense—'

175

'No, it's true. Have you any idea how poor Olma used to suffer with those headaches? But since you mixed that remedy, she's not had the smallest trouble. It's as good as anything the Wayfarers could have offered, she says. Better, indeed, for it came from a friend, someone she knows she can trust.'

A sharp little chill went through Carys at Juda's mention of the Wayfarers. It was some time since she had thought about her encounter with the old matriarch, but now the memory came back, and with it a sense of unease. Juda could not know . . . could she? No, ridiculous. The Wayfarers did not break their promises, and she herself had never breathed a word to another human soul. Neither Juda nor Olma nor Gyll nor anyone else could possibly have divined the truth about her newly revealed 'talent'. They could not, did not, and must never, ever know about Robin.

Carys had kept her promise to Robin, calling to him on the night after Garler's potion was made and waiting for him, as she was accustomed to do, by the yard gate. They had walked in the woods, he listening silently while she told him of Deenor's pleasure and gratitude at the gift, and then she had explained her plan to repay her friends and neighbours. She had glowed with happiness when Robin kissed her and told her that she was the kindest soul in the world, and under the shelter of the beeches and oaks they had loved each other with a passion they had not shared for a long time.

That night had been, perhaps, the most perfect of all the nights they had shared. It was only a shame, Carys thought, that she had seen so little of him since then; in fact, when she stopped to consider it she realised that their only meetings had been when she had needed his help in preparing another of her remedies. The trouble was, she was so busy these days. Almost every daylight hour was taken up with work about the farm, and when the sun set she was so tired that she wanted only to retreat to the bedroom she had made for herself – a very pretty and cosy bedroom it was now, too – and sleep until morning.

If he could have shared that room with her, it would have been different. She had asked him again why he could not, but again he had been unable or unwilling to explain in a way that she could comprehend. *It is impossible for me*, was all he could tell her. On the rare occasions when Carys did not fall asleep almost as soon as she laid her head on her pillow, she fretted over his words, his refusal, until the fretting became a tight, hard little knot inside her that only a night's rest alleviated.

And now winter was approaching. It was all very well, she told herself, to tryst with her lover in the woods or on the hill, out under the sky and the stars, when the weather was warm and fine, but when the rain had ice in it and the wind cut like a knife, what then? There had to be a better way for them.

Then, on the first day of Reed-month, winter did come, not quite with the predicted vengeance, but with a sure hand and the promise of a hard and uncompromising time ahead. The previous day had been perfectly pleasant, almost warm, but an inscrutable instinct was at work in Carys, and when the evening milking was done she told Lob not to turn the cows out again but to leave them be. By the time she woke the following morning, everything had changed. Rain had come in while the world slept, and a spiteful north wind was blowing down from Crede Hill and turning it to sleet.

Garler Shepherd, in oiled hide coat and heavy boots, came to the farm in the grey early light, concerned for Carys's livestock and anxious to offer his help. He was surprised to find the cows peaceably chewing hay in the byre, and looked at Carys with a new and surprised admiration.

'I reckon you must be the only one hereabouts who hasn't been caught out this morning,' he told her. 'There's cattle in most of the pastures looking miserable as dark sin, and the holders over north of Crede are in a proper to-do.' He eyed her slantwise. 'What made you decide, then? It was mild enough last evening.'

'I know,' said Carys. 'But I had a feeling it wasn't to last.'

'Well then, that's a blessing, isn't it?' Garler lifted his shoulders and peered out at the foul day. 'We don't want too much of this too early. Bad for the sheep if winter comes on fast; there'll be losses. That Lob, now; might you spare him to me for an hour or two this

177

afternoon? I reckon it would be as well to look over the hurdles, just in case, and the boy's got brawn if not brain.'

'Have Lob, and welcome,' Carys agreed. 'I won't need him for the cows today, and there's no especial work for him anywhere else on the farm.'

Garler nodded his thanks. She expected him to go then, but instead he hovered. He seemed to be mustering the will – or courage – to say something else, and after a long pause it abruptly came out.

'That medicine, now.'

Garler looked almost embarrassed, and to help him Carys prompted, 'For your cough?'

'That's the one. I was wondering, like, if there might be some more . . . ? No hurry, mind, the bottle's still quarter full. But what with the change in the weather and all . . .'

'Of course,' she said. 'I'll mix it as soon as I can, and bring it to you.'

'As to payment—'

'I'll take none, Garler. You know that.'

He nodded again, slowly. 'Well, that's kind and neighbourly. Kind and neighbourly.' Then he cleared his throat. 'Our young mare, the one we drive to market. She's none too fit at the moment.'

'Oh?' said Carys. 'What's amiss with her?'

'We don't rightly know. Merion looked at her three days back, and what he gave her helped some. But she's still not right. I wondered . . .'

Carys was taken aback. 'You think *I* might help? But I don't know about animals, not the way Merion does. And I wouldn't want him to think I was interfering.'

'No, no,' Garler assured her. 'It was Merion himself said I should ask you. What you've done for people – well, everybody knows about that. So why not the same with animals, that's what Merion says.'

She was astonished, and, she had to admit, not a little flattered. *Could* she cure the mare? Impossible to say without seeing the

178

animal, and of course consulting Robin . . .

'Well,' she said at last, cautiously, 'perhaps I might come over and look at her? I can't promise that I can help, but—'

'Oh, I know, and I wouldn't expect it.' Garler sounded relieved. 'But just to see. It would be a kindness.'

'Very well. Then maybe this afternoon?'

'You don't want to turn out in this rain!'

She glanced at the sky. 'It'll stop by noon.' *How did she know? She simply did, that was all there was to it.* 'Yes,' she added, trying not to notice the look of astonishment that Garler was giving her. 'This afternoon. I'll be over to see the mare then.'

Carys called to Robin that night. It was near on midnight; the rain had stopped as she had known it would, and the wind had dropped with it, but the air was bitingly cold. If the sky cleared – as it well might – there would be frost before dawn, and even in her heaviest coat Carys shivered as she waited for Robin to come.

Suddenly he was there at the gate, holding out his arms to her and smiling. Carys let him hold her tightly for some moments, savouring his warmth, then drew back a little from him and said, 'Robin, I need your help again.' Her breath misted in the cold as she told him about Garler's sick mare.

'I walked over to see her this afternoon,' she said. 'She looks in a bad way – lying down in her stall, and sweating all the time. When I went up to her she rolled her eyes and snapped her teeth at me. Garler says she's suddenly become like that with everyone.' She hugged herself, rubbing her upper arms. 'The trouble is, they say they don't *expect* me to cure her, but I know they do. I can see it in their eyes. I tried to tell them, I tried to make them understand that I don't know what's wrong, but they don't believe me. Because of the potions, they don't believe me.' She sighed heavily, her breath fogging the air again. 'Robin, what am I to do?'

Robin was frowning, thinking. 'If I could see her for myself . . .' he said gingerly.

Carys seized on his words. 'Yes! Oh, yes, you can, you must!

179

We could go there together, now, you and I! Please, Robin – come with me, and help me!'

'They mustn't know, Carys. Your shepherd and his family, they mustn't know anything about me.'

'They needn't,' she said. 'They'll all be long asleep anyway. The only problem could be the dogs.'

He smiled an odd, lopsided smile. 'Dogs don't bark when I come near.'

That was true, she realised. Even Fleet never made a sound when Robin came to the farm, and he never tried to follow when Carys left the house at night. 'Well, then,' she said eagerly. 'Will you come, Robin? *Will* you?'

He hesitated, then nodded. 'Very well. For you.'

It was a hard, uphill walk to Garler's homestead, but it seemed to Carys that only a matter of minutes passed before they were approaching the long, low house in a fold of one of the shallower valleys. The stables lay beside and at a right angle to the house. As Robin predicted, the dogs made not the smallest sound, and Carys unlatched the stable door and slipped inside. Robin hesitated a moment on the threshold, then took a deep breath – she heard that, and found it curious – before following her.

The mare, whose name was Ready, was in the last of the three stalls. As before, she was lying down, and the feeble light of one high-hanging lantern was enough to show the sheen of sweat on her flanks and neck.

'Ready . . .' Carys spoke the mare's name in a soothing, singsong tone that of late had come naturally to her. The mare turned her head, showing the white of one eye; she gave a low, ominous whicker and they heard the sound of her teeth snapping threateningly.

Then she saw Robin. The threat display stopped, and her ears, which she had laid flat, pricked forward with a different kind of interest. Robin whistled softly through his teeth, then moved noiselessly towards her, hunkering to a crouch at her side. Ready's breathing was unnaturally rapid; she watched as Robin ran a hand quickly, smoothly, along the length of her neck, across her withers, then down her face from brow to muzzle, pausing a while with his eyes closed and fingers clamped lightly over her nostrils. Carys watched intently, too, her own breath pent, then Robin rose and turned to face her.

'You didn't tell me about the foal.'

'Foal?' Carys's face was blank. 'What foal?'

He frowned. 'Inside her. You didn't know?'

'Garler said nothing! Do you mean—'

'I mean there's a foal growing in her, and it seems that no one has realised.' Robin looked down at Ready again, and shook his head in a silent comment on human short-sightedness. 'Its position is bad, and it's causing her pain.'

Carys stared at the mare in wonder, asking herself how Robin could possibly know and finding no answer to the question. 'There's so little sign of it,' she said, still only half willing to believe. 'Her belly's hardly distended, no more than if she'd been overeating.'

'It hasn't grown to its full term yet,' Robin told her. 'By rights it shouldn't be born until well into Elder-month. But it can't stay in her much longer, not if it and she are going to survive. It will have to be brought out in the next few days, or they'll both die.'

'But that can't be done!' Carys was appalled; she had heard of such things happening before, but always the mare had had to be cut open, and thus killed, to save the foal. Merion had told her a story once . . .

She shook that off and grasped Robin's arm. 'Can *you* help her?' she pleaded. To lose Ready would be a cruel blow to Garler and Deenor, and in more ways than one, for Ready was young, and good young working horses did not come cheaply. 'You have skills – powers – that are beyond the reach of humans. Can you use them to save her and make her better?'

There was a long silence before Robin answered, 'I can't interfere, Carys. Not directly; it wouldn't be right.'

'It *would!*' she protested. 'Listen to me, *listen*. Garler and Deenor are dear friends who have done all they can to help me, even though

181

they wanted to buy my farm for themselves. Now they need me, and I can't let them down.' Her mouth tightened, making her jawline hard suddenly, and she added with an edge to her voice, 'I *won't* let them down, Robin.'

Whether he sensed the challenge she was implying, the challenge to his promise of loyalty and service to her, Carys did not know. But her words had the effect she wanted. Robin's face flushed – even in the gloom it was noticeable – and he seemed to shrink in on himself, as if an invisible hand had struck him.

He said, in a voice so low that she could barely hear him, 'I understand.'

She swallowed. 'Then . . .'

'I still can't do it.' A pause. '*I* can't. But I could teach you the way.'

'Then you must! Tell me, show me what to do. I want to save her *and* her foal!'

He sighed. 'Very well. But you must make me a promise in return.'

'What is it?'

'That what I teach you . . . you will never use for any purpose other than to do good.'

She was shocked, almost insulted. 'Of course I will not! What do you think of me, if you believe for one moment that I—'

He held up both hands in an apologetic gesture, silencing her. 'Peace, my love, peace. Forgive me; I meant no slight. But I have to ask it of you, and hear you pledge it.'

Carys calmed down. 'Yes,' she said, 'I understand. And I do pledge it, Robin, I do.' She hesitated. 'Is my word good enough for you?'

Was there an answering hesitation? She could not be sure, but she suspected there was, before his shoulders relaxed and he said, 'Yes.'

They turned together to concentrate on the mare again, and Robin spoke quietly. 'The only power that can help Ready is not medicine or healing in the sense that your friend Merion Blacksmith, or even your apothecary, knows. It's a gift of another kind, love. You have it within you, locked away, and what I shall do is turn the key that unlocks it.' He gazed keenly at her. 'Are you ready for that? Are you ready for the responsibility and the consequences it could bring?'

Carys didn't stop to consider what his question might imply; all her thoughts were on the mare, the unborn foal, her desire to help.

'Yes,' she said resolutely.

'Very well. Then give me your hands, my Carys. Let it begin . . .'

Chapter XVI

When Carys arrived at his house shortly after dawn, Garler Shepherd was surprised. When he heard what she had to tell him, he was astounded. And to begin with, he did not believe her.

''Tisn't *possible*,' he said, shaking his head firmly. 'No slight to you, Carys, but if things had been so, we'd have known about it long since.'

'We did put Ready to the stallion last winter,' Deenor, who had come from the kitchen to hear the tale, said tentatively. 'Around the start of Rowan-month, wasn't it, Garler?'

'Maybe so,' Garler acknowledged, 'but we reckoned at the time that she didn't take, and Merion says the same. Why, you only have to look at her to see that there's no foal!'

'But there is,' Carys insisted. 'And it's the cause of all her trouble – please, Garler, you must trust me!'

'You seem so certain, Carys,' said Deenor, 'but how can you know? Yesterday when you came you were as perplexed as Merion, and now this morning all's changed. I don't understand.'

'I . . . thought about it,' Carys dissembled, aware that she could never, ever tell them the truth. 'Long and hard, into the night. I thought and thought, and . . . it came to me. I remembered, from . . . from my childhood, when something like this happened to a neighbour's horse, and . . .'

She didn't finish the explanation, because she could see from Deenor's face that she doubted every word and knew Carys was being evasive.

185

'She *is* in foal, Deenor,' she finished helplessly. 'I simply *know* it. And she needs help.'

Garler and Deenor looked uneasily at each other. At length Deenor said, 'If Carys has her reasons, Husband, then perhaps we should go along with them, at least for now. We've nothing to lose by trying, and Ready'll get no better for leaving her alone.'

Garler stroked his beard, his brows coming together in a frown. 'We-ell, now,' he said ponderously. 'I'm not sure if I agree. Sometimes, meddling only makes things worse.'

'Carys isn't meddling, Garler. Look how her wisdom has helped before.'

'Yes, yes, I know that, and like I say, I mean no slight.' Another lull followed, while Carys seethed inwardly with frustration. Then finally Garler made up his mind.

'I reckon I should speak to Merion Blacksmith again, that's what,' he said, in his voice the relief of a man who after much effort had solved a very difficult conundrum. 'If Carys is right – and mind, I'm not saying she is – then Merion will know what to do. Yes, I'll speak to Merion.' He smiled kindly at Carys. 'This evening, I'll ask him to come.'

'Will you sup with us tonight, Carys?' Deenor asked quickly. 'And Merion shall bring Gyll – we'll make a pleasant company of it, yes?'

Carys bit back her despair at their slow obtuseness and nodded. 'Yes, Deenor. Thank you, I'll come, and gladly.'

She only prayed that Ready would last until then.

'The fact is, Garler, I don't see that you've got anything to lose.' Merion stood, hands on hips, staring down at the suffering mare. 'I'll admit that for the life of me I can't see any sign that she's foaling, but life and nature take strange paths sometimes, and it isn't for us to understand them all.'

'I agree,' said Deenor. 'I said to you, Garler, didn't I; we've nothing to lose by trying what Carys says.'

Four heads turned and four pairs of eyes looked at Carys where she stood, a little apart, in the shadows beyond Ready's stall. She found it hard to meet their gazes, for she was all too aware of their unspoken questions, the curiosity, even the suspicion they felt as they asked themselves: *if this is true, how can she have known?*

'Well, Carys,' Merion said at last, gently. 'What must we do?'

She swallowed. This would be the hardest part, persuading them to go along with what she wanted. All very well for them to agree in principle, but when they witnessed it with their own eyes and ears, how would they react? She could well imagine what they would think, and her mind, flicking back, conjured the image of Jone standing frowning in the cow-byre when she brought back the Wayfarers' cure for Placid. Superstitious nonsense, he had called it.

Yet if her work today resulted in a living mare and a living foal . . .

Carys drew a deep breath to steady her nerve and said, 'If you'll all draw closer to Ready's stall, though not so near as to crowd her. Then . . .' She glanced nervously from one to another of them. 'Pray for her. And while I do what I must, *will* the foal to come.'

A little less than two hours later, Ready was delivered of a living foal.

Carys sat on a hay-bale, head bowed to her knees, hands limp at her sides, while the dizzying aftermath of what she had done slowly ebbed from her. It had been the strangest and possibly the most exhausting experience of her life, as the skill that Robin had unlocked – her gift, as he called it – had allowed her to link her mind with that of the unborn creature in its mother's womb. She had chanted to it, the eerie, singsong chant that Robin had taught her, weaving a spell that stirred it from its growing place and called it into the world.

At the end they had needed Merion's strength and a good length of rope, for the foal, as Robin had said, was badly positioned, and the act of birth had been a struggle for all concerned. But mother and child were both alive. Now, Ready lay in a deep bed of fresh straw, and the foal – a little colt – lay beside her. He was at least a month premature, smaller than any foal Carys had ever seen, and too weak to do more than raise his head a little and stare at the bewildering new world around him. But with care, he would survive.

A hand touched Carys's shoulder, and she looked up to see Deenor gazing down at her. Her eyes were as full of wonder as the foal's, which made Carys want to laugh.

'How are you feeling?' Deenor asked softly.

'Tired, that's all.' Carys quelled the laughter and smiled instead.

'I don't know what to say,' Deenor continued. 'We had not the least idea . . . How can we ever thank you, Carys?'

'You don't need to,' Carys told her. 'After all you've done for me.' With an effort she stood up, pressing fingers into the small of her back, which ached fiercely, and nodded towards the foal. 'He'll need the greatest of care for a while, and so will Ready. I can make cordials for them both, to strengthen them. I'll bring them over tomorrow.'

'I'll *fetch* them tomorrow, and no nonsense about it!' Deenor insisted. She, too, looked at the little one in his straw. 'I want to call him Miracle, because that's what he is. It's for Garler to decide, of course, but I think he'll agree.'

Carys nodded, then yawned, and at once Deenor was solicitous. 'My dear, you're so weary you can hardly stand, and it's little wonder!' she said. 'Come to the house, come and eat.'

'No . . .' Carys held up her hands. 'Thank you, Deenor, but I *am* so tired that I think I should rather go home and sleep.'

'Then Garler shall take you back straight away. Husband!' she called. 'Husband, Carys cannot stay longer. She needs her rest.'

In fact it was Merion who took Carys home, driving her in his own cart. Deenor sat beside her, which was as well, for Carys would likely as not have fallen from the seat through sheer tiredness. Deenor also wanted to help her indoors and up to bed, but Carys said no, she would be well enough, and so they left her at the door, Deenor with a hug and kiss, and a look of admiration that spoke more than words.

With the last of her failing energy Carys went to bed and fell asleep in her clothes. But at Garler's house, where Merion and Deenor had returned, no one had any thoughts of sleep. The supper had been eaten, and Deenor and Gyll had gone to the kitchen to wash the dishes, leaving Garler and Merion to sit by the fire and talk. It was better that the men should broach the subject that preoccupied them all, and by the time the women returned to join them, they had done so.

'The thing that baffles me,' Merion was saying as Deenor and Gyll sat down, 'is where she *learned* such a thing. Carys, of all people.'

'And that's saying nothing of how she knew about the foal,' Garler added, nodding soberly. 'It's a mystery to me.'

'She's been hiding her light, that's what Juda says,' Gyll ventured. 'You know she cured Juda's headaches? *I* believe she has a gift, and it's only now that she's starting to discover it.'

'Only now?' Merion looked at her and frowned. 'You mean, since Jone went?'

'Well, perhaps.' Gyll sounded defensive. 'Jone was a good man, but . . . he probably wouldn't have approved, would he? You remember when his Placid took sick in the spring, and Carys went to the Wayfarers for a cure? Jone didn't like the idea, and he took some persuading to try it.'

Deenor spoke for the first time, thoughtfully. 'Maybe what Carys did was something the Wayfarers taught her? Could that be, do you think?'

'It's possible,' said Merion, 'but I doubt it. The Wayfarers haven't been back since – they didn't come for harvest this year – and if Carys had learned from them, why did she wait for so long before showing it?'

Gyll met his eyes. 'Maybe Jone . . .'

'Didn't approve? All right, Wife, I see now what you were getting at a few moments ago. But I don't give the idea any credence. How long did Carys spend at the Wayfarers' camp – an hour? Two at most? Whatever the nature of this "gift" of hers, she couldn't have learned it in so short a time.'

'I agree with Gyll,' Deenor said slowly. 'I think the gift Carys has was always with her. And . . . and instead of questioning it, and worrying about it, I think we should simply be thankful that it's there.'

There was a silence as the others considered this. Merion's first impulse was to rebuke Deenor for her foolishness. This was too serious a matter to be accepted lightly; it should be considered and discussed, as much for Carys's sake as for their own. But in the stable outside was a sick mare who had been cured, and a new-born foal which, without Carys's intervention, would have died. Merion was a fair man, and he couldn't help but acknowledge – privately, at least – that there might be a modicum of pique in his disapproving feelings. Carys's knowledge had proved greater than his own; he had failed to help Ready, but she had succeeded. Perhaps, as Deenor suggested, they should simply be grateful. Perhaps any other attitude would be petty and mean-spirited.

Garler, too, was pondering his wife's words. He was a more staid man than Merion, narrower in his thinking and slow to accept anything new or unusual in his dealings with the world. But Carys Jonewidow was a virtuous girl, a good neighbour. There was no harm in her.

He said aloud, 'When Jone's Placid took sick . . . I recall he told me something about that cure the Wayfarers gave him.' He drew on his pipe but it had gone out, and he took it out of his mouth, staring at it meditatively. 'Reckoned he had to make a proper fool of himself, saying special words and such, and all at night under the light of the moon. Proper flummery, he said.'

'But it worked,' Gyll pointed out gently.

'Oh, yes.' Garler nodded. 'Oh, yes. It worked.'

'Just like what Carys did tonight,' said Deenor.

Garler tapped his pipe on the arch of the fireplace and fished in a pocket for his tobacco pouch. He didn't make any further comment.

After a silence of some seconds Merion sighed gustily. 'So maybe our wives aren't so far wrong, eh, Garler? Maybe we should accept what Carys has done, and what she can do, and thank the kindness of Providence for it.'

Garler's pipe was full again. He lit it with a spill from the fire, puffed until smoke began to curl from the bowl, then said, 'I don't hold with witchcraft, mind.'

'It isn't—' Gyll began, but Merion waved her to silence.

'Nor does any right-thinking person, not in the way that I suspect you mean. But if Carys's gift *is* a kind of witchcraft, it isn't the wrong kind. She'll not try to blight crops or make trouble or hurt people in any way. She's an innocent child; such a thing would never enter her head.' Suddenly and broadly he smiled, as a flash of inspiration came to him. 'Her skills and the dark powers – they're opposites, like the difference between the seasons. The dark powers are things of winter. But Carys is a *summer* witch.'

Gyll and Deenor both gave little cries of approval, and Gyll looked at her husband in open admiration at what seemed to her a positively poetic explanation. Garler scanned their faces, hesitant still, wary. But he was outnumbered.

'We-ell . . .' he said cautiously. 'If it's only to be used for the good . . .'

'Can you imagine Carys doing anything else?'

Garler rarely imagined anything, but he nodded. 'True. That's true. She's a good-hearted girl.'

Gyll and Deenor exchanged a quick, triumphant glance. Gyll had known that Merion would see sense, Garler she had been less sure of. But his friend's influence had swayed him, and his doubts were receding. Not, Gyll reflected, that anything could have been done to stop Carys's activities; she was a free soul (though the men might naturally tend to forget that from time to time) and could choose her own path. But they could have made life difficult for her. She might have been snubbed, excluded from local society, forced into isolation. If people did not trust their neighbours, they easily became prejudiced against them. That, though, would not happen to Carys, not if Merion and Garler and others like them led the way of opinion. In fact Gyll would have taken a wager that, far from declining, Carys's popularity was set to increase markedly once the news of tonight's triumph got about.

And Gyll, of course, would make sure that it *did* get about. That, she considered happily, was the least she could do for her dear neighbour and very good friend.

The first real snow fell ten days before Midwinter-feast. There had been flurries in the preceding month, but nothing that settled for more than a day, then one morning clouds began to build up in the north-east, and by noon the sky was a solid leaden bank, tinged with a dull, angry pink that warned of something foreboding and imminent.

The local sages had not predicted the blizzard that began as the sun (invisibly) westered. But Carys Jonewidow had, and those who had heeded Carys's warning were in the majority, and had reason to thank her. Cattle still out on Crede Hill were driven home to yard and byre; sheep were hastily hurdled and given what shelter could be provided; while in houses and holdings farmers' wives gathered extra water from their pumps or wells or springs to keep them supplied through the first onslaught.

The snowstorm continued through the night, driven by a cruel wind that rattled the roof tiles and made the farmhouse creak like a ship in a high sea. Carys lay wakeful, listening to the noise of it, listening, too, for any sounds of trouble from byre or sty or barn. None came. She had had willing help to secure her animals, and the buildings were all sound enough (a few tiles loose here and there, but Merion had made some hasty repairs for her this afternoon and would complete them properly as soon as the weather allowed). All was well, and at length, lulled rather than disturbed by the wind, she slept soundly.

She woke at dawn to a white, alien world. It was still snowing, but the wind had dropped and now the flakes fell more gently, though thick and relentless as ever. Looking out in the first grey light, Carys estimated that the snow in the yard would be up to her calves; deeper where the wind had piled it. She could see icicles hanging from the eaves of the farm buildings, and in the byre one of the cows was lowing, as though passing her own reproving comment on the change.

Carys considered the scene spread out before her. The snow would stop for a while this afternoon, but tonight the heavy clouds would march in again and bring more. Two days, perhaps three, then the sky would clear. But that meant frost, heavy and hard, and it was set to last for some time. She had seen all the signs, but more significantly, she *felt* it in her marrow, a certainty as sure as the fact that day followed night. Part of the gift. Part of the unlocking. It was still a heady feeling at times, but she was growing used to it now.

Turning from the window, she began to dress in her warmest clothes. Snow or no snow, people would begin to arrive soon: Izzy and Lob – Merion would bring them if his cart could get through – and probably the village girl, too. Then Garler. No weather would ever prevent Garler from doing what he considered his neighbourly duty, and doubtless he would have some small gift from Deenor, a pie or a cake or a piece of bacon, to show their gratitude for her timely weather warning. Which reminded her: Deenor's hips and legs always ached badly when the weather turned cold. Garler would not ask directly for help, but he was likely as not to drop a hint this morning. So she would have something ready to ease Deenor's trouble . . .

Carys smiled. Garler would be as impressed by her foresight as by the potion itself; it would not occur to him that it had more to do with observation than with magic. Ah, well. Another feather in the cap of her reputation. It did no harm.

She finished dressing, pushed her feet into her wooden-soled shoes, through which the cold of stone-flagged floors could not penetrate, and went downstairs to riddle up the range and begin the day.

The snowfall lasted for as long as Carys had foretold, and, again as she had foretold, was followed by clear skies and a ferocious frost that clamped down on the land like a vice. The soil in the fields froze solid, bringing the root-crop harvest to a halt. Sheep could not forage, and the shepherds were obliged to toil over Crede Hill with cartloads of hay to keep the flocks from going hungry. Water pumps seized, and wells developed crusts of ice that had to be broken by dropping large stones down into the depths. The ice, indeed, was everywhere, even encroaching into houses, where it obscured windows and formed each morning on the surface of the water in bedroom wash-bowls. Jem Apothecary was called on to treat great numbers of bumps, bruises and sprains caused by falls on the slippery ground, and one unfortunate horse, coming to grief outside the chapel, broke its leg and had to be put out of its misery by the slaughterman.

But the bad weather was nothing that the people of the parish were not accustomed to. It had merely come a little earlier than usual this year (the natural penalty, said the pessimists, for a good summer), and on the whole life went on much as usual. Garler was suitably impressed by Carys's newest potion, and Deenor's aches improved. The village girl who helped with the chickens and cows developed bad chilblains; Carys made up some ointment and gave her a pair of oversized but warm boots instead of her usual eggs and butter, as payment for her work. Gyll, tramping intrepidly across the fields to pay her good friend Carys a visit and hatch plans for the Midwinter celebration, brought the newest gossip from the village. The preacher had at last proposed to Tally Rigswidow and it looked like being a spring wedding, maybe even a double one if Tally's son stopped dithering and married Carys's sister Thomsine. Ina Bartelwife's youngest had had the croup but was better now (and why Ina hadn't come to Carys was something Gyll would never understand; really, the girl had no more wit than a chicken). Bensel Taverner had ordered new boots from Corl Shoemaker, but now claimed they didn't fit and was refusing to pay Corl . . .

'Oh, and there's news of your other sister,' Gyll added, a little diffidently because she had some inkling of the rift between Carys and her family, even if she did not know the details. 'Things aren't going too well with her and the coming child. Apparently she's been quite ill; they called Jem in, but he hasn't improved matters.'

'Oh,' said Carys unemotionally.

'Yes . . . The child's due in Ash-month, and of course that's not so long away, but Jem fears it might come early. *Too* early.'

Carys nodded, and stared into the fire.

Gyll paused for some moments, then decided not to hedge any further. 'Carys, I know matters aren't friendly between you and Nellen, but . . . blood *is* more than water. If she's in trouble, don't you think you might put aside your differences and help her . . . ?'

She wondered if she had said too much, overstepped the bounds. But Carys showed no sign of anger. Instead, she continued to gaze at the fire's heart for a few more seconds, her eyes oddly narrowed and seeming to focus on something beyond the flames and invisible to Gyll. Then her face relaxed and she said calmly, 'Nellen doesn't need my help. She'll be well enough, and the child will be born alive and healthy.'

Gyll drew in a sharp breath. 'How can you know?'

A shrug. 'I do know, Gyll. I just do.' She turned her head and gave her friend a reassuring smile. 'Like you say, blood's more than water.'

Gyll recalled the discussion that she, Merion, Garler and Deenor had had on the night that Ready's foal, Miracle, had been born. Garler had been suspicious of Carys's insight, calling it witchcraft, while Gyll had preferred to call it a gift. Now though, she wondered a little. Carys's predictions were proving to be uncannily reliable, and as for her ability to cure ailments . . . well, she was a natural healer, no possible doubt of it. It wasn't that Gyll was afraid of her friend's talents, not that exactly . . . but it *was* just a morsel discomfiting at times. After all, if Carys could foretell the future, then as well as knowing when something would come to good, did it not follow that she also knew when it would come to bad? That conundrum made Gyll shiver inwardly, and suddenly she had to know the answer.

'Carys,' she said.

Carys looked at her and smiled again. 'Yes?'

'If . . . if something . . . dreadful was to happen. Say, to – to me, or any friend – just as an example, mind, please Providence that it won't . . .' She hesitated, licked dry lips. 'Say someone was to be taken serious sick, or – or even – even die . . . Would you know, before it came about?'

Carys considered for a while, then: 'I can't say, Gyll. It's never happened to me.'

'Not even when Jone . . . ?'

She shook her head. 'No, not then. Not at all.'

Gyll nibbled her lip, which didn't help the dryness. 'But if it did. Just say it did, and you *did* know, and it was me or Merion.' She swallowed. 'Would you tell us?'

The silence lasted for what seemed a long time. Then Carys asked gently, 'Would you want me to?'

'I . . . don't know. I truly don't.' Gyll was floundering, and beginning to wish she had never allowed this train of thought to develop. What she had wanted to say, wanted to explain, had more to do with the principle of the thing than the actuality, but somehow her intentions had twisted themselves around and rebounded on her. 'I suppose . . .' she got out at last, 'I suppose that if you foresaw something good, I would want to hear of it. But if it was something bad . . .'

Carys nodded. Her expression had suddenly become a little closed, though Gyll was too preoccupied to notice. 'I understand you,' she said. 'And – if it helps, Gyll – I think I should feel very much the same.'

Gyll visibly relaxed. 'Well, then, there's probably no more to be said.' She was glad to have an outlet, a chance to escape from the tangle she had created. 'What a silly goose you must think me, to be so morbid!' A pause. 'There *isn't* anything, is there? Anything you've not said . . . ?'

'Oh, no. Nothing at all – I promise it.'

Which was true. But all the same, Gyll's hesitant question had raised an uncomfortable dilemma in Carys's mind. It was all speculation thus far – but if she were to have a premonition at some time in the future, what then? *Would* she have the courage to tell the truth? Would she, indeed, have a duty to tell it? Or were such things better left unspoken, shut away in a mental closet and never allowed to see the light of day? The quandary was one that couldn't easily be resolved. All she could do, perhaps, was pray that it would never happen to her . . .

Gyll was talking again, but her words flowed through Carys's consciousness without penetrating; all that registered was a change in tone, a lightening of the mood that Carys suddenly and desperately needed. With an effort she made herself snap back to the present, the reality of the crackling fire (which needed more wood) and the pot of tea (which needed refilling; Gyll never said no to another cup) and Fleet sprawled and snoring on the floor as close to the hearth as he could contrive.

'I'm sorry.' She interrupted Gyll, but not rudely. 'I must have been daydreaming. I didn't hear . . .'

'Oh, I was just saying that Merion and I would dearly like it if you'll come to us for Midwinter-feast. Merion has already invited Garler and Deenor, and Juda and Elios will be there of course, and Olma, and we're killing the goose tomorrow, so we shall have a veritable banquet, and then games and talk, and of course Merion or Garler will drive you home. Will you come, Carys? Say you will!'

Midwinter-feast. Carys did not want to spend it here, even with her friends about her. In the village, at Merion and Gyll's home, she would be drawn into a warmer, livelier spirit, which at this moment was something she felt that she needed. There was Robin . . . but she had made no promises to him, no arrangement with him. Robin would understand.

'Yes, Gyll,' she said, rallying with a smile in which Gyll did not detect the ache of relief. 'I shall be very glad to come.'

Chapter XVII

Though Gyll had planned only a small Midwinter-feast celebration, in the event more than two dozen people crammed into the parlour of the long, low house beside the village smithy. A partial thaw had set in on the previous day, and as slush was marginally less hazardous than ice, people felt more inclined to venture out. So the gathering of invited guests was swelled by a number of impromptu callers, including Jem Apothecary, Corl Shoemaker and his wife, Bartel Carpenter with his entire family, and even, for a short while, the preacher and Tally Rigswidow (though not, to Carys's relief, accompanied by Tally's son and Thomsine). Everyone brought some contribution in the form of food or drink, and the evening grew livelier by the hour. There was no room for dancing, but talk was loud and genial; they played Stick-Stacks and The Old Grey Mare and Riddle-Me-Round, then Garler recited a verse tale, and Olma another, and Merion performed a comic mime that had everyone rocking with laughter.

As midnight approached, the company sobered a little, enough to listen for the chiming of the chapel clock. When it came, carried on the still, cold night and sounding distant and ethereal, they all rose to their feet as though at some unspoken command. Joining hands to form a circle with the centre of the room as its focus, they then sang the old Winter Song, a thanksgiving for the year that was passing and an invocation of hope for the new year to come. As she raised her voice with the rest, Carys felt a sudden pang of loneliness, a sense that, though she was among friends and surrounded with good cheer, she was not truly a part of this

199

celebration but one step out of kilter with it all. Strangely, she had been thinking of Jone tonight. Their marriage had not lasted long enough for them to spend even one Midwinter-feast together, and in a peculiar, inexplicable way Carys missed him. For all their differences and all her dissatisfactions, he had been *her* man, and since his death she had been alone in a way that was completely new to her. There was a blank, empty space in her life.

And the one person who might have filled that space did not, and could not.

The Winter Song ended, and with the formalities observed and completed they all relaxed again. Juda was prevailed on to sing some ballads to Garler's accompaniment on the whistle-pipe, and Merion broached another keg of beer.

As mugs were refilled, Jem Apothecary moved from his place near the door and took a vacant place on the bench where Carys sat. She smiled at him, and when he began to talk to her about this and that she thought nothing particular of it. Until, after a few minutes, Jem said, 'Mistress Carys . . . I would be most happy to drive you home tonight.'

Carys looked at him in some surprise. He was smiling at her, diffidently but with a distinct gleam of hopefulness, and understanding dawned. Jem was a single man, she a young and pretty widow. He had a good trade, she a farm. In his eyes, therefore – and no doubt in the eyes of others, if they paused to think about it – what could be more logical than to court her, and see what might come of it? It would be an eminently suitable match.

Except that Jem was also past forty, with a balding pate, spindle shanks and a reputation for being miserly. No doubt it would please him very well to take Carys for his wife.

But it would not please Carys.

He was waiting for an answer to his question. Carys wanted to tell him that no power in the entire world would persuade her to drive with him, be it to her home or ten paces along the village street, and that if he thought otherwise he might buy himself a looking-glass and answer his own question. She did not tell him that. Instead, she cast her eyes modestly down and replied, 'Thank you, Jem, but it's already arranged that I shall drive home with Garler and Deenor.'

'Your farm is out of their way. I can save them the trouble,' Jem persisted. 'Really, it would be my great pleasure—'

Carys did not let him get any further. 'Thank you,' she said again, 'but we – Garler and I – have some . . . matters to talk over. Farm matters,' she added, knowing that Jem knew nothing whatever about farming and so could not offer to advise her in Garler's stead.

'Ah. Of course.' He was disappointed, but tried to swallow it. 'Then perhaps on another occasion . . . after chapel, possibly . . .'

Carys smiled pleasantly but did not encourage him by saying anything. She also made a mental note to be sure to drive herself to chapel, preferably with a friend, for the next month or so.

And inside her, deep inside, something gave a sour and angry little twitch.

Garler was yawning and Deenor nodding on the cart seat as they and Carys, all wrapped and muffled against the cold, drove from the smithy under a cloudy sky diffused by moonlight to a blank pearl-grey. Trusty plodded steadily along, the reins slack on his back; if all three of his passengers fell asleep he would find his way surely home. Carys, however, was wide awake, though thankful that Garler rarely talked unless he had something specific to say. She did not feel like talking. Instead, she stared around her, stared at the shapes and shadows of the familiar landscape made unfamiliar by darkness, and tried unsuccessfully to banish the gnawing sensation of dissatisfaction within her. Tonight had been a pleasant and happy occasion; why, then, did she feel a sense almost of resentment in the wake of it? She couldn't blame Jem Apothecary; his overture might have been unwanted, but it had not been made in any disagreeable way. Besides, the feeling had been growing in her before Jem spoke. Isolation. Solitude. The sense of being an outsider, looking in at the worlds and the lives of others but having no real world or life of her own.

Which was utter nonsense, of course. Carys made a quick movement, partly a shiver and partly an impatient shake of her shoulders. Garler looked sidelong but did not comment, and as he turned his drowsy attention back to the road, she railed scornfully at herself. How long was it since she had lain awake at nights *craving* the freedom she now possessed? How long since she had longed to be no man's property and at no one's beck and call? Yet here she was, envying Gyll and Deenor and Juda and all the other women who still had husbands. What was the matter with her? What did she really *want*?

The trouble was, Carys knew the answer to that question. What she wanted was something she could not have, at least, not in all the ways that she desired. There lay the maggot in the fruit of her freedom, souring the sweetness, burrowing its way towards the core.

She sighed impatiently, drawing another look from Garler.

'Nearly home now,' he said, misinterpreting. 'We'll all soon be warm in our beds, never you fear.' He chumbled thoughtfully, as if chewing something. 'That was a fine do Merion and Gyll put on. A fine do. Don't you reckon?'

'Yes,' said Carys, forcing herself to smile.

Garler ruminated for a few moments. Then: 'I saw Jem Apothecary speaking to you. Not jealous, is he?'

Unsure of his implication, Carys repeated cautiously, 'Jealous . . . ?'

Garler chuckled throatily, and spat over the side of the cart into the hedge. 'Deenor said to me, she said, maybe Jem's pressing Carys for some of her recipes, for potions and the like. Maybe he's getting worried, in case Carys takes his trade away.'

Despite her mood Carys laughed too at the thought that Jem might look on her as a rival. 'I don't think so,' she said. 'He certainly didn't ask me anything about potions.' She paused. 'He just wanted to drive me home.'

'Oho,' said Garler, nodding sagely. 'We-ell, stands to reason, doesn't it? Him and you. I can see how he'd think it, logical-like.'

Another few moments of consideration. 'Not that he's got much to his name, for all his pretendings. You could do much better than Jem Apothecary, and that's a fact.'

'Better than Jem?' Deenor had stirred, and heard her husband's last remark. 'Who said anything about Jem, Husband?'

Garler nodded at Carys, who shrugged. 'Oh, it's nothing, Deenor. Jem offered to drive me home tonight, that's all.'

'The nerve of the man!' Deenor said indignantly 'Whyever would you look twice at *him*? Or even once? I hope you didn't encourage him, Carys!'

'No!'

'Good, for there's certainly no need for you to take the first proposal that's made to you. With your standing, and the farm, and your youth and good looks, you can afford to take your pick.'

Carys did not reply. She thought: *they don't understand. Even now, they can't see that I might want something other than to marry again, and there's no point in trying to explain.*

But wasn't that a reversal of what she had been thinking only minutes ago? Confusion filled Carys, and for no reason that made any sense she was sorely tempted to snap at Deenor, tell her to look to her own business and stop thinking, stop *assuming*, that she had any right to probe. The impulse passed, like a light breeze, and was quickly gone. But the dissatisfaction remained.

They were on the so-familiar home track by now and Carys's farmhouse was vaguely visible ahead, a rectangle only slightly darker than the surrounding night. Trusty wanted to turn for his own home steading, but Garler flicked the reins and clicked a warning with tongue and teeth. Reluctantly the horse obeyed, and they skirted the house, approaching from the back where the path was wider. Past the barn, then the edge of the byre came into view, reflecting a gleam of light from the lamp Carys had left in the kitchen window as a welcome and a guide. The lamplight spilled across the yard, almost to the gate—

Deenor said suddenly, sharply, 'Who's that?' She caught at Garler's arm. 'Husband, stop!'

203

Garler tugged the reins so hard that Trusty tossed his head in surprised protest, and Deenor's voice dropped to a whisper. 'There's someone there. Look.'

They all peered into the dark, and after a long, tense pause Garler said, 'Where to, Wife? I see nobody.'

'By the gate . . .' Deenor was frowning. 'There *was* someone, I'm sure of it. But he seems to have gone now.'

Garler shook his head. 'You've taken too much of that cider Merion brews, that's what,' he declared, and laughed wheezily. 'Eh, Carys? Eh?'

Carys didn't answer. She was still looking in the direction of the yard, and her pulse was throbbing and racing so hard that it was almost physically painful. Garler had seen nothing; Deenor had glimpsed but was oblivious now. But *she* had seen, clearly and surely, in the moment before the figure flitted away.

Robin, at the gate, waiting for her to return. At the sight of the approaching cart he had gone, concealing himself, she suspected, in the deepest shadow by the barn, but she had the feeling that he had deliberately waited for her to see him before fleeing.

'Carys?' Deenor inquired. She slipped one hand into Carys's, squeezed her fingers. 'Garler's right, there *is* no one there. I must have imagined it.'

Carys nodded, but couldn't trust herself to reply.

'Would you like us to come into the house with you?' Deenor persisted. 'Just in case . . . ?'

Garler grunted disparagingly, and Carys shook her head. 'No – no, thank you, Deenor, I'll be well enough. There's no one there, as you say, so I've nothing to fear.'

The cart moved on to the gate. Garler climbed down, unhooked the latch, then returned and drove slowly through the gap. Carys knew she must not look back, but she could feel Robin's invisible presence as the cart halted again and Garler helped her down.

'Now, are you *sure* you don't want—' Deenor began.

Carys interrupted, though kindly. '*Truly*, Deenor. We're all tired, and you've a way to go yet. Good night. Good night, Garler.'

She watched, trying to contain her impatience, as Garler slowly and carefully turned the cart around. She could hear Fleet snuffling on the other side of the kitchen door, but he did not bark, and nor did she open the door to give him the greeting he wanted. The cart started off, stopped again for Garler to close the gate (frustration roiled in Carys at the ponderous deliberation of his every movement), then finally they were away and the night enclosed and swallowed them.

As the sound of hooves and wheels faded, Carys stumbled across the slippery yard at a run.

'Robin?' Slithering to a halt she peered into the dark by the barn but saw nothing, 'Robin! They're gone, it's safe now . . .'

He emerged, not from where she had thought him to be but from another, further hiding place.

'Carys.' He didn't come to her but stayed a few steps off, gazing at her. 'You didn't call to me.'

'No . . .' she said. 'I've been to Merion Blacksmith's house. For Midwinter-feast.'

'Ah.' He looked down at the ground. 'I thought you would see the turning of the year with me.'

A twinge of guilt made Carys defensive. 'We have so many other nights, Robin. This was . . . I was invited. A special occasion.' She did not want to tell him that the prospect of shivering on the hill or in the woods on Midwinter night, even with him, had been less appealing than the prospect of a warm fire, food and drink and cheerful company. That would have been unkind, even though it was the truth.

Or was it? Back came the old confusion yet again, and Carys shook her head, trying to push away what she could not understand.

'I'm here now,' she said, not sure whether the trace of resentment she felt spilled into her voice. 'There's time enough left for us – isn't there?'

A ghost of a smile showed on Robin's face. 'Yes. There's time.'

He did come forward then, hands outstretched to take hers and lead her away. 'Robin, no,' she said. 'It's so *cold*. If you can't come to the house, at least let us go into the barn. That must be possible for you?'

He hesitated. 'It is. But the woods—'

'*No!*' It was vehement, adamant. 'I won't go to the woods.'

'Even if I pledge to keep you warm?'

'Even then. I'm *tired*, and I'm already chilled half to the bone. The barn it must be, or . . . or I will not stay with you tonight.'

She wondered briefly if she had misjudged, and he would rise to her challenge and walk away. He did not. His fingers traced a light pattern over her hand as he held it, and he said, 'Very well. Let it be as you wish.'

The heavy barn door groaned and scraped open, eliciting soft rustles from among the hay-bales as the six cats stirred at the disturbance. Carys saw one pair of eyes, amber sparks in deep gloom, then they vanished and all was silent again.

Robin entered slowly and, it seemed to her, a little reluctantly, staring into the darkness but saying nothing.

'Wait,' Carys said. 'There's a lantern . . .' She found it and a flint-box, carefully lit the lantern and set it on a ledge well away from the bales.

Robin rubbed his eyes and blinked, as though he found the light uncomfortable. He gazed around, still silent for some moments. Then: 'So many things . . . They were his? Your husband's?' He paused. 'They must remind you of him.'

It hadn't occurred to Carys to look at the barn's mundane contents in such a way. Scythes, pitchforks, spades, the plough (which this year must have new shares; the old ones had been honed so many times that there was barely anything left of them). To her, they were simply the everyday implements of the farm, and had no particular connotation with anyone or anything.

'There's no reason why they should remind me of Jone,' she said. 'They're only tools, and besides, they're mine now.' She gave a self-conscious laugh. 'Do you know, people are already calling this "Carys's farm"?'

'Yes,' Robin said. 'So I've heard.'

'Oh.' She had hoped to impress him, but shrugged off her disappointment (though a part of her asked: *how* did he know? *How* had he heard?). 'Well, it's fitting, I suppose,' she continued lightly.

'Indeed. You've done well and bravely.'

'And will continue to do so. I'm determined on that.'

'And it makes me happy to hear you say so. You know, don't you, that my only purpose and pleasure is to help you gain your heart's desire?'

'Yes.' She nodded. 'But . . .'

She didn't finish, and he prompted, 'But?'

'Ohh . . . You *can't* give me my heart's desire, can you? You know what it is – it's to be with you, *truly* with you, not just in the night but in the day as well. I want you to be always here, at this farm, at my home.' Abruptly and directly she looked him in the eye. 'Isn't it yours, too? Isn't it the reason why you came tonight, without my calling you? Midwinter-feast, the turn of the year. You *needed* to be with me.'

Robin sighed. 'That's true, yes. But there's something else as well. Carys, I – I have to go away.'

'*What?*'

'Wait, hear me out. It won't be for long; a month, perhaps. But I *must* go. I've no other choice.'

Carys's hands clutched at his upper arms. 'Where?' she demanded. 'Where are you going?'

'I can't tell you. Please, love, believe me when I tell you I don't want this. As I said, I have no choice. I *will* come back, though. I promise it.'

She took a grip on herself with difficulty, and when she spoke again her voice was calmer. 'A month . . . ?'

'Or perhaps a little more, I can't be certain. But if you call to me on Plough Night, I'll answer you.'

Plough Night . . . the beginning of Ash-month. It seemed an eternity into the future, and Carys's spirits shrank dully from the thought of it.

'I don't understand,' she said unhappily. '*Why* must you go, Robin? It isn't fair to me – or to you.'

'I know. But nothing we say or do can change it.'

'How will I bear so much time without you?'

He smiled, an odd little smile. 'You'll have a great deal to occupy you, I suspect. You might even forget all about me.'

'*Never!*' she flared, her hands gripping him again.

'I trust not.' Another, kindlier smile suggested that he had merely been jesting with her and acknowledged that the joke had been misplaced. 'But while I'm gone, there is something you can do for me, if you will.'

'What is it?'

He hesitated. 'It might seem a strange request, but . . . this coming year, when you sow your land, put up a scarecrow in the field by the woods.'

A small, uncanny chill stirred in Carys. 'Why?'

'Because I ask it of you. Please. Will you do it?'

If it was what he wanted, how could she refuse? 'Yes,' Carys said. 'I will.'

'Thank you, dear love. And please . . . make this scarecrow anew, with your own hands and without help from anyone.'

She was perplexed and inexplicably unnerved by the request, but she would do as he asked and trust in him. She nodded, and Robin's demeanour visibly eased. He drew her to him, stroking her hair.

'This is our last night for a while, then, my Carys. Shall we make of it what we can?'

His hands moved gently, cajolingly, over her body, and she felt the answering call of her own desire beginning to awaken. She tensed a little, felt his warmth, the touch of his breath on her face.

'Come,' she whispered. 'Here, with me, where the hay is deeper.'

She drew him with her towards the further end of the barn, where the bales were stacked high. Past the wall of the highest stack they turned – and Robin stopped, staring at what was suddenly revealed.

Carys had forgotten the Harvest King. After the feast, when the

208

old King was burned, he had been carried back to the farm where he was created, and here he would stay until summer came again, and the crops ripened, and it would be time for him to give up his crown and his place to a new successor. Now he stood huge and silent, faintly illuminated by what little lamplight could reach him, dull gold against the dimmer gold of the bales.

The warm colour had drained from Robin's skin. For some time he and the King regarded each other, and to Carys's imagination it was as if some unspoken, unnameable communication passed between them, with a significance that she could not hope to comprehend.

Then, abruptly the spell broke and Robin turned away.

'Not here,' he said hoarsely. '*Please.*'

Grasping hold of her hand he all but pulled Carys back to the other side of the barn, out of the King's sight, out of his reach. A cat slid quickly away at their approach, and they found a place where some of the bales had been cleared and there was a hollow, shielded to either side by the higher walls of the stacks.

Robin said, 'Here,' and drew her down with him, reaching out to her, embracing her tightly as if she were a refuge. 'Hold me,' he said. And Carys did, not knowing what troubled him, unable to ask, only aware that he needed her and that, at this moment, it was he and not she who was afraid.

Chapter XVIII

Carys was woken by the lowing of the cows in the byre. For several seconds she could not think where she was, then, as her eyes adjusted to the pearl-grey dawn, she remembered. The barn, the hay, Robin . . . She sat up, wincing at the protests of muscles stiffened by cold, and peered into the dimness around her.

He had gone, of course, vanished with the first omen of sunrise. And she had not been awake to bid him goodbye. She hadn't wanted to fall asleep, but the feast and the lateness of the hour and their lovemaking had all conspired against her, and eventually she had had no choice. Her last memory before sleep had come was of Robin's arm about her waist, and Robin's face looking into hers, and of one kiss, light and gentle, almost a salute, but lingering on her brow.

And now she would not see him for a month or more. The thought made Carys feel hollow and empty, as though some vital part of herself had been stolen away while she slept and left her only half complete. She wanted to cry, but sternly held the tears back, telling herself that weeping was a fool's distraction and the time would pass and be gone soon enough. Robin had said, again, that she would have much to occupy her in his absence. He had also said: 'Use your gift well', and something in his voice had made it sound like a plea, as if he thought – or feared – that she would *not* use it well. Carys made a sound that hovered between laughter and a choked-off sob. No need for him to fret. Who could have anything to fear from her?

The cows' noise was becoming more insistent; their udders were heavy and tight, and they wanted the relief of milking. And she was so *cold*. There would barely be time to stoke up the range and ease the sensation of ice in her bones before Izzy, Lob and the village girl all arrived and the day's work must begin. Was it really only last night that they had celebrated Midwinter-feast? Doubtless there would be a few sore heads around the district this morning. Izzy for one; for all her righteous airs she liked her tipple, and suddenly, despite her mood, Carys smiled. She had a remedy for too much drink; a little drastic, but reliable. Perhaps it would be as well to mix a pot and set it to brew . . .

Still stiff, and moving awkwardly, she climbed from the nest of hay and rubbed briskly at her numb legs before leaving the barn. Outside, the light was growing and with it an unpleasant north-east wind. As Carys started across the yard, Fleet began to bark in the house, as though he sensed her presence. He must have wondered at her long absence, but throughout the night, while Robin was here, he had not made a sound.

The wind came nipping and biting, making her shiver. Pushing her hands into her sleeves, Carys quickened her pace, anxious for warmth and the kitchen and a good, hot breakfast.

The days after Midwinter-feast settled into a mundane routine of necessary work, with little leisure time and few excuses for any festivity to brighten the long evenings. Carys had warned her neighbours that the thaw would be short-lived and the frost would return before long, which proved true. She also continued to mix her simples for those who asked, and for a few who hoped but did not have the courage to ask, and their efficacy, coupled with her uncanny weather-sense, built further on the reputation she was acquiring.

Then, at the beginning of Rowan-month, ring-fever came to the district.

Ring-fever was especially dangerous to children, and all the more so when it struck in the depths of winter. Jem Apothecary's remedies brought some relief from the symptoms, but if the disease got a firm hold on a child there was nothing he could do, and survival was a lottery of luck and the child's own constitution. Carys had no illusions that her own potions were any better than Jem's; Garler's cough and Deenor's aching bones were one thing, but this ailment was too serious to be cured by hedgerow herbs. There was another possibility, however, but she was reluctant to use it.

Until one morning Gyll came to call, and sombrely told her that Padlow Holder's youngest daughter had taken the sickness and, despite Jem's best efforts, was failing fast.

'She's such a *sweet* child,' Gyll said worriedly. 'Good as gold, always bright and lively – until these past few days, that is. The terrible change in her is enough to break your heart. Padlow and Honna are beside themselves with fear.'

'You've seen her for yourself?' Carys asked.

Gyll nodded. 'Yesterday evening. Merion was called to mend a wheel at Padlow's holding, and I went with him, to inquire . . . Oh, Carys, there must be *something* that can be done!'

The child's symptoms, Carys discovered on further questioning, were advanced: high fever, red blotches on her face, neck and chest, and a racking, rattling cough that did little or nothing to clear the phlegm clogging her lungs.

'Jem has despaired,' Gyll said. 'He won't say so to Padlow and Honna, of course, but he confided to me . . .' She paused, looking at Carys keenly. 'You haven't sensed anything, have you? A premonition? If the little girl will – will live, or . . .'

'No.' Carys shook her head, glad that it was the truth.

Gyll sighed. 'All the same . . . there's little hope. She's so *weak*.' Again she hesitated, then: 'My dear, I – I know I shouldn't ask this of you, but – might there be some way in which *you* could help her?'

Carys had been waiting for this, dreading it. Gyll and all the others had such faith in her skills; they seemed to think her infallible, and it was hard, the hardest thing in the world, to make them understand that she was not.

'Gyll,' she said, 'I know no more than Jem Apothecary. Less, for he's schooled, and he has years of experience behind him. My potions are just simples. They might ease birth pangs or help a wound to heal, but they can't cure anything as serious as this!'

'But if you were to see her—'

'It would do no good! *Please* don't ask this of me, Gyll. I could achieve nothing of any use.'

Gyll bit her lower lip, as if summoning up the courage to speak bluntly. Then at last she said: 'I'm not talking about your potions, Carys. I'm talking about something else.'

Carys sat very still. 'What do you mean?'

'You know what I mean. We all remember very well what happened with Ready and Miracle. You saved both their lives, not with a simple but with . . .'

Gyll stopped. Carys knew that she had wanted to say the word *witchcraft*, but at the last moment her nerve had failed. Her meaning was clear in her eyes, though, as she looked at Carys steadily, almost challengingly.

Her gift. A spell, a weaving of natural forces, a calling to the old powers, to save the life of a child . . . *Could* she do it? Carys asked herself. To try would be to raise Padlow and Honna's hopes. If she failed, they would be more devastated than if she had done nothing at all.

Yet if she succeeded . . .

The internal arguments warred furiously, and Carys did not know what to do. But then she thought: what was there to lose by trying? If she turned her back on her neighbours in their time of need and their little girl died, could she live with the knowledge that she *might* have saved her? No guarantees or promises, perhaps not even much hope. But she surely could not deny the child a chance. Her gift.

Use it well.

She said: 'I'll go over this afternoon. Just to see . . .'

Quaking in her mind and in her shoes, Carys arrived later that day at Padlow's holding on the other side of Crede Hill. Padlow and

Honna were waiting anxiously, and Carys was a little dismayed to find Gyll and Juda there too, like spectators waiting for the play to begin.

The child was in a small upstairs room. The curtains were drawn and febrifuge herbs burned in a small brazier, clogging the air with a strong, acrid stench. Aware of the watchers crowding in behind her, Carys crossed to the bed. It took no expert knowledge to tell her that the child was mortally sick; as Gyll had said, her skin was covered with ringed crimson blotches, and her eyes were puffy, lips dry and cracked and throat visibly swollen. As Carys bent over her she went into a horrible spasm of coughing; Honna ran to her side, raising her and trying to make her spit up the foul stuff in her throat and lungs, but she could not, and after a few minutes she fell back, too exhausted even to cry.

Later, Carys had no clear memory of what she did. All she could recall was that, ignoring all protests and questions, she had crossed to the window and flung it wide open, letting in the daylight and the cold air. Smoke from the brazier eddied and was sucked away, and again Carys stared down at the child, feeling with her mind, her inner senses, for the hard, red core of the sickness. Padlow and Honna and Gyll and Juda seemed to fade away, retreating into some distant and meaningless otherworld, and when Carys found what she was looking for she began – so Gyll told her afterwards – to chant. She did not know how long the chanting went on, or what she said, or what, if anything, happened in the room. All she knew was that suddenly it was over, and she stood blinking and swaying on her feet, feeling as though she had surfaced from some deep, dark place and returned to the light.

She could hear the child breathing. Ragged, uneven. What did it mean? Had she achieved anything at all, or had this been to no purpose?

'I think . . .' she said in a weak, faraway voice, 'that I would like to go home . . .'

No one argued with her. Honna was staring fixedly at the stricken child, her face displaying an awful, twisted look of hope and dread combined. She did not follow the others as Padlow, pallid and haggard, led them back down the creaking staircase. He tried once, haltingly, to offer Carys a brew of tea but seemed relieved when she refused. Outside, Spry waited in the shafts of the small cart; shaking her head at Gyll's suggestion that she and Juda should see her home, Carys drove slowly away.

The sun was setting when Juda's gig came flying to the front of the farmhouse. It pulled up in a scatter of stones, and Juda jumped from the driving seat and rushed to the door. Her face was alight with incredulous excitement, and as Carys listened and tried to take in the garble of words, she proclaimed the news. An hour after Carys's departure, Padlow's daughter had suffered her most violent fit of coughing thus far – and the foulness inside her had come out at last. She had then begun to sweat profusely, a sure sign that the fever was breaking. And now, Juda added joyously, *now*, though still too weak to sit up unaided, she was asking for water and a little broth!

Carys shut her eyes and sent up a silent prayer of thankful relief. No matter whether she had truly had a hand in it or whether the breaking of the fever was mere coincidence, it had happened, and that was the important thing, the *wonderful* thing.

Juda departed for the smithy to impart the news to her good friend Gyll, and Carys sat down in the parlour and stared into the fire. Fleet came wriggling to her side, pushing his cold, wet nose into her hands where they lay slackly in her lap. After a few minutes she fondled his head, got up again and walked a little unsteadily into the kitchen.

It seemed the child would live. She was so glad.

She did not allow herself to think of what might have followed if the little girl had died.

The retrieval of Padlow and Honna's daughter from the very door of death (as it was viewed) was the talk of the parish within two days. And so was the means by which it had been achieved.

Gyll and Juda were wise enough, and respectful enough of

Carys's privacy, to have made no mention of spells or witchcraft or anything of that nature. But Padlow and his wife had no such reservations. Over and again they told their tale of what Carys had done, what Carys had said, the magic Carys had performed. The story grew with the telling, as stories always do, until Carys took on the stature of a wisewoman and miracle-worker the like of which had never been seen in the district before.

She knew little of the gossip to begin with. The sheep were suffering in the renewed cold weather, and she and Garler and any other hands they could muster had as much work as they could cope with to keep the toll on the flocks to a minimum. Carys was often to be seen tramping the hill pastures in a man's oversized coat, breeches and heavy boots, a broad-brimmed hat jammed on her head, a crook in her hand and Fleet shivering but resolute at her heels. Izzy managed the house, more or less, and several of the cows were in calf and thus needed no milking, but there was no room to spare for visits to the village or comfortable fireside chats with friends. Even her chapel-going was neglected; there simply wasn't time.

Then, midway through Rowan-month, the unexpected callers began to come to ask for her help.

Some, as before, wanted nothing more than a medicine, either for themselves or for their animals. But some sought a little more than that. A cow was soon to calve: could Carys say whether the calf would be a bull or a heifer? A spring had inexplicably stopped flowing: could Carys divine the cause of the trouble? Three kestrels had flown in line abreast over a holder's field this morning: could Carys say what the omen portended?

To her own surprise, Carys found that she was able to satisfy most of the petitioners who came to her door. As she had 'looked' for and found the core of the disease in Padlow Holder's child, so did she find the answers to their questions. She could not say how she did it, but the knowledge came; a part of her gift, a part of herself. She would take no payment for the help she gave, but she soon found that small tokens of appreciation were being left at her door. Woollen gloves. A length of ribbon. A cake. Goose eggs.

After a while, however, the nature of the requests started to change. The first inquirer was Bensel Taverner, keeper of the inn in the village, who drove to the farm one afternoon with his wife in her best visiting clothes beside him. Carys barely knew Bensel's family; Jone had not frequented the inn, and women did not go to such places without husbands to conduct them, so she was both surprised and intrigued by this unexpected call. The couple were clearly ill at ease when she invited them in, but they sat down in her parlour, and haltingly Bensel explained. The tavern was suffering from a run of small, nuisancy troubles. First it had been an inordinate number of breakages; then a rat had got into the larder and gnawed at all the foodstocks so that they had to be thrown away; then two casks of new beer had split for no apparent reason and caused a flood. They were, it seemed, being dogged by bad luck. Could Carys – *would* Carys – give them a charm to ward it off?

That night, when Izzy had gone and she was alone, Carys opened her front door to the waxing moon and, kneeling on the doorstep, made a good-luck spell for the tavern. She drew the symbol of it – an image inexplicable to her, but she knew it was right – on a scrap of paper, and when Bensel returned the next day she told him to place the paper under his taproom hearthstone at midnight and then, while holding his wife's hand, bow three times to the moon and say a prayer. The last instruction was pure invention, but Carys was wise enough to know that merely hiding the paper would not satisfy her customer's need for some element of drama. Bensel went away with cautious hope in his eyes, and Carys went to bed and dreamed a disturbing dream, in which Robin, in great pain, was calling to her, but however desperately she searched she could not find him.

Bensel Taverner's charm had the desired effect, and, like Padlow, Bensel was a talkative man. New word spread round the parish that Carys Jonewidow was not merely skilled in healing; she had *other* powers – and within days she also had other visitors seeking

218

to make use of them. On the whole they were simple requests. A young wife, heavy and terrified with her imminent first child, begging for a spell to ensure that nothing would go wrong. A lovelorn boy, hoping that a magic charm might succeed where natural charm had failed. A father whose son was travelling far away, asking the boon of a talisman to protect him from harm. They all came to Carys Jonewidow. They all came to the girl they were beginning to call their white witch.

Carys found the demands on her tiring. The casting of spells left her physically and mentally drained, and it was especially hard when her rare free hours were interrupted, as they often were, by yet another plea for help. But she could not bring herself to turn people away – and she had to admit that in truth she found great pleasure in her new fame. To be admired and liked and sought after; it was a happy feeling, a *good* feeling. Robin, she thought, would be glad for her.

Not that she had had much time to think of Robin since their last meeting on Midwinter night. Now and then she felt the lack of him, more so if she should happen to wake in the dead of night, when feelings of loneliness are at their most acute. But she did well enough without him. And soon the month would turn, Plough Night would come, and they would be together once more.

She had, however, fulfilled the last promise she had made to him. The new scarecrow was in the barn, half completed and sitting like a giant doll on a straw bale near the feet of the Harvest King. They made a bizarre pair, like two players in a cryptic mumming masque, and the scarecrow was very lifelike; disturbingly so in the opinions of Merion and Gyll and Izzy, though none of them liked to make any overt comment. Lob, for his part, would not go near the barn now, and even the stolid and unimaginative Garler thought it most peculiar that Carys should take so much trouble over what was, after all, only a device for keeping the birds from her newly sown crops.

Carys did not know what her friends were thinking, and if she had done, she would not have cared. The slow, painstaking creation of Robin's scarecrow was an absorbing occupation, and one in which she took fierce pride. She was even making clothes for it – jacket, trousers, neckcloth, all in bright colours and decorated with scraps of braid or ribbon to give them a festive air. Sometimes, late of an evening, she carried the doll into the house, sat it in a chair by the ingle and measured it for its finery. Occasionally, she talked to it. It was comforting to confide her secrets to a silent listener, and the scarecrow could never repeat them.

On one such evening, she and the scarecrow were keeping each other company when someone came to pay a call. Fleet, who had been asleep in his usual place on the hearth, woke, sprang up and barked a warning, and moments later Carys heard the crunch of hooves outside. A single horse, not drawing a conveyance of any kind but ridden. Fleet barked again, and tapping his head lightly to tell him to be silent, she went to the door.

The rider was dismounting, and by the light of the small lantern he carried she recognised Jem Apothecary.

'Jem . . .' A flicker of unease; what could he want with her at this hour? 'Is anything amiss?'

'No, no.' Jem smiled. 'Forgive me, Carys, I know it's an unusual time to call. But I need to speak with you.'

He had tied his horse to the wall ring and was approaching. Carys hesitated. Should she allow him in? Oh, nonsense; Jem was no threat, that wasn't his nature. Besides, she had Fleet to protect her if the need arose.

She stood back and he came into the parlour, removing his hat and making a courteous little bow to her as he stepped over the threshold. Fleet eyed him suspiciously, but Carys held up a warning finger and the dog subsided, though still alert.

'Sit down, Jem,' she said. 'And tell me what's to do.'

Jem made a move towards the ingle, then saw the scarecrow. He stopped, staring, his expression so astonished that Carys had to stifle a laugh.

'You – ah – you already have company,' he said pallidly. It was his attempt at a joke, and a means of trying to cover his confusion.

'Oh, that.' Carys waved a negligent hand. 'It's for Plough Night; a little amusement that Gyll Merionwife and I are planning.'

'Oh,' said Jem. 'Yes, I see . . .' He took a chair as far from the scarecrow as space allowed.

'You'll take tea?' she asked. 'Or would you better prefer cider?'

'Oh – ah, cider would be most pleasant. Thank you.'

He was staring at the scarecrow again when she returned with a jug and two beakers, and he jumped visibly as she came into his field of view. Carys filled the beakers, handed him one, then sat down herself and waited for him to explain his mission.

'Carys.' Clearly this was not going to be easy for Jem. 'I hope you won't think me impertinent.'

Carys said nothing.

'Impertinent, or . . . or hasty.' He licked his lips, gazed nervously into his cup. 'I have been greatly impressed by your – by the talent you have lately shown in curing sickness.' Looking up, he ventured a tentative smile. 'Perhaps I am in a better position than most to appreciate it, for it tallies so closely with my own calling.'

Thinking she knew where this was leading, Carys said, 'I trust my small efforts don't offend you, Jem? I wouldn't dream to try to poach your ground.'

'Oh, no, no, no, not at all!' Jem assured her hastily. 'Quite the contrary, indeed *quite* the contrary.'

'Ah,' said Carys. She had been wrong, then.

'I *admire* what you have done,' Jem went on. 'And it occurs to me that, as we are both – so to speak – striving for the same end and good, it would be the soundest of common sense to – to combine our skills, as it were.'

Carys was taken aback. 'You mean, you would like me to work with you?'

'Most certainly,' Jem smiled. 'Don't you think it an excellent idea?'

Carys certainly did not. However, neither was she anxious to offend him, so she chose her words carefully.

'Jem what you say is . . . most flattering, and you're very kind.

But I'm not an apothecary! I merely have some small ability with herbs and the like.' She smiled disingenuously. 'I never could be as wise or as clever as you, and I wouldn't pretend to be.'

'Of course you could not,' he agreed. 'You mistake me, dear Carys. What I am suggesting is not a partnership – at least, not in the sense of mere business.'

Carys tautened. 'Then I'm afraid I don't understand.'

'Don't you? Or is it shy modesty . . . ? Carys, I am proposing that you should become my *wife*.' He reached out as if to take her hand, but she drew back from him. Undaunted, he continued, 'Think, Carys, of what we could achieve together. I, known and respected and, I like to believe, admired in my profession; you by my side, my assistant and helpmeet. What could be more fitting? And what better solution to our mutual dilemma?'

Under cover of her apron, where she had pushed them, Carys's hands clenched into fists. 'What dilemma is that?' she asked.

'Well, it is twofold, isn't it? We are both lone souls in need of company. And we are both dedicated to the succour of our fellows. Yet that can give rise to confusion. A man falls sick: should he turn to Jem Apothecary, or to Carys? How much better if his solution were immediately obvious – to go to Jem Apothecary and Carys Jemwife together!' He smiled in his turn now, and sat back, satisfied that he had put his case and would receive a favourable answer.

Carys stood up. 'Jem,' she said. 'I am sorry, but I don't want to marry you.'

'Now now, my dear – I understand that it may be a little soon yet; you've been widowed only a few months and I'm not about to press you. All I ask now is your promise.'

'Which you can't have,' said Carys. 'I'm sorry. My answer is no.'

Jem sighed, smiling with the air of a patient mentor. 'My dear, you're still very young, and youth is impulsive. But I must be scrupulously fair. Very well, I shan't ask for a promise not yet. Take time to consider, and perhaps in a month or so—'

'*Jem.*'

Something in Carys's tone stopped him in mid-sentence. He looked at her with a blend of surprise and annoyance, and she said, 'It seems there's no kinder way to say this, so I'd best say it bluntly and leave no room for doubt. I will not marry you, Jem, not now, not next year, not ever. If you were the only eligible man in the entire district, I still wouldn't accept your proposal.' She turned to look at him, and there was an angry fire in her eyes. 'I may be young, but I'm old enough to see your motives. Yes, it would suit you well to have me for your wife, wouldn't it? You would own my property and be master of me, and you would see to it that my skills, which you compliment me so prettily on, were used only with your permission and under your direction. You don't want *me*, Jem Apothecary. You only want what I possess. Well, I tell you now, you shan't *ever* have it!'

Carys had never made such a speech in her life, and it was almost as much of a shock to her as it obviously was to Jem. He stared at her for some moments. Then, stiffly, he rose to his feet and placed his beaker carefully on the settle.

'I will take my leave of you, Carys.' His voice was severe and he was no longer smiling. In fact, there was a look in his eyes that Carys did not like at all. 'I'm sorry that you feel as you do. And I think you are making a grave mistake.'

'I do not think it,' said Carys.

'Clearly not. Time will judge which of us is right. I bear no grudges, I'm not that kind of a man. However . . . I think you will find your . . . *services* . . . a little less in demand in the future.'

Carys's eyes narrowed. 'Are you threatening—'

'I do not *threaten*, Carys. I simply state a fact. I have my living to consider. And, of course, the honour of my profession, which I cannot see brought into disrepute by charlatans.'

Her jaw clenched. 'Please leave my house.'

Jem bowed, gave her one last, cold look, and went. Leaning against the door, which still vibrated from the force with which she had slammed it, Carys heard his horse canter away, and as the hoofbeats diminished a thunderhead of rage came welling up in her. She had never *known* such anger; even when her father had tried to coerce her into giving up the farm to him, her fury had been controllable. This was *not* controllable. It was a colossal, all-consuming surge of hate.

She did not stop to consider; at this moment the ability wasn't in her. Launching herself away from the door, she strode to the middle of the parlour, spun round and raised her arms, stretching them out before her with fists clenched so tightly that the colour drained from her knuckles. The will was there, the knowledge was there; nothing else mattered, and she fired the full mental force of her hatred out like an arrow, hurling it into the dark, straight and irresistible, in the wake of Jem and his horse.

As suddenly as it had come, the bitter fury was gone, leaving her drained and weak and more miserable than she could remember feeling for a very long time. Tears prickled her eyes; she wiped them away. From the hearth, Fleet whined a concerned inquiry, and his tail beat against the flagstones.

Carys went slowly to the ingle. She did not sit down in her own chair; instead she sank to the floor at the feet of the scarecrow. Fleet wriggled to her, wanting to lick her face. She hugged him, and pressed her cheek against his rough, warm fur.

And slept.

As Jem Apothecary approached the village, something that might or might not have been a badger scuttered across the road in front of his horse. The animal reared, slipped on the half-frozen slush of the road, and fell, with Jem still in the saddle.

Barring a few bruises, the horse was unhurt.

Jem broke his leg.

Chapter XIX

The news of Jem Apothecary's accident put Carys in a ferment. Guilt at what she had done was rapidly followed by the dread of being found out, and for the best part of a day she went about the farm like a blank-eyed puppet, her mind roiling over her predicament and made worse by Izzy's gleeful determination to relate every detail of the incident that she knew, and a good few that she didn't.

But when evening came, and Izzy had gone, reason finally came to Carys's rescue. Firstly, no one knew about the curse she had flung after Jem, and unless he could see through solid walls, not even Jem himself had the least idea that she had done it. Secondly, she in her turn didn't know for certain that her action had caused the horse to slip and fall. The accident might have happened in any case. And thirdly, Jem would recover from his injury. Not to say that a broken leg wasn't serious, but it would mend. At least he wasn't dead (though last night she had wished . . . No, she told herself, don't even think about what she had wished). So, then. No one would link the mishap with her – according to Izzy, Jem claimed he was riding home from a visit to a patient, so clearly he did not want his true whereabouts to be known. She was safe from discovery, and the harm done was not irreparable. Some good might even come of it, for it would serve as a salutary lesson to control her temper.

Plough Night was approaching, and preparations for it were under way. The occasion was as its name suggested: heralding the time of ploughing for the spring-sown crops. There would be celebrations, though not on the same scale as harvest or Midwinter-feast, but more important to the farmers and holders was to ensure that animals and implements were fit and ready for their work. It was a busy time for Merion Blacksmith, Bartel Carpenter and others in like trades. And it proved to be a busy time for Carys, for with Jem laid up, the nearest available apothecary was three villages away, too far for anything but the greatest of emergencies. So, naturally, anyone who was ailing turned to Carys, and suddenly she found that the trickle of people coming to her door became first a stream, then a veritable flood. They sought her help and advice for everything from mild headaches to violent fits, and though she did her best for them all, Carys began to find the demands they made on her very tiring. They seemed to forget that, unlike Jem, she did not make her living from curing illness. She had a farm to run, and there simply were not enough hours in the day to cope with everything.

Matters came to a head on Plough Night itself. Carys had invited just a few of her closest friends to celebrate with her: Merion and Gyll, Garler and his family, Elios and Juda and, a little reluctantly (but it would have been unthinkable to exclude her) Izzy. The feast was a simple one, and the revelry would not go on late into the night, for the frosts had relented enough to make the land workable. Tomorrow at the chapel the preacher would invoke blessings for the work ahead, and the day after that the ploughing would begin.

They had finished the bacon and pease pudding and creamy potatoes, and Carys was serving a fine apple pie, when Fleet's sudden barking announced a new arrival, and moments later an urgent knocking came at the front door. Carys's heart skipped as she remembered her last unexpected caller, and she waited uneasily as Merion went to answer the knock.

A plump boy with a pockmarked face was outside. Carys did not recognise him, but he clearly knew who they all were, for breathlessly he said, begging Merion Blacksmith's pardon, but there was someone ailing and in trouble, and Jem Apothecary could not be called, and could Mistress Jonewidow come as quick as possible?

Carys, overhearing, went to join Merion at the door.

'Who is in trouble?' she asked the boy. 'What's amiss?'

He bobbed his head nervously. 'It's the baby, Mam; Missus says it's coming, and it's too early, and Young Missus is taking on something awful and—'

'What baby? Whose?'

Merion spoke before the boy could. 'This is Jemp Holder's farm boy, Carys. He must mean your sister, Nellen.'

The concern that had been rising in Carys abruptly faded. 'Oh,' she said disinterestedly.

'Hurry, Mam!' the boy pleaded. 'I got the cart waiting, and Missus says there's no time to lose in case she might die!'

'She won't die,' Carys told him. 'I've said this before and I'll say it again: there's nothing wrong with her, and the child will be born healthy. Go back and tell her so. And tell her that it will all be done by tomorrow noon.'

The lad gaped, and Merion said, 'Carys, she's your own *sister*.'

Carys shrugged.

'You'll not go?'

'No. There's no need.'

The other women exchanged uneasy glances, and Deenor said, 'Surely *someone* should help? If there's only Jemp's mother to cope with it all . . . I've dealt with lying-ins before now. I'll see what I can do.' She stood up, gathered her shawl and gave the boy a reassuring smile. 'Don't fret, lad. Mistress Jonewidow is . . . too busy to help now, but I shall come with you.'

Everyone else was looking at Carys; she could feel their disapproval like a palpable colour in the air. She turned away, pretending to busy herself with the apple pie, and only looked round again when the door had shut behind Deenor and the boy. They were all still looking, and there was silence for some while, until Gyll broke it.

'Well,' she said, a little sadly. 'I must confess I'm surprised, Carys.'

'I'm not,' declared Izzy. 'Sister or not, that Nellen Jempwife's no friend to her and never has been. All her airs and graces; nice as you please when it suits her, and rude as you please when it doesn't. If you ask me—'

'That's enough, Izzy,' Carys interrupted sharply. It was true that dislike of Nellen had played a part in her decision, but there was more to it than that. This latest incident had simply been the final straw; yet another intrusion on her time and her life, with the blithe assumption that she had nothing better, or even nothing else at all, to do. She would have refused anyone tonight.

Especially tonight.

So she tried to explain to her friends, and they tried to understand. But the men were frowning, and the women – excepting Izzy – were uncomfortable, and the ease had gone out of the occasion. It wasn't long before the guests started to take their leave, Garler to Jemp Holder's house to see how Deenor was coping, the others to their various homes. Merion and Gyll took Izzy with them. They were the last to go, and as Merion helped Izzy into the gig, Gyll came back to where Carys stood at the door.

'Don't worry too much, Carys,' she said quietly so that Merion should not overhear. 'I do understand your feeling. Besides, you've known for a long time that all would be well with Nellen, haven't you?'

Carys nodded.

'And if you thought it would not, you'd have gone to her tonight.'

Another nod. There was no point in telling Gyll the truth, it would serve no purpose.

'You'll be at chapel for the blessings tomorrow?' Gyll went on.

'Yes, I – expect so.'

'Good. I'll see you then.'

'Good night, Gyll.' Impulsively, Carys hugged her. 'And thank you, for . . .' she didn't know quite how to finish.

Gyll smiled. 'I know. Good night, my dear.'

Carys did not go to chapel the next day, for that night, just as he had promised, Robin returned.

228

As if he had been waiting just out of sight of the house, he was there at the yard gate mere moments after she sent out her silent call. Carys ran to him and flung herself into his arms, kissing his face, his hair, his hands in a rapturous tide of welcome that took him aback.

'My love!' His face lit with delighted astonishment. 'What is this? Do I deserve it?'

'I've *missed* you so!' Carys told him. Which perhaps was not entirely true, but in the wake of this evening's small calamity she felt a great need to believe it, and to ally herself with him against the difficulties that the rest of the world seemed to be trying to heap upon her.

In the barn – well away from the Harvest King – she showed him the scarecrow, now almost complete. Robin was pleased, or perhaps relieved was a more accurate term, Carys thought curiously, though he did not explain why. And now that she looked more clearly at him, it seemed to her that he was not his customary self. The glow of health and energy was lessened, as if he had had some malaise from which he was not yet fully recovered.

'Robin,' she said, 'are you well?'

'Well?' He smiled brilliantly – but was there a touch of strain? – at her. 'Of course! How can I be anything else?'

'I don't know. To me, you look tired. As though something had drained the energy from you.'

'Oh, that . . . it's nothing. The season. I'll be right as a rainshower before you know it.' He kissed her. 'And I'm still strong enough for *you*.'

They laughed together, and out of sight of the Harvest King they became lovers again. Tonight, though, Carys did not fall asleep afterwards in Robin's arms. She wanted – needed – to talk to him, confide her troubles in a way she could do to no one else, not even Gyll, who understood far better than most.

So she told him of Nellen and the spoiled party.

'Did I do wrong?' she asked him. 'Should I have gone to her because she is my sister?'

229

Robin sighed. 'I can't answer your questions for you, Carys. It isn't my place – or my nature. It must be for you, and your conscience, to decide.'

A frown creased Carys's forehead. 'The child *will* be all right,' she said. 'Won't it? You can answer that question.'

'But don't need to, for you already know what the answer is.' He squeezed her hand. 'Trust yourself. Remember your gift.'

She nodded, and was silent for a few moments. Then: 'You told me to use my gift well. Before you went, you told me that.'

'I remember.'

'Well . . . once, I did not.'

'Ah . . .' said Robin.

Carys told him the sorry tale of Jem's visit and what had followed. He made no comment as he listened, and when she finished he still did not speak.

At last Carys could bear the silence no longer. 'Are you angry with me?' she asked in a subdued voice.

Robin seemed genuinely surprised. 'Angry? No. How can I be?'

'You have the right. You gave me the gift to use.'

He sat up, the hay rustling. 'No, Carys, I did not give it to you. It was yours from the start. I only unlocked it, and as such I have no right to say how it should be used.'

'But you told me—'

'I *asked*, love. I can do no more than that. The ultimate choice – and the ultimate responsibility – is yours.'

His words stirred a memory of the Wayfarer matriarch. She had spoken of responsibility, when she gave Carys the spell that had first called Robin to her. Carys wondered what she would have had to say about the incident with Jem, then put the consideration out of her mind. What did it matter what the matriarch thought? She might be wise, but she was not infallible and her word was not law. So long as Robin excused and did not censure her, she was content.

They stayed together in the barn for a while longer, talking more lightly and idly to relieve the mood before it could cloud their time together. Then Carys began to yawn.

'You're weary,' Robin said sympathetically. 'I've been selfish, kept you too long and too late.'

'Ohh . . . I'll do well enough.' Carys swallowed the largest yawn of all, and smiled an apology.

He kissed her nose. 'You should sleep. You'll have hard work in the days ahead; you need your strength.'

She hesitated, then reluctantly nodded. 'I've so enjoyed being with you tonight, Robin.'

'And I with you. As I always do.'

'But perhaps I should go.' She could, she knew, have settled down with him in the hay and slept in his arms until the sun rose. But memory of her last awaking here, the cold, the stiffness, the prickling discomfort . . . Her soft bed in the warm house was a more appealing prospect, even without Robin to share it.

She swung her legs over the edge of the stacked bales and let her feet dangle. There was a sense of contentment in her body and, though to a slightly lesser extent, in her mind. She had satisfied something within herself, and now it was time to be practical.

'I don't know when I can call you again,' she told him. Another yawn. 'It may be some days.'

'I'll wait.' But a shadow filled his eyes briefly. Seeing it, Carys was discomfited and looked away.

'Well, then . . . good night, dear Robin.' She slid down to the barn floor, straightening and brushing at the hay on her skirt.

'Carys . . .'

'Yes?' She turned. He was kneeling in the hay, watching her, and the shadow was still there.

'I can't tell you what you should do in any of your dealings with the world. But I can offer you advice – if you're willing to hear it.'

She frowned slightly. 'Of course,' she said.

'Then . . . take care of yourself, love. Your gift is a precious thing, but it's heady, like strong wine. And you are fragile.'

'Fragile?' Carys laughed, thinking of the work she did, the way her days were spent. 'Oh, no. I don't think so.'

231

'I mean it in a very different sense, and in that I think I'm right. So I only ask, for your sake – and for mine – take care of yourself.'

Carys was about to laugh again, but quelled it as she perceived a disturbing intensity in Robin's tone.

'You're not *afraid*, are you . . . ?' she said.

He did not reply immediately. When he did, his face was grave.

'Yes,' he said. 'A little. I am a little afraid for you.'

Nellen Jempwife's child was a girl. The labour had been hard and excruciatingly painful, but the mother survived and the baby was healthy.

They named her Tibba, after her grandmother, and the baptism took place at the chapel when ploughing was over and Nellen sufficiently recovered. Carys was not invited, and would not, anyway, have gone. She could hardly remember when she had last set foot in the chapel; once or twice since Jone's funeral, perhaps, but that was all, and the last occasion must have been months back. There was always so much else to do, and anyway, the preacher's sermons and the psalm-singing held no appeal for her; the one was not uplifting and the other was barely tuneful, so there seemed little point in it all.

She heard an account of the baptism from Juda, who had been there and was eager to regale her with details of hats, quarrels and gossip, including Powl Miller's ire at the fact that his first grandchild was not a boy. Apparently, said Juda, he was so put out that he had withheld a promised gift of money to Nellen and her husband. Guessing where Powl had expected to find that 'gift', Carys surmised that, for all his show of annoyance, he was probably relieved to have an excuse to break his promise.

As the first signs of spring began to show, the farmers and holders of the district consulted Carys, asking if the weather would soon allow the crop sowing to begin. Carys studied the land about her, and cast her runes (a new practice; she had not learned it in any structured way but, somehow, she knew what to do and that it was right), and said at length, yes, the season would be kind enough.

So, in a spell of quiet, almost windless days, lines of men and women bearing wooden boxes and with sacks on their backs could be seen moving like a slow tide over the fields, strewing the new furrows with the seed of the summer corn.

Like haymaking and harvest, the sowing was a communal affair, the work carried out field by field and everyone joining in. Carys took her turn with the rest, trudging steadily over the heavy ground amid a small army of neighbours and casual labour hired from the village and further afield. A fair number of the hired hands were strangers to her, but if she did not know them, it seemed they knew her, at least by repute. The women either smiled shyly or refused to look directly at her, but the men were more openly curious and interested. Some of the younger men tried to engage her in flirtatious talk. At first Carys was inclined to ignore them, but after a while her attitude thawed. A little harmless banter helped leaven the tedium of the work, and one or two of her admirers were quite handsome. It made a pleasant change to be in the company of men who were neither married nor at least twice her own age. She felt flattered by the attention. And if the women disliked the fun, and glared instead of joining in, that was no concern of hers.

When the sowing was over she held an impromptu celebration at the farmhouse, to which all who had helped were invited. Food was simple, drink plentiful and the parlour rang with noise and merriment. It delighted Carys's heart to see the house come alive in such a way; in Jone's day such a thing would have been unthinkable, but now Jone was gone and she was mistress here and could do as she pleased. So when a spontaneous band consisting of fiddle, shawm and two pipes struck up inexpertly but enthusiastically, she joined in with the younger revellers for two hours of exuberant dancing.

First one partner and then another and another claimed Carys, and by the time the band admitted defeat, having played every tune they knew at least three times, she was breathless and dishevelled and glowing with excitement. Of her friends – her older friends – only Gyll and Juda still remained. Garler and Deenor, who had

233

become more subdued as the party grew livelier, had left some time ago, and soon afterwards Merion and Elios had also departed, leaving their wives to stay to the end and help as promised with the clearing up. Gyll and Juda had joined in one or two dances but then refused any further invitations; they looked a little uncomfortable, but Carys was enjoying herself too much to give them more than a passing thought.

Eventually, though, she did call a halt to the revelry.

'It's well and good for the likes of you,' she said to the broad-shouldered, curly-haired, cheerful youth with whom she had danced the final dance. 'But some of us have *real* work to do in the morning!'

The youth, whose name was Rofe, grinned and replied saucily, 'I could work for *you*, Mistress. All night, if you wanted!'

Carys had had a lot of cider, and her burst of laughter turned heads. 'Go on with you!' She made a playful swipe at him. 'Go home and dream your dreams!'

At the door he put his arm round her waist, then, emboldened when she did not rebuff him, kissed her full on the mouth. Carys did push him away then, scolding him for his impudence, but her cheeks flushed pink with pleasure, and she watched from the threshold until he and his companions had vanished noisily into the night.

Gyll and Juda were already carrying dishes to the kitchen when she came back inside. The three of them cleared in silence for a while; Juda poured a kettle of hot water into the sink and began washing up, while Carys dried and Gyll went about setting the disarrayed parlour to rights. Then, as Gyll returned to the kitchen, Juda said with apparent casualness, 'That Rofe's a young rip. Handsome though, with his bright eyes and splendid hair. No wonder so many young girls sigh after him.'

It was as if her comment was a prearranged signal – which, Carys thought later, in all probability it was – for Gyll gave a light, artificial laugh and replied, 'Too many, by all accounts. You know Etty, Cotty Baker's eldest girl, is with child? Rumour is Rofe's the

234

father, though neither of them will own up to it.' She glanced at Carys, as apparently and unconvincingly casual as Juda. 'You should take care Carys, and not allow him too many liberties.'

Carys was too tipsy to take offence. 'Oh, nonsense!' she said. 'What's the harm in a few dances and a goodnight kiss? He's not wed to Etty, or anyone else.'

'That'll soon change, if his father has his way,' Juda told her. 'He wants Rofe to marry Sarl Farmer's daughter, over to the east side of Crede. Sarl's as keen for the match as he is, and she's a better catch than a baker's girl.'

Carys laughed immoderately. 'So he'll do as he's told, will he? Like Tally Rigswidow's son, with my sister!'

'As to that—' Juda began, but a shake of the head from Gyll, behind Carys's back, silenced her. A snippet of talk they had both heard a few days ago . . . but it was better not to impart it to Carys. If she did not find out, well and good; if she did, Gyll preferred not to be the one to blame for telling her.

'All the same,' she said, returning to the subject of Rofe, 'it's better to steer clear of the lad. He and Sarl's daughter *will* marry in time, no doubt of it. They're as good as pledged, whatever Etty's family might say.'

Carys shrugged. 'So, I wish them both well. But it hasn't happened yet, and until it does, why shouldn't Rofe enjoy himself as and where he pleases?'

'True,' said Gyll. 'Just so long as it isn't at your expense.'

Carys smiled at her, almost slyly. 'Oh, have no fear of that, Gyll. I'm not such a fool as Etty!'

Gyll and Juda left soon afterwards. No more had been said about Rofe; they had made their point and, for now, could do no more. Whether or not Carys would heed their advice remained to be seen, but as they climbed into Juda's gig and Juda turned the pony for the homeward drive, their faces were pensive and their thoughts concerned.

In the house, windows were darkening one by one as Carys extinguished the lamps and prepared to go to bed. She would lie comfortably and happily tonight, think of her party and savour, just a little, the brief flirtation she had enjoyed. As the gig departed, Gyll thought that she glimpsed a flick of movement where the track began. But it was gone in a moment, and the gig lamps revealed nothing, so she put it down to a trick of the eye (she was very tired) and quickly forgot it. Neither she nor Juda was aware of the shadowed figure that watched them go, then looked toward the house. The figure stayed for some time, motionless, patiently waiting. But no one emerged. Soon all the ground floor windows were in darkness, and a few minutes later the single light in an upstairs room dimmed, faded and was gone.

Only then did Robin turn and leave. His shoulders drooped as though in defeat, and the light had gone from his eyes. Once, from a distance, he looked back, seeing through the dark as no mortal man could have done. Then the patch of night around him shimmered and warped briefly, and the track was empty.

Chapter XX

The rumour that Gyll and Juda had heard concerning Thomsine's prospects did not reach Carys's ears for some while. Carys rarely had the time or the need to make the trek into the village, and those who came to the farm, whether to work or to make use of her skills, did not mention it.

Ash-month settled to a period of quiet, almost spring-like weather, which pleased Carys, who had forecast it, and the farmers, who had paid heed to her predictions. The corn seed came through the earth in a soft fuzz of new green shoots, and Carys duly placed her scarecrow, now completed and looking startlingly realistic, in the woodside field as Robin had requested. She meant to see him, to tell him what she had done, but somehow the chance did not arise. She was simply too busy.

And there was a new distraction in her life.

She had not been entirely surprised when, three days after her celebration, Rofe called at the farm. His mother had a touch of the ague, he said, and would be obliged if Mistress Carys could kindly mix her a posset to ease it. What with Jem Apothecary being laid up and all, if Mistress Carys could see her way . . . Carys smiled and said yes, she could, knowing all the while that the ague – if it existed at all – was a flimsy excuse. It was nearly evening, the day's outdoor work ended. Rofe had hoped to find her alone, and hoped to be invited to stay for a while.

She did invite him. It was harmless enough: a little chat that veered occasionally towards the suggestive, if not bawdy; a little flirtation; a kiss when he left that lasted longer than the first had

237

done. He went away under a bright moon, leaving Carys feeling oddly contented. There was something very *real* about Rofe. His solid, broad-shouldered build, the power of his laugh, which seemed to barrel out from somewhere deep inside him, the wholesome, earthy smell of his skin and his clothes, sturdy wool and leather that made her think of warm-furred animals and mulled beer and all manner of unlikely, foolish, homely things. Substantial, that was the word for him. Substantial, and very, very *human*.

Twice more Rofe came calling, and each time the talk became a little more intimate, the flirting a little more overt. Then, on his fourth visit, Carys found herself at a crossroads.

Rofe was already daring to touch her in ways that only Robin had touched her before, and she took delight in the light-hearted and, so far, harmless amorous play in which they indulged. But on this particular night the play grew more serious. Carys was highly aroused, and though she tried to draw back from the brink, the illicit excitement they both felt was too great a temptation. She knew she was encouraging him, she knew she should not, and she knew that unless she called a halt within the next few minutes they would pass the point of no return. She did not call a halt. Instead, as he pawed her body and nibbled her ears and her neck and writhed hungrily against her, she gripped his biceps and breathed a single word in his ear.

'Upstairs . . .'

She left lamps burning, the kitchen uncleaned, Fleet unfed, and without so much as a candle to light the way led him stumbling and laughing and still intimately touching up the creaking staircase and along the landing to her bedroom. The sheets were cold, which excited her still further, and when Rofe began eagerly to tug her undergarments away, she moaned her pleasure, all but overwhelmed by the surge of her desire.

He spread her legs, covering her body with his, and paused. 'Carys . . .' he said.

'Don't talk!' she mumbled, trying to bite his shoulder. 'Go on, go *on*!'

'No . . . I mean, what if – if anything *happened*? If you got . . .'

She realised what he meant, and laughed a throaty, sensuous laugh. 'Don't fret,' she told him. 'If I did, I'd know what to do about it. You're safe.'

'Sure?'

'*Sure!* Now don't talk, don't talk! Just—'

The command was cut off as he kissed her with all the greedy passion pent-up in him. The passion lasted only a minute before he spent himself uncontrollably in her. But he stayed, and in the night he took her a second and then a third time, and when the first streaks of dawn showed, Carys woke sated and contented with him sound asleep beside her.

She woke him, gave him breakfast and saw him go on his way, hurrying to his own home. The long walk would give him time in plenty to think of an excuse for his night's absence, and even if the excuse was not plausible, he would tell no one the truth about where he had been. He would not dare.

Carys smiled, flexed her back which ached deliciously, and went to fetch the pail for the morning milking.

It wasn't until Carys took time to pause and consider that she suspected her assurances to Rofe had been just a little glib. If anything were to happen . . . 'I'd know what to do about it,' she had told him. But would she? Turning the question over in her mind, she realised that in fact she would not. Amid all the skills her gift had given her, the knowledge of how to prevent an unwanted child, or to get rid of one already conceived, was not included. There had not been the need for it, after all. No one had ever asked her for such a remedy, and with Robin there had been no danger.

Now, though . . .

The thought of it nagged her all the rest of the day, and the night and day that followed. The answer to the dilemma was obvious, but Carys found it hard to face the prospect of summoning Robin and telling him what she wanted. He would ask her why she wanted it, and if she lied to him, she had the uncomfortable feeling that he would know it, and perceive the real truth.

She wished she had not been such a fool as to allow Rofe into her bed. Gyll had warned her about letting him take liberties, and though Carys had dismissed the advice at the time, she now saw the sense in it. She tried to cheer herself by thinking that probably there would be no repercussions.

But if there were, what then? What would she do?

Rofe came to the farm again that evening. Carys had not expected that, and was chagrined and, at first, a little aloof towards him. But she relented enough to let him into the parlour. And then she discovered that, as well (so he ardently declared) as wanting to see her again, he had another motive for this visit.

It seemed that the rumour about Rofe getting Cotty Baker's daughter with child was true. Cotty was raging about it, and he was a big, violent-tempered man; all he needed was one word of confirmation and Rofe would have a stark choice between marrying Etty and waking up bruised and broken in a ditch somewhere one morning. And that, Rofe added dismally, was to say nothing of what his own father would do. So far, Etty had refused to confess anything despite her family's threats. But that might change – well, girls were fickle, weren't they? You could never be sure which way they would jump. So . . .

'So?' Carys prompted when his tongue failed him at this point.

She knew what he wanted, of course. She herself had put the idea into his head as they lay in her bed together. A potion to rid Etty of her shame, and to put Rofe's hide out of danger.

It gave her the excuse she had been looking for.

This time, Rofe did not stay all night. But he did stay long enough, and again left Carys feeling sated and pleased, though perhaps with a faintly sour edge to her pleasure that had not been there on the previous occasion. She had seen Rofe's real colours tonight, and they were not quite as bright and unstained as she had at first believed. He was not in love with her, for all that he declared it to the rafters at the height of his amorousness. He simply lusted after her, as he had lusted after Etty, and she had been fool enough to be

240

flattered to the point where she gave him what he wanted.

Ah, well. It had been what she wanted, too, there was no denying that, and no call to feel piqued that she was merely one more notch on Rofe's tally-stick. If she wanted to look at it that way, she could always say that he was just one more notch on hers. Carys giggled to herself at that thought. It was nonsense, of course; it wasn't in her nature to behave like a trollop. She had enjoyed an interlude, that was all, and now, for the sake of good sense, it was probably time to call a halt. Probably. She would decide that when the moment came. Meanwhile, she would procure what Rofe wanted, and save him from Cotty Baker's wrath.

That night, she did at last summon Robin. When he appeared, he was reluctant to go with her to the barn but instead hung back, beyond the gate.

'It's a fine night,' he said to her. 'Can't we walk, as we used to?'

Carys was too preoccupied with other concerns to hear the wistfulness in his voice, and she shook her head. 'No, Robin, not now. I need your help again.'

She told him about the unwanted child, though she was careful not to mention any connection between herself and Rofe, implying that the plea had come from Etty. When Robin realised what she wanted, his expression changed.

'Carys, I don't want you to do this,' he said.

'Why?' Her voice became sharp suddenly. 'What do you mean?'

'I mean that you shouldn't be a part of it. You haven't the right to interfere in a matter like this.'

'Etty *asked* me to interfere!' Carys pointed out angrily. 'It's not *my* choice!'

'But it is. And if you do it, it will also become your responsibility.'

'Oh, responsibility, responsibility!' She pulled a face, then added sulkily, 'You sound like one of the preacher's sermons!'

'Don't you think that the preacher's sermons have some truth in them?'

Carys sighed exasperatedly. 'Robin, please don't be so dull! Etty is in straits and has asked for my help. Why should I not give it? It makes no difference to me, but it will make every difference to her. And there is a way, isn't there? There must be.'

'Yes,' said Robin quietly. 'There is.'

'Then tell me of it. Come, Robin, smile a little, and tell me. Why should we quarrel over something so unimportant?'

She touched his face. He didn't pull away, but she had the feeling that he wanted to, and, a little offended she withdrew her hand. 'Come,' she said again, with an edge to her voice. 'Or do you not care for me any more?'

His face flared. 'You know I do!'

'And anything that I ask of you, you will do if you can.'

A pause. ' . . . Yes.'

'Then do what I ask of you now. You must.'

He nodded. 'Yes. I must.' Slowly, he reached out with one hand. 'Come with me. I'll show you where to find what you need, and teach you the use of it. But Carys . . .'

Half-way through the gate she stopped. 'What is it?'

'Be careful in what you do. Please. Be careful.'

Carys closed the gate behind her and took his proffered hand. 'You dear fool,' she said tolerantly. 'Of course I will.'

Carys returned home with the remedy she wanted, which was part herb and part spell and, Robin had assured her, would not fail to work. She had also cajoled him into teaching her another spell, which would prevent a woman from conceiving if she did not wish to. That would also be passed on to Etty, and it might be useful, she thought, to remember it for herself in case of need.

She had let Robin make love to her in the woods as he wanted. But she had taken little real delight in it; to her it was more like payment, a favour given for a favour received. Robin might be more skilled a lover than Rofe, but Rofe was – what word had she used for him? Substantial, that was it. Substantial, and human in a way Robin could never be. The contrast, now that she had had the chance to test it, surprised her.

And in truth she was beginning to find Robin just the smallest piece boring. When she called him dull she had been teasing, but on reflection she felt that the tease was closer to the truth than she had realised. He was so intense, so serious; more like a faithful dog than a man. In the past she had found that delightful, but now, more often than not, it was tedious.

He had not asked her about Rofe. Whether that meant – as she hoped – that he had not the least inkling of what had happened, or whether he suspected but could not bring himself to challenge her, she did not know. Either way, it was a relief not to have that to contend with. Robin's attitude to her newest mission had been tiresome enough, without heaping more coals on the fire.

But no matter; she had gained what she had set out to gain, and that was what counted. When Rofe returned the next evening she told him to send Etty to her in two more days, when the full moon had passed – not before, she said, the moon must be waning. The time did not matter and nor did the pretext; Carys's household would not presume to question what Carys did. Rofe tried to express his gratitude by kissing her and hinting at more, but a sudden worm of discomfort moved in Carys and she pushed him away, telling him that enough was enough and he could thank her if the cure worked.

It did, and quickly. If Izzy speculated on a possible link between Etty's stammering, blushing appearance at the farm and the news, a few days later, that she had lost what she had never bargained for in the first place, the old woman knew better than to reveal her curiosity. Etty's family, too, kept their counsel; they were simply thankful that the whole thing could be swept out of the door and forgotten. And Rofe, of course, had his own reasons for staying silent.

But hints went round nevertheless. They came to Gyll's ears via Juda, who had heard them from Bensel Taverner's wife, who had been told directly by Tally Rigswidow (who, as Gyll was aware, had cause to be interested in Carys's doings). Tally in her turn had heard them from . . . well, Bensel's wife did not know, but she gathered it was a good friend, one who had Tally's best interests at heart.

When she had heard what Juda had to relate, Gyll was troubled. Tally Rigswidow was now officially betrothed to the preacher, so would certainly have told him this same tale, and that could spell trouble. The preacher did not approve of what he termed 'dabbling' with matters that, in his view, were the rightful domain of Providence. If Carys *was* responsible for Etty's relief, he would not look kindly on her at all. Gyll thought that Carys should be warned. But how to do it, when she could not be certain that this latest rumour was true? If it was not, Carys would be rightly outraged by the slur and Gyll would risk losing her friendship, which she most certainly did not want to do. But if it *was* true . . .

If it was, then it meant that Gyll's assessment of Carys was not as sound as she had fondly believed. On the night that the foal, Miracle, had been born, Merion had dubbed Carys a 'summer witch', which still seemed to Gyll to be an ideal description of the kindnesses she performed. Now, though, it seemed that a cold touch of winter might be creeping in to taint the summer brightness. Admittedly it was just one dubious deed – assuming, of course, that it had happened at all. But if it had, then it had cast a shadow on what Gyll had thought to be a strong and stainless character.

Uncertain and a little afraid, she did not know what to do. To ask Merion's advice was the obvious thing, but somehow, Gyll could not bring herself to do that. Men did not see things in the way that women did; to them, a thing either was or it was not, with no middle ground between. Merion would support Carys outright or condemn her outright, and it was not time, yet, for a decision like that to be made. So Gyll listened, and said nothing, and did nothing, and continued to worry.

What Gyll did not know, and Carys did not tell her, was that there was a new influx of callers at the farm.

It began with Rofe, who brought her two pairs of white stockings. Carys sensed that they were a gratitude gift from Etty or possibly even Etty's mother, a tacit acknowledgement of the service she had done the family. Rofe, though, pretended otherwise. He claimed that he had bought the stockings himself at Fendrow Draper's in town last market day, and he made it abundantly clear that he expected to watch Carys put them on, then take them off again with his own hands and a good deal more after that.

At this blatant suggestiveness something in Carys shrivelled. 'Rofe,' she said, 'don't be so foolish.'

'Foolish?' he repeated, grinning lasciviously. 'Oh, yes. Oh, *yes!*'

Echoes of Jem Apothecary reverberated in Carys's mind, and she turned sharply away. 'I'm not gaming with you, Rofe. Go away.' Suddenly she saw him as a child, despite the fact that he was a year older than she was. A silly, selfish child, who had had his pleasure with her and now complacently wanted to carry on the play as and when it suited him. Something Izzy had said yesterday came to mind, and she added, 'I hear that you're to be wed.'

'What?' He looked surprised she saw, as she glanced at him over her shoulder.

'To Sarl Farmer's daughter. I hear it's all arranged.'

'Oh – oh, that. Well, yes. Now that the trouble with Etty's over—'

'You can have the dowry Sarl Farmer's offering for his girl. You'll live well on that.'

Rofe shrugged. 'Well enough.'

'And until you're wed, you can continue to have your dalliances. So long as they're *safe*, of course.' She smiled coquettishly at him, knowing that he would not see the pretence in it. 'Maybe even after you're wed, eh? If she doesn't turn out to be exciting enough for you.'

Rofe turned red, but another grin spread across his face and he advanced a step towards her. 'Well . . .'

'Go away, Rofe,' she said. 'Go away from my farm. I don't want you here any more.'

He was nonplussed. 'What have I done?'

'You've done enough. You've had your fun, and so have I, and now there'll be no more.'

'But why, Carys?'

'Because I say so. Take your bride, and behave properly to her, and if you've any sense at all, don't go looking for other girls.'

Some glimmer of the truth dawned and he said, 'You're jealous, aren't you? There's no call – I love you, Carys, I do!'

Carys laughed. 'Yes, yes. Just as you love Etty and I don't doubt plenty of others; any who'll give you encouragement!' The laughter subsided. 'Well, *I* don't love *you*. I'm tired of you. So go away.'

She knew she had wounded his pride, but she was unmoved; in truth it would probably do him good, and for two days she thought no more about it. Then, early one morning, the next callers came. Two girls – sisters whom Carys knew only by sight, and whose father had a smallholding a few miles away – who giggled and whispered at the yard gate before finally plucking up the courage to venture to the byre where Carys was milking. Lob was there too, putting new straw in the cows' stalls. He gawped and dribbled at the new arrivals until they turned beetroot-red and hid their faces, and Carys was obliged to steer him out of the door and set him to a new task before she could get any sense out of her visitors.

The girls, it seemed, were acquaintances of Etty's, and they clearly knew her story. What they wanted was the same 'witching', as they put it, that Etty had been given to stop her from making the same mistake again.

Carys saw no point in refusing. The girls obviously intended to do what they should not, with or without the means of doing it safely; better, then, to help them avoid the consequences. With a sigh she told them to return in two hours. When they did, she gave them what they wanted, adding a sharp warning not to tattle about it, as she had better things to do than spend all her time saving silly feather-heads from their own folly. The girls looked askance at this – Carys was hardly older than they – and then one whispered something in her sister's ear. Carys heard only two words, but they were enough.

' . . . *with Rofe* . . .'

Something in her turned to acid, and as the girls made to leave she said tartly, 'Haven't you forgotten something?'

They looked blank. 'Forgotten . . . ?' echoed the whisperer.

'Yes. Payment. Money.'

'But we thought – Etty said—'

'Etty says altogether too much, in my view,' Carys retorted. 'From you, I want payment.' She held out one hand and named a sum; not much, and she knew they could well afford it, and smiled grimly as they dutifully handed the coins over. Lob came shambling from the chicken arks to stare again as they left. Carys shouted at him to get back to his work, then went into the house and slammed the door.

Damn those two giggling geese! The money in her hand felt unclean, and she smacked it down on the parlour dresser, not wanting to have any contact with it. She had *never* asked payment before, but that last, petty incident had triggered her anger and she had demanded the money almost before she realised what she was doing. So, Rofe had been bragging, or at the very least hinting, about their encounters, had he? She should have anticipated that. She should have had more sense.

Then, suddenly she began to see the funny side of it. She might have been a fool, but Rofe was a bigger one, to go braying like a donkey about his own prowess. Most boys boasted, and few people believed them. It was nothing to her. Nothing at all.

She looked at the dresser. Her sense of principle was nagging her to give the money back, but her heavy boots needed mending, and it would just cover the cost nicely. So perhaps she would harness Spry in the trap, drive to the village and leave the boots with Corl Shoemaker, then pay a social call on Gyll. Just for once, let principle be damned.

She scooped the coins up once more (they did not feel so tainted now) and put them safely, comfortably in her purse, away from Izzy's curious eyes.

It made a pleasant change to be driving rather than walking, and on a level road rather than a rutted track. The trap spanked gaily along, with Spry living up to his name in the shafts. He was so exuberant that several times Carys had to check him from breaking into a spirited canter, and with the sun shining and the wind light, she found herself catching his mood.

At the start of the long village street she slowed Spry to a walk. A number of people were about, and most smiled or nodded a greeting to Carys. A few, though, only looked at her in silence and then turned away. Carys was not altogether surprised, and it did not concern her. The silent ones were spiteful tabbies for the most part, and bound to disapprove of anyone who did not entirely follow their own small-minded ways. Most were not of their ilk. Ina Bartelwife, for instance, dawdling at the gate of Bartel's yard, beamed and waved at her, and as she passed the inn, Bensel Taverner looked up from rolling casks to his cellar and shouted a cheerful 'Good day.'

Carys drew up outside Corl Shoemaker's door, tied Spry to a handy ring and went through the low door with its pinging bell and three steps down into the shop. Corl already had a customer: a plump woman whom Carys did not know. They smiled at each other but said nothing, and the woman left a few minutes later.

Corl greeted Carys cordially, almost effusively. Most surely he could mend the boots, yes, all could be restitched, and as for the soles, did she simply want the worn patches strengthening, or would completely new ones be preferable?

'Well, I don't know,' Carys said. 'What is the difference in cost?'

'Ah . . . now, it may be that . . .' Corl took a peek through the thick glass of the window, as if to be sure that no one else was likely to come in. Then he cleared his throat. 'It might be, Mistress, that there will be no charge at all. We might call it, payment in kind . . . ?'

He made a question of the last statement and waited, eyebrows raised invitingly, for her to respond.

'Oh,' said Carys. 'Well . . . what is it you would want from me?'

Corl looked relieved. 'Normally, of course, I wouldn't dream to resort to – oh, please, sit down, sit down!' Carys sat and he continued.

'I wouldn't dream to resort to such measures, but in truth, Mistress Carys, I am at my wits' end. It's Bensel Taverner – I don't doubt you'll have heard the story, it was all over the village . . .'

'Ah,' said Carys. 'The new boots?'

'Indeed, the new boots. Bensel *still* refuses to pay for them! He says they don't fit, and this is wrong and that is wrong, and though I have turned myself upside-down and inside-out in my efforts to accommodate him, he now wants to give the boots back and pay me not a grain for any of my work. Well, I ask you, how can I resell boots to one man that were made to fit another? I am a *craftsman*!'

Carys said sympathetically, 'I'm very sorry to hear of your trouble.'

'Thank you, you're most kind. So *in* your kindness, I wonder – can *you* make him pay the money he owes?'

'Me?' She was startled. 'How?'

'With one of your spells. An enchantment, a bewitchment, to gain my just due.'

There was a brief silence. Then Carys said, 'I'm sorry, Corl, but I think you make a mistake. I'm not a witch.'

Corl's eyes narrowed perceptibly. 'Oh, come now, Mistress Carys. Everyone knows what you can do. And it doesn't stop at cures for ailments.' His look became sly. 'I've seen the charm you gave Bensel, you know.'

It occurred to Carys to ask what Corl had been doing in the tavern at all if he and Bensel were at such odds, but she did not pursue that.

'I'm sorry,' she said again, thinking quickly and looking for a way out. 'I might have some small talent for charms and the like, but what you ask . . . I can't do it. I don't know how.'

Corl looked so crestfallen that she added impulsively, 'I would help you if I could, Corl, truly. But this is beyond my skill.'

Corl nodded and sighed. 'Ah, well. I had hoped . . . but there, what is, is, and we must accept it. Now, your boots. I am a little busy at present, but I believe I can have them ready in four days' time. Will that suit?'

Carys left the shop a few minutes later. She had insisted on paying Corl in advance, which seemed to make up to some degree for his disappointment, and he ushered her out with an affable smile.

Climbing into the trap, she turned Spry's head in the direction of Merion Blacksmith's forge, which lay at the far end of the village, beyond the chapel. Passing a side street, she did not see the figure that emerged and stared after her; only when her name was suddenly and unexpectedly shrieked, like the screech of a wildcat, did she start with surprise and turn her head.

A young woman was running along the road towards the trap. She had hitched up her skirt and was holding her hat to stop it blowing away, and instinctively Carys reined in to allow her to catch up. Someone in need of help – but then the supposition collapsed as she recognised the racing figure. It was her sister, Thomsine.

'*You!*' Thomsine slewed to a halt in front of the trap and grabbed the bridle, making Spry lunge with fright. Jerking viciously on the reins she screamed, 'You slut, you trull, you serpent! I hate you! *I hate you!*'

Carys's jaw dropped. 'Thomsine—'

'Don't speak to me, don't *dare*!' Thomsine's face was twisted and grotesque, and her cheeks burned apoplectic scarlet with a rage that was completely out of control. 'You know what you've done, don't you? *Don't you?*' She raised a quaking fist, as though it held a knife. 'My whole life's ruined, *everything's* ruined – *and it's all because of you!*'

Chapter XXI

'Hold the pony!'

'Mind, he'll kick you!'

'Thomsine! Come *away*, girl, don't be so foolish!'

'Making such an exhibition—'

'Now, shouldn't we all calm down and be sensible—'

The noise and flurry as a dozen or more people intervened in the fracas had Spry rearing in the shafts and Carys almost flung sideways from the trap's driving seat. At last, though, some measure of order began to emerge from the chaos. Spry stood still, though tense and shuddering, long enough for Carys to scramble down to the ground, where she held on to the high wheel-guard as she caught her breath. Faces crowded round: traders who had come running from their shops, two women who had been gossiping on a doorstep, and the preacher, summoned from his house beside the chapel by an agitated child convinced that someone was being murdered. Thomsine stood shaking and crimson-faced on the edge of the small crowd, held back by an older woman and man who had no desire to see such a murder done. Then, as the chattering and questions and opinions started to swell again, the preacher elbowed his way to Carys and laid an authoritative hand on her arm.

'You'd best come to my house and rest for a few minutes,' he told her firmly. 'Someone will see for your pony. Come along, now, come along.'

Thomsine shouted, '*She isn't*—' but the preacher turned a basilisk stare on her.

'Enough, Thomsine! If you have something to say, you may say

251

it at a proper time. Go home to your mother.'

Carys and Thomsine were steered away in opposite directions, Carys towards the preacher's house, Thomsine in the midst of a cluster of sympathetically clucking women. Carys still had not the least idea why Thomsine had attacked her in such a way – something about her life being ruined, and it all being Carys's fault – she couldn't imagine what had happened.

She was soon to find out. Though the preacher's manner towards her was benign, his face was not friendly, and when he led her into his parlour he wasted no time.

'Well, Carys,' he said. 'A very sorry business, and it was quite wrong of Thomsine to behave in such an unseemly way. But one cannot entirely blame her, can one?'

'I'm sorry,' Carys told him. 'I don't understand. Why should she turn on me in that way?'

The preacher looked surprised. 'Surely even you must acknowledge that she has cause! Or do you consider the spoiling of your sister's marriage chances a trivial thing?'

Carys's jaw dropped. 'Spoiling of her chances? Whatever do you mean?'

'You're saying you don't know?'

'Know *what*?' Carys was becoming more frustrated by the moment. 'All I've heard is that my sister is likely to wed Tally Rigswidow's son. Do you mean she's not to after all?'

The preacher looked searchingly at her, and belatedly realised that she was not up to date with the news. 'Of course,' he said at last, musingly. 'You've not ventured to the village for some time, have you? Not even to chapel.' This with a faint barb in his voice.

'I've been too busy,' Carys said defensively.

'Ye-es. With Jem Apothecary laid up, I imagine you have . . . Well then, I'd best tell you and have done with it. Your sister is *not* to marry Tally's son, for I – and Tally – have forbidden it.'

She was astounded. 'Why?'

His mouth pursed. 'It pains me to have to put it bluntly, but I must. Thomsine is your sister; no fault of hers, but a fact

252

nonetheless. And it simply would not do for a preacher and his wife to be associated, even at a remove, with a person of your character.'

Carys could only stare at him. She barely believed what she had heard, and her mouth worked spasmodically as she struggled to find an answer. At last she got out, 'My – my character is *good*! It has never, *never* been called into question!'

'I wish that were true,' said the preacher. 'Sadly, it is not.'

Carys had started to shake. She wanted to stand up and confront him on his own level – he was not a tall man – but at this moment she could not trust her legs to support her. 'Who?' she said savagely. '*Who* has defamed me? What are they saying?'

The preacher looked sternly sorrowful. 'Child, it isn't a question of *who* has defamed you or *what* they have said. The facts speak for themselves.' He paused. 'For example, need I mention the name of Cotty Baker's daughter?'

Carys sat very still.

'Or a certain pair of girls who are no better than they should be and who have been heard boasting that they can behave like harlots without fear of the consequences?'

The colour drained from Carys's face until even her lips were white. *They had babbled. She had warned them, but they had babbled* . . .

The preacher went on relentlessly. 'And then there is the matter of Jem Apothecary's accident. Or should I say, the ill wish that *resulted* in his accident?'

'*What?*' Now Carys did scramble to her feet, though her apparent outrage was only a thin and desperate disguise for terror. 'Are you accusing me of—'

'I accuse you of nothing. It is not my place. Jem, however, believes he has good reason for suspicion. After all, are you not rivals now?'

'Of course we are not! I only—'

'Cure people of their malaises, just as Jem does, and doubtless receive payment into the bargain.'

'I do not take payment!'

The preacher smiled grimly, and named a sum of money. It was exactly the sum that Carys had demanded from the two girls.

'To help one's neighbours is fine and good, and the proper duty of us all,' he continued, satisfied by her silence and feeling no further need to elaborate. 'But when helping becomes a cloak for the use of dark and wicked means to an avaricious end, then it is time for decent people to speak out against it.'

During this last speech Carys had had time to gather her wits. Inwardly she was anything but calm; outwardly, composure had returned.

'Well,' she said, her voice almost if not quite steady, 'It seems that I'm condemned without a chance to defend myself, doesn't it? Not that I've got anything to say to you, because what I do is my business and none of yours.' She picked up her hat and put it on with what she hoped was a degree of dignity. 'I shan't trouble you any more. As for my sister – well, if she's forbidden to wed Tally's son because you disapprove of me, then all I can say is, she's better off single!'

The preacher raised an admonitory finger. 'Now, Carys—'

'Don't "Now, Carys" me!' she fired back. 'You are – you are a *humbug*!'

It was the best insult she could think of on the spur of the moment, though it didn't go half-way towards expressing her real feeling. Head high, shoulders back, she marched out of the preacher's house to where Spry and the trap were waiting. Several people were standing around nearby, doubtless loitering in the hope of further excitement. Carys ignored them all, climbed into the trap and gathered up the reins. Merion's forge was further on down the village street, and Gyll would be there . . . But suddenly Carys could not face even Gyll, for all that she would be kind and understanding. She was too shaken and angry; she wanted only to go away, to go home.

She turned the trap round. Curious and speculating eyes watched as she drove away. But Carys did not look back.

* * *

At the farm, Carys hurled herself into a frenzy of work that lasted until sunset. Then, as dusk closed in she told Izzy to take herself home (no, there was *no* more to do; Izzy could *go*; why did she never *listen*?) and, when Izzy had huffily departed with Lob in tow, she slammed into the dairy, shutting the door in Fleet's face when he tried to follow her. There was a pan of new cream waiting to be turned into butter; the churning would settle her temper and help her to think more clearly.

For think she would. The urge in her mind had been brewing since her return from the village, and now it had turned into a resolve. She had warned the two girls; no one could say she hadn't warned them. If they chose to defy her warning, they should learn that defiance brought reprisal. A small blighting, just enough to put across a clear message and ensure that her rules would be heeded in future. And it would have a salutary effect on the likes of Rofe and Jem Apothecary when they heard of it. A warning to hold their tongues. It was not wrong, Carys told herself. It was simply a matter of self-preservation, and those who sought to malign her had only themselves to blame.

She made her butter, and by the time it was done she felt calm again. Extraordinarily calm; her mind was at ease and her spirits surprisingly buoyant as she prepared for the enchantment she was about to perform. Earlier she had used her weather eye, and had concluded that a spring thunderstorm was a possibility tonight, though by no means assured. Well, she would assure it. But the storm would be localised, confined, in fact, to the fields of one particular smallholder. He would not know why he alone had been afflicted. But his daughters would.

The working took upwards of two hours. Carys had not expected that; when she had cast a spell to control the weather once before, the power had come far more easily to her. But she persevered, and at last it was done, though it left her pallid and weary. She went to bed, satisfied with what she had achieved. And if, as she closed her eyes, a voice came out of the distance of the night, calling her name like a soft, mournful plea, she either did not hear or did not heed it.

She slept.

It was Gyll who brought the news, shortly before noon the next day. As soon as she saw her friend's face Carys knew that some calamity had happened, but until Gyll told the story, the connection did not dawn.

Oh, there had been a storm last night. A freak storm of extraordinary ferocity that concentrated its entire force over one small area. Three fields belonging to a holder had been washed out and the newly burgeoning crops in them devastated. But that was not the worst of it. Not by any means. For at the height of the tempest a bolt of lightning had struck the roof of the holder's house. The thatch had caught fire, and the entire house had burned to the ground.

'The family escaped with their lives, praise be,' said Gyll. 'The man and his wife, two daughters and a baby son. But they've lost everything they had, and they weren't well-off to begin with.' She shook her head in sorrow at life's cruel twists. 'Merion has gone over with Bartel Carpenter, to see if anything can be salvaged from the wreckage, and Juda and I and some others will follow later to help where we can.' She paused. 'Do you have time to spare to come with us, Carys?'

Carys's heart was pounding sickly under her ribs. 'Ah . . . no, I – I'm so busy that I can't spare so much as a moment,' she said pallidly. 'But – but perhaps I can do something else . . .' She turned from side to side, her gaze frantically raking the kitchen. 'Some pots and pans, and utensils . . . yes, and some linen, they'll need linen . . . And foodstuffs, eggs, milk . . .' *Oh, I feel so sick, please, please don't let me be sick!* 'Tell me what they want and I shall give it. How much can you take in the gig with you now?'

'Carys, that's kind and generous,' Gyll said. 'I'll carry as much as I can, and when I've seen the situation for myself I'll let you know if there's anything more that's urgently needed.' She smiled warmly. 'I knew I could rely on you!'

Carys only just managed to keep down the nausea inside her as she and Izzy helped Gyll to load the gig. As Gyll climbed into the driving seat – gingerly because of the heavy load – Carys suddenly caught her hand.

'Gyll – if they should ask where these things came from . . . there's no need to tell them, eh?'

Gyll looked puzzled. 'Whyever not?'

'Because . . . oh, I don't know, they'll be grateful and feel indebted to me, and I don't want that. They have enough troubles, without heaping obligation on top of it all. So just say they are from someone who wishes them well.'

Gyll smiled and nodded and agreed, praising Carys again for her kindness. But as she drove away, her face and her thoughts were sombre. Gyll had heard about yesterday's incident and what lay behind it, and she was no fool. This morning rumours were already rife in the village, and the word *revenge* had been nervously whispered. People were weighing up the ingredients of the tale, and they were forming a murky mixture.

Gyll did not claim to know the truth. But the look on Carys's face when she heard the story, her eagerness to help and yet her desire to do it anonymously, all pointed in the direction that Gyll dreaded.

She would – could – do nothing, not without positive proof of her suspicions. But she could no longer entirely trust Carys. And she was beginning to feel deeply afraid.

In chapel five days later, the preacher delivered an impassioned sermon on the evils of witchcraft. Carys was not there to hear it. She had not been near the village again and had no intention of doing so. Izzy had collected her mended boots, but until the current furore died down Carys preferred to stay within the boundaries of the farm.

Even on her own land, though, there was trouble enough. One morning, soon after the freak storm, a hail of stones was flung at her from behind a hedge as she walked the fields inspecting her crops. Then a patch of new corn was mysteriously trampled, though the damage was not severe. And, most unpleasant of all, she was making her way back from Crede Hill, where the sheep were now roaming freely again, when a man's burly figure emerged from the cover of a hawthorn stand and blocked her path. Carys halted uneasily. She could not tell who the man was; dusk was gathering, and he was muffled in a scarf that disguised his features. All she could see was his flint-cold eyes staring at her from under a pulled-down hat, as he leeringly told her that he wanted the same from her as Rofe had had.

Carys acknowledged later that she had had a very lucky – and narrow – escape. She had taken Fleet with her to the hill, but on the walk back had allowed him to go off exploring on his own. She knew that he was out of whistling range, but it seemed the dog had a sixth sense, for as her would-be assailant made a lunge towards her, a piebald streak appeared from the gloom and Fleet came flying to his mistress's defence. The man staggered back under the onslaught, then turned and fled. Fleet would have followed, but Carys called him back, holding him by the scruff until the running figure was out of sight. Then she ran, too, over the ridge and down the valley slope, shocked and frightened and badly in need of the safety of home.

Those were the worst incidents. But other, smaller things were adding to her tribulations. Izzy worked in the house as diligently as always, but she had become very taciturn and seemed to avoid Carys's company whenever possible. Garler, though he tended her sheep with the same meticulous care as his own, was no more than pleasantly civil now, and never gave his opinion or made a ponderous jest. And neither Deenor nor most of the other women Carys considered her friends had been near the farm for days. Even Gyll had only called once; too busy, she explained apologetically, with helping the stricken holder's family to have time for social pleasures.

Carys wished with all her heart that Gyll did have more time.

She desperately wanted someone to talk to, and Gyll was the only person in whom she would have dared confide. Not all the truth, perhaps; she did not have the courage for that. But a part of it, enough to ease some of the agony of her conscience.

Through wakeful night after wakeful night Carys had suffered torments over what she had done. As with Jem Apothecary, she had not *meant* matters to go so far. All she had wished was for a downpour to soak the holder's crop and set it back a little. This, though . . . it was monstrous. It was *wicked*. She had tried to atone for her deed, firstly by donating as many items from her house as would not look too suspicious, and then by contributing more than generously to a fund organised by Gyll and Juda to relieve the holder family's straits. But it was not enough. Nothing could be.

The one person she could have talked to was the one person she was most desperate to avoid. Robin. How could she face him now? What would he think of her, what would he say to her if she were to confess to him what she had done? She had a feeling – intuition, but it was very strong – that Robin wanted to reach her, but that only served to make her dread him the more, for it must surely mean that he already knew the truth. So she forced away the yearning to cast herself before him for judgement and, perhaps, be shriven, and struggled through the days with the fear and pain and confusion growing worse with every dawn.

Then came the preacher's sermon. The chapel congregation received it with astonishment and awe, for never in all his tenure had he preached with such inflammatory zeal. His homily was not quite an incitement, but it came close enough to inspire some of his more hot-headed parishioners, and Gyll, who sat with Merion in their customary place half-way between the pulpit and the door, saw the looks on certain faces and felt uneasy. Outside afterwards, those same faces could be seen muttering and whispering away from the main crowd, and her unease increased. Unless she was very much mistaken, Gyll thought, trouble was brewing. Tomorrow, she had best go to see Carys, and do what she could to warn her.

Tomorrow, though, proved too late.

* * *

When she went to bed that evening, Carys was feeling better. She had resorted to drink to help her sleep; under normal circumstances it was something she would never consider, for she was no sot, but this once she had decided to gamble. And the gamble seemed to be paying off. She drank a mug of cider before her evening meal, three more with the meal, and another two afterwards, sitting in the ingle with Fleet's head on her outstretched foot. Now, her mind was sluggish and the room looked faintly unreal, swelling and fading before her eyes. She had the beginnings of a headache and would doubtless regret this in the morning, but her eyelids were beginning to droop and a sense of real, healthy tiredness was washing over her like a balm.

She left the table and the kitchen uncleared, pushed Fleet gently away from her foot and went upstairs. Progress was slow and she had to hold the banister rail to steady herself, but she reached her bedroom at last and, without troubling to undress, fell thankfully on to the mattress.

She was asleep almost immediately, and slept until well past midnight. Then, something disturbed her.

Carys opened her eyes blearily, staring into the dark. For a few moments she was confused, then the tight, sharp pain in her forehead focused her memory. Her mouth felt dry. Sitting up, she fumbled for the mug and ewer of water that she kept near the bed, wishing she had thought to drink some earlier to counter the effects of the cider. Finding what she wanted, she gratefully gulped a long draught, then lay down once more. Something was troubling her. She couldn't pinpoint it, but it was there, a feeling of unease, a sense of . . .

Menace? Carys sat up sharply again as the word came out of nowhere and fixed itself in her mind. Something fearful, threatening . . . Here, at the house? She was out of bed in a moment and stumbling to the window. But there was cloud over the moon and the night was too dark for anything to be seen.

Then, fleetingly, she heard something. Faint, distant, a sound that rose and fell on two repeating notes. A name being called. *Her* name . . . Memory whirled her back, and the pounding of her heart increased. Robin was calling to her. He had come without her bidding, and he was calling.

'*Caaa-rys. Caaa-rys.*' So familiar . . . Yet there was an urgency in the sound that was not familiar, and it set the fear prickling through her again. Robin had not come to the farm; in fact she knew that he wasn't anywhere close by. Something was wrong.

'*Caaa-rys! Help me . . .*'

Gooseflesh broke out on Carys's arms. 'Robin . . .?' Her voice quavered and the word came out as a whisper.

'*Hurry, love . . . hurry . . .*'

'Where are you?' Still she whispered; there was a tightness under her ribs that choked back anything more. And then abruptly she knew where he was, felt the pull of his presence, a compelling sixth sense that flowered into absolute certainty. The field by the wood . . .

'*Help me, Carys!*'

Fleet began to bark at the sound of her clattering steps on the stairs. He sensed her agitation and jumped around her, wanting to join in, wanting to help, but Carys pushed him away and, pausing only to tug shoes on to her feet, ran from the house.

Across the yard, through the gate, and she was racing on her way to the wood. Moonlight slanted in fitful bursts through breaks in the clouds, lighting the track but casting treacherous shadows that hid the ruts. Time and again she stumbled and once fell, landing awkwardly on one elbow. Pain throbbed but she ignored it, scrambling to her feet and hastening on. She could no longer hear Robin calling, though in a distant copse a fox had begun to yelp and the sound of it was like a warning, a goad spurring her, *faster, faster*!

Then, ahead and below, where the track levelled out, lights flickered in the darkness. Three of them – the moon was hidden again, but the lights flared brighter and Carys realised that they were the flames of newly lit brands. The silhouettes of human

261

figures showed near the flames; they were closing together, moving in on something—

'*Carys!*' Out of the night, so suddenly and unexpectedly that Carys cried out in shock, Robin came running. His eyes were wild, his hair and clothes in disarray. Reaching her, he caught hold of her arms in a desperate, vice-like grip.

'Carys, stop them! Don't let them do it, don't let—' His plea cut off in a scream, and to Carys's horror he reeled back, flinging up both hands to cover his face. '*NO! NO! Carys, HELP ME . . .*'

He spun away from her, staggering from the path and into the young corn, twisting, writhing in agony.

And below, the flames joined together and leaped up with new energy—

Realisation slammed into Carys's consciousness as she saw the shape at the heart of the fire. Humanlike, arms outstretched, tied to a pole that was tipping and tottering. The scarecrow – they were burning the scarecrow!

Robin screamed again on a hideous note, and an answering cry bubbled up in Carys and erupted from her throat in a banshee shriek of horror and fury and anguish. She flung herself down the track, running, racing, heedless of her own safety, wanting only to reach the raiders, beat them with her fists, hurl them aside, *do* something. In the jumping firelight figures turned, faces registered alarm, someone yelled a command and suddenly the figures were fleeing, scattering and bolting like rabbits, leaving only their blazing handiwork behind.

Carys could not reach the scarecrow. The flames had too great a hold; she made one frantic attempt but the heat scorched her face and hands and drove her back. She fell to her knees, staring numbly, blankly as the scarecrow blackened and burned and, at last, collapsed to a pile of detritus on the hot ground where the pole had stood. Sparks spiralled up, dispersed on the wind, winked out, and the last small tongues of flame licked at the earth before dying down to embers.

The night was frighteningly quiet. Carys knelt motionless,

staring, struggling not to acknowledge what had just happened but forced, finally, to believe.

'Robin . . .' She whispered his name then with a dawning sense of horror. Where was he? What had happened to him?

'*Robin!*' This time it was a shout, and she clambered to her feet and ran back to where she had left him. He was not there, and though she called again and again, sobbing now with fear for him, there was no reply, and no trace of him to be found.

Except for one thing. Carys did not know, did not dare ask herself, what it meant, but she found one telltale sign: a small patch of young shoots twisted and blackened, as if something had burned there and then vanished into nothingness.

The tears stopped at last, and when they did she turned and stared at where the scarecrow had stood. The flames had died and nothing was visible. The raiders, too, were gone, but as Carys's senses attuned, she felt the echo of their presence. She could not tell who they were; that was not in her power. But she knew how to ensure that they would never commit an outrage like this again . . .

Time passed and Carys stood still and steady as an oak tree on the track. Resolve was forgotten, caution scorned and discarded; only hate burned in her now, as hot as the fire that had devoured the scarecrow. Hate, and a hunger for revenge.

In the woodland that encroached to the trackside hedge, two owls began to call to each other. The mournful sounds had a sinister ring to them; after a while the calling ceased.

Only then did Carys emerge from her trance and slowly, deliberately, turn her steps towards home.

Chapter XXII

It wasn't exactly a rumour that reached Gyll's ears early the next morning; but the odd murmured word, and her ability to make a picture from a few disparate scraps, were enough to alert her. She persuaded Merion, who trusted her intuition, that they should visit Carys without any delay, and so as the sun started to climb they drove from the village and towards the farm.

The blackened patch where the scarecrow had stood was clearly visible from the road – and so was something else. The raiders must have done it before they set fire to the figure on its pole, and now in daylight it stood out for all to see. Scratched and scraped into the ground among the young corn, a clear and vindictive message:

LIKE FOR LIKE

Gyll and Merion exchanged disquieted looks. Then Merion flicked his whip sharply over the pony's back and the gig hastened on towards the farm.

The yard was deserted when they arrived, but there were noises in the byre, and there they found the village girl belatedly milking the cows. She stammered that Izzy was somewhere about, but Missus, no, she didn't know, she couldn't say, and she'd been told not to go up to the house.

Izzy was at the chicken arks, and was almost as cryptic. 'There's no getting sense out of her this morning and that's a fact,' she grumbled. 'Just about chewed my hand off, and all I gave her was

265

a good day and asked after her health.' She would have elaborated, but Gyll was too concerned to wait and turned at once for the farmhouse.

She opened the back door and stopped, surveying the kitchen in consternation. It was a mess: unwashed dishes piled untidily, the table cluttered with remnants of yesterday's meal, the kettle empty and cold beside the range, which itself was almost out. Merion said, 'You'd best look for her. I'll see to the fire,' and swung out of the door again to fetch wood.

Carys was in the parlour. She did not look up as Gyll entered; she was sitting hunched on the inglenook settle, staring into a fire that had clearly gone out some hours ago. The room was cold, but she wore no shawl. And a familiar sound was missing. It took Gyll a few seconds to place it but then she realised that the clock had stopped.

'Carys?' She advanced cautiously into the room. 'Carys, are you ill?'

Carys raised her head and looked at her, but Gyll had the unnerving feeling that she was seeing someone, or something, else entirely.

'It's me – Gyll,' she added. 'Carys, whatever's *wrong*?'

Carys's mouth trembled, then distorted. 'He's gone,' she said flatly.

'Who's gone? What are you talking about?'

'They destroyed him. I called and called but he didn't come back, and I can't find him.'

Gyll thought she understood. 'The scarecrow . . . Yes. We saw, Merion and I. Merion's here, he's seeing to the range for you. Who did it, Carys? Do you know?'

Carys shook her head.

'Well, we shall find out,' Gyll declared angrily. 'And when we do, something shall be *done* about it!'

Carys laughed bitterly. 'There's nothing to be done. I told you, he's gone.'

She was speaking, Gyll thought, as if the scarecrow had been a living thing. Shock, she decided. It must have temporarily unhinged her . . . 'Then we'll make another one,' she said soothingly. 'You and I together, we'll make another, and—'

'*How can we*?' Carys almost screamed. 'We can't, we can't, we *can't*, because he's *gone*, and he won't come back, *ever*!' Then, like a dam breaching a wall, her emotions broke, and she burst into a storm of sobbing.

It took Gyll nearly an hour to comfort Carys and calm her down. Merion looked in twice, but his wife shook her head and he went away again to make himself useful in the yard. When the tempest did finally subside, Gyll made tea, then took Carys's hands and looked into her face and said solemnly, 'Now, my dear. Tell me what I can do for you, and it shall be done.'

Carys looked steadily back at her. She felt *so* calm now that it was almost frightening; as if she had entirely detached herself from reality and was looking down on the world from some remote height.

'Thank you, Gyll,' she said quietly, 'but there's no need for anything. I'll be all right now.'

'The scarecrow—' Gyll began, but Cary interrupted with a quick shake of her head.

'There's nothing to say. It's done, it's over.'

'We *will* find out who was responsible,' Gyll persisted, mistakenly thinking that that would help Carys. 'Whatever some people might think or say, this sort of deed is wrong – and firestarting's a serious crime. Think if it had been your stacks, or even the house!'

Immediately she could have kicked herself – the last thing Carys needed was an alarming idea to be put into her head – but to her relief Carys did not seem to have taken the words in. She was sipping her tea now, frowning at some private thought, and Gyll decided it was probably best to leave her alone. She would recover in a while, and the most useful service she and Merion could perform for her now was to return to the village and see what could be done about finding and punishing the wrongdoers.

Carys was still sitting in the ingle when her friends left. Fleet, who had been shut out of the house all morning, tried to follow the gig, but a stern command from Merion sent him slinking back with his head and tail drooping. As they passed the fateful place again, Gyll looked carefully at the surrounding area, but nothing there held any obvious clues.

'The chapel bell's tolling,' Merion said suddenly.

'What?' Then Gyll heard it too, intermittent on the wind.

'Someone's died,' Merion went on, and sighed. 'One of the old folk, I suppose.'

But it was not, as they discovered even before they reached their home. Nor was it merely one death; the mournful bell was tolling for two brothers, who early this morning had met with a freakish and completely unpredictable accident, when two apparently sound walls of their barn had caved in while they were inside fetching straw bales. The pair had been crushed under a rain of falling stones; the bodies (according to gossip) were dreadfully mangled, and Bartel Carpenter had been asked to make two coffins in double-quick time so that the horrible remains could be hidden from view as soon as possible.

Gyll and Merion had no reason to connect the accident with the events that had taken place last night in Carys's field. Only Carys, when she heard about it, was aware of the truth. And if two or three other men suspected, they were too afraid for their own lives to speak a word to another living soul. Their only consolation was that the dead brothers had been the ringleaders and had incited the rest, who had let the effects of an evening's drinking sway them from their better judgement. They had not really wanted to go, and if sober would not have dreamed . . .

They were fortunate, for there were no more reprisals.

And there were no more attacks on Carys's farm.

Alder-month and Willow-month passed, and almost before anyone knew it Hawthorn-month had arrived, bringing the first heralds of summer. The spring had been kindly on the whole, and the corn was growing sturdily, while the grass in the hay-meadows was almost ready for cutting.

At Carys's steading, life continued in a round of quiet normality. The worst of the gossip had long since died down; when the story of the burned scarecrow came out, the preacher in a fit of conscience delivered another thunderous sermon, this time inveighing against disorder and anarchy and like wickednesses. Carys did not hear that sermon, either. She had not set foot in the village for months now, but though a few tongues wagged darkly over that, and speculated as to the reason for it, every topic of gossip eventually ran its course and before long there were newer, and thus more interesting, matters to distract attention.

Besides, there were Carys's skills to be considered. Jem Apothecary was on his feet again, but some people still preferred to make the trek out to the farm to seek advice or remedies. Carys was as generous as ever, giving help with a good grace and asking no payment. But many noticed the change in her own self; her manner was distant in a way it had not been before, and she was not willing to linger and talk with her customers as she used to do. Cold, they said, there was something cold and more than a little strange about Carys Jonewidow these days. Subdued, she was, kept herself to herself and no longer joined in with local life. But perhaps, some added, that was no bad thing. There was still a smack of witchcraft in what she did, and everyone knew that through the winter and early spring there had been some peculiar coincidences – such as Jem Apothecary's mishap – that might not be quite as coincidental as they seemed. Even the business over the scarecrow ... Carys had been uninterested in bringing the culprits to book, and that was a little ... well, surprising, to say the least. Not, of course, that anyone was actually casting suspicion. *But* ...

They balked, however, at voicing the smallest hint that there just might be a link between the scarecrow and the death of the two brothers. The preacher himself had spoken sternly on the folly of idle talk, and anyway, no one in their right mind could think Carys capable of such a diabolical thing. It was even being mooted that her sister Thomsine would be allowed to wed Tally Rigswidow's son after all; a sure sign (*if* one were needed) that Carys was absolved.

Life went on. On the first day of Hawthorn-month the preacher and Tally were married, and Thomsine, who was bride's attendant, looked smug enough to confirm the rumours about her own nuptials. On the twelfth day, Carys walked the boundaries of her farm with Fleet at her heels, and decided that the hay cutting could begin.

She delivered that news to Garler Shepherd in the way that had become her custom of late: coolly and impersonally, almost as though she were throwing the information away. Garler nodded and said, yes, well, he would see what could be done about hired help, she might leave all to him if she chose. Carys did choose. She was uninterested in the tedious business of hiring casual labourers; who came and who did not, and who most needed the work and who did not, were of no concern to her. The task would be done and she would pay the money, and that was an end to it. It didn't matter. Nothing mattered any more.

Carys had indeed changed. On the night that the scarecrow was burned, something within her had shrivelled and died along with it. For the best part of a month after it happened, she had tried to tell herself that Robin's plea for help, his pain, his screaming, had been a mad dream and not part of her waking reality. She had refused to believe that he was gone, and for five more nights she had called to him from her window, willing him to come to her and for things to be as they used to. He had not come, and when at last she had been forced to acknowledge that he would not, she had railed and raged and execrated him, calling him a treacherous and faithless deceiver, until the false mask of fury collapsed and exposed the terror that truly drove her wrath. Eleven nights followed then, during which she roamed the fields and the woods and the ridges of Crede Hill with only Fleet and the moon for company, searching, calling, shouting, crying to her lost love and begging him to return.

Robin did not return, and at long last Carys's tormented mind admitted defeat. Whatever she did, however long and hard she sought, she would not find him, for he was not there to be found. Was he dead? She did not even know if he *could* die, though she feared that possibility above all others. Her only certainty was that he had gone from her life and her world, and she could not summon him back.

She thought, sometimes, about the two brothers who had met with such an unlikely end. And the more time passed without Robin, the stronger grew a vindictive sense of justification at what she had done. To begin with, the act had shocked her to the core; now, though, it seemed a rightful recompense. Not that any vengeance could make up for her loss. But it satisfied, or at least silenced, some bitter gall inside her that festered and refused to heal. Maybe it was a kind of madness; if so, Carys no longer cared. Robin was gone, and with his going, the light had been snuffed out of her life.

So it did not matter that, when a man came to her asking for a spell that would inflict his wife with a swollen tongue for her nagging, Carys gave it. It did not matter that another man, jealous of his neighbour's prize cow, wanted the beast's milk to dry up; the thing was done and Carys was unmoved. Many people still asked only for beneficent things, and these too she was equally willing to give. The difference was that she made no moral judgement and felt no moral qualms. To her, it was all one.

On the morning when the haymaking was to begin, Carys rose at dawn as usual. The day was fine, as she had known it would be, and despite the prevailing mood of its mistress there was an eager air about the farm as first Izzy and Lob arrived, then Garler and his sons and the first of the hired hands, who mustered in the yard with their scythes.

Carys came out from the kitchen where she was preparing dough for the day's batch of bread to feed the workforce. Garler greeted her pleasantly, and said, 'There's five here now, Carys, and another dozen or more to come.'

Carys nodded. 'You had no trouble finding people?'

'Oh, no. Oh, no. Piece of luck, you might say, for there's new arrivals in the district just since yesterday noon, and they're sending men for the scything and some of their womenfolk for the pitching and turning.' He looked over his shoulder and nodded to the distant slopes beyond the yard. 'There, now, they're coming, see?'

Carys looked . . . and a tight sensation clutched at her stomach. Heading across the fields from the direction of the village was a group of people dressed in clothes of a bright and colourful motley that no villager would ever have dreamed to wear. A tall, high-shouldered man led them, and walking at his side was a woman. Carys stared at the woman with the horror of dawning recognition, for she was old, and in stark contrast to the others she wore grey clothes, and her hair was grey too, plaited into five long braids.

The matriarch raised her head then, and even across the distance her gaze seemed to lock with Carys's own. As Carys stared back fixedly, one gnarled hand made a small gesture that might – or might not – have been a greeting.

The Wayfarers had returned.

She knew that the matriarch would come that night, and when the soft knocking sounded it took all her courage to walk (calmly, *calmly*!) to the door and open it. Haloed in silver by the low moon, the old woman stepped over the threshold without a word spoken, and Carys followed, closing the door quietly. Fleet, who was lying by the hearth, raised his head and stared; the crone smiled at him, said something in a tongue Carys did not understand, and Fleet settled his head back on his paws and went to sleep.

'You'll . . . take tea?' Carys asked, finding her voice at last. 'Or – or something stronger—'

'I'll take nothing.' The voice brought back memories, and Carys suppressed a shiver. The matriarch gazed meditatively around the parlour for a few moments, then: 'We're alone.' It was a statement rather than a question, but even so Carys nodded. 'There's just Fleet . . .' she said.

Another smile. 'Oh, we won't mind him. Animals are too wise to worry overmuch about our human follies.'

The word *follies* sent a spike of apprehension through Carys, and in an attempt to cover it she looked for something, anything, to say.

'I knew you would come,' she got out.

'Of course you did. And you know why, too.'

No answer. The matriarch sat down in the best chair, and Carys subsided on to the settle. Fleet began to snore; the matriarch touched his head and the snoring stopped, though he did not wake.

'Well then, Carys Jonewidow. What have you done?'

Carys's mouth worked convulsively. 'He's gone . . .' she whispered.

'Yes, he has. And the fault's your own.'

Because that was so close to the accusations she had hurled at herself, Carys rebelled. 'I'm not to blame!' she protested. 'It was you who began this!'

'Oh no, girl. It was *you* who began it, with your longings and your wishings and your thoughtless hurry. Remember what I told you back then? Once it's done it can't be changed, I said, and the responsibility's on your shoulders and no one else's.' She paused and gave a clipped, cynical little grunt. 'Well, that's burden enough for you by now, isn't it? For it seems you've also forgotten something else I told you: that to use magic to force another to act against their nature is a shameful and wicked thing, and dangerous into the bargain.'

'I didn't—' Carys began, then stopped, aware that with this woman, unlike anyone else, she could not dissemble and not deceive herself.

The matriarch nodded, satisfied. 'Yes, you begin to see now, don't you? When it's almost too late.'

One word, just one, caught Carys's attention, and her head came up sharply. 'Almost . . .?' she repeated.

The matriarch did not reply. Instead, she took the clay pipe that Carys remembered – or one very like it – from a bag slung over her shoulder.

'I have tobacco,' Carys said quickly. She had grown into the habit of keeping some for Garler or Merion. 'Here, in the jar—'

'Thank you, I'll use my own.' She stuffed the pipe, lit it with a spill from the fireside. 'So, you're wondering why I said "almost".'

Carys swallowed. 'If there's any hope – any hope at all—'

'Of finding your Robin again? Well, girl, you made him, so you should know the answer to that.'

'*I* made him?' She was stunned. 'What do you mean?'

The woman raised an eyebrow. 'Mistress Echo, I called you, as I recall. Seems you haven't changed.'

'Please!' Carys begged in distress. 'I *don't* understand, and I don't pretend to! If you can help me . . .'

The words tailed off under the matriarch's steady, flint-eyed scrutiny. Smoke rose from the pipe bowl, and one of Fleet's paws twitched, as if he was dreaming. After a silence that seemed endless to Carys, the old woman sighed and leaned back in the chair.

'Ah, well,' she said. 'What's done's done, and I own I'm not entirely innocent in this turmoil. All right, then, Carys Jonewidow. I won't explain the whole of it – that's not my way, and you wouldn't understand if I did – but I'll tell you a few things, and what you make of them, good or bad, is up to you.'

Mouth dry, Carys nodded and waited for her to continue.

To her surprise, the old woman began with a question. 'Answer me this,' she said. 'What *is* your Robin?'

Carys blinked. 'He is . . . he . . .' Beads of perspiration started to form on her brow. 'I don't know . . .'

'Mmm, you don't, and that's the truth. Very well, then: what do you think he *might* be?'

Carys's mind floundered. There was an answer on her tongue but she didn't want to utter it, for she had tried from the beginning to push it away and bury it in a part of her brain that would never allow it to come back. But the ancient gaze was still unwavering on her face, and she found that she could not evade it. The thing, the suspicion and the fear, *had* to be said.

'Is he . . . the scarecrow?'

The matriarch gave a little laugh. 'No, he's not,' she said, to Carys's enormous surprise and relief. 'Or not in the way that you're thinking. He's more than that, *much* more. But the scarecrow

274

is . . . well, let's say it's an aspect of him. Or he of it; same thing when all's said and done, only that's another truth most people can't understand. When you fixed your daydreams on that old scarecrow in your field and played let's-pretend with it, you made a link, see? A link between *it* and *him*. So when you called him to you, that's what he used to give himself solidity.'

'You mean . . . Robin isn't real?'

The matriarch laughed so loudly that Carys jumped.

'Oh, he's *real*, girl! Far more real than you know or I could begin to tell you!' Then her face sobered. 'But his kind of reality has a wider and more enduring compass than this fleeting little world of ours. So in his dealings with you he needed an anchor. Something of this world, to give him focus in this world. Do you begin to understand now?'

Carys's hands were trembling where they lay in her lap. 'So when they burned the scarecrow . . .' The hands moved abruptly and convulsively, and she covered her face. 'He begged me to help him, but I couldn't. He was screaming – in such pain—'

'Yes, he would have been. But that part of it's over with now.'

Carys hung her head miserably. 'He's dead, isn't he?' she whispered.

'Tush,' the matriarch said contemptuously. Instantly Carys's head was up again and she stared at the old woman, who shrugged almost carelessly. 'He can't die. You called him to you, so you of all people should know that.'

'But I *don't* know!' Carys all but shouted at her. 'I *don't*! Do you think I've not tried *everything* I can think of to find him again? I need him, I *love* him—'

'Oh, you do?' Suddenly there was steel in the old woman's voice, so cold and hard that Carys physically recoiled. 'Love him so much that you broke your promise never to use what he taught you for evil ends? Cursed your own neighbours if they offended, so that they started to fear you? Let things come to such a pass that they burned that scarecrow where it stood in your field, and so broke the link? Look in your heart, girl. Look, and tell me who

275

took your Robin away from you that night!'

Something in Carys's throat swelled, making it hard for her to breathe. 'I didn't mean . . .' she choked out. 'I didn't want . . .'

'No, you didn't mean and you didn't want. But you did what you did all the same.'

Tears started to fall on Carys's hands. 'How can I change it now? How can I make amends? Please, please—' she reached out in entreaty, hardly aware that she was doing it. 'If you can, if it's within your power, help me now!'

For a minute, perhaps more, the parlour was very quiet. The matriarch relit her pipe and drew on it, her face thoughtful as though she debated some private matter in her mind. Carys dared not speak, barely even dared to move. She only watched the wizened old face before her, trying to interpret every blink of the eyes, every small movement of the mouth as the old woman considered. Then a long, resigned sigh broke the hiatus, and the matriarch looked at her again.

'One more thing I'll tell you. Maybe I'm a fool to do it, but I still sense some good in you, and as I had my own part to play I suppose I'm obliged to back my hazard.'

Carys waited, the tension in her close to breaking point.

'You've lost the link you had with your Robin through the scarecrow,' the matriarch continued after another pause. 'But if you want him back, if you *truly* want him, there's another.'

'*What*? *Where*?'

She received a hard smile. 'The answer's in full view, if you've the wit to see it. In your own barn. The link's already made, and you should know, for you had a hand in it.' Stiffly but abruptly the old woman rose to her feet. 'And now I'll be on my way. We've taken enough of each other's time.'

Confounded, Carys protested, 'But you haven't explained!'

'Nor will I. I've said all that's needed to set you on your way; the rest's for you to fathom.' She looked down, with something akin to pity in her eyes. 'Good night to you, Carys Jonewidow. And I hope you'll learn wisdom.'

Carys couldn't speak. She wanted to ask so much more, but the words would not come, and all she could do was follow the old woman to the door and watch dumbly as she opened it and stepped out into the warm, quiet night. Then the matriarch turned to face her once more.

'I think we'll not meet again,' she said matter-of-factly. 'So rather than good night, I'll say goodbye. I don't know if I should wish you fortune, but there; I do, and that's my burden and not yours, eh?' She started to move away, then paused again. 'You'll dream of those two dead brothers tonight, but it'll be the first and last time, for it isn't my place to judge you. That's for your own conscience to live with as it may.'

And with that parting shot she walked away into the darkness.

Carys stood frozen on the doorstep, shocked to the core and with a tight, twisting sensation in her stomach. So the matriarch had known all along; yet she had said not a word about it, not until the very last moment before she took her leave. No accusation, no condemnation. *It isn't my place to judge you* . . . But her words *were* a judgement of a kind; Carys was aware of it, and aware, too, that tonight's dream was not a prophecy but a promise. She feared it. She only wished that Robin could be here to help her when the time came to face it.

Then as her chaotic thoughts turned to Robin she recalled what the old woman had said about the link. That another existed, and the clue to it was in her own barn . . .

She ran to the kitchen, snatched a lantern that hung on its nail from one of the beams, and hurried across the yard to where the barn loomed black and solid. She had not set foot in here after darkness fell since the night she had spent among the straw with Robin, and the memories of that came sharply and painfully back as, lamp held high, she advanced slowly into the cavernous space, peering among the skipping shadows for a clue to the riddle. The market cart, bridles and harnesses on their hooks . . . racks of implements neatly arrayed, the great pile of rick-covers laid ready for when the hay was all in and the stack built . . . Nothing here to hint at the solution. She moved on, accompanied now by a new shadow as the cat called Little Black dropped noiselessly down from where he had been sleeping on a partition and padded in her wake for sheer curiosity. Deeper in, to where the straw bales rose like walls and their dry, dusty scent tickled her nostrils. Then round, and—

She had forgotten, and she should not have done, for it was the only answer there could possibly have been. He stood where he had stood since Harvest-feast, tall and motionless and silent, a slumbering giant waiting for the year to come full turn once more, and for the ultimate celebration and culmination of his reign. The Harvest King gazed sightlessly down on Carys, and Carys gazed back.

'Robin . . . ?' she said softly.

The figure did not respond, nothing changed. But Carys felt a strange, intuitive excitement stir within her. Slowly she stepped forward, aware on another, distant level of her consciousness that Little Black was purring. This was right, it *had* to be. Months ago, when she had brought Robin to the barn, he had faced the King and something significant had passed between them. Another aspect of himself . . . she had had a hand in its making, and thus, as with the scarecrow, a link had been formed . . .

This was her means of calling Robin back.

She touched the King's feet, and her fingers tingled with something more than the rough sensation of straw. Carys smiled and, quietly, calmly, spoke.

'I'll bring you to me again, my Robin. No matter how long it may take, I'll discover what I have to do, and I'll find you . . .'

Chapter XXIII

The good weather held until the end of haymaking. The Wayfarers, too, stayed to the finish, swelling the ranks of those who laboured from dawn to dusk in the fields to scythe and turn and carry and, finally, stack the sweet new crop. But after the first day, the old matriarch was not seen among their number.

Carys had worked as hard as anyone, and, as Gyll observed privately to her good friend Juda, she seemed more at peace with herself and the world than she had been in recent months. Gyll and Juda did not know of the matriarch's visit to the farm, nor of the long night that had followed, through which Carys had cried and sobbed and screamed in her sleep as the promised nightmares came marching out of the dark to torment and terrify her. Only Fleet had sensed something of what was afoot, and for hours had whined and scratched at the stairway door, wanting to offer comfort to his mistress but unable to reach her.

But, as the matriarch had also promised, the dreams had come only once, and their tide had been a kind of cleansing that lifted some of the burden from Carys's heart and spirit. She bitterly, bitterly regretted what she had done, but for the first time since it had happened she found herself able to face it, rather than thrust it away and bury it beyond conscious reach. She could not atone for her wrongdoing; no amount of penitence could be enough and she must live with her guilt for the rest of her days. She would never forget, and she would probably never forgive herself. Yet perhaps as her life went on she could make some amends, by using her gift in the ways that Robin had wanted her to do. Kind ways, benign

279

ways, that would bring only good and not harm. She had learned a lesson, she told herself, and learned it at a cruel and terrible cost. But it had gone home and taken root, and from now on the darkness might start to fade and the light return.

And every night, when the last of the haymakers had made their weary way home, Carys went to the barn and crouched before the Harvest King, seeking to unravel the Wayfarer matriarch's conundrum.

To begin with, she talked to the straw figure on its makeshift throne as if it were Robin. She told of her day's work, confided her secrets, laughed and sighed just as she would have done with her lover of the woods. But her words and laughter fell away into silence, and the figure made no response. It was a doll, nothing more.

Carys did not know what to do. Recalling the scarecrow – the first scarecrow, which she had carried to the wood – she thought of repeating the game she had played then. But something in her shrank from the prospect. There was something forbidding, almost menacing, about the great straw image, and to treat it in such a way felt irreverent.

How, then? She didn't know. But she recalled the promise she had made, to herself and to Robin. *No matter how long it may take, I'll find you.* The matriarch had given her hope, and she must hold to it and not give up. There *was* a way to reforge the lost link – and one day, somehow, she would discover it.

The final loads of hay were carried in, and as if to celebrate the completion of the last stack on the last farm, the fine weather broke in a spectacular thunderstorm. Villagers converging on the chapel for the traditional ceremony to mark the occasion saw the sky blackening to the south, and by the time Carys arrived with Garler and Deenor, the first heavy drops of rain were falling. The rain intensified as Garler helped his passengers down from the trap, and they had just hurried the last few yards into the chapel building when there was a colossal flash of lightning and the heavens opened.

Heads turned curiously to look as the three of them joined Merion and Gyll, who had saved places for them. Carys knew that everyone was greatly surprised to see her here after so many months' absence, but any speculative whisperings were drowned by a bawl of thunder that rattled the windows. The preacher noticed and made a point of smiling at Carys, though the smile had a false ring to it. Then, as the thunder died away he nodded to the choir, the musicians in their stall struck up, and the ceremony began.

Throughout the proceedings, Carys was aware that the rest of the chapel-goers were far more interested in her than in what the preacher had to say. She could almost physically feel the covert glances – though people were quick to turn away whenever she tried to catch their eyes – and once or twice, in quiet moments, snatches of muttered comment reached her.

' . . . after all these months?'

' . . . in here just as if nothing had happened and she'd never . . .'

' . . . mended her ways, and high time too . . .'

Carys began to feel angry. She had not expected to be welcomed back with open arms, but she had thought that her neighbours would at least receive her with some measure of kindness. Enough time had passed for the gossip and rumours to abate, and – at least, as far as anyone else knew for certain – her worst offence had really been no more than indiscretions. Yet here they were, whispering about her like spiteful tabbies, judging, disparaging, censuring. There was no cause for it, she told herself.

The whispering continued and Carys's sense of grievance grew. By the time the preacher got up to deliver his sermon, Garler and Deenor were looking distinctly uncomfortable; they too had overheard the comments and Carys suspected that they regretted inviting her to come with them and wished they could distance themselves from her. The spark of anger in her was beginning to turn into a flame of ire. And when the preacher, looking (Carys thought) directly and trenchantly at her, announced that his theme today would be 'Penitence and forgiveness', the flame flared up.

Skin prickling with a flush of outrage, Carys looked at the nearest window. The storm showed no sign of passing; the outside world was blotted out by hammering rain, and lightning and thunder had punctuated the ceremony from its beginning. Carys felt her willpower gathering like a reflection of the thunderclouds, dark and heavy and relentless. *Penitence and forgiveness*, indeed . . .

The rage in her coalesced, found its focus—

The thunderbolt struck the chapel bell tower in a gargantuan flash that turned the air to livid, blinding blue, and a simultaneous detonating roar shook the building from end to end. Debris rained down from the roof: splintered wood, smashed slates, the remains of an old bird's nest – the preacher yelled in shock, cowering and covering his head with upflung arms, and others were screaming too, clutching each other, ducking and grovelling to evade the falling rubble. The chapel bell swung out of control, clanging and resonating wildly on the remains of its ropes; high in the tower wood creaked and groaned, then more slates fell . . .

'Everyone, leave!' Outdoor ceremonies in the worst of weathers had given the preacher powerful lungs, and his voice bellowed out over the racket and disorder. 'Outside now, hurry, *hurry*!'

There was a scramble for the door and the congregation piled out, heedless of the pouring rain. Carys was carried along in the rush, but there was no sense of panic in her. The bell would not fall, for she had not willed it to. A bad fright, a little damage, just enough to pay them back for their contempt. She smiled. She was satisfied. She felt numb.

No more debris fell and no one was hurt in the general exodus; within minutes the entire congregation was clear of the chapel and milling outside. It seemed that the storm had peaked with the thunderbolt, for soon the lightning became faint and the thunder distant, then the rain at last began to slacken off. Any thought of completing the disrupted ceremony was out of the question, though, and while some people hurried for the shelter of the meeting hall, others gathered round talking and exclaiming and peering up at the chapel roof to see how much damage had been done. Merion and

Gyll were among this group, and so were Izzy and Lob. Lob was in the throes of some sort of fit, flapping his arms and dancing on the spot; his mother pulled at his coat and shouted at him, trying to make him go with her to shelter, but her efforts were only making matters worse.

Then suddenly Lob saw Carys. He stopped dancing and stood rigid, gaping at her while his mouth jerked convulsively open and shut. With half the village watching and agog, he raised a hand and pointed straight at her.

'*Bad* Missus!' he cried. '*Bad* Missus!'

Carys's cheeks blanched under the streaming tendrils of her hair and she backed away a pace. Lob still pointed, though the sounds he made were no longer intelligible, and a gaggle of wide-eyed faces stared silently. Izzy hissed, 'You stupid great loon, what do you think you're at?' but even as she said it she too was looking, sidelong, nervously.

There was a flurry of movement and the preacher pushed his way through the gathering. He patted Lob's back, saying, 'There, boy, there!' then shouldered his way past him and towards Carys. Carys looked at him once, blindly. Then she swung round and walked away.

'Now, Carys!' the preacher called, sounding surprised and offended. 'Carys, come back!'

But Carys kept walking, out of the gate, on to the village street. A sharp turn to the left and she was striding away in the rain without a single backward glance.

'Going home, I reckon,' an old woman said, loudly and in a tone laden with disapproval. 'Good riddance, then! If you ask my opinion, what's just happened was a sign that her sort aren't welcome in a place of decent folk.'

Gyll was standing close enough to hear. She had wanted to call after Carys, but she had not. Instinct told her that at this moment Carys would pay no heed. Izzy now had Lob under control and was dragging him away, still berating him, and beyond them Garler and Deenor were walking towards their trap. They both looked subdued and embarrassed, and Gyll had the feeling that they were glad Carys had gone and thus freed them from any responsibility to her. They climbed into the trap, and as they drove away, Gyll and Juda exchanged a look.

Juda said, 'You don't *really* think she . . . ?' She glanced towards the chapel.

Gyll put up a hand to her soaked hair, trying to squeeze some of the water out of it. Her eyes were worried. 'I don't know, Juda, I truly don't,' she replied sombrely. 'But the looks people gave her . . . She must have heard mutterings. And then Lob . . .'

Juda nodded. 'They say, don't they, that idiots often sense truths that the rest of us can't?' She paused. 'And I can't stop thinking of the other occurrences. Jem Apothecary. The holder whose house burned down. And—' But she did not say the two dead brothers' names aloud. Gyll knew what she was thinking; the hint was enough.

Gyll stared along the street. 'I think someone should go to the farm.'

'Yes . . .' said Juda.

'This afternoon, when I've dried and changed my clothes and seen for Merion's dinner . . . I think it would be as well not to leave it longer.'

Juda nodded again. 'I'll come with you,' she said. 'Just in case . . .'

'Yes,' said Gyll. 'Yes, Juda, thank you. I'd be grateful for your company.'

No one saw Carys on her long walk back. She had turned off the road as soon as was possible, and she went cross-country, field by field, until her home came into sight.

With the rain turning everything to grey, the deserted farm had a desolate air. Even the cattle weren't in sight; they had moved off to find shelter under the trees beyond the brow of the hill. The only sign of life was a sudden eager barking from the house as Carys opened the yard gate and Fleet sensed her. Carys ignored him. She had stopped half-way through the gate and was standing motionless, staring blankly at the buildings before her, oblivious to the steady, dismal rain. All the way home, the numbness that had come over her in the chapel after the thunderbolt struck had held her in check, enabling her to behave – on the surface – with some semblance of normality. She had walked home without conscious thought or effort, and with nothing in her mind beyond the simple goal of reaching the house and changing her wet clothes. Now though, the numbness was beginning to leave her, and beneath it, pushing up and cracking the shield it had created, was a terrible, sick realisation. She had lost control. All her resolve, all the pledges she had made to herself; in the space of a few seconds she had smashed them to shards and let the bitterness take her over again. In her mind the sorrowful face of the Wayfarer matriarch rose like a haunting, and she shut her eyes tightly, trying to blot it out. But the image only changed to the face of Robin, gazing at her with a sad, silent and disappointed accusation that cut her to the bone.

The rain streamed from Carys's hair and ran like tears down her face. But there were no real tears. She desperately wanted to cry, but she couldn't, the ability simply wasn't in her. Yet something was struggling, bursting to get out; a feeling, an emotion, an enormous, agonising, rising tide of grief and shame—

Suddenly her paralysis snapped, and she ran. Fleet's barking rose to a crescendo, but Carys swerved away from the house and raced towards the barn. The tall door juddered on its hinges as she wrenched it open, and she ran inside like a hunted animal, dragging the door shut behind her. The noise of the rain abruptly faded, as did most of the bleak daylight. Carys lifted the inside bar and slammed it into place, then plunged into the gloom, stumbling, staggering, until she rounded the familiar corner of the straw stacks and the figure of the Harvest King confronted her.

'I'm sorry!' Carys's voice cracked from her throat in a sobbing moan. 'Robin, I'm sorry, I'm sorry – forgive me! You have to forgive me!'

The full force of her emotions erupted and she scrabbled to the King, clutching and clawing at the straw that formed him, locking her arms around his giant form as the tears she had been incapable of shedding broke free at last. The King rocked precariously, throwing a great, dim shadow over her, then suddenly the figure unbalanced, tipped and started to keel over. Carys saw it toppling towards her but could not get out of the way, and the King crashed down on top of her.

The impact knocked the breath from her lungs, but that was all. Shaken and gasping, she disentangled herself from under the fallen image, and found herself staring into the King's face, no more than a handsbreadth away from her own. There was a dark smudge on the face where eyes might have been, and for one heartstopping instant they looked—

Real.

Every muscle in Carys's body locked rigid, then, as the Harvest King *changed*. The rough, sculptured face became sun-browned skin; plaited straw became long, abundant hair; a pair of eyes the blue of a summer sky opened and gazed at her with a pain that sent daggers through her mind.

And a so-familiar voice, Robin's voice, said: '*Why did you call me back, after this?*'

'Carys?' Gyll knocked again at the door, sending Fleet into a new frenzy of barking. 'Carys!'

Juda came hurrying round the side of the house. 'I've looked in all the windows and I can see no sign of her,' she said worriedly. 'Perhaps she didn't come home after all.'

'She did, I'm certain of it.' Gyll's intuition told her that Carys was somewhere on the farm, and her intuition was usually reliable. 'She might be upstairs. I think we should go in and see.'

'It's an intrusion . . .' Juda said dubiously.

'I know. But after what happened at the chapel, I truly think we should make sure that there's nothing wrong.' Gyll looked at the back door. 'There's a trick for opening this, Carys showed me once. Here, now . . .'

The door opened and Fleet came rushing to meet them, barking

ecstatically and wagging his tail. 'Hush,' Gyll said. 'Good dog.'
She peered around the kitchen.

'The kettle's cold,' Juda told her. 'And the fire in the range has
gone out.'

Gyll went to the foot of the stairs. 'Carys?' she called again.
'Carys, it's us – Gyll and Juda! Are you there?'

No reply, and when they went upstairs, both the bedrooms were
empty.

'Well, she's not in the house, that's for certain.' Gyll stood, hands
on hips, looking around as though for some clue they had missed.
'We'd best try the outbuildings. Or maybe—' She broke off. 'What's
that? Has someone arrived?'

There was the noise of a cart in the yard, and when they went to
the nearest window they saw Garler's trap, with Garler and Deenor
on board.

'Perhaps they know something.' Juda's eyes lit eagerly. 'Perhaps
that's why they're here.'

But Garler and Deenor did not know. In fact, as Deenor
explained, they too had been concerned about Carys, and so had
driven over now that the rain had cleared away, to see her and
ensure that all was well.

Garler gazed around the yard and scratched his head. 'Well, one
thing's for sure, whatever way she took, she wouldn't have got
herself lost on her way home. I reckon she's here.'

'Maybe she's gone to fetch the cattle?' Deenor suggested.

'No, Wife. We came that way remember, we'd have seen her.
I'll wager she's in one of the buildings. Byre, maybe, or the barn,
though Providence knows what she'd want to be doing in there.'

The byre, which had Faithful and Spry's stable attached, seemed
the more likely place, and the three women hurried away to
investigate. Garler, meanwhile, walked unhurriedly towards the
barn. Fleet had been shut in the house again. They had tried urging
the dog to 'Find Mistress!' but with so much rain there was no
scent to be followed, and Fleet had only run round in confused
circles, getting under everyone's feet. Garler doubted that they

would find Carys in the barn, for he could not imagine what she could possibly want to be doing in there, but he would check, to be sure.

When he tried to open the door he found he could not. The interior bar was in place; the door moved an inch or two then held fast. Garler rattled it a few times, frowning as he thought the matter through in his slow, methodical way. He was still deliberating when Gyll crossed the yard to join him.

'We've looked in the byre and stables,' she said. 'Then Deenor thought of the chicken arks, so she and Juda have gone to see if she might be working there.'

Garler nodded. 'This door, now,' he said. 'Seems it's barred on the inside.'

'The *inside*?' Gyll looked at the door with quickening interest. 'Then she's in there, she must be!' Clenching her hand into a fist she hammered on the wooden planking and shouted Carys's name, but no answering call came from inside.

'Maybe she's fallen asleep,' Garler said.

'Or she's ill.' Or something else, Gyll thought . . . 'Garler, could we dislodge the bar from outside? See, there's a gap in the door. Is it wide enough, do you think?'

'Reckon it's worth a try. There's a pitchfork there, look, not been put away. You fetch it, and we'll try with the shaft.'

It took some prising, but at last they got the pitchfork pole through the door and wedged under the bar. Garler levered it, putting all his strength into the effort, and abruptly there was a clatter from inside the barn as the bar fell from its slots.

'There,' said Garler. 'That's done it. I'll look, you go and tell the others what we've found.'

Gyll went, and Garler opened the barn door and went quietly inside. It took his eyes some moments to adjust to the gloom, but when they did he saw at once that there was no one in the immediate area, so he ventured further, walking on to where the bales were stacked. He turned the corner—

'Why, Carys!' Garler's face broke into a relieved smile. 'There now, we've been looking all over for you, and here you are safe and sound.' He paused, his face creasing with puzzlement. 'Whatever are you doing?'

Carys stared back at him from where she crouched among the jumble of bales that the Harvest King's collapse had dislodged. Her hair and clothes were still soaking wet; clearly she had made no effort to dry herself since returning home. The King himself lay supine beside her. To Garler, it was just a giant straw doll. But to Carys, it was something else entirely.

She said harshly: 'Go away. Leave us alone!'

Garler flinched a little. 'Now, lass, there's no need for that,' he told her, sounding hurt. 'It's only me. And Deenor's hereabouts, with Gyll and Juda too. We were worried for you.'

Carys's mouth jerked in a rictus of a smile. 'You needn't be. I'm perfectly well. Go *away*, Garler – we don't want you here!'

Belatedly, it dawned on Garler that she said *we* where any normal person would have said *I*. There was no one with her, only the great dumdolly of the King, and that didn't count. He began to wonder if she was ill; a fever, brought on by shock at what had happened in the chapel, or perhaps by trudging all that way from the village in the rain. Garler was a kindhearted man, and for all the embarrassment he had felt today at Carys's reception in the village, he was not about to abandon a neighbour so obviously in need of help.

'Come along,' he said benignly, moving forward and holding out a hand to her. 'I reckon you're not quite yourself, eh? Come along to the house, and Deenor and the others will see for your comfort. Can't stay in here, can you, all wet and bedraggled as you are. You need warmth, and some good food. Come along, now.'

She shrank back from him with a movement so violent that he was quite disconcerted. 'I said, *go*!' she snarled. 'We don't need you!'

'We?' said Garler. 'Who's we, Carys? There's only you and me here, nobody else. Now, I know it wasn't easy for you at chapel today, people talking and whispering and all. And as for that bolt

289

of lightning – well, that's enough to upset anyone, isn't it? Little wonder, little wonder. But it's past now, and all's well.'

Carys stared at him with mounting fury and frustration. How dared he intrude, how *dared* he? Just when she had succeeded, just when the link was about to be reforged, completed, *whole* again! She had been on the brink of touching Robin's mind and bringing him through to her, and now *this*! It was not to be *tolerated*!

Garler had taken another step towards her. 'Come along, lass,' he coaxed again. 'You've taken a touch of fever, that's what, so you don't want to be staying out here all cold and wet.' He reached out one hand. 'Come with me, now.'

If, at that moment, Carys had been capable of sane thought, she would never have done what she did. But she was not capable. A scarlet fog was filling her head, a fog of sheer, blinding rage, so that suddenly the man standing before her was not Garler Shepherd, friend and neighbour, but a stranger, an interloper, an *enemy*. Her eyes narrowed to slits, like an animal's eyes; she reached behind her, grasping hold of the Harvest King, gripping him, drawing strength from him, and she felt power flowing through her. She had given this old fool his chance. Enough was *enough*.

She smiled a terrible smile, and said: 'Damn you.'

Then she focused her will.

The three women were half-way across the yard when they heard the animal shriek that echoed out of the barn. Fleet, in the house, started to bark and yelp hysterically, and the women stopped, staring towards the barn in shock.

'What in the name of Providence . . . ?' Deenor hissed.

Gyll said: 'Come on!'

She was the fastest runner, and she reached the barn ahead of the others, barging through the door in a flurry of skirts and pounding feet. As she rushed through, a figure streaked out of the gloom, cannoned into her, rebounded—

'Carys!' Gyll's voice went up on a shrill note. 'Carys, what—'

She stopped dead as she saw Carys's demented face and realised that her friend did not know her. Then Carys thrust viciously, jabbing her, pushing back and to one side, and as Gyll reeled off balance she had a last glimpse of Carys darting through the door and away. Juda and Deenor called after her in astonishment, their calls sounding like bird cries, but Gyll did not follow. Her heart was pumping and there was sickness in her throat as she looked deeper into the barn and felt a dreadful premonition.

She had to see, had to steel herself and be certain. Slowly, cautiously, she moved to the straw bales. Their wall rose up to meet her and she almost lost her nerve; closing her eyes she murmured a short, fervent prayer, then she made her eyes open again, and stepped round the edge of the bales.

The shock was not as horrifying as she had feared, for she had been prepared in some measure. But one look was enough. Gyll's brain took in the figure of the Harvest King, standing tall and upright and faintly sinister on his base of straw. Then her gaze travelled down, and she saw what lay at the King's feet, like a newly offered sacrifice . . .

She met Juda and Deenor at the barn door.

'We ran after her, but she was too quick for us!' Juda said breathlessly. 'She went towards . . . Gyll?' Her expression changed as she saw that her friend's face was grey. 'Gyll, what is it?'

Gyll took an unsteady step forward and touched Juda's arm. 'Tell Deenor to stay out here,' she said very quietly. 'Whatever you do, don't let her go in. I . . . I'm going for Merion. He'll know what to do.' She swallowed back bile. '*He*'ll know.'

Chapter XXIV

Strange to think that the wheel of the seasons had come round again and another whole year had gone by since last the harvest was gathered. As she walked slowly across the yard of Carys's farm – which, one day, must be given another name – Gyll Merionwife looked around with troubled eyes, and reflected, as she did all too often, on the tangled and fateful chain of events that had ensnared them all since last summer. Their lives had been ordered and peaceful then, with no sign of storm-clouds on the horizon. Jone had been alive, Carys had been blossoming (or so Gyll believed) as chatelaine of his house, and they had all been such good friends. They had been *happy*. And now . . .

Garler had had a fine and solemn funeral, one that was fitting for such a kindly, gentle man who had been much loved and would be sorely missed. Almost the whole parish had turned out for it, and copious tears had been shed. For Deenor's sake the preacher had confined his oration to a eulogy of Garler's life, with no reference to the manner of his death and certainly no mention of Carys Jonewidow. But everyone *knew*. Half of them had joined in the long and extensive hunt for Carys, which had lasted more than a month before it was reluctantly accepted that she was either dead or fled so far away that she would never be found. Gyll hoped she was dead, for if she was not and she ever was captured, her death would be slow and agonising. The village would see to that. This time, the memory and the desire for revenge would not fade.

Gyll sighed to herself, and continued on across the yard. She still had to muster her nerve before entering the barn with its dreadful associations, but she had promised Merion that she would look over the big cart and the implements, and let him know if any needed repair before the harvest began. There seemed to her something incongruous about using Carys's equipment to harvest Carys's crops on Carys's land, but they had all agreed that, whatever the circumstances, it would be a crying shame to let good corn go to waste when it could be used for the wider benefit. They would sell it, and the money they made would go to poor Garler's family; Deenor had declared she did not want it but Merion believed she could be persuaded for the sake of her sons. The whole farm would probably be sold when a little more time had passed, though no one would dream, now, to suggest that Deenor's eldest should buy it as he had once hoped to do. Nor would it go to Powl Miller; even greedy Powl had balked at the prospect. Possibly a stranger would come, someone from a distant parish who had no connection and no memories here, who would not be affected by what this place had become . . .

The barn was a cool, dry haven from the humid summer day, and when she had paused on the threshold for long enough to convince herself that no ghosts lurked, Gyll settled to her task. After a while she moved further in, and looked at the Harvest King who sat waiting to play his role in the celebration that would mark the end of the reaping. Gyll felt a small pang of sorrow, for this King would not fulfil his destiny. As the preacher had said, to carry him in triumph over the fields when he had been made by Carys's hand was wrong, and would surely bring bad luck to the harvest. So the women who worked on the new King were making a second, a substitute to go to the burning. As for this figure in the barn . . . well, no one knew for sure what his fate would be, but it was most likely that he would simply be dismantled, strand by strand, and cast away. No ceremony, no prayers, simply a dissolving of the past that would, they all hoped, help lay the spectres to rest.

So, then. In five days, if the weather held (Carys could have told them, but Gyll tried not to think about that), the field labourers would come with their scythes and their songs, and the harvest would begin. Gyll reached out a hand and, very gently, touched the feet of the luckless King.

'I'm sorry for you,' she said softly. 'It wasn't your fault. How could it have been?'

Moments later, a sound like a mournful sigh whispered through the barn. But Gyll thought only that it was the breeze blowing among the rafters, as she turned to go back to her work.

She knew it was beginning. She could feel it as a prickling in her marrow, sure and certain, as she made her wary way to the edge of the wood from where she could see the wide sweep of the fields. She had not dared to venture this far from hiding before, but a compulsion was on her, a need to witness the commencement with her own eyes. So she went, and she watched.

She was, now, expert at concealing herself, and with the help of the power *he* gave her she could be sure that no one who chanced to look this way would notice anything but the trees. They would not see the gaunt human figure, with her hair in matted strands and her torn and grimy clothes hanging from her, shrouds which her emaciated body could no longer fill. They would not see. And if they could, they would not know her.

She was motionless, staring at the line of slowly moving labourers and thinking her own thoughts, when she sensed movement behind her. Her head snapped round, and from the dappled shadows under the leaf canopy a voice said, 'Carys . . .'

Robin had come silently from the heart of the wood, and for a moment Carys felt a spark of dark anger. She had not summoned him to her side, not given him leave to follow her . . . But then the impulse gave way to another, and instead of scolding she went to him and slid her arms around his neck and said, 'I love you.'

His blue eyes dulled and she knew that he wanted to turn his head away and avoid her kiss. But he could not, for she did not want that, and what she did not want, he must not do.

His lips tasted sweet, as they always did, and she made the kiss linger. 'Dear Robin,' she told him when finally it ended, and laughed. 'They've come, do you see them? The harvesters. They're going to reap my land for me.' Another laugh, broken, deranged.

Robin tried to free himself from her grasp, but her fingers tightened on him and her face grew menacing. '*No!*' she said. 'You can't. You mustn't. I *want* you; you're *mine*, and you will stay!'

He did not reply, for he knew this litany all too well, and knew, too, that it was true.

'They won't burn my King,' Carys said, her thoughts skipping and wandering as they so often did. 'I know, I can feel it. They're making another. So the link I made will remain, won't it? Doesn't that please you? Tell me it does!'

'Yes,' said Robin pallidly. 'It pleases me.'

'"My love",' she prompted. 'Call me "my love", as you always used to.'

'My love.'

But she scowled, for he did not say it now in the adoring way he had done during those early, balmy days. So long ago, they seemed, and try as she might she was never able to quite call them back. That thought brought the anger bubbling up again, and she swung round, narrowing her eyes to stare at the fields and the distant, toiling human figures.

'I want it to rain,' she said after a few moments. 'I want the crop to be spoiled.'

'Carys, *why*?' he asked her sadly.

'Because . . .' Ah, there were so many reasons. Because she hated them all. Because they were stealing what was rightly and justly hers. Because . . . because she *could*. That was the nub of it. Because she *could*. *He* had granted her that. He had had no choice.

She didn't answer his question but laughed at him, then ran past him and away into the wood, merging in seconds with the trees and vanishing. Robin waited to see if she would call him to go after her, but she did not, and at length he allowed himself to relax a little. He moved to the trees' edge, where he sat down, shifting his form into the likeness of a hewn stump, and gazed out at the harvesters. There was a leaden weight on his spirit, crushing it like a leaf trodden into the ground by a careless foot. If Carys wanted rain to ruin the crop, then rain she would have, for she would command him and he had to obey, because he – this part of him, this aspect that had haunted the woods since she had called him back – was hers to do with as she chose.

And the road Carys had taken had turned from a bright, straight track to something twisted and bleak and abominable. She was mad. He had seen it in her eyes in the hour that she used her gift to call him back; through the medium of the Harvest King, her other link with him. And he had known it beyond all doubt when she had killed the old shepherd for the simple fault of trying to be kind when she did not want kindness. That evil act had been the breaking of Robin. He had been brought back, made manifest again, to find himself the bound servant of a human woman who could not resist the temptations of the power granted to her. Carys's mind had been slowly warping, until at last it cracked like an undetected fault opening in rock, and darkness had flowed out to eclipse the light. He had tried to help her, then tried to warn her, but after a while she had listened only to the voice of her own whim and impulse. She had never truly loved him. How could she, when she was mortal and he was not? They were worlds apart, and at most their liaison could only have been fleeting, until she found a real and human love. He had expected that; it was the nature of the task for which he had been summoned. But he had thought the game would be harmless, even benign. He had not expected her to want him in this way, for the powers and skills that were his true reality. He had not expected her to usurp those powers and use them to further her own twisted pride. He had not perceived the deadly flaw in her, and he had not foreseen what could come of it. He was a *fool*.

But she had called him and trapped him with the very skills that he had taught her, and now there was nothing he could do. At the fateful moment when Garler had come to the barn, he had still been held within the shell of the Harvest King. Then later, when the crime was done and she had fled to the woods and was safely concealed, Carys had cast the spell that brought him back to his old form, the one she had known and wanted to know again. He had begged her to set him free from his obligation, but she had only laughed in his face and told him that she needed him now as never before. Since then Robin had done her bidding. When men with dogs and staves and ropes came searching for her, he sheltered her. When she wanted food, he fed her. When she wanted him to lay her down on the forest floor and take her, gently or violently, he obeyed. And when she took a mood against some hapless, unknowing soul, and demanded from him the knowledge that would blight them, he had no option but to give it.

Once, he could have healed her. That, he suspected, was what the Wayfarers' matriarch had hoped when she offered Carys a second chance. But her judgement had been badly awry, and now it was far too late.

Unless . . .

But Robin did not believe he could do what *unless* entailed. There had been a chance, but something Carys had told him had snuffed out the spark of hope. He might try to break out, defy her long enough for the thing to be done, but he did not think he had that strength. Not now, not as he was. The summer witch had become a witch of cruel winter, and he could not stand against her.

From the wood, distant but insistent, came a call.

'Robin . . . Robin . . . I want you. Come to me, Robin . . .' Such a soft voice, but there was nothing soft about the intent behind it. Robin rose. The stump became, briefly, a young sapling, which then faded and vanished, and with a heavy heart he turned to answer the summons that could not be refused.

In a few more days the last loads would be carried in. Gyll thought she had never known a harvest so dogged by ill fortune. As if the weather had not been enough to contend with, there had been outbreaks of fever and sickness among the workforce, and then that plague of biting insects, and finally the eerie lightning-storm, with no rain, that had come up so suddenly over Crede Hill and caused havoc. More than twenty sheep and cattle had been killed by the lightning, and three labourers had had a narrow escape when a giant oak tree was struck and fell close to where they were working. Gyll could almost believe that some supernatural agency had taken against the district and had set out to wreak spiteful havoc.

She consoled herself with the thought that it was nearly over now, and today, at least, the weather had been kinder, without rain or wind or tempests to battle with. Now, at noon, she was preparing the small mountain of food for carrying by cart to the hungry army in the fields. With conditions so unpredictable, the harvest needed every available hand; even Juda was working with the rest, so Gyll had no one to help her. She was untroubled by it; the sorting of loaves and cakes and hams and cheeses was simple enough, and it was peacefully pleasant to be alone in the yard with the sun shining down on her and no need for urgency.

When the unfamiliar voice spoke her name at close hand, she jumped. She had not heard footsteps, nor had a shadow fallen across her, yet when she looked up, the young man was standing not two paces away. Recovering herself, Gyll opened her mouth to ask if she could be of help . . . then the civil greeting died on her tongue as intuition clutched her vitals.

He said again, 'You are Gyll Merionwife.'

'Yes . . .' Gyll stared, unable to take her gaze from him. Though she was certain that she had never seen him before, there was something achingly familiar about him. A manner, a mien, like something half remembered . . .

She found her voice again at last. 'Can I – is there anything you . . .'

'I need your help,' he said. She saw then that he looked ill: his face was haggard and devoid of colour, and he was swaying on his feet. Sweat glistened on his skin. She thought he must have a severe fever.

Then he said the thing that shocked her to the core. 'You were Carys's dearest friend. If you ever loved her, then I *beg* you to help me now.'

299

Gyll's eyes widened. 'Carys . . . she's alive?'

He nodded, swallowed.

'Where *is* she?' Gyll cried. 'Please – if you know, then tell me!'

'I can't. I daren't. Gyll Merionwife, I – this is hard for me, to appear to you like this; it takes a toll on me and I can't maintain it for long. If she calls, if Carys calls me, I may not be able to resist, so—'

'What do you mean? I don't understand!'

'I know, and I can't explain to you, there isn't the time left. Gyll, please – you must do two things for Carys. They're her only hope of salvation. And . . . and mine.'

Gyll's mind reeled. 'Who are you?' she whispered. 'Does Carys know you?'

He nodded. 'You know me, too, Gyll Merionwife. You all do, after a fashion.' He hesitated, then: 'I am the one who gave Carys her gift, the skill to heal or curse.'

Gyll's mouth worked. '*You* gave . . .'

'Yes.' There was such a wealth of misery and grief in his voice that she could have wept for him. 'I believed in her. I believed she was strong enough to hold what I gave her and use it wisely. I was so wrong . . .'

'We were all wrong,' Gyll said more gently. 'It was a terrible, terrible mistake, and we all had a part in it.'

'There's only one way to take the power from her,' he said. 'I have to break the link that binds me to her. But I can't do it alone, I don't have the strength any more. If—'

'Tell me!' she said. 'Tell me what I must do, and I swear that I'll do it!'

'For Carys?'

'Yes. For the Carys that used to be.' Gyll paused. 'And also for you. Though I don't think I even know why.'

He looked at her, a strange, shining, unfathomable look, then he stepped forward and kissed her cheek. The scent of honey caught in Gyll's nostrils, and something that felt like the essence of summer seemed to tingle where his lips had touched her skin.

Awestruck, and realising something akin to the truth, she started to say, '*You are*—' But he put a finger to his mouth and she found herself silenced.

'Yes,' he said. 'I believe you know what I am.'

Then he told her what he wanted her to do.

Moving the Harvest King was the hardest part. The straw figure seemed to have a will of its own, lurching first to one side and then to the other, wanting to go everywhere but in the proper direction as Gyll wrestled and heaved it across the barn floor. Every so often Gyll stopped to rest, and each time turned to look back at the still, silent form lying in the straw where the King had stood. He was as tightly bound as she had dared to make him, wrists and ankles tied together, arms pinned to his sides. She had not wanted to bind him but he had gently insisted; if Carys should summon him, he said, then unless he was physically restrained he must go to her, and that would be the ruin of everything.

His vivid blue eyes were closed now and he looked as if he was asleep, though Gyll felt instinctively that he was not. The sense of awe she had felt earlier came back to haunt her again and she shivered. He had told her about Carys's gift and the madness it had awoken in her, and he had asked pardon for the tribulations of the harvest. When Gyll realised who had been at the root of those troubles, the thought that Carys could have gained mastery over such a one as him chilled her blood. Carys *had* to be stopped. That was why the thing that he had begged her to do must be done, and quickly.

She manoeuvred the Harvest King to the door at last, but when she tried to push him through, the door jammed and would not open. Gyll was fighting with it, and saying words that she knew no woman should ever say, when a voice shouted from the direction of the gate.

'Gyll! Wife, are you there?'

'Merion!' Through the narrow gap that was all the barn door would allow, Gyll saw her husband and two other men walking into the yard. The half-loaded cart was still there; the harvesters must have wondered what had happened to their meal, and a deputation had come to find out.

'Help me, Merion!' she called. 'Hurry!'

He came at a run, and stopped when he saw the King's head wedged in the doorway. 'Quickly!' Gyll urged. 'It must be taken outside. I can't explain now, but it must!'

To her relief he didn't stop to argue but put his shoulder to the jammed door and forced it open. Gyll all but fell out, dragging the King's form with her, and together they hauled it fully into the yard. They dropped it thankfully to the ground and, straightening, Merion gave her a long, stern look.

'What are you *doing* with this, woman?' he demanded. 'What's afoot?'

Gyll drew a deep breath. 'It's Carys,' she said.

'*What?*'

'She's still alive, and she's not far away. Please, Merion, don't ask how I know, because there isn't time to explain now – just believe when I tell you that the trouble she's made isn't over yet, and if we don't do what we have to, it'll go on and become even worse!'

'What do you mean? What have we to do?'

'Get fire,' she said. 'A torch, a brand, anything. Get it, and bring it here. We have to burn this King. And we have to do it *now*.'

Perhaps something of Robin's own will was channelling through Gyll at that moment, or perhaps it was simply that Merion Blacksmith knew his wife and trusted her, and was aware that she would never ask so bizarre a thing of him without very good reason. He took a quick glance round the yard and said, 'Take this further from the barn; stand it there – the others will help you. I'll find kindling and a brand.'

They stood the King upright. The men were curious and uneasy, and one ventured tentatively, 'This wasn't the way it was meant to be, Missus . . .' but Gyll gave him such a look that he dared say no more. As Merion returned with wood, brand and a tinder-box, a peculiar, brassy shadow seemed to fall on the yard. Gyll looked up quickly, expecting to see the sky dulling as though another storm were on the way. But the sky was still blue and the sun still shone. Nonetheless, she shivered with a sense of foreboding. Something was not quite as it should be . . . Goaded by an abrupt instinct she shaded her eyes again but gazed this time along the track that led down to the woods. Nothing there. Or *was* that something moving? A distant figure, it looked like, running . . . but when she tried to focus more clearly it faded with the landscape and was gone. Imagination, it must have been. But suddenly Gyll felt a pressing need to hurry.

Merion had heaped the kindling at the King's feet, and now he was trying to strike fire from the tinder-box. But a capricious wind had suddenly blown up, and every spark he made winked out before the tinder could catch. Merion frowned and muttered.

And suddenly, in the distance, Gyll glimpsed the running figure again. Something about it was horribly familiar . . .

'Husband!' She grabbed at his arm, making him start. 'Look – on the track!'

Merion was noted for his long sight, and he needed only one look before his body tensed. 'It's her! It's Carys!'

Gyll's heart contracted with fear. 'Light the pyre, Merion, *quickly*! She mustn't reach him; whatever happens, *she mustn't reach him*!' She tried to snatch the tinder-box from him but in her panic dropped it.

The wind pounced, whipping the tinder away. Calling her a fool of a woman Merion ran to retrieve it. And the running figure was closer.

Suddenly, shrilly, a cry of pain rang out from the barn.

'*Great Providence!*' Merion jumped as though an invisible fist had punched him. 'There's someone in there!'

'No!' Gyll screamed. 'Don't go in, you mustn't, you mustn't untie him – *ohh*!' For Merion had ignored her and was racing towards the barn, the tinder-box forgotten. Desperation slammed through her; she couldn't stop him, and Carys was running, and there was no *time*—

She took off like a hunted hare, sprinting for the house. The wind (and it was Carys's doing, she knew it was) tried to slam the kitchen door in her face, but she hurled herself against it and smashed it back. A lantern, a lantern – she found one, burned her hand as she lit it from the range, and fastened the glass pane tightly.

'You try!' she spat savagely to the wind as it rattled the windows in their frames. 'You just *try*!'

The lantern was a shepherd's light, made to withstand the weather's onslaught, and though the wind whirled into the kitchen, tearing at Gyll's hair and clothes and whining like a maddened hornet, it could not blow out the flame. Gyll ran back outside as though in the midst of a small tornado. Merion and the other men were nowhere in sight but she could not waste attention on them. The Harvest King was rocking on his pyre, and she staggered towards him, clutching the lantern to her breast when the wind tried to rip it from her grasp. She reached the King, braced her feet—

The wind dropped. And there in front of her, shoulders hunched, head down, was Carys.

Gyll stared at her, appalled. The girl she had known was gone, and in her place was this – this *thing*, no longer human but something degraded and demented and utterly lost. Carys was as thin as a scarecrow herself, and as tattered. She had the aura of some dark, deadly bird of prey, a phantom from a nightmare; her hair was an unclipped hedge of detritus, and through its filthy tangle her eyes glared ferally.

The shoulders rose higher, the head dipped lower, and in a voice Gyll could barely recognise Carys said: 'Give it to me!'

A hand, the nails broken and the fingers clenched into talons, jerked out, demanding the lantern. Gyll clutched it tighter, shaking her head, unable to speak.

'*Give it*!' She took an ominous pace forward. Gyll backed away. 'You will. I can make you. *We* can make you.'

'No,' Gyll said, her voice no more than a squeak. She sucked air into her lungs, trying to give herself strength. 'You can't. He doesn't want to.'

Carys stopped moving. She put her head on one side as though considering this – or listening for something. Then, horrifyingly, she smiled.

'Oh, so *that's* how it is. I see.' A peculiar glimmer of light rippled over her, and Gyll felt a chilly breath flicker past her own face.

Then Carys raised her head and called out with a ferocity that shocked Gyll to the marrow.

'*Robin!*'

From the barn came a yell – Merion's voice, shouting in surprise and alarm.

'*Robin!*' Carys cried again. More shouting, but this time there were several voices, with Robin's rising desperately above them. 'Hold me back! Stop her, don't let her get in – *ahhh*!'

It was a scream of sheer agony, and at the sound of it Carys screeched in triumph. But Robin's warning had struck home to Gyll; she knew what would happen, and when Carys launched herself towards the barn she flew at her, blocking the way, grabbing for her arm, her hair, her clothing, anything to drag her back and keep her from her quarry. Her fingers clamped on wool, and Carys screeched again but on a very different note. With the agility of a cat she spun round, and her nails raked Gyll's face, missing her left eye by a fraction. Gyll reeled back, Carys twisted in her grip – she heard fabric rip, then she lost her balance and fell sideways to the ground as Carys sprinted for the barn door.

Gyll struggled to her feet, her cheeks blazing and her eyes watering from the pain. The world had blurred, she couldn't see – then as she swayed dizzily, Robin screamed her name. It was a plea, an invocation, a last desperate hope, and it shocked Gyll out of her stupefaction. *The lantern* – she had dropped it in the struggle with Carys, but as her vision cleared she saw it lying two paces away. The glass was unbroken – the metal cage had protected it – and the flame still burned, though oil was leaking from the reservoir. Gyll snatched it up, and as she did so the spilled oil caught fire and flames seared her hand, but she held on and ran for the pyre. The Harvest King's shadow loomed over her; clenching her teeth and willing a silent, headlong prayer to the heavens, Gyll thrust the now blazing lantern into the heart of the kindling.

The pyre went up with a roar and a blaze of light that sent Gyll tottering back so that she almost fell again. Through eyes that streamed now she saw the King begin to burn, still tall, still proud, but wreathed in a corona of fire that rose higher and higher as though it would challenge the sun.

And from the barn came a sound that she hoped she would never, ever hear again. The sound of someone – or something – screaming its agony and yet its triumph, as it departed the mortal world. The scream shrilled out, and as it did so, the blazing creature of straw turned his head and looked at Gyll, and a face that, for one shattering instant, was Robin's face, smiled down at her.

Gyll was a strong and courageous woman, but even her strength was not proof against that. Her eyes widened, her breath stopped in her throat – and she dropped to a dead faint on the cobbles.

An unpleasant burning smell brought her round, and she opened her eyes to see Merion casting aside a charred chicken feather which he had been holding under her nose. The Harvest King's pyre was still blazing, and Gyll wanted to laugh at the idea of the feather remedy when there was so much *other* fire to be had. But when her eyes focused on her husband's face, the impulse died.

Merion said quietly, 'You'd better come to the barn, my dear.'

Gyll sat up. 'Carys. Is she . . . ?'

'She's there, and alive.'

'And he . . . ?'

Merion did not answer. He helped her to her feet, and together they went through the tall door. It was very quiet inside the barn; even the cats were not in evidence. Round the edge of the bales . . .

The other two men had been standing guard, but they drew back silently as Merion and Gyll approached. Carys was kneeling in the straw. She was smiling, and she was hugging something to her, rocking back and forth and cradling it in her arms as though it were the most precious thing in the world. Gyll braced herself to look . . . then realised that there was nothing to fear. All Carys held was a bundle of ropes.

'We've tried to speak to her,' Merion said, 'but she won't answer us. She just says a name over and over again.'

'Robin,' Gyll murmured.

He looked at her in surprise – and Carys looked, too, alerted by the word. She saw Gyll, and smiled a peculiar, crimped smile, like that of an idiot child.

'He's gone, Carys,' Gyll said. She felt contempt and pity for the human wreck before her, but not hatred. Somehow, that wasn't in her. 'He's free, and you can't have him back.'

'I can.' Carys nodded emphatically. 'I *can*.'

'You can't, for he never truly belonged to you. He'll never belong to anyone in that way. I know who – and what – he is. He told me, you see, he . . .' But the words tailed off, for what was the point in trying to explain?

Carys stared at her. 'He didn't talk to you. I wouldn't let him. He's *mine*, not yours.'

Gyll could have said, 'He is everyone's and no one's, Carys', but she knew, again, that it would serve no purpose. She sighed, and turned away, feeling tears springing to her eyes.

Carys started to rock again, and to croon an odd, high-pitched song to the coils of rope. Merion spoke quietly to the other two men, and when they went to her and took hold of her arms, she did not resist but went meekly with them, though she still clung possessively to her prize. As she was led slowly past, Gyll said, 'Husband . . . what will they do to her?'

Merion stared at his boots. 'I don't know.'

'Will they . . . kill her?'

'I think it's unlikely. The law won't demand it; it's too cruel a thing to execute those who – well, who are like her.'

'Mad.'

He nodded.

'Poor Carys,' said Gyll. 'She *was* our friend, once.' Then she summoned the courage to ask him the thing she most needed to ask. 'Merion . . . did you see him?'

Merion nodded again. 'He was lying in the straw, tightly bound. He pleaded with us not to release him, but we thought . . .' He shrugged helplessly.

'I know,' she said. 'If I had not understood, I would have done the same.'

'And then, when you set fire to the King, he – he *screamed*. That was all, just one scream. And a moment later, he was . . . gone. Only the ropes were left.'

Gyll said nothing. She had the answer she wanted.

They started to move towards the door. 'We'll send for Juda,' Merion said as they emerged into the sunlight. 'She is kind. We must also tell the preacher; perhaps he might help in some small way. And Carys's mother . . . I know they did not get on, but, well, family is family . . .' Abruptly he stopped and looked at Gyll. 'Who was he?' he asked.

Gyll gazed at the pyre. The King was burned to ashes. But another would rise in his place; this year and every year when the harvest came home. That was the way it had always been, and the way it would always be. In one guise or another, they would meet Robin again.

She looked at Merion and wondered how to answer him. She could have said all that she had just been thinking, and more than that. He is the land. He is the spirit of life and the seasons. He is the Harvest King, and the Man of the greenwoods, and the patient scarecrow guarding the burgeoning new crops in their fields. All those things, and so much else besides.

Bu there was no need. One name would suffice for all of it, and be enough.

'I think,' she said very softly, 'that he was the *true* summer witch.'

Merion considered that for some moments. Then he smiled a slow, thoughtful, gentle smile.

'You always were a fanciful woman,' he said.

The Summer Witch

His arm was around her shoulders as they walked towards the house. And from the distant fields, far away down the track that led past the woods, the breeze carried the sound of someone whistling.

Epilogue

They told her that it had been nearly fifteen years. She found that hard to believe, but time and the steady routine of this place had instilled the habit of believing what they said. She did not *feel* fifteen years older, nor, on the rare occasions when she was allowed to look in a mirror did she think she looked it. But then, who was she to judge? All the old points of reference had gone, together with so many of her memories, and the person who had come here so long ago was not the same person who would leave the shelter of these walls on this bright summer morning.

They said that an old friend was coming to fetch her. She wondered who, and whether she would remember them. She hoped she would, or, if she did not, that she would feel a kinship with them, and they with her. So she stood in the little anteroom, fingering the small, linen-wrapped parcel that was the sum of her worldly goods, waiting for her unknown future to begin.

The gig arrived just before noon. Turning in at the gates, Gyll suppressed the chill little shiver that assailed her each time she came here. Not that she had visited that often; seven or eight times, maybe, in all the years that Carys had been confined in the asylum. She would have come more often, but the distance and the busyness of her own life had conspired against it.

Besides, in the early days there had been little point; it had taken a long time for the healing process to take a hold on Carys, and several years had passed before even a glimmer of it had begun to show.

Now, though . . . Gyll was wise enough not to make too many

311

predictions, but there was hope of a new life and a new chance for her one-time dear friend. She had been told that Carys recalled very little of those last, dark days before her mind collapsed. She was not aware of the crimes she had committed, and it was unlikely that she ever would be. That was the reason why the law had been merciful, and Gyll believed it was for the best. Not, of course, that Carys could ever return to her old home, for the farm had long been the province of a new owner, and had quietly prospered in his hands. But there were other options. Carys would need care and friendship, like an orphaned and bewildered child. It could and would be done. Gyll had made that promise, and she would keep it.

The track up to the big stone building was a long one and the pony was in no hurry, so, wanting to marshal her thoughts and prepare for the meeting, Gyll let him pick his own dawdling pace and cast her mind back to the previous evening. So strange, that had been. With the reaping about to begin it was time, again, for the creation of the new Harvest King. This year – ironically, perhaps – it was Nellen Jempwife's turn to host the making, and the women had all been together in the barn, chattering and laughing as they wove the straw and shaped the frame. Gyll had only intended to step outside for a few minutes, to breathe cooler air and rest her aching fingers (with advancing age she no longer had the dexterity of her youth).

But then *he* had come.

She knew him at once, for he was in the same guise he had taken at Carys's farm all those years ago. He had smiled at her, and complimented her on the making of the King, and then he had said, 'Be kind to her, Gyll. Be her friend, as you were before. She'll remember little, and nothing of me. But be assured that I will always be here. Keep her from the shadow, and let her turn her face to the sun. The rest will follow.'

Gyll had stood very still. Voice trembling, she said wonderingly, 'You do not . . . hate her?'

The being whom Carys had called Robin smiled gently and shook

312

his head. 'It isn't in me to hate. Only to live, and to watch over all else that lives.'

Gyll glanced anxiously towards the barn. 'The King,' she said. 'She used him once, to gain control of you. If . . .'

He knew what she was thinking, and held up a hand to forestall what she had been about to say. 'Don't fear that she might do the same again. She made my images in the King and the scarecrow, but it was the Wayfarers' spell that enabled her to call me through them and bind me to her service. Once both images were burned, the chain was finally snapped, and without the spell's magic it can't be forged again. That will never happen. It will never be *allowed* to happen.'

Gyll gazed down at the ground. 'Then her power is gone . . . ?'

'Yes, it is gone, and even if she should remember what she once was, she will never be able to call that part of herself back to being. It's past, and it's over. Help her to live in peace.'

Gyll had nodded, slowly, thoughtfully. Still looking at the dusty ground, she had begun to say, 'I shall do whatever I—'

Then she had looked up, and there was no one else in the yard.

The noise of the gig wheels changed as the rough surface of the track gave way to the grass, and Gyll came out of her reverie to find the shadow of the asylum's grey walls looming over her. The pony stopped of its own accord, and with a butterfly quickening in her stomach Gyll climbed down.

The door opened as she approached, and two people stepped from the dim interior into the daylight. One, Gyll did not recognise. But the other . . .

She was thin, too thin, and there was no glow of health in her cheeks. Her hair showed signs of grey at the temples, and that was far too early for her age. Her eyes were quiet but dull, as if she had forgotten what it was to look at anything but the closest of vistas. But a certain way of tilting her head, of moving her hands, brought familiar memories flooding back to Gyll's mind, and she ran forward to enfold her in an impulsive embrace.

'Carys!' Her voice was warm. Carys looked at her, smiled

hesitantly, then dropped her gaze to her own feet. Did she remember? Gyll couldn't be sure. But she thought she detected a glimmer of response that was more than mere politeness. For a moment Carys's hands rested on her arms, squeezed slightly.

'Gyll . . .' she said.

Gyll felt tears prickle behind her eyes. Blinking them away, she said, 'Oh, my dear . . . welcome back to the world!'

She could see the effort with which Carys was striving to recall. Her lips parted, she hesitated. Then: 'Merion . . .? How is . . .?'

So she did remember. Gyll's smile modulated to sad fondness. 'Merion died, my dear. A year ago. But it was peaceful, and we had a good life together. I'm alone now, like you. So would it not be good and fine for us to share our lives together?'

Carys hesitated again. Then shyly, she whispered: 'I believe that I would like that very much . . .'

The asylum attendant who had come out with Carys was saying something about the formalities and a paper to be signed or marked, but Gyll only nodded without listening. Carys was holding both her hands now, hanging on as though the clasp was something rare and precious which she would never again lose her hold on. Which, perhaps, was close to the truth. *She is a child again*, Gyll thought, her heart overflowing with compassion. *And like a child, she must be nurtured and helped to grow. Let her turn her face to the sun . . . She will never see him again. She will never know him again. But he will always be there.*

'Come, my dear,' she said aloud. 'The darkness has gone, and I'm a silly old fool for crying. Come: I will take you home.'